Blood Will Out

DAVID DONACHIE

Allison & Busby Limited
11 Wardour Mews
London W1F 8AN
allisonandbusby.com

First published in Great Britain by Allison & Busby in 2019.

A CIP catalogue record for this book is available from
the British Library.

First Edition

ISBN 978-0-7490-2175-7

Typeset in 12.25/16.25 pt Adobe Garamond Pro by
Allison & Busby Ltd.

The paper used for this Allison & Busby publication
has been produced from trees that have been legally sourced
from well-managed and credibly certified forests.

Printed and bound by
CPI Group (UK) Ltd, Croydon, CR0 4YY

To Stephen and Alice Bates
with much affection
And, of course, Harry

CHAPTER ONE

Henry Tulkington could make little sense of what had just happened. The multitude of angry shouts had registered, likewise the fusillade and muzzle flashes of muskets going off, followed by the subsequent cries of pain, without any real idea of who had suffered. In the melee, his right-hand man, in pulling him to the ground to then follow through, had landed heavily on his chest, leaving his less than robust employer winded.

'Stay down,' John Hawker commanded, as he raised himself to shout. 'Put up your weapons all, or die where you stand.'

That his own men obeyed was hardly to be commented on: Hawker was respected by all, as well as the source of their prosperity. Their opponents did likewise and quickly, which came more from dread than command for the man issuing the instruction had a brutal reputation. Besides, they were outnumbered and had already suffered casualties, not least their own leader.

Dan Spafford was rolling on the ground, groaning and cursing, this mixed with earnest cries to the Almighty, pleas seeking what he had just witnessed was an illusion: his dearly loved but wayward son Harry, the cause of so much trouble in his life, shot by his father's closest lifetime companion. Jaleel 'Daisy' Trotter had put a ball between Harry's sneering eyes, cursing him as he did so.

Hawker's instruction came in time to prevent anyone reloading their weapons, which left him carrying the only primed and cocked pistol, this waved menacingly and just visibly in a clearing now poorly illuminated. The lanterns initially employed had been dropped when the shooting commenced.

'Get some proper light on matters. And disarm these damned Spaffords.'

Tulkington sat up, immediately feeling his ribs for any sign of impairment, relieved to feel no pain. Retrieving his own dropped lantern, he looked around to observe the ensuing activity: a couple of Hawker's men taking muskets off Spafford's crew, others picking up said lanterns to provide increased visibility with the man who'd ordered their activities circling, looking for others wounded, able to confirm, fortunately, it included none of his own followers.

By Tulkington's right hand lay the spread-eagled body of Harry Spafford, eyes wide open to show the shock of what had so suddenly befallen him. Gone was the conceited, unctuous smirk which nailed his disreputable character, to be replaced by a rictus expression of disbelief on the puffy, at one time handsome face. At Harry's feet lay the crumpled and riddled body of his nemesis, the pistol Trotter had grabbed from the belt of Dan Spafford still in his hand, the barrel smoking slightly.

'Spaffords, look to your master,' Hawker barked. 'And for the sake of Christ Risen, shut him up.'

Hawker came to stand over Henry Tulkington, holding out a hand to raise him to his feet, the one hissed word, issued when upright, a whisper into the Hawker ear. The men surrendering their weapons had not been the primary target of this ambuscade, indeed they'd not been expected. The real objective, who had, was plainly not present.

'No sign of Brazier, your honour,' Hawker said quietly. 'He and his tars was bringin' up the rear, so got the chance to run when the shooting started. I'd set one of my men to cover them, the best with a musket. Marker says he sent a shot after Brazier and saw the sod stagger, so it might be he was hit. Must have got clear, regardless.'

'So you could be said to have failed,' was the bitter response.

The tone of accusation was not well taken, so the reply was terse. 'You'se still breathing, unlike the pair at our feet, so I'd say a thank you might be in order. Daisy Trotter could have put a ball in you as easy as he did Harry Spafford, given you was standing right by him. You was also in the firing line when Trotter got his reward, which is why I hauled you down.'

A glance at Trotter's crumpled corpse brought home to Henry Tulkington how close he had come to a similar fate, which caused him to shiver and clutch at the muffler round his neck. He could now see in his mind's eye the whole event as it unfolded, no more than a few seconds in extent, though seeming an age when recalled. The stand-off, as the shocked Spafford gang, caught in the centre of the clearing, halted in confusion. To their rear, less well-lit but just as surprised, Edward Brazier and his armed support.

He'd sneered at their crass ineptitude, crowing at the way he'd humbugged both Brazier and Spafford senior. The latter had come to rescue his boy from what he saw as the grip of Tulkington's clutches, unaware Harry was more than happy with such an estate. His pa had beseeched, if not grovelled, for his son to come home to the family hearth, an offer ridiculed and cruelly dismissed. So busy had Dan been with his begging, he'd not felt the pistol being lifted off his belt, nor had anyone else seen it happen. Only a few paces separated Daisy Trotter from the contemptuous Harry and they were quickly covered. The bitter words spat out were now printed on Tulkington's memory.

'An end to this, you ungrateful little shit.'

Right before him was the pointed pistol, as well as the determined eyes of the man holding it, quickly followed by the flash and bang

9

of the discharge, replicated by many more, weapons mostly loosed with little in the way of aim. Trotter was the main but not sole target and Hawker had spoken aright: had he not dragged his employer down, one or more of those balls could have stuck him, which made a retraction necessary.

'The shock made me speak too harshly, John.' Hawker waited for a more fulsome apology but this was, as it had ever been, in vain: Tulkington's main interest was still paramount. 'Where did Brazier go?'

'Didn't see, but if he had any wits, he'll have scarpered back to Deal.'

'We need to find him.'

'Mr Tulkington,' was delivered with an impatient sigh. 'We need to sort out what's afore us first. Dan Spafford has a belly wound that could be mortal, so we either put him out of his misery or call in a sawbones, one who can keep his mouth shut. There could be two more who'll need seein' to before we decide what to do with those unharmed, as well as two dead bodies.'

Tulkington ran an eye over the corpses once more to give himself time to think. There was no gainsaying Harry Spafford was deserving of the description by which Trotter had labelled him. He was indeed an ungrateful shit, as well as a dissolute drunk and lecher, who'd mocked his father with glee. In life he'd been no more than a tool for Tulkington's needs, which precluded any feelings of remorse at his passing. Trotter he barely knew, so he was of even less concern.

Yet it did nothing to assuage the current predicament. For a man who held himself to be in control of every aspect of his life, Henry Tulkington was at a stand, stuck with a whirling set of possibilities and no clarity. His attention was drawn by a loud call, to say someone was coming from the house; hardly surprising, since the crack of multiple gunshots must have been heard several miles away.

'Get everyone back to the slaughterhouse, John,' Tulkington commanded as, lantern in hand, he rushed towards the waving lights of those approaching. 'Wounded and dead included.'

The cursing such an instruction induced, heartfelt as it was, didn't carry to Tulkington's ears given the difficulties. But, even repeatedly expressed, there was nothing to be done other than obey.

'Shut the bastard up, I say again,' Hawker cried, pointing towards the groaning Dan Spafford. 'Gag the sod if need be. One of you, go fetch the cart we came in and double quick.'

The lights towards which Henry Tulkington was hurrying jerked unevenly, as those carrying them moved closer, until he could identify a pair of his servants.

'Hold there, all,' he called.

The voice was recognised and, given such individuals feared to disobey him, they stopped immediately, leaving him to make the approach. Close to, he identified Grady and Creevy, the first who ran the house, the other the keeper of Cottington Court's gardens. Behind them, wrapped in her outdoor cloak, stood his sister Elisabeth.

'What's going on, Henry?'

The peremptory tone of her demand rankled and rendered his response inappropriate. 'None of your damned business.'

'Guns going off in the middle of the night? It sounded like a war had broken out.'

'We was concerned when it was found you weren't in the house, your honour.'

'Poachers, Creevy,' Henry claimed hurriedly, the obsequious remark from his toadying head gardener giving him a second to think. 'And, given the incursion has been seen to, it would be best if you all returned to your beds.'

The way the servants had split allowed Elisabeth to push through, creating an arc of light, one strong enough to render visible her features, which reeked of suspicion. It also showed, under her partly open cloak, she was fully dressed.

'Don't tell me you took a slug like Harry Spafford with you to catch poachers. He'd be more likely to aid them than contest them and drink away anything gained. Come to that, given your aversion to the gun, it's not a duty I see you undertaking either.'

'How do you know Spafford was with me?' This demand was issued before Henry realised the obvious: the servants, Grady probably, would have told her, but he had to stay off it as a subject. 'Given you know so little of me, sister, I'm surprised by such certainty. Now go back to the house as I have commanded.'

'These poor creatures are bound to obey you, Henry, for fear of dismissal. I will choose if I do so or not.'

'Then you will be out here alone in the moonlight, for where they go, so goes the lantern light.'

'I don't fear the dark, Henry, as perhaps you should, for the devil will take what passes for your soul if he encounters it, only to find, in evil, he is much surpassed.'

The bitter laugh, loud and wounding, which came as his sister made to turn away, had Henry Tulkington wish he had brought a pistol, as well as the will to employ it in the same manner as had Trotter. But he did have a way of exacting retribution for her insults, which did not require firearms.

'Grady, Creevy, leave one of your lanterns and do as I bid. You, sister, might as well wait and hear what I have to tell you. It will be of much interest, though of little cheer I fancy.'

Elisabeth spun back to glare at him, taking from Grady the lantern he was holding. That Harry Spafford was dead, which would relieve her, must remain a secret for now, but it was secondary. They stood, eyes locked in mutual loathing, until Henry reckoned the servants far enough off not to overhear his softly spoken words.

'Brazier came for you again.' He heard the catch in her throat, which was heartening. 'And, as before, he fell afoul of a more acute mind.'

'The shots?'

'Do you ask if he has been killed or maimed? I wonder if I should tell you anything. Perhaps best if I leave you to stew.'

'Resist telling me if he'd been shot? You couldn't contain yourself.'

'A pleasure I will have to forgo. Brazier ran like the coward he is. When you next choose a lover, perhaps it would be best to find one with a degree of backbone. Lord help the King's Navy if Brazier's an example of those who command his warships.'

'He's ten times the man you'll ever be and has proved it.'

'How repetitious you are for your paragon. Well, know this – if he sets foot on my property once more, he will indeed be shot and out of hand. No magistrate will blame me for what is a clear case of repeated and egregious trespass. So, if you've found a way to communicate with him, which I assume you have, since you're up and dressed in outdoor clothing, I presume in preparation for an attempt at flight, it would be wise to tell him so.'

It was pleasing to see the face, so defiant and superior to begin with, crumple as he spoke. Much as Elisabeth tried to maintain her composure, the information he was imparting made it impossible. Then the countenance suddenly cleared as realisation dawned; he had as good as told her, much as he might hope otherwise, Edward Brazier was unharmed.

'If I could tell him anything, Henry, it would be this. I will wait for him both day and night until he finally comes to take me away from you and everything this house represents.'

Elisabeth spun round, to make her way back towards the house, leaving her brother wishing he could say with certainty what John Hawker could only imply. Instead he was left to call out after her retreating figure, 'Which you will do in vain as long as I have blood in my veins', which even to him sounded very feeble.

13

'Water fills your veins,' was Elisabeth's parting shot. 'You're too miserable a creature to run to blood.'

He watched the light from her lantern fade and, for reasons he could not quite comprehend, felt at a loss. There was, in addition, a slight sense of absurdity, given he felt in no position to move. He could not contemplate returning to the scene of the recent clash, the clearing up of which he had no desire to become involved in, seeing it as beneath his dignity. Yet nor could he bring himself to follow in Elisabeth's footsteps and merely return to the house, there to face the thoughts his servants would harbour but dare not show.

This left him feeling, in his sense of indecision, like an interloper on his own property. Silently he cursed the name of Edward Brazier, the sod who lay at the seat of all his recent difficulties. He was the major disturber of what had hitherto been a peaceful polity, his arrival and aims spreading ripples of trouble into areas in which he had no concern. What should have been a minor inconvenience, soon dealt with, had become a major impasse; nothing he had said or ordered to be carried out seemed to do anything to deter the man.

The heavy beating, administered after Brazier had made his intentions towards Elisabeth plain, seemed to have strengthened his resolve, not weakened it. The ploy, which Henry saw as a stroke of genius, to thwart both him and his sister by marrying her off to Harry Spafford, was now worth nothing, the same as the putative husband. The sod was dead, and Elisabeth was a widow for the second time.

Henry shivered, which he mistakenly ascribed to the night-time chill, not his worrying cogitations. He pulled his coat tight as a hand went to his temple, to feel for any unwelcome heat, the kind which might precede the kind of fever that would play havoc on an extremely delicate disposition. In truth, he had no idea how to proceed, while the complications extended beyond the thought his sister would keep hoping to escape.

There was little doubt Brazier, assuming he was still fit to do so, would keep trying to snatch her away. Turning, he could see a multitude of bobbing lights, which brought back the reality of what he'd left John Hawker to clear up, the first of the problems being the use of weapons which had only been intended to threaten.

What explanations and complications would arise from this night's events? He might consider Dan Spafford a gnat, not a threat, but badly wounded he could be more trouble than he was whole. His wastrel son would not be missed except by his pa and the local whores and tavern keepers, but there was Trotter's body to dispose of too.

If he didn't know the man, he knew of his inclinations, for Hawker had told him. His disappearance would surely be marked by those with whom he shared what passion he possessed, the denizens of the Middle Street Molly-house: their orientation rendered them clannish and protective of each other out of shared necessity.

There were the wounded to be dealt with, who once recovered, and added to those of Spafford's crew who were unmarked, would be difficult to keep silent. This he must leave to his subordinate for now; let Hawker do that for which he was employed, which was to ensure no evidence of what had occurred was there to be seen when the sun rose, ensuring neither curiosity nor speculation on the estate.

He would consult with Hawker on the morrow, perhaps to give him his way, for he'd suggested a disposal of the entire Spafford gang not a week past, obviously put out by his employer's refusal to contemplate a mass disposal of those who had troubled their trade. A return to the house it must be, for he could not stay out here and risk his health, added to which there would be a fire in his study to see off any chill. When he began to move, he was wondering if what had been suggested previously might serve now. Hawker's notion had been to take the whole gang out in one of their own luggers, lashed to the hulls, then sink them beyond the Goodwin Sands.

It had been declined on compelling grounds: such an act, the disappearance of a known rival in the smuggling trade, however insignificant, must draw too much attention to the business in which they were engaged, one which required a degree of discretion. For all his prominence, indeed power locally, it rested on a solid base of understanding with the leading citizenry.

Some knew something, if not all, regarding his activities, while the rest expressed no desire to enquire. Many benefitted materially from the level of smuggling he and his forbears had brought to the East Kent coast. Others in the town turned a blind eye merely to avoid trouble, for it was known crossing the Tulkington family – and Henry was the heir to several decades of their undertakings – could be at best expensive and at worst painful.

All would look away as long as the public peace remained undisturbed. Minor infractions could be covered over and frequently were, but a major breach of the peace, the kind which brought interest from outside the district, even the military, might force them to act against him on the grounds of self-preservation. It was essential no word of this night's events should spread and this indicated the need for drastic measures.

This did nothing to resolve the problem of his sister's relationship with Edward Brazier. Perhaps he would be required to reprise a notion previously put aside, given the disposal of a post captain in the King's Navy could not even be considered: the ramifications of such might go anywhere. Could he have Elisabeth locked away as mentally deficient, which would serve two requirements, first to keep her out of her paramour's clutches, the other allowing him to continue to control both her affairs and her considerable personal wealth?

Grady was waiting to open the front door as soon as his master came into view, there to disrobe him once indoors. The suspicious glare the servant got as Henry Tulkington stood, waiting to have his coat and muffler removed, did not register. Grady kept his gaze firmly fixed on a point just above his master's head.

'My sister?'

'In her room, sir, and the door locked once more.'

'Do I sense an opinion, Grady?'

'Such a thing is far from my place, Mr Tulkington.'

'Keep it that way and ensure you're not alone. I won't abide gossip, d'ye hear?' Taking assent for granted, he added, after a weak cough, 'Hot brandy and sugar in my study.'

'Henry.' The sharp call from halfway up the staircase obliged him to respond. There, wrapped in a dressing gown and under a mob cap, stood his Aunt Sarah, her face lined with concern. 'What's going on?'

'Going on?' was a growl, one which sent Grady off to do his master's bidding.

'Shooting, Henry, which I could not help but hear, then everyone rushing out of the front door as if we were under attack.'

'It's not something with which you should concern yourself. Indeed, it would be best if you go back to bed.'

'Do I not qualify for some kind of explanation?'

Henry lost his temper then, the frustrations of the night building to boiling point. Before him stood someone he could shout at without fear of response or sarcasm.

'I am not required to explain anything in my own house, which you would do well to remember, since you so recently have felt the need to set such a constraint aside.'

'Your tone is unbecoming,' was delivered in a hurt tone.

'Have a care your being here does not render itself unbecoming. You reside at Cottington Court on my sufferance, which is mine to grant or withdraw.'

There was so much Sarah Lovell wanted to say in response but dare not. Henry had bellowed the plain truth; she was wholly dependent on his goodwill for the room she occupied and the food she ate. Yet there had to be some kind of retort, one to imply she was not totally submissive.

'I will do as you ask, nephew, and wait until the morning, when I hope your mood will be more congenial.'

Henry replied as the weight of all which had happened this night bore down upon him. 'It would be best not to presume it to be so.'

CHAPTER TWO

Such a loud exchange could not but penetrate the locked door of Elisabeth's room. Her brother, normally icy cold in his relations within these walls, was clearly troubled enough to shout at their aunt. This might induce some comfort, but it did nothing to relieve her major anxiety; her lover had tried to rescue her for a second time and had, once more, failed. What would happen now?

There were many things beyond the door to trouble her, not least Henry being in control of matters. Then there was the threat from Harry Spafford, the man she had been drugged into marrying, a person she'd never met prior to the nuptials. He'd declared his intention to come and claim those rights which fell by law to a husband, however questionable the marriage.

She detested him and would have done so however they'd encountered each other. In his utter dissolution, he stood in total contrast to everything in which she believed, as well as the manner of her prior existence. This was based on only what she knew; the truth of his debauched way of life was likely many times worse, so it was terrifying to imagine him brutally forcing himself upon her in a place where there existed no protection.

Such thoughts, as well as visualisations of the ordeal, were whirling through her mind, only to be disturbed by the soft knock at the door.

Startled, she immediately concluded it could not be Spafford: he, no doubt full of wine and brandy, would have banged and demanded entry, thus it must be a servant or more likely her Aunt Sarah. Even so, there was a whispered obligation to make sure, added to an assurance of her being alone, before the key was turned. Face to face with her did not incline Elisabeth to being benign, given Sarah Lovell was as complicit in her difficulties as her brother.

'Henry is in a foul mood.'

'I heard.'

'I must ask if you know why?'

'I have no more notion than you.'

'I will not have him address me so. I will demand an apology come morning.'

The look accompanying this statement might be one of defiant determination, but Elisabeth knew it to be braggadocio without fear of consequence: Sarah Lovell would say nothing to further upset her nephew and, since Elisabeth ate in her room, her niece wouldn't be there come morning to nail the lie.

'Am I allowed to remark on your being up and fully dressed at this time of night?' This came with a meaningful glance at the outdoor cloak, which had been thrown on the bed. 'Also, awoken by the sound of guns going off, I saw you leave the house with the servants.'

'Remark upon it by all means,' was the cool reply.

Lovell's age-creased lips pursed with pique. 'So, I can conclude a purpose, which leads me also to think myself cruelly used. You must have had an arrangement to leave, which I suspect could only have been put in place by a deceit practised upon myself.'

There had been no arrangement, just a requirement she be ready, the only message her friend Annabel, with Sarah Lovell in constant attendance, had been able to pass on, and it had required a diversion caused by Annabel's children so as to permit a whisper.

Yet what was exercising Elisabeth was the notion her aunt could in any way consider herself a victim, she who'd complied with Henry's demand she witness the marriage to Spafford, pleading she had no choice. About to confirm the suspicion, Elisabeth held it in check; let her wonder without knowing the truth.

'Please leave.'

'Elisabeth, I'm doing my best to protect you.'

'Given the damage your aid has so far visited upon me, please desist. If you do not wish to consider Henry's invective just now as of no account, do as I ask.'

'I'm the only friend you have in this house.'

A cold look was enough to oblige departure, leaving Elisabeth, once the key was turned again, to ponder what the future held: terror or release.

'Please try again, Edward,' was a whispered prayer before she lay down, still fully clothed, to try and sleep. Somehow the hooting of an owl promised disappointment and brought on a wave of despair.

The same sound was heard by the quartet who'd come to Cottington with Edward Brazier, one of whom had just advanced a questionable proposition, to which the reply was scathing.

'Split up, is you mad?' rasped Dutchy Holland. 'With scarce a moon and who knows what might be lookin' out to put a ball in our back?'

'We can search wider,' countered Peddler Palmer. 'An' so far no soul's come after us.'

His tone lacking confidence, it was as good a way as any of telling Dutchy he was right. There might have been no evidence of a pursuit from the grounds of Cottington Court, as well as no more sounds of guns going off, but it did not render them safe. For now, their protection lay in being out of sight, within the small wood in which they'd taken shelter.

'We's got to find the captain,' Peddler insisted.

'Be daylight in short order,' Dutchy admitted. 'We'll look for him then.'

'We'll be easier to spot, sunup,' was the piqued response.

'Happen he's headed back at the Navy Yard,' suggested Joe Lascelles, as much to stop the argument as for any feeling it might be the case. 'Would he not head for there if he could?'

'So that's where we should go.' This came from Cocky Logan, the fourth of the old barge crew Brazier had called to his side when the town of Deal turned perilous. 'Captain's no an eejit.'

'His horse might decide the way,' Dutchy mused. 'Recall the wound and the way he lost his footing from the blow? Took him in the shoulder is my guess.'

'You'd ken, being hard by.'

'Like I stopped to look, Cocky. He was slumped over the neck when we sent the mare goin'. Keeping it headed where he wanted to go might be beyond him.'

'Well I hope my bugger knows the way home,' Peddler moaned, 'since I'm never puttin' my arse on his back again after this night.'

'His?' Joe scoffed. 'She's a mare too.'

'Peddler never did ken the difference, Joe,' joked Cocky, 'man or beast when it came to comfort. Spent the odd night in the manger, he has.'

'Havin' elbowed you aside first, you Sawney Jock.'

'Will you lot put your mind to what's to be done and stop gabbing your nonsense.'

Having been Edward Brazier's coxswain, the man who ruled aboard the captain's barge, Dutchy was the man to be deferred to by those who'd crewed it. Thus, mumbled regrets were in order, as was a subsequent silence. This allowed Dutchy to think and eventually come to a conclusion, which, after a long silence, he passed on to his mates. With the time since parting being past half a watch, and many miles of open country around, there was no telling how far the captain's horse, if he was in no state to control it, could have taken him.

But he could have managed its course, so it made sense to look first in the places he might be. Staying still and hoping was not wise; their escape had been blessed with luck while the threat of yet being pursued remained a reality. In daylight it would become more potent and, as Peddler said, they'd be sitting ducks in the open.

'Joe, you need to go back to the Navy Yard an' see if he's there.'

'On my own?'

Given his near-black skin, Joe's face and reservations were invisible, but the tone left no one in doubt of his feelings: safety lay in numbers. Dutchy pointed out they messed with the sailors attached to the yard. Being Brazier's servant, he could go places they could not, like the officers' quarters where the captain had been given a berth.

'And us?' Peddler asked.

'I say we call in at the Old Playhouse. The Riorden woman is a bit soft on the capt'n and she'd take him in if he turned up hurt. We'll go by the other Irish cove's stables first and drop off the mounts, which'll tell us if the mare's found the way home.'

'Walkin'?' Peddler demanded.

'You can if you want, if'n you don't mind being left behind.'

'Remind me to dig out a better set of shipmates.'

'Dinna exist, Peddler,' Cocky responded. 'An' what others would put up wi' ye?'

Once out of the copse and a moaning Peddler mounted, there was no doubt about direction: given a sky of mixed cloud, the sea reflected the half-moon when it showed, which fixed their course. Moving in such indifferent light was not without obstacles, these usually being sensed by the horses rather than seen by the riders. Thick hedgerows made a straight line of progress impossible, while drainage ditches were hard to spot when clouds obscured both moon and starlight.

Progress was eased once they made the marshes to the north of Deal. Joe Lascelles being sent on foot towards the flaring beacons of Sandown Castle. The others turned inland to skirt around the town, relieved when dawn began to show, a thin strip of grey light in the east. By the time they made the stables owned by Vincent Flaherty it was full daylight, with the owner already up and doing his work. A man who would normally have given them a loud and friendly greeting, such a thing did not materialise this day. The looks on the trio of faces didn't allow for his customary cheerfulness.

'I can take it, Mr Flaherty, Captain Brazier has not come by?'

'You can, Dutchy.'

'Thought Bonnie might know the way home.'

'And why would she need to?'

Dutchy shrugged but didn't reply, which got a jaundiced look, especially aimed at the long musket slung, like those of his companions, over his shoulder, as well as at the two spare mounts, Canasta being one. The pony had been hired by Brazier's lady and, so fond had she become, she'd expressed a wish to buy him.

'It might be a notion to tell me what it was you were all about last night, not that much of a brain is required to guess. And I ask again, why would Bonnie need to know the way home?'

'Can I get off this damned animal?' called Peddler.

'Sure it's a miracle you're still on the cuddy.' Cocky and Dutchy slid to the ground as Flaherty went to help Peddler down, before loosening the girth on the mare, speaking over his shoulder. 'What you're askin' suggests Edward would struggle to come back this way unaided. It tells me also, since you're enquiring of him, you've no idea where he is.'

'Best tell him,' Cocky murmured.

The response wasn't immediate; it had to be weighed, though the looks Dutchy was getting from his shipmates underlined there was little option. Without Brazier they were adrift, and this was not a comfortable place to be, especially when they had no idea what the repercussions of the night's events would be. As he related his tale, likewise unsaddling his mount, it was to an increasingly incredulous Irishman.

'Muskets you took along, for all love. Sure, I never had Edward for a fool, though I will own, passion makes eejits of us all.'

'They were for threat, no more,' Dutchy protested.

'But loaded nevertheless?' That got a nod. 'He took a wound you say. How bad?'

It was shaming to admit they had no idea, having loaded him on to Bonnie, slapping hard on her rump to get her going without a care for where it might be. They were then obliged to look to their own safety, which meant aiming said muskets through the gate from which they'd just escaped, to deter anyone in pursuit. When none showed, they took the horses and retired, taking refuge in the nearby clump of trees.

'And Bonnie?'

'I'd say she was headed north to begin with; after that, who knows?'

'From where she might turn in any direction?' There was no choice but to acknowledge the truth of Flaherty's conclusion. 'The condition of Edward would dictate the matter.'

This got no answer either, even if already discussed, just head dropping so their eyes would not meet those of the man seeking answers. No one wanted to admit the obvious: with no certain knowledge of the nature of the wound, only a suspicion it might be serious, the possibility existed their captain might not still be alive.

'Christ,' Flaherty huffed, 'we'll know the truth of it soon enough, will we not? Expired or living, he will be found, wherever he's ended up. A man with a wound can't just disappear.'

Asked to answer for his whereabouts or his condition, Edward Brazier would have been unable to reply. He lay, face down and unconscious, on a straw-filled mattress as the man who'd found him at first light examined his naked back, more the small hole high on the shoulder with severe bruising around it, which he suspected had been made by a pistol or musket-fired ball. The soaked shirt testified to what blood had been lost already, this stemmed by pressure: in falling off his horse, the victim had landed on the wound.

No true assessment could be made while it was covered, which explained his being stripped to the waist, only a feeling that if left unattended it could prove mortal. There was bound to be cloth in such a wound, carried from the clothing this officer had been wearing when struck. If such extended to an unclean shirt, or part of his uniform coat, putrefaction would set in and it would, in time, prove fatal.

'What brought you to my fence?' was an oft-repeated comment from the man doing the tending. 'And what's a captain in King George's Navy doing riding around this part of Kent at night, getting shot at, an' you such a meaty soul to boot.'

It had been a struggle, once it had been established the flat-out figure was still breathing, to get this strange apparition indoors and disrobed. Zachary Colton was not the man he had once been; age had sapped the strength for which he had been noted. Catching a horse intent on grazing between the trees of the orchard had been easier, the fine bay mare now tied to a rail outside.

'I say it must be God's will to bring you here,' he continued, bent over to get an up-close view of the wound, seeing the minute trail of trapped white thread, material from the linen of the shirt, clear to the naked eye now the sun was up, light streaming through the opened shutters. 'Never thought to see a wound like this again, but seen them I has.'

Zachary then crossed himself, for he was a deeply religious man. 'It will be his grace which sees you living or his wish if you should pass over.'

Colton wondered if he was seeking to absolve himself, should matters turn out badly, which was not Christian. He must do his best and, if it did not suffice, then some of the outcome must lay at his door. This accepted, he went to an old and battered sea chest with faded gold lettering on its front, which, when opened, revealed it to be lined in metal, sufficient to keep out vermin. There he knelt down to take out and lay aside much of what it contained: a meagre amount of clothing, spare shirts, an oilskin cape and a blue brass-buttoned jacket, plus a couple of blankets.

At the bottom, by a small pile of books and a medicinal bottle, lay the instruments bequeathed to him, never used since the surgeon/barber who'd been his master, and to whom he'd acted as an assistant, had come home from the Americas. The surrender of the British Army at Yorktown had put paid to any hope of holding on to the thirteen colonies and, with the 3rd Regiment of Foot no longer engaged in fighting, he'd returned home to East Kent, bringing Zachary with him.

As he took out the instruments, he sought to recall the procedure, worried a lack of memory might cause him to act imprudently. Still kneeling, he clasped his hands together and mouthed a prayer, asking God to guide his hand. The instruments were then laid out on the floor beside the cot, the most important being the retractors, with which he would be required to find and, if it was safe to do so, remove the ball he suspected was embedded in flesh.

Before acting, he crossed to the hearth to fetch the pot of hot water earlier placed there to boil. He also fetched the needle and thread commonly used these days to mend his clothing, also previously made ready for use. A final look to an invisible sky for more divine assistance was made before he commenced his task. Taking up a probe, he pushed gently into the wound, a cloth whipped from the pot and squeezed to dampness being used to wipe clear the increasing flow of blood. The insertion caused severe pain, which could not be in doubt; the body jerked in spasm and a low moan escaped through compressed lips, which had to be ignored.

Speed was better than care and his first task was to get out the ball and, if his effort lacked subtlety or finesse, the swiftness, once he took up and employed the retractors, was commendable. Luckily the ball had not penetrated too deeply, surely due to the amount of clothing it had had to pass through before striking flesh. As he pushed, he felt the ends come up against bone, so he sought to close them, his heart lifting when they refused.

The extraction was made with scant grace but, on exit, there was a round ball, from a musket by its size, clasped in the grip. This was cheering, but blood was still flowing, which made his next task so much harder: he used tweezers to extract, once located, the bits of what he suspected were shirt linen, a task he now recalled he should have carried out first. To keep on for too long was as dangerous as the thought some might remain; blood was being lost too quickly, so a clamp was applied to close the wound.

This had been his task in the past, be it on a horse or a human, to hold it while the surgeon stitched the flesh. It was obvious one man alone could not accomplish both, so he held on, to sit for a good hour in deep prayer, interrupted by regular glances to see if the bleeding had ceased. When it stopped, he went to work with the needle to join flesh to flesh in a pattern which was far from perfect; the wound, if it did heal and if the victim survived, would form an ugly scar.

Once completed and with his patient comatose, Zachary left to go about his daily tasks of pruning and paring, with the additional need to take the man's horse, which he reckoned a fine animal, to the field of pasture where he kept his donkey, leaving the pair to sniff each other out.

CHAPTER THREE

It had been a trying night for John Hawker, even if being up till dawn was a far from uncommon experience given smuggling, of necessity, had to be carried out in the hours of darkness. To oversee such operations induced tension certainly, but they were meat to his soul, for the element of risk, or rather the need to negate it and safely land a cargo, fed something in his being. What he had just been about carried hazards, no doubt, but they were not of the kind to bring satisfaction, even when successfully completed.

He'd got his charges, both his own men and those they'd taken prisoner, back to the slaughterhouse-cum-tannery he ran on behalf of Henry Tulkington, to place Spafford and his gang in parts of the building they'd only very recently vacated. This was the second time their activities had landed them as captives, all because his employer had not seen the wisdom of capping their depredations with the right remedy on the first transgression.

Not really a man for introspection, Hawker could not avoid rumination now, given he had no one with whom he could share the thoughts which troubled him. This was not a factor to induce concern; he'd been a self-contained entity, man and boy. The notion of sharing problems was anathema: such required trust and that was not an emotion to even be considered when his early years had been so full of betrayals.

Now he was brooding, alone, in his office above the slaughterhouse, halfway through a strong pot of coffee being kept warm on the stove, the remains of a breakfast brought in from the nearest tavern congealing by his side. The place was coming alive below his feet, if this could be considered the right expression for the sound of lowing cattle. They were being led to the pens they would occupy, prior to being stunned, slain, butchered and salted, before being packed in barrels, noisily knocked up by the cooper.

The lowing had a soothing quality, so different from the squealing of pigs facing the same fate. It was as if the bovines had no inkling of what was to come, while the porkers knew instinctively or could smell death. Right at this moment he felt closer to the latter than any herd of cows. He wanted to make as much noise regarding his own fears but was concerned it would be futile.

'You've buggered this up good and proper,' was applied to a mental image of Henry Tulkington.

Talking to himself induced no feeling of eccentricity. If he would never admit to being lonely and would have smashed in the head of anyone who suggested such a thing to be the case, he was, in truth, isolated by one if not both of his employments. No one loves a tax collector, unless they can bribe him to ease their burden, something best never to raise with John Hawker. That aside, there were a multitude of folk who had reason to be cautious of a man known for violence as well as one who revelled in his reputation. Better to be feared than loved was a saying he had heard ascribed to some famous cove from ancient Rome. It was one which suited him well.

The words just uttered brought on a welcome and rare feeling of denigration; normally he kept his opinion of Henry Tulkington and his ways well buttoned up, for to allow them free rein was to lose control of where they might lead. At the base of this was the sure knowledge his present employer was not half the man his father had been, and recent events underlined the fact.

'Soon as Spafford laid hands on our goods, you should have slit the sod's gullet, or let me do it for you. That's how you clap a stopper on thieving.'

Dan Spafford had done it twice, stolen smuggled cargo and sold it for his own gain and, Hawker suspected, for the added spice of tweaking Tulkington's nose. Unlike his willowy and weak-chested son, Acton Tulkington might not have left such a task of chastisement to John Hawker or anyone else. He was man enough, if need be, to do the deed himself.

The sound of footsteps on the wooden risers had Hawker set aside such disturbing thoughts, lest they show in some way to whom he suspected must be coming. Few ascended to his office without first issuing a warning shout, to ensure it was allowed. Sure enough, the silk-edged tricorne hat appeared, adorning the visitor's head. When the whole of his being emerged, it was, as usual, well protected with a heavy coat and muffler.

Also familiar was the look, which ever needled John Hawker on his employer's arrival: one of condescension, as if even to be in this place, full of the smell of blood and tanning, was a dent to his dignity. As ever, there was a plate of rosemary by the coffee pot, being warmed to alleviate the troubling odours.

'I trust all went well, John.'

'As well as could be managed, with Dan Spafford screaming like a trapped fox.'

It was not necessary to add he'd been silenced by a thud from Hawker's pistol butt; Henry Tulkington would not wish to know. For the man administering the blow, if the bugger expired, it was no more than he deserved.

'Is he still . . . ?' The uncompleted enquiry was delivered over a shoulder; as usual his first act had been to remove his gloves and warm his hands over the stove.

'Breathing? Far as I know.' The sigh this produced obliged

31

Hawker to add, 'I'd be told the minute he was not, which would scarce serve us ill.'

'The problem is serious, is it not?' *All because you're too lily-livered to act right* remained unspoken, as Hawker acknowledged Tulkington's conclusion. 'I still have doubts as to your proposed remedy.'

Turning to look at Hawker, his demeanour serious, he added an obvious point. 'In one sense the situation has not altered. To dispose of so many people, especially when one is as well-known as Spafford and the rest are Deal men, cannot be done without engendering dangerous rumours.'

'I say it can, if it's done right, and we've got to cover for Daisy Trotter being dead regardless. If they just disappear and one of the Spafford luggers is gone with them, it will be supposed they've either been had up over the water while loading, or sunk on the way there or back, which has happened to enough folk afore.'

'How simple you make it sound. And I note you make no mention of Harry Spafford.'

'He's not one to be missed. Him you could dump by the roadside and it would be taken as just deserts.'

Hawker was not the only one harbouring unspoken thoughts, and Henry's pressing one was how inappropriately the man before him had behaved. He'd been too vocal in his pursuit of whoever had thieved their contraband, acting as if it was his own property, his behaviour utterly lacking any degree of subtlety. He'd dragged a drunken and pleading Harry Spafford, known to be a weakling, all the way to the slaughterhouse along the Lower Valley Road, the busiest thoroughfare in Deal.

Questioning a terrified Harry had provided proof of what Spafford senior had been up to, which was a good thing. But too many folk had witnessed him being manhandled as well as where he'd been taken. Given the wastrel had been used to thwart Brazier's intentions, he'd been out of sight of the locals ever since, either at Cottington Court or, for a brief spell, debauching himself in Chatham. Talk would have begun as soon as he was hauled away and could only have grown with his continued absence. This was among the thoughts upon which Henry had fretted before retiring for the night. He had returned to the same problems as soon he awoke, which continued both through being shaved, this followed by a silent breakfast in the company of his Aunt Sarah.

There was little doubt a deed such as Hawker proposed could be carried out, but could what it would spark be controlled? Rumours would arise regarding the fate of Spafford and his gang. There was the nature of Deal and its surroundings, with a population ever eager to invent something, if no other wild tale was doing the rounds. What might be whispered long afterwards was not a cause for concern, as long as it could be contained in the immediate aftermath.

'I ask you to consider what else we can do, Mr Tulkington?'

The response was terse. 'Don't you think I've done that?'

'You can't fix up Dan Spafford without a sawbones and, as said already, it would have to be one you trust or can pay enough to stay quiet, which is for you to know. He might die under the knife as he should, but what happens with him recovered, about and with nowt to lose? He's sure to gab about what happened with his boy and blame you.'

Acknowledgement came out reluctantly, with Hawker quick to drive home what looked like agreement.

'T'other sod has a flesh wound, which even I can manage to stitch, but it's his tongue and those of his mates I can't sew up. Walking free, I would not be trustin' to any promises they made. A few pots of ale, or a whore's head on a bolster and it would be bound to spill.'

'What of your men?'

It was typical of Henry Tulkington to leave out the crux of the question, just another example of him being so much more squeamish

33

than his pa. Why not just come out and ask if they were up to doing murder, for he had obviously decided it must be so?

'Might need a reward, but they'll do as I bid. Any who look to be doubtful will join the Spaffords in the deep six.'

'Can it be as simple as you say?'

'I'll grant it as a problem. Ground needs waterin', word spread Spafford has gone on a crossing and will be looking for folk to buy his cargo. There's a tale I can set in motion and it'll be all over in no time.'

'How long?'

'Couple of days would see it common gossip. After that is up you, but I'd say the sooner we see the disposing finished, the better.'

'Then I must give my consent.' Tulkington gave Hawker a look as he said it, which told his man, if he was agreeing to the deed, there was no enthusiasm.

'Then I'll set the rumours going this very day.'

'We must turn to other matters.'

'Next cargo's due?'

'Of course.' The voice, hitherto far from firm, became strong now. 'And this business you propose must not do anything to impede a safe landing.'

If the forces of law and order moved in the English counties, it was not with haste. For the post of High Sheriff of Kent, it could well depend on the load under which the man in office was presently labouring. This took no account of the office being an annual Crown appointment, something which rendered variable the ability and enthusiasm for enquiry into felonious matters of those called upon to fill it, not generally held to be high.

The latest incumbent, Mr John Cottin, was different to the normal run of placemen. New to his office and, having followed on from a set of indolent predecessors, he was determined to make his mark.

In visible activity lay the opportunity to place his name on the lips of those in the county who could guarantee further career elevation, which might even extend to Whitehall.

Not many would have acted on the matter disconcerting him now, even if zealous, given the distance. This involved travelling from Westerham to Deal, a journey of nearly eighty miles, with two changes of coach and an overnight stop, thus one not to be undertaken lightly. He'd been advised in writing of a serious crime, one he saw as an occasion in which a reputation might begin to be forged. Thus, unlike those who'd gone before him, he declined to accept assurances all proper procedures were being followed.

A dead body had been found after riotous assembly and the burning out of a private house. The Deal coroner, duty-bound to advise him of the circumstances, had laid out the bare bones of the matter, saying the victim was unidentifiable, with too many potential miscreants to nail a culprit. He thought they could, as was the custom, handle it locally. John Cottin disagreed and wrote to tell them so.

Thus, the Canterbury stagecoach, the third he'd been required to take on a two-day journey, deposited him at the Three Kings fronting Deal beach, where he had written to arrange accommodation. Here, as required by the summons also sent ahead, there should be waiting the local officials whom he required to answer to him: said coroner, two local magistrates and the official responsible for oversight of the town watchmen who were supposed to and had clearly failed to maintain law and order.

'A room has been prepared for your use, Mr Cottin, and it be a signal honour you chose my humble establishment to go about your occasions, the honour of which will not go unremarked upon. The gentlemen you need to see are awaiting you.'

This obsequious greeting was provided by the proprietor, a fellow named August Garlick according to the board above the entrance, a man utterly unsuited to the name under which he'd been baptised, given there was nothing either elevated or sunny about his disposition. With his long, pallid face, dominated by a purple imbiber's nose and framed by excessive side whiskers, he had about him a manner which tended to induce a degree of caution. There was also a look in the watery eyes, added to a certain slight cant of the head, hinting at an untoward level of inquisitiveness.

'You'll find no better place to undertake your business than the Three Kings, sir. And should you want for anything, then August Garlick is here to provide it. I can say, without peradventure, no one knows the town as I do, for I make it my business to keep an ear to the ground.'

The invitation that this should be followed by enquiry was in the proprietor's expression, one intended to imply he could be trusted to provide information not vouchsafed to mere mortals. John Cottin saw instead a probable busybody, who would be the fount of every rumour going, possibly more likely to distract from the truth than reveal anything useful. It was, however, politic not to close off any avenues of enquiry.

'Rest assured I'll bear it in mind, Mr Garlick. Now, if you would be so kind?'

The hint being taken, Cottin was led up the stairs to a room overlooking the Deal Roads, the busy anchorage hemmed in and protected by the Goodwin Sands, packed with maritime activity. He was afforded a brief glimpse of what lay within its waters: vessels of all shapes and sizes, either recently returned from far-off destinations or preparing to weigh and set off for the same places, all fed by an endless stream of boats and hoys carrying the many articles they would need on their voyage.

As he was shown in, four soberly suited men stood to greet him, none wearing a smile. They saw before them a fellow too slight for such a high-sounding title. He was young-looking even for his thirty-five years, sprightly in his step, with a clear, good-looking countenance, an open expression emanating from a steady brown-eyed gaze. Hat off, it revealed a full head of light-coloured hair, the greeting accompanying the act followed by a broad and disarming smile, which faded when not returned.

Cottin reckoned he was about to be confronted by people seeking to test his mettle, just as he reckoned to know why. The nature of this place could be said to constitute common knowledge throughout the county; indeed, it probably extended to half the country, Deal being seen as exceptionally lawless, an opinion publicly endorsed by no less an authority than William Pitt, the King's First Minister. Frustrated by the level of smuggling on the East Kent coast and the subsequent loss of revenue to the Exchequer, he'd brought in soldiers to burn every boat on the strand a mere three years' past. Not that it had seemed to have much effect: craft were quickly replaced and the nefarious trade was held to be as lively as ever, with Cottin wondering if by his efforts he might effect change.

Introductions made, he first asked the coroner to lay out the case.

'Which I wrote you about, sir, in some detail.'

'Oblige me with a reprise, Mr Cavell. No written missive can fully cover the facts. It struggles with interpretation.'

The short period of silence which followed, added to the exchanged glances from those before him, underlined how they judged his presence. There would be many occasions when matters, which might have fallen to the judgement of the High Sheriff of Kent, or even the King's Bench Court, had taken place here, disreputable occurrences which had been kept within its boundaries, lest enquiries lead to places the locals wished to keep opaque.

Cavell related what had occurred in a monotone voice, which lacked any indication of either shock or sympathy for what had surely been the innocent victim of a crime. When asked what had set the riot in motion, he could offer no clue, this backed up by the

37

slow shaking heads of his companions, who acted as if wrongdoing of any kind was beyond their comprehension. The disturbance had taken place, Quebec House had been set alight for no known reason, by persons as unidentified as the charred corpse discovered in the ruins.

'You do not yet have a name?'

'Time has not permitted us to press our enquiries to uncover such a fact.'

There was little point in saying how many days had passed. 'Your letter implied he was not alone in occupation?'

'No.'

'So who else was living there?'

'A certain naval officer.'

'Can I assume he has a name?'

'Edward Brazier . . .'

'Rank, Mr Cavell?'

'Post Captain.'

'Anyone else – apart from the victim, of course?'

'It's been suggested to us he had with him some fellows rumoured to be members of his old crew.' It took raised eyebrows to get Cavell to add, 'Four in number.'

'Their names?' This too got looks of ignorance. 'Do you know if they were within the building?' It was hard to contain frustration in the face of a quartet of blank expressions, but John Cottin managed it. 'From which I take it you have yet to institute any enquires at all?'

One of the two magistrates, Phineas Tooke, other than having been introduced when Cottin first entered the room, spoke for the first time, his words silently backed up by vigorous nods from Gould, the fourth fellow attending.

'You must surely understand, Mr Cottin, we are busy men with our own affairs to see to, which must take precedence over the business of the town. Added to which we have no proficiency in the investigation of crimes – this lies with an office like your own. It would not be proper to usurp such duties, sir, so once informed of your intention to come to Deal, we felt it best to await your arrival.'

Cottin looked at the written report he'd been sent on the morning after the riot, now open on his lap, taking his time in the sure knowledge doing so would render these men uncomfortable. To a mind like his, there was only one explanation for such inactivity: a complete indifference to the execution of even the most basic functions of their positions. One fact was very pertinent – there was no one else waiting to meet him.

'The whereabouts of this naval officer? He's surely available to be questioned?'

'Ah!' was Tooke's expression, which meant what followed was no surprise. 'He chose to reside at the Navy Yard, but on enquiring of him late last night, in order he may be available to you this morning, there was no sign of his presence. Nor were any of those who we think shared the house with him. It is quite possible they have departed Deal altogether.'

It's very possible you hope they have done so, Cottin thought, as he looked back at Cavell's letter, thinking about the choices before him. Whatever the cause of the events described, these four worthies wanted it to go away. A Crown official with sweeping powers poking about in their known den of iniquity was anathema. He could comply, and allow Cavell to convene a court at which the whole affair would be put down to death by misadventure.

No opprobrium, Cottin knew, would accrue to him and nor, given no one had come forward to say they could be related to the corpse, would anyone bother to enquire if he had properly executed his duties. Later he would wonder if it was just cussedness or the obvious determination of these four sods not to cooperate with him which made him go on.

'Your letter tells me the proprietor of Quebec House was not on the premises at the time of the fire?' A nod greeted the question; again, no information was about to be volunteered. 'A Mrs Riorden?'

'The name is correct, sir, but we have no knowledge of her matrimonial estate.'

'Yet, as landlady, she would surely know who lived on her property?'

'It could be so,' Tooke replied, before adding, on the receiving end of a sharp look from the coroner, 'then again, perhaps not. I believe a lawyer handles her affairs.'

'Let us assume it to be the case. I suggest she be the first person to whom I speak. You will, I assume, be willing to direct me to where she resides?'

'We will enquire on your behalf, certainly,' came from Tooke's fellow magistrate, Tobias Sowerby, who could not conceal he was struggling to hide his frustration. 'When we find her, I take it you would like us to send the information here?'

'I'd be obliged.'

'Then, if you don't mind, Mr Cottin, the needs of our undertakings and those of the town never cease to call upon our time.'

The way they all stood as one gave Cottin no choice but to accept the meeting was over, forced to stand himself and respond to their murmured good days. Once they were through the door he sat down again, deep in contemplation, seeking an avenue by which he could proceed without their help. After a few minutes, an interval decent enough to ensure they had departed the premises, he went down to the hatch where he'd met the proprietor, ringing the bell to summon him.

'Mr Garlick, do you know where I could find a lady by the name of Riorden?'

'At the Old Playhouse, sir, as all know. She's a person of some significance in the town.'

'Which is where?'

'In the Lower Valley Road.'

'From the name, this being called the Beach Street, can I take it Middle Street is on the way?'

'You can. Might I enquire as to why you wish to know, sir?'

'What I wish, Mr Garlick, is for directions and no more.'

CHAPTER FOUR

Having confirmed the details regarding the latest expected cargo of contraband, set for any suitable day in the coming week, Henry Tulkington left the slaughterhouse in a far from settled state. Even if he'd agreed to what Hawker proposed, it gave him scant comfort, seeming to him to fall into the same box as the night before, namely a loss of control. He'd been pushed to approve a plan not of his devising and one about which he still had serious reservations, which led to conclusions already considered.

Hawker appeared to think any misgivings he harboured about the way matters were being run remained hidden. But his employer was adept at smelling the slightest degree of dissent and he was sniffing it now, troubling since it underlined a feeling he'd been increasingly aware of these last weeks, namely the man seemed to have forgotten his place. The way the enterprise was constructed, and for reasons of security, meant only one person could be in possession of all the strands and it was him. Financing, added to the distribution of contraband, were separate elements to those overseen by Hawker, the actual physical landing of the cargo.

He seemed to be questioning his employer's judgement, something hitherto unknown and which could be dated. The first manifestation surfaced over his dealings with Dan Spafford, a fellow he had hitherto taken great trouble to avoid. The reasons had more than just business at the core; Spafford was a ruffian, who looked, acted and sounded like one, the kind of low, ill-educated cully who still lived in the manner of Henry's grandfather.

Corley Tulkington had, by sheer effort, sharp cunning and a degree of violence, hauled himself up from a mere beach smuggler to a position of affluence, though he'd apparently never lost his coarse, Lower Deal manner. This had seen the family shunned, even when they took possession of the dilapidated estate of Cottington Court, lavishing much expenditure on improvements, to turn it into one of the finest houses and farm properties in East Kent. Two generations later, the case was much altered, as a result of which Henry was conscious of and jealously guarded his status as a gentleman. The likes of Spafford, a smuggler of an older school, stood as an uncomfortable reminder of the stock from which he came.

Much persuasion had been required before he'd agreed a meeting, this originally proposed at the behest of the now deceased Daisy Trotter. Spafford's lifetime collaborator had contacted John Hawker to suggest it take place, insisting there was profit to be had for the Tulkington trade. Once Hawker extracted the nod, the only insistence being it happen out of sight of prying eyes, the pair then set a time and place, even if the aim still remained mysterious. Once revealed, far from being tempting, it had received nothing but ridicule larded with insults from Henry Tulkington.

But it was not the nub of the problem. Meeting over, he'd declined to inform an inquisitive employee what had passed between them. This had not gone down well: John Hawker felt he had the right to be included when, in truth, it was none of his business. A man who'd come by inheritance, he'd never hidden his admiration for, or his gratitude to, Henry's father. This was seen as very proper and, hitherto, he'd proved both loyal and efficient.

To keep it that way Hawker would need to be reminded of his

43

place in the scheme of things. If he didn't like it, then he would have to move on, a thought to open up an obvious conundrum: how to replace him, for such men were not ten a penny. He would be hard to substitute, quite apart from the fact, though he was reluctant to entertain the notion, Henry Tulkington had no idea of how to go about it.

By the time his coach was passing the entrance to the Old Playhouse, his thinking had moved on to the problems of his sister and how to contain her. Harry Spafford was no more, which was a pity given the threat he posed was one to keep her in check. His coach stopped, having become entangled in a mess of conveyances, from vans to dog carts, added to which was much bustling humanity, none willing to surrender the way, a feature of the Lower Valley Road.

An idle glance out of the side window drew his attention to a group of men, sailors by their garb, being let in through the front door, one a blonde giant, another black, the other pair nondescript. He failed to recognise them, which was hardly surprising: the habit of keeping his affairs in boxes gave him no chance to put a name to the former members of Edward Brazier's barge crew. Vincent Flaherty had preceded them and thus remained unseen, for his face would have been familiar; indeed, it was only due to his calling that the party had been admitted at all. An establishment which stayed open late, to entertain both the locals and the numerous visiting seafarers, did not welcome early morning custom.

'Sure, I hope there's some purpose to this.'

Called from her upstairs apartment, Saoirse Riorden still managed to elicit a degree of admiration, for she had declined to appear before them without at least the most basic toilette. With a mass of red hair and a fine if pale complexion, she was a striking woman. Added to this, as the owner of the Old Playhouse, run by her single-handed, she was not of the kind to be trifled with.

'Tell her, Dutchy,' Flaherty murmured.

A big man and confident with it, the cap Dutchy wore was nevertheless snatched off his head with speed, a gesture duplicated by his companions.

'It be about the captain, ma'am. I take leave to ask if he's here or has come by.'

'He has not,' came with flashing green eyes, a look which sought to convey the nature of the enquiry was untoward, given what it could imply. 'Nor has he reason to.'

About to explain, Dutchy was interrupted by loud and imperious banging at the door. Saoirse impatiently gestured for the maid who'd come downstairs with her to respond, which left everyone standing in silence. There was no admitting whosoever was doing the banging. The door closed once more, the maid came to whisper in her mistress's ear and hand over a card, the effect mystifying.

'All of you, out of sight till I see to this.'

'Who is it, Saoirse?' Flaherty asked.

'A fellow no one in their right mind wants to have callin', but one I must admit. Go into the Card Room and shut the door. And for the love of Christ, stay quiet.'

Joe Lascelles protested. 'What we're about is serious.'

'I daresay, but it will have to wait. Now get moving. Dottie, admit the caller when all is right and show him to my sitting room. Then make a pot of coffee.'

If you excluded Dottie, John Cottin entered an empty hallway, being gifted a curtsy from her before he was led up the stairs. Vincent Flaherty, peering through a crack in the door, saw him but this provided nothing in the way of enlightenment, though the sight of a good-looking cove calling on Saoirse at such an hour, given his feelings for her, was not something to induce comfort.

If he was in the grip of disquiet, Saoirse was a damn sight more uncomfortable, the only relief being this official had come on his own, so it was no raid. Like most folk in the town who traded for profit in anything to do with relaxation, her cellar was the repository of much in the way of untaxed goods, wines and spirits bought through the agency of John Hawker. She had firm opinions on who was behind him but it mattered little; he was the man with whom she did business.

This made her ragingly curious as to why she was being called on by such an official, yet there was just as much wonder to what a man of his standing was doing in Deal, given the local elected officials would have done nothing to encourage a visitation. The law, from high sheriffs through to lord lieutenants, the military and officers of the Excise were best kept at arm's length. Then, if he was here on official business, which the production of his card indicated, why was she being called upon when there were any number of places even more complicit in the avoidance of taxes?

It was essential to appear calm, so she disported herself on a settle, forcing down the feeling of tense anticipation by the application of several deep breaths. Cottin, shown through the door, appeared slightly thrown by what he saw sat before him: whatever he'd expected it was not a beautiful woman lounging in a silken dressing gown and one who addressed him in a steady voice.

'Mr Cottin, is it?'

His hat came off with the same alacrity as Dutchy's headgear. 'I'm unsure how to address you . . .'

'Miss Riorden will serve, sir.'

The hat was used to request permission to sit, granted by a nod. 'Forgive me for calling at what appears to be an inconvenient hour.'

'The hour apart, I am deeply curious as to your reasons, sir?'

'Quebec House?'

It took a high measure of control to merely respond with, 'What of it?' given the purpose was far from what she'd expected. In the name of all holy, what was a high sheriff doing poking his nose into that mess?

'You are the proprietor, I gather, and were renting it to a certain naval officer.'

'You seem well informed, sir,' was mere hedging, buying time to think.

'The information was vouchsafed to me by the coroner. A Captain Edward Brazier, I was told.'

There was no alternative to admission, though doing so did nothing to quell the measure of concern engendered, so her next question was asked to gain time.

'Have you come far?'

Seen for what it was, it got a composed, if firm response. 'As far as my duty demands, Miss Riorden.'

'Duty, is it? Sure, we're not accustomed to such eminent folk as your good self coming to the coast on official business, or even just to take the air.'

'The occasion requires it. A man died in circumstances which warrant enquiry, and those who are responsible locally for such matters have no idea who he is. I was hoping you could enlighten me.'

Saoirse was sure, without knowing precisely why, acceding to such a query would be unwise: it never did to act openly with those representing the law. Her mind was also occupied with the appearance of Dutchy Holland and his mates in the company of Vincent Flaherty. They too had been asking about Edward Brazier, in a way implying something untoward. Whatever else she was going to be told, by their expressions it did not bode well. The natural caution about husbanding information, which came as much from her Irish background as anything in Deal, made her disinclined to volunteer the truth, which would be to admit the victim was a one-time groom at Cottington Court, recently dismissed from his post.

Anything to do with the name of Tulkington was to be avoided and, besides, she could only guess at the reason Upton had ended up in Quebec House, which rendered it territory into which it was unsafe to wander. But this damn sheriff had come here, sent by whom? What had already been said? It was necessary to take a chance he'd been given little.

'The only person I had dealings with was Captain Brazier. I was aware he was not in sole occupation but, beyond that, I saw no need to enquire. As long as my rent was met it was his affair.'

'So you have no names for the other occupants?'

'None.'

'And the present whereabouts of Captain Brazier?'

'You will appreciate he's no longer my tenant.'

'For obvious reasons.' The head dropped as if in disappointment, but it was really a stratagem to create disclosure, aided by the next question and the complete change of subject. 'What do you think caused your house to be the target of a mob?'

'I don't see the house had anything to do with it.'

'The occupants, then?' came with the faintest hint of exasperation, which led Saoirse to conclude he was asking a question to which he already knew the answer. Equivocation thus would not serve.

'There was a rumour doing the rounds – and to be sure there is ever one or more – hinting Captain Brazier was acting as a spy on behalf of the Excise and William Pitt. If you ask about, you'll find Pitt's not popular in these parts for his past actions. It's a name likely to unleash high passions in those who make a living on Deal Beach.'

'Do you say they are responsible?'

'Mr Cottin, I have no idea. I was not party to what took place, so I have no knowledge of who or what set the disturbance in motion.'

'You say "rumour". It was not, then, established fact?'

'I have no awareness it was.'

'I took the liberty of passing the shell of your house, which I would suggest represents a grievous material loss. Odd you don't seem able to see a connection to do with my purpose here.'

'Which is?'

'To find out who is responsible for what was plain murder.'

'The house was torched by a mob and it's not the first time this has happened in Deal.'

'Such disturbances are often set in motion to serve the purpose of one or more individuals. If, as you say, the name of William Pitt was invoked, then I would scarce be surprised to find a number of folk locally, if it was true, had a great deal to lose.'

'Have I not already said enough to convince you? I don't know what you suggest is fact.'

'Indeed, Miss Riorden. My task now is to find Captain Brazier and ascertain from him the identity of the victim.' The tone of voice changed to one of deliberate irony. 'I cannot but believe *he* knew the name of someone in occupation of a house in which he was also resident. If you have any contact with him, please request he calls on me at the Three Kings.'

Cottin stood, his attitude now lacking warmth, nor was there humour. 'I shall bid you good day. For now.'

Saoirse sat for a good two minutes after Cottin left, as much to ensure he was out of the door as to deliberate on what had just taken place. But sitting thinking was not going to get her anywhere and there was the other matter to attend to. So she went back downstairs to the Card Room, demanding on entry to be told what in the name of the Holy Virgin was going on.

As before, it was left to Dutchy to do the talking.

John Hawker had gone back to brooding, now on the meeting with Henry Tulkington, nurturing even more the feeling matters were not as they should be. Ever since he'd taken over from his sire, with the very rare but not serious glitch, operations had run smoothly; if their relationship had never been one of mutual affection, it had endured. Tulkington was too cold a fish for friendship and Hawker was disinclined to intimacy, which left it as one of mutual dependence:

both had their roles to play and it worried Hawker to admit grit had entered the connection and he could nail the cause.

It would be a blind man who'd fail to see the arrival of that sod Brazier as the source of some of the recent troubles. Usually steady and calm in his deliberations, Tulkington had been knocked off balance by a man seeking to marry his sister, making strenuous efforts to discourage him, none of which seemed to have worked. Hawker wanted to visit upon Brazier a more drastic fate than the beating he'd been asked to arrange, having, after that, been physically humiliated by him and his men. The blow to stun him, delivered in the dark in the grounds of Cottington Court, had been bad enough, but worse followed.

Still not recovered, Hawker had been taken as a sort of hostage, dragged halfway back to Deal by a rope attached between his wrists and a horse's saddle. This had caused him to repeatedly stumble and fall, afforded no mercy when he did. Endlessly mocked, he was finally dumped in a ditch, his clothing torn and filthy, forced to sneak back to the very place in which he now sat so as not to be seen in such a disordered state.

To a man with his degree of pride, and the memory was fresh, it was too demeaning to be borne. He'd determined to make Brazier and his crew pay, even going so far as to contravene instructions from Henry Tulkington so he could get his revenge. If his plan had worked, there would have been a whole heap of bodies in the remains of Quebec House, not just the one. But it had not so it was still, to him, unfinished business.

He needed to put it to the back of his mind. It was a coincidence and certainly nothing to do with the difficulties which had arisen with Dan Spafford. What had he and Tulkington been gabbing about when they met, and why wasn't he told? Informed, he might have been able to nip the problems which arose in the bud. Keeping him in the dark had caused real trouble, with the added embarrassment of deliberate and blatant impudence.

It was bound to come out eventually, the fact Spafford had managed to filch part of a cargo Hawker had been tasked to see landed, going on to catch in transit a cartload of tea, everything stolen having disappeared without trace. Such a story would spread quickly if the half-dozen men now locked up in the slaughterhouse were let loose to talk. Clapping a stopper on the gossip would be even more trouble and bloodier than what had just been agreed. More tellingly it would affect the way he was seen, tempting others to copy the act.

John Hawker was proud of his reputation. He saw himself as respected by all – most would have said feared. This applied even to those whose station in life was more elevated than his own, which could not have been predicted from his early upbringing. In a town having more than its fair quota of street urchins, with paid-off sailors coming and going from the busiest anchorage on the East Coast, the pickings for ragamuffins could be constant. This might have been his destiny had good fortune not put him in the path of Henry's father.

Acton Tulkington had singled him out on first acquaintance, not that it looked auspicious at the time. As one of the most generous patrons of the Blue Coat Charity School, he'd been visiting on the day a pupil had seen it as necessary to put a man seeking to teach him, or to Hawker's mind humiliate him, on his back, which he did with a single blow. In the commotion which followed, the miscreant had found himself before the principal as well as a distinguished visitor, where the case to examine him and no doubt chuck him out was to be heard.

Oddly, this patron had actually laughed when he heard what had occurred, which did not please the cleric who ran the place, though he dare not say so for fear of causing offence.

The well-dressed benefactor then asked Hawker to give his side of the story. In a halting way, young John had insisted he was not to be practised upon in such a manner. The class had been set a question regarding a quite complex money sum and, after a few quick scrapes on his slate, Hawker had answered quickly and correctly, only to be accused of cheating.

When he protested, the teacher had lifted his stick to beat him, the boy's blow delivered to forestall the act. Questioned, the principal reluctantly admitted the boy did show a facility in numbers, but set against this was a bad attitude and a bullying nature, one just demonstrated. What followed from this visiting worthy was nothing short of astonishing.

'My brothers and I were never seen as saints when we attended here, quite the opposite. We gave the divine who then ran the place no end of grief and would have been chucked out had our pa not made a sizeable donation.'

'But you have prospered despite bad behaviour, sir,' simpered the present occupant. 'No doubt aided by natural abilities; God has seen fit to endow you with much good fortune.'

'I rather think it was my father who did that, sir, not the Almighty, though it scarce matters. Now, boy, tell me who you are and from where you come.'

There was little to tell; born at the dilapidated North End of the town, which edged the marshes, and raised in a hovel, his father had been a body for hire. The son declined to name him as a useless drunk hardly ever present, who could never hold down anything lasting in the way of employment, being ever willing to argue with those prepared to give him a day's work. A further enquiry regarding his mother elicited no more than a shrug; John was not going to describe a woman who, for the price of a flask of gin, was willing to sell him, even in his very tender years, to men coming off the visiting ships in search of young boys on which to gratify their lust.

The interrogator, whose name he didn't know, pressed for no more information than the youngster was prepared to volunteer, probably because it was too common a tale.

'What would you say if you were offered a place aboard ship?' he'd been asked. 'With a head for figures you could prosper. There are any number of visiting captains who would take you aboard.'

The vehemence of his objection brought surprise, but his reasons were again his own. The sailors he had been sold to as a nipper were not of a type he ever wanted to encounter again.

'Well,' came with a meaningful look at the principal. 'I doubt it would serve for you to be expelled. If you show a talent for numbers, then it should be encouraged.'

'He struck his tutor, sir.'

'How I wish I'd done so in my time.' There was a long pause before the visitor added, 'I want this young fellow to be kept on, though he will be required to apologise and contain his temper. Let him have extra instruction in mathematics, for which I will provide the means.'

'Say thank you, boy,' was a bitter response from the cleric, who clearly didn't agree.

'If you gain enough by it, perhaps I will have for you a place in the future.'

And it had come so to pass, with both his known attributes honed till he'd become an increasingly important cog in the Tulkington undertakings and not just in numbers. As the family increased its grip on the town, John Hawker had become the face of the enterprise, trusted to collect taxes and bills for goods supplied, as well as to collect payments from the local tradespeople of the more common kind, regular sums to guarantee they could operate in peace. Failure to cough up was met with a visit from the men John Hawker led, with predictable consequences.

Acton Tulkington was not one to leave everything of this nature to an underling, being quite capable of exacting retribution himself. Extreme reckoning would be visited on anyone threatening the smuggling operations, a task not always delegated: he wanted those who suffered to know the name of their nemesis. This did not apply to Henry, who talked as if he was the same, but was, in truth, living in a land of make-believe.

'Not a tenth the man your pa was,' Hawker growled out loud.

He raised himself to go about the necessary business of the day. While he was going about his tasks the rumour must be spread, to let folk know Dan Spafford was close to going off on a crossing, no need to name the purpose. When he and his crew failed to return, the assumption of malign fate, aided by more rumour spreading, would gain currency over mere misfortune: losses at sea were far from rare in a coastal community.

CHAPTER FIVE

The sole escape for Elisabeth lay in early morning walks, taken when her brother had either left the house or she could be sure he was locked away in his study: on this occasion his coach had left quite early. As for Harry Spafford and the danger he represented, he had never shown the least sign of being a pre-midday riser, so she could be fairly certain not to meet him. Even if she did, it would be in the public parts of the house, in which he could scarcely act out his threats.

Grady was waiting in the hall when she emerged, which led her, not for the first time, to wonder at his acute ear. He knew when his presence was required even, it seemed, merely from the sound of her unlocking the bedroom door. Having been in service at Cottington Court from his first youth as an under footman, he'd known her both as growing child and young woman, one of the many servants present on the sunny day she had married her childhood sweetheart.

He was required to be very careful in his behaviour towards her, but she knew he was no enemy in this sense: while overt aid was risky, he could and had turned a blind eye wherever possible. He would need to be doubly careful now after the departure of Lionel Upton, given the suspicious nature of his master. Upton had been very active in trying to help her escape, only for his attempts to be discovered, which led to immediate dismissal. The risk of exposure as well as the consequence had been known and, given she could do nothing to provide material aid, Elisabeth advised him, if trouble ensued, to search out Edward Brazier who would, for her sake she was sure, see to his welfare. For now, and assuming he had done as advised, it seemed only fitting to invoke his name in her prayers.

'As you know, Miss Elisabeth,' Grady said, his tone very correct. 'I am obliged to inform your aunt on your being out of the house.'

'It is a duty I know you must perform.'

The servant's voice dropped to a near whisper, possible because, when helping her into her cloak, he was very close. 'Can I say it would be as well to attempt nothing untoward? Your movements are being closely watched.'

The reply was equally soft. 'Something to which I have become accustomed.'

His voice returned to normal as he moved backwards. 'No, Miss Elisabeth, Mr Spafford is not in his room. In fact, he did not return to the house last night.'

She had to admire the way this was delivered, in a servile disinterested monotone, answering a question she'd not asked, but one he knew would be of much interest. Knowing it would be unwise to ask for more, this formed her thoughts as she walked out into the crisp fresh air, to cross the parterre and exit through the gate which led to the kitchen garden. This would take her down to and round the lake.

Grady had to show great care to avoid being overheard by anyone, Henry most of all, but also her Aunt Sarah. What of the others, the footmen, maids and kitchen staff, who must surely wonder what on earth was going on? It had been possible to assume the servants were well disposed, but this was all it could be for their respective positions mitigated against direct enquiry. That too would have changed with Upton's abrupt departure: she didn't employ, feed and house them, Henry did, and he had shown how he reacted to his wishes being challenged.

The evidence of Grady's warning was not long in showing itself. First was the gardener Creevy, seemingly working away, but in a location which could not be considered normal. As she progressed there was a feeling, and sometimes a fleeting glimpse of humanity, which underlined Creevy was not alone in carrying out discreet observation. Walking slowly took her mind back over the years in which she'd lived here, to wonder if it had always been thus with some of the servants, even in her father's day, something to which she'd never given much thought. Growing up with domestic staff, as with everything else, you took them for granted, even to the point of rendering them invisible, which applied especially to those who toiled outdoors.

She blushed to recall how many times, as a girl, she'd thrown precocious tantrums, which those who served the household indoors had to accept with a meek apology or studied indifference. Was she worse than others of her station? It was shaming she had no idea. It had taken life in the West Indies to even contemplate the needs of those who saw to her every whim, brought on by the fact of their being her husband's slaves. It was the excess of power which had focused her mind: the knowledge that, if disapproval in England must be stoically borne, dismissal for a sugar plantation household slave was not the same: it would be a sentence to back-breaking toil in the cane fields.

Now it was she who was the equivalent of a slave, unable to leave what had been her family home without permission from Henry. No means of transport would be provided without his approval of the destination and this would include, as chaperone and informer, her aunt. A horse was out of the question, while even walking had been rendered impossible since the rickety old and secret gate by which she'd met with Edward Brazier had been sealed up with battens.

For a multitude of times since coming home, she'd wondered how he had become the man he now was: cruel, despotic and prepared to go to any lengths to get his own way. Not that he'd ever been cheerful company, quite the reverse: even as a boy Henry seemed to find jollity alien, which was why, added to a substantial difference in age, they'd never been close. How different Cottington Court had been in the past, a house those who lived locally were eager to visit, for her father enjoyed entertaining and was lavish and generous with it. The high point had been, as she recalled it now, even if her father had not been there to see it, her wedding day. The sun had shone, the guests were delighted at such an engaging couple, with Stephen Langridge, her childhood sweetheart, looking so handsome.

Even Henry, who'd given her away, if not cheerful throughout, had managed a smile when they kissed, albeit in a wan fashion. For once, the Reverend Doctor Joshua Moyle, Vicar of Cottington, had been sober, at least for the actual ceremony. This didn't last very long; by the time of the wedding feast he could barely speak, while walking was beyond him, just another day when his long-suffering wife had to see him carried home.

But nothing could mar her own joy. She was joined in holy matrimony to the man with whom she desired to spend the rest of her life, which would be away from the likes of Henry and Moyle in Jamaica. How cruel was the fate, or was it the endemic sicknesses, which cursed the Caribbean, which took him from her so soon, smiling and robust one day, near a skeleton within weeks?

She came back to find Henry had turned Cottington into a sort of morgue; there was no laughter or gaiety at all, something she'd determined to change by organising a fete, with games, good food and a flowing rum punch. Added to her intention to cheer things up had been the vague hope Henry, extremely eligible in terms of affluence, might catch the eye of a suitable bride-to-be. Every eligible maid for miles around had been invited, along with mothers eager to push them forward. It was something to produce an ironic laugh now: God forbid any poor creature should be saddled with her brother as a spouse.

Walking brings on more than unhappy recollection. Elisabeth yearned for someone to talk to, anyone precluding her brother or her Aunt Sarah. Her friend Annabel Colpoys would be a welcome companion right now, able perhaps to give some advice on the dilemma she had of being forcibly married, added to the need to keep it unconsummated so annulment remained possible. Even a benign sounding board would help, perhaps to formulate some plan.

Annabel, initially disinclined to take her part, had in the end proved stalwart, in the way she'd passed on a message from Edward Brazier saying Elisabeth should be ready to depart at a moment's notice. Yet now and above all, and it could hardly be thought odd, it was him she most wanted to share her immediate concerns with; that and their hopes for a shared future.

It would not have served her, at present, to enter his fevered mind, for she figured not at all. In his currently troubled reveries, there was a lack of any structure to his imaginary wanderings, though all had some link to his life as lived so far: a cosseted child who became a callow midshipman, then a naval officer, rising through the ranks until he took command of his first ship. There had been several to follow, the last being the frigate HMS *Diomede*, which, when it entered his dreams, had aspects so troubling he more than once cried out loud.

In the main his recollections were benign: maternal warmth and childhood scrapes, which morphed into the early acts of a new recruit to the King's Navy, not least fights with faces familiar or strange. The captains and crews, with whom he'd served and associated, came and went in a jumble of mixed and outlandish images, the fancies of a man in a coma. Barely conscious, he had been fed soup while still lying face down, most of which had ended up on the cloth set to catch the dribbled spill. This too had lacked reality, given the person spooning it took on the aura of an ethereal creature, not human but a deep-voiced chimera, which soothed but could not kill off the pain racking his upper body.

Freedom from such agony came from going under again, to a

state closer to semi-consciousness, where he began to range across his boyhood, more idyllic in a dream than it could possibly be in reality: there were no disappointments, no cuts or bruises or foul weather which threatened to blow out the windows of the family home. Nor was there scolding for his escapades and misdemeanours, added to stern warnings telling him if he did not pay attention to his letters and numbers, his Latin and Greek, he would end up a beggar.

Lucidity, when it came, and it did so frequently, brought more agony, which the man tending to him eased with tincture of laudanum from a bottle which had lain unused in the chest for years. It induced a deeper sleep as well as dreams of a more formed nature, vividly taking him back to the actions in which he fought off the Azores and the Cape of Good Hope. Then he was off the north coast of Ceylon, on a scorching day, a lieutenant preparing to go into a land battle with fleet marines, sepoys from the British East India Company, as well as a strong party of sailors who'd landed and hauled into position the ship's cannon, to batter the walls of the Dutch forts of Trincomalee, in a bloody encounter in which his pistols would not fire and his sword, however hard he tried, would not swing.

His Good Samaritan watched as smiles turned to frowns and back again, as the lips twitched, the mouth opening often in what appeared to be silent shouts, arms seeking to move and fists clenching, wondering what animated such expressions and brought forth the occasional groan. Then he saw the eyelids flicker, one eye opening first, the mouth forming the beginnings of a grimace of pain, one he could no longer do anything about: he had no more tincture with which to ease it, the bottle now empty.

With care he raised the pad he had placed over the wound to look at the rough stitching, a red scar surrounded by dark-blue bruising, pleased to see no sign of putrescence. Fever notwithstanding, there was a high chance his charge would recover. He was on his knees already, so giving thanks to God came easily. Through one open eye and lying face down, Brazier struggled to make out his features. On his knees, hands clasped and lips moving silently, the man was so close he could feel his breath.

It slowly dawned on him, even in what was limited light, he was looking at an elderly black man, skin wrinkled, hair white and tightly curled, rendering the fact of his race and age obvious. Sense, aided by the pain in his shoulder, began to intrude; if Edward Brazier had no idea where he was, it was clear he was alive.

'Who are you?' he croaked.

'The man who found you, sir.'

'Where?'

'Down by the stream, which edges my property.'

'What stream?'

'Does it matter? Best think, sir, on how you came here with a musket ball in your back.'

The recollection came slowly, of what had happened at Tulkington's place: the shock of discovery, guns going off, he and his companions fleeing, the thud of impact as he was hit. There was vague recall of his argument with Dutchy and the others, followed by being thrown on to the back of a horse, one soon galloping, then nothing.

'How did I get here?'

'On a fine mare, and "here" is my smallholding.' Brazier's eyes closed again and it was clear from his expression he was feeling waves of pain. 'You need to rest, sir, and hope God grants you a happy recovery.'

'I must . . .' faded to silence, as feeble as the attempt to raise himself up; the amount of pressure to stop the movement was minimal, so Brazier was soon back with his head on the feather-filled bolster, which muffled what came next.

'There are things I must see to.'

He passed out again, to the sound of a deep chuckle.

* * *

By the time he arrived at his destination, Henry Tulkington was in a more sanguine frame of mind: matters with John Hawker would be resolved. The Freemason's Lodge by which he alighted served as a meeting place for the Brotherhood as well as a social club, where local worthies could take their ease and ensure their businesses prospered, with the added need to keep those not so fortunate in some form of order, behaviour which did nothing to threaten their collective hold on the town.

The mood was not diminished by the first person he encountered, if anything it was enhanced by the nature of their relationship. Tobias Sowerby was someone who relied on him, a fellow raised from paucity to prosperity by his association with the Tulkington family. Even better was the serious look with which he greeted Henry, taken as evidence a recent warning about his failure to cover certain losses had hit home. Sowerby had failed to fully compensate Henry for the loss of a cartload of tea, stolen by Dan Spafford.

'Why, Tobias, you look concerned,' Henry exulted, for it pleased him to twist the metaphorical knife. 'There is no need, I do assure you. Our recent difference is quite forgotten.'

Sowerby wanted to scream 'Liar', but it was essential to allow nothing of the sentiment to show. He knew it was not, just as he knew he was talking to a man who would and could see him reduced to penury if the fancy took him. It was he who owned the carting company contracted to transport the Cottington farm produce. More profitably, he moved the recently landed contraband from where it was stored to where it was to be sold, which involved despatching his horse-drawn vans to many parts of Kent, as well as filling a barge to carry smuggled goods up to London.

He was well rewarded, indeed overly so for the activity, and now enjoyed a comfortable life. Yet he lived constantly with the fear common to those who start with nothing: namely, by some stroke of ill fortune, they will be returned to such an estate.

The recent disagreement with Henry over recompense had brought home to him just how vulnerable he was, and it was an uncomfortable place to be. Also, as an accomplice in what was a seriously illegal activity, he had no option of retaliation.

'I had hoped it would be so, Henry,' he dissembled, 'but, as of this moment, it's not that which concerns me and I'm not alone. There could be trouble for the town on the horizon.'

'You intrigue me.'

'We have just been visited by the High Sheriff of Kent.'

Henry shrugged. 'What is a placeman like him doing hereabouts?'

'Can you not guess?'

'Please, Tobias,' was delivered with a look of mild frustration, the voice a touch less friendly. 'Do not trifle with me.'

'He's interested in the fire at Quebec House. More, it should be said, in the discovery of the body in the embers.'

Sowerby related the details: how this High-Sheriff had failed to behave as had his predecessors, who would never have travelled all the way to the east coast, leaving it as a problem to be dealt with locally. The present incumbent had come to look into the matter himself, seemingly intent on doing so with some application, despite it being made plain, if not vocally explicit, his presence was not welcome.

It was Henry's turn to be guarded; it had been his idea to have Hawker work up a mob and force Brazier out, though no one was supposed to set fire to the place, just as no one was supposed to die. A thorough drubbing for him and his companions by a mob was the notion, which would serve as a final notice to desist in his pursuit of Elisabeth. The only shortcoming was it had failed in its object, leading inevitably to the mayhem of the previous night.

'An accident, surely? The mob got carried away, I'm told.'

'He sees it as foul murder, following on from a riot, one set in motion by persons unknown for purposes as yet undiscovered.'

'Does he have any reason for such an assertion?'

'He seems to think so, but granted us no details.'

'Us?'

Sowerby named those who'd been at the Three Kings, then, very elliptically, referred to what was at stake. If Sowerby was deeply involved in the business of smuggling, his fellow jurats and leading citizens were not much better placed. All happily and regularly purchased untaxed goods, some making good money selling them on to family and friends away from the coast. When it came to the trade itself, a judicious blind eye was the common attitude.

Various excuses had been conjured up over many decades for such an approach, the primary one being it could not be stopped and, if such was the case, it was best to seek the kind of oversight which kept the most dangerous aspects under control, not least the violence that came from competition. This was not easy when every boatman on Deal beach could readily cross to France if the wind and weather were right, and they could find the purchase price of contraband, returning with brandy, tea, silks and the like for discreet local sale, the proceeds of which, in many cases, kept them from dearth.

Too heavy a hand had led to disturbances in the past, with those standing out against the trade finding their homes threatened. Thus, legality was put aside in favour of security and it was no good the likes of Billy Pitt and the government in London railing against it; he and they didn't have to live with the consequences. Nowadays, the only people at risk were those who advocated temperance and deplored drink and criminality from wherever it came.

When one family, not without a degree of less than subtle brutality, began over time to consolidate their enterprise, it was seen as a corrective and an improvement, though small-time smuggling still went on. Their increasing domination cooled the endemic rivalry of the beach boatmen, as well as the bloodshed such uncontrolled activity encouraged; in short, they brought peace to replace the kind of disorder which put at risk those of means.

'It would be unwise to have such a fellow poking about,' Sowerby continued. 'We discussed a notion afterwards. If he persists, we'll have to find a culprit to hand over.'

'Come, if he's here it cannot be for long. He'll soon get bored and go back to wherever he comes from to fiddle with his quill. Believe me, Tobias, I have heard of the kind of cully who fills such a post and they are, to a man, lazy and ineffectual.'

'Not John Cottin.' A pause to note the enquiring look. 'That's the name and he's determined to question people who may know something. After we left him, he was spotted calling on Saoirse Riorden, which leads us to suspect he means to stay until he has the truth.'

It was natural to then ask, 'Anyone in mind?'

'One of my carters tells me Dan Spafford was at the forefront of the mob, him and his gang of ne'er-do-wells. Fellow denies being there himself, of course, but that's by the by. He'll want for work if he talks to Cottin, but we could give up Spafford and I reckon it might be something you'd welcome.'

'Why do you say so?' was sharply delivered.

'Will it not get him out of your hair?'

Sowerby realised he had said the wrong thing as the face before him closed up in what he took to be anger. In truth, Henry was trying to contain himself, stopping the words which nearly came out unbidden. Spafford was *not* anywhere near his hair, he was a nobody to be swatted like an annoying fly. He was really more concerned by what he could not ask: if Tobias Sowerby thought Spafford was the leader of the mob, and it could be an opinion held by many, on what grounds had they come to think it so? Was there anything to suggest the truth, which was he had set the whole affair in motion?

Sowerby spoke quickly, seeking to recover ground. 'I just thought you might want to join us in reeling him in. The whole neighbourhood would surely be better off without him and his kind.'

The difficulty this posed immediately surfaced. Spafford not only had a bullet in his gut, he knew it was his idea to force Brazier out, indeed it had been the price of he and his men originally being released from the slaughterhouse and any retribution, after his son Harry had fingered them as the original thieves of Henry's cargo of tea. What would happen if he sang, always assuming he could live to do so, and not just about the riot?

'Might it be an idea to put out feelers to find out where he is?'

'Let's wait and see how far this Cottin is prepared to go.' Knowing he must return to the slaughterhouse, Henry stalled even more. 'I doubt offering up Spafford would be a good notion, anyway, given the certain risk he would have of the rope. Who knows whom he might incriminate if we do.'

The inference was obvious. Dan Spafford had to have knowledge of who shifted the Tulkington contraband and perhaps a lot more besides, maybe even where to, since he had known where to intercept and rob a load of tea.

'I care not who we give Cottin, Henry. But if we want to see the back of him, I reckon we have to offer up someone.'

'Best haul up a creature from the beach, there are enough villains there to fill a prison hulk, some of whom are known to rob their own. Then get a few people to swear to the guilt.' It was a notion Sowerby was thinking on when Henry added, 'Now if you will forgive me, Tobias, I have some important business to which I must attend.'

CHAPTER SIX

Being a sensible woman, Saoirse Riorden made sure those who'd come to see her at such an ungodly hour were fed, time she used to dress properly and think through what she'd been told: that it beggared belief went without saying and this applied only to what they knew for fact. None seemed to have a clear idea of what had been the final outcome, except Harry Spafford had taken a ball between the eyes and was likely gone from this earth, which was no loss. As for the rest, it was mislaid in the fog of their own reaction.

Plain as day was the evidence of Edward Brazier's naivety, which surprised her: teaming up with a character like Dan Spafford showed terrible judgement. She recalled their first meeting, which certainly gave no indication of such folly, quite the reverse. His air of self-assurance generated more interest than the kind extended to the average newly introduced client, the man doing the introductory honours, Vincent Flaherty.

If she had a soft spot for him it was based on a love of horses and riding, a shared background, added to a degree of amusement at his fecklessness, held to be a national trait with the Irish and one to which Vincent gave much credence. Allow him a guinea and he would spend it on wine – good-quality wine, it had to be said, for he was no drunk, which was even more foolish on an endemically constrained purse.

It was telling how little presence her fellow Irishman had compared to Brazier, though there was, of course, a marked difference in height and build: the one was tall and imposing, whereas Vincent had the build of the ex-jockey he had been. Yet there was more. Those attached to the Navy Yard were frequent visitors to the Old Playhouse, but somehow he seemed dissimilar, with his saturnine, captivating countenance, added to a sardonic smile utterly lacking in any kind of condescension, and an ability to command the space around him.

Dismiss it she might, and she had, but Saoirse had found him arresting, as much for the way he contained the same feeling in regard to her. Attraction had been evident in his eyes, but without – which was unusual – him seeking to take it further. In this regard the contrast with Vincent was doubly striking, often so eager to impress her he engendered more sympathy than the kind of feelings he sought.

Many of those who frequented the Old Playhouse, those who made their wants plain, might see her as a woman devoid of emotion, but this was far from the truth. It was the well-honed carapace of protection an attractive woman required to stave off untoward advances, something to which she was bound to be subjected when running a place of entertainment. Men took it for granted a lady in her position was in need of their company, even a degree of protection; Saoirse went out of her way to make it plain she required no such thing.

Tending to Brazier following the beating he'd suffered, not yards from her front doorway, also had an effect, though she saw it as no more than what would be granted to one who'd quickly become a friend. Some people, if and when they heard the tale of her taking him in, would suspect much more. Had not Dutchy Holland hinted at the possibility of such a deeper connection in her hallway not minutes past? Saoirse would decline to argue it was not the case; there was no point in pitting truth against rumour.

'My hair now, Dottie, if you please.'

Her maid came forward with the brush, to run it through the long auburn tresses, the act doing nothing to dismiss the feeling Saoirse had, given the way matters had turned out, this being somehow she was responsible for the trouble he'd brought down on his head. By being open with Brazier about the stories surrounding Henry Tulkington, and they could be no more than opinions lacking hard evidence, she might have set much in motion which would have been best avoided.

'Enough!' she said quite forcibly, putting an end to depressing speculation.

If he'd got into trouble, it was of his own making, all down to his love for Tulkington's sister, added to his determination to effect a rescue. How could she hold herself to account for what followed, which ended up in the torching and utter destruction of her own property? The death of the poor old soul of a groom, who'd been chucked out of Cottington Court, could not be laid at her door. As for the sheriff, let him find out the identity from others, not her.

'Holy Mary, for all that, Edward must be found.'

'Miss?' Dottie asked, her worried face plain in the mirror; her employer was not given to sudden outbursts.

Saoirse gently took the brush from her hand. 'Thank you, Dottie, that will be all for now.'

Downstairs she found Dutchy and his shipmates sitting at a table laden with empty dishes, talking quietly, Vincent having gone back to his stables. The expectant way they looked at her was annoying, given what it implied. Why should she have any more idea of a way to proceed than they? But there was agreement, which said sitting doing nothing and waiting would not serve.

'You will have to go to where you think he might have ended up to ask if he's been seen, maybe taken in by some kind soul. A wounded man cannot just be ignored.' The gloomy looks obliged her to add the obvious. 'If he's suffered more than we hope, there's nothing more to be done.'

69

'Other than burying him' was an unwelcome thought and Saoirse knew, as the four heads dropped to look at the table, it was one shared. Having just a moment past been slightly irritated at their attitude, it softened to something akin to sympathy, for in this reaction was a degree of affection bordering on something greater. She knew they respected their old captain in the way men do a good and decent commander, but this went beyond mere admiration.

'Happen we should let word out,' Dutchy suggested. 'The more folk lookin' the better.'

'Best not for now.'

Such an abrupt answer was given for any number of reasons. The message would get to the likes of John Hawker in no time, so they wouldn't be the only folk searching. But there was the damned sheriff to consider as well, with him being on the hunt for criminality. Being armed and breaking into private property was not something to bring to his attention, however high-sounding the purpose.

'Let's see what you can find on your own for now. Head the way he might have gone and ask around. But say nothing about his carrying a wound unless you have to.'

'Long shot for just four of us,' Joe muttered.

'Best one for now. If you can get him back here and he's in need, he can be attended to.'

'Can we berth at the Navy Yard still without him bein' present?' Dutchy wondered.

'Best do so, like you said last night, in case he shows up,' was Joe's answer.

'And if they start asking for him?' Peddler asked. 'What's we to say? Likely we'll be out on our ear.'

'I can put you up here,' was the response from Saoirse.

'Got tae thank you, ma'am, fer such kindness,' Cocky Logan said.

Kindness? More like foolishness, Saoirse thought. What I should really do is show you the door and forget all about Edward Brazier.

* * *

70

'It's too dangerous to carry out your plan at present, John, with a high sheriff grubbing around. The slightest slip could be fatal.'

'Then what do you suggest, Mr Tulkington?' The query lacked any sense of supplication; it was more pique. 'Keepin' them here for more'n a day or two will be hard to cap a stopper on. Daisy Trotter worked out where they were afore an' it's no good thinkin' it were guesswork. There be any number of our own workers coming and going, even more folk bringing their animals in for slaughter. It was never a sweet idea first time round and it's even less of a one now.'

'It's as sound as dragging Harry Spafford along the Lower Valley Road for the whole town to see. And for all anyone of those who witnessed it, he's still here! Can you not see the consequence if anyone whispers his name into the wrong ear?'

'They'd pay for crossing me.'

'Dammit, as if you'd ever know.'

Such a sharp rebuke hit home with someone already in a less than happy mood, which went beyond his previous rumblings of disquiet. He'd been called back to the slaughterhouse, Tulkington having sent a couple of his men out to find him, not that such a thing was hard: he was a person whose passing was marked by many. But the demand had irked by the nature in which it had been issued and delivered.

'I had it planned to end tonight,' was conveyed almost as a wish.

'We must hold our hand until this Cottin fellow has gone.'

Trying and barely succeeding in containing his concerns, Henry knew from Hawker's piqued expression he'd spoken too abruptly but his own mood precluded subtlety. Since departing the Lodge, he'd allowed his imagination free rein, inducing much uneasiness. Feeling the need for haste, in case Hawker had already begun to act, he had eschewed his carriage, with the chance of being held up once more, to walk hurriedly along Middle Street, a route he normally avoided. Nothing he'd witnessed in the narrow, teeming thoroughfare made him want to repeat the experience.

Even in broad daylight, flasks of gin were being dispensed through street-level windows by numerous naval widows, to customers already well oiled. The two penny whores of all ages and specialities were at work and they, spotting a finely dressed gentleman, saw him exposed first of all to offers he found insulting. This turned to loud, carnal and demeaning ribaldry as, with a level of blushing hauteur, he'd passed them by.

'Whatever you say, but I would want them moved from here.'

'Perhaps back to Cottington would be best?'

Delivered with a serious expression, John Hawker knew what the reaction would be and was not disappointed: Cottington was out of the question but it pleased him to pay back in kind an employer acting out of character and, to his mind, with a degree of unwarranted fright.

'Can you be serious, man? I had you with more wit.'

A stricture applied ever since it was purchased, anything to do with the smuggling business had to be kept away from the house. At all costs the Tulkington family must be seen as upright country gentlefolk of independent means. They had no difficulty in justifying their wealth: tax-gathering aside, Henry had inherited a well-run stud farm, added to many acres of productive fields. He also did profitable business in parts of the lower town as well as the countryside around, where he now owned all but one of the flour mills, with high hopes of a clean sweep, once this present business had died down.

Tempted to point out such a policy, thanks to the actions of Brazier, had already been twice breached, Hawker knew it to be unwise: he could only afford to needle this man once, so wisdom dictated a degree of humble pie.

'Then I is at a loss to know what to suggest, your honour.'

The pacing up and down which followed was another indication of Hawker's state of mind: normally he was very controlled, signs of tension well concealed. He was now lacking his normal composure, which was far from comforting. Unknown to Hawker, such an emotional state applied to his employer as well, induced by the deepening feelings already experienced. Matters had got out of hand and Hawker's actions in the matter of Harry Spafford might bring on consequences over which he could have no control.

It was natural, given Henry's nature, to blame this on other people. Thus, as he had navigated his way along Middle Street, everyone who'd irked him these past weeks became subject to mental censure, even Hawker just castigated. His ingrate sister was roundly damned for thwarting his will, Brazier likewise for aiding her and setting things off-kilter. Even his aunt was cursed for questioning his judgement and last, for no one could be excused, came his Uncle Dirley in London, a very vital hub in the entire operation, for contacting Elisabeth by letter, without informing Henry of his intention to do so.

Sowerby and his like he blamed for the presence of this damned sheriff, which showed, to his mind, nothing but plain stupidity; another concern then surfaced, and it was a far more troubling one. Did they suspect him, even if they dare not say so, to be at the root of the fire at Quebec House? If they did, how far would they go to ensure no opprobrium fell upon them? They were, as his mood grew increasingly darker, lily-livered scum who were happy to accept his largesse while secretly plotting behind his back to save themselves.

'I needs an answer, Mr Tulkington, cause I can't think of one.'

It was near a minute before Hawker got his reply. 'They must be taken to Spafford's place and kept there. This can only be for a few days and it will be easier to move them from there to where their luggers are beached, so it will better serve your purpose.'

The look Hawker got took immediate cognisance of his doubts, but Henry was not going to be defied. 'You brought them here in a covered van, did you not?' A slow, far from enthusiastic nod. 'Then move them tonight, and that, I must add, is my final word on the matter.'

A long moment of mutual staring was required before Hawker acceded, with Henry feeling it necessary to soften the atmosphere they had, between them, created. He was sure his tone of voice posited honest feelings and regret as he repeated his reasoning; to his employee the silkiness and slightly weening tone raised hackles of mistrust.

'We have had our troubles recently, John . . .'

Your doin', not mine, stayed unspoken.

'. . . which should never have occurred. But properly handled, they will pass and we can go back to the peaceful pursuit of our operations.' Still sensing discomfort, he added, 'If I have spoken bluntly, I ask you to consider the burden I carry.'

'Whatever you say, Mr Tulkington.'

Passing to the north of the slaughterhouse as this conversation was taking place, three of Edward Brazier's old barge crew were heading in the direction they'd traversed the night before, Joe Lascelles again having been left at the Navy Yard in case the captain showed up. The notion of splitting up had been discussed, only to be dismissed. With no knowledge of what threats they might face in daylight, in unfamiliar country, small comfort came from safety in numbers.

The notion it was a fool's errand might be in all their minds, yet it was not raised: staying put and doing nothing would drive them mad. Each carried a sack containing bread, cheese and beer supplied from the Old Playhouse, the intention being to stay out once darkness fell, resuming the search in a wider arc throughout the following day. Saoirse had sketched them a rough map showing the various parishes around Deal, the aim to head first for the spires of Sandwich, then turn vaguely east and south in the hope of a sighting.

Luck got them an empty cart heading along the Sandwich Road, no more than a rutted track, which ran between a distant Cottington Court and the shoreline. Dutchy having, to no avail, quizzed the carter, stood the whole way, his eyes ranging over the landscape, both reed-filled marshland as well as the cultivated, ditch-crossed fields further inland, seeking any sign of a saddled horse or, worse, a wake of feeding crows.

They took to walking as they came level with Cottington, exchanging words with those working in the fields – not many, it was true. No details were volunteered, but the negative responses were enough to ensure there had been no sign, which had to be taken as true: anything untoward would catch their attention. The marshier parts of the landscape, also crossed by deep ditches, seemed an area of more promise, even if one very obvious fact emerged. Spread out to cover as much ground as possible, what they were about was going to take time. They were traversing a flat and featureless coastal plain, long stretches of which lacked any evidence of humanity, covered with long, deep grass, which bent in the wind.

'He could be a'laying in that lot and we'd never see him.'

Peddler pointed this out as they gathered and squatted by a riverbank to eat some of the food. The river itself was slow moving and muddy, twenty feet wide and probably just as deep. The remark got him a cussed look from a pair of companions who had no notion to curse their endeavours by harbouring negative thoughts.

'An' don't go tellin' me we should be seeking his cuddy, there bein' no surety the beast would've stayed around if'n he fell off.'

'Ye got another notion, Peddler?' Cocky asked, through a mouth full of bread and cheese.

'None of us have,' Dutchy snapped, 'so I'd be obliged if you'd both clap a stopper. There's no way this here water can have been crossed, so once we've followed it down to the shoreline, we can double back and head inland.'

'Should've got the horses back. We'd have covered more ground.'

Which got Peddler enough abuse to shut him up.

The wait for the light to fade gave John Hawker too much time to think, none of it coming out as encouraging. Tulkington might say

75

matters would settle back to normal but to his mind such a state had gone for good; a malevolent spirit was out of the bottle and there was no putting it back, which meant vague thoughts of moving on had surfaced. He did not want for money accumulated over the years, yet any serious consideration saw them dismissed: where else would he find employment to both suit his gifts and satisfy his character?

He'd just have to take Henry Tulkington as he found him, carry out the work he undertook with as much efficiency as he'd shown hitherto and let other matters take care of themselves. For now, he had to get Spafford, the men he led and the bodies of Trotter and Harry to the farmhouse outside Worth, without it being noted by any nosy bugger, including those in the still busy slaughterhouse.

Killing was over for the day, but there was butchering being carried out, as well as barrelling and salting of the day's slaughter, before the knocked-up casks could be sealed with pitch, hot irons then used to burn on the source, the date and the nature of the contents. Likewise, lamps had been lit in the tannery so work could go on in the curing and drying of hides. There was the need to get rid of piles of bones, which would go to the glue maker, as well as bloodstained sawdust, which the vegetable gardeners who worked strips behind St George's Church took off his hands, so carts coming and going should be nothing to remark upon.

When he judged the time right, he went to the outside storeroom in which his captives were held. Dan Spafford lay on the straw-covered floor, his normally ruddy face pale, eyes closed but still breathing. The bodies of Trotter and Harry Spafford, now rigid, were wrapped in sackcloth, while the gang member with the flesh wound sat against the wall looking wan.

'Gag 'em, Marker, old Dan as well. If the bugger wakes he'll raise Cain.'

'Where we goin'? Mr Hawker?' This plea came from a fellow called Dolphin Morgan, sporting a bandaged arm, who was reckoned to be

76

as thick as a beachside berthing post, which to Hawker summed up the whole lot of them.

'You're goin' home, Dolphin,' was the jesting reply. 'Afore long you'll be toasting your toes by the farmhouse fire, just like days of old, and maybe a muffin as well.'

Dolphin must have wondered why those words had Hawker's men chuckling, but he asked nothing more. The gagging was carried out without protest; no one wanted to rile a man who, rumour had it, was capable of cutting up dead bodies, packing them in barrels, then sending them off to parts foreign in place of pork.

The outhouses in which they'd been housed backed onto the track to Sandwich, so getting them out and into the van without attracting too much attention was possible.

What would draw the curious eye, and this edge of the town had a fair number of nosy hovel-dwellers, would be John Hawker mounted and leading a dozen hard bargains bearing muskets, half in front of the van, the rest to the rear. They were well away from any building before the torches they'd brought along were fired up, a couple of men going ahead to light the way in the fading light.

Twilight made what Dutchy and his mates were about close to pointless. Having reached the mudflats at the mouth of the Stour, then looked along the long strand of beach which fronted the Sandwich Flats, they turned to make their way back towards the Sandwich Road, now devoid of people either carting or walking between the twin towns. There was no searching to be done now; with the light fading they needed to follow the lighter sky and find somewhere to rest up.

'Be best in a wood, Dutchy. Chill will come later, so we need tae light a fire.'

'I spotted some trees earlier, Cocky, not far off on t'other side of the road. We'll rest up there.'

'Give me a ship any time,' Peddler moaned. 'This walkin' lark is for dolts.'

'Should make you chipper, then.'

'Will you stow it, Cocky? I'm not in the mood for your digs.'

'Furst it was the bluddy mare you couldn'a be doin' wi', an' now it's Shanks's pony. Best grow wings, mate.'

'Hold up,' Dutchy hissed, an insistent command which brought silence, his own actions making the next words hardly necessary. 'And get down.'

If John Hawker had not been mounted, riding between a pair of flaring torches, all Dutchy would have seen was a man on horseback. Nor would his identity have really registered with Cocky or Peddler, who'd seen him but once and very briefly in Middle Street. Dragging him along in the dark on the end of a rope, from the seat of a horse he had just been a shape cursing and spitting. Nor had they had a confrontation, one to one with the bastard, as had Dutchy the day he arrived in Deal. He'd squared up to the sod as he manhandled a fair-haired young lad, drunkenly pleading to be set free, and it had come close to blows before Hawker dragged his captive off.

'What is it?' Cocky asked softly, now kneeling in the tall grass.

'Hawker.'

'Ye sure?'

'I am. There's a cart with men ahead and a party followin' too.'

'Out on the hunt for the captain?' Peddler suggested.

'Not in the dark, mate.'

'Happen he's in the cart. But where would they be heading?'

'It ain't goin' to be hard to find out.'

CHAPTER SEVEN

'You must understand, Mr Cottin, Captain Brazier is not on the Downs establishment and even if he was, not being in command of a ship in my area of responsibility, I'm not sure I would know of his whereabouts.'

'Admiral Braddock, he is resident here, is he not?'

'On a temporary basis, yes. Couldn't leave him to fend for himself, having his place of residence burnt down. Least a fellow salt could do was to give him somewhere to lay his head.'

A knock at the door allowed for the entry of the clerk Braddock had sent to the guest suite, to see if Brazier was there, who'd returned previously with a negative answer, only to be despatched to the quarters set aside for the lower ranks.

'Found Captain Brazier's servant, sir, though no sign of the others you mention. He's waiting downstairs for your visitor.'

'Mr Cottin,' Braddock said, eyebrows lowered to the papers on his desk, an obvious invitation to depart.

'If I could see him in here, sir? I have some questions to which I require an answer.'

'I think not, Mr Cottin,' was imparted in a gruff tone, as Braddock began to shuffle said papers, though the sheriff didn't think this had any real purpose. 'Wouldn't be fitting, at all, common seaman in my office. Everyone has their place, what?'

Cottin responded by standing up and retrieving his hat. 'Then I can only thank you for your cooperation.'

The parting got a sharp look from a naval officer ever wary of being practised upon. Nothing in Cottin's arch expression diminished the deliberate sarcasm, which to him, after a trying day, was appropriate, Braddock having been as helpful as everyone else he'd spoken to, which was to say not at all. His trawl of the drinking dens of Deal, normally in any town a sure source of information, had produced naught. Added to which, he couldn't be sure if the silence and blank looks to which he'd been subjected were prompted by ignorance or folk being evasive, while any admission of his office seemed to have no effect; he could have been the Cham of Tartary for all being the High Sheriff dented the willingness of anyone to speak to him.

They would not admit to there having been a riot at all, never mind what subsequently came from the disturbance. Cottin would have been even unhappier had he known what his enquiries set in motion. A message ran quickly through the town, sometimes even ahead of him, one simple to impart and suited to the inhabitants, especially those – and there were a high number – who'd been part of the mob at the torching of Quebec House: 'Tell the sod owt and the Lord help anyone who blabs.'

Following the clerk down the stairs, Cottin sensed something amiss by the way the man's head spun from side to side as he came in sight of the wide hallway.

'I told him to wait here.' After a confused look, he added, 'Perhaps he's returned to his quarters. I'll go and see.'

Tempted to say 'Don't bother', Cottin held his tongue, his suspicions confirmed as the shame-faced clerk returned to admit the fellow was nowhere to be found.

'I don't suppose you have his name?'

'No, sir. But he's a blackamoor and they're not numerous round these parts.'

Walking out through the main doors of the headquarters, into the gloomy dusk, Cottin passed under a pair of huge lamps, fired up to illuminate the portico. Thus, Joe got a good sight of him, being himself well hidden by a pillar.

'Marked you, mate,' was his conclusion, having no idea who he was: the clerk hadn't said.

He'd only been told there was an official waiting to question him regarding the whereabouts of the officer upon whom he attended. To Joe Lascelles, anyone looking for Edward Brazier, outside a half-dozen people known to be friends or well disposed, could only wish him harm.

Zachary Colton came in from his daily toil, carrying a basket and a pail, to find his patient sat on the cot, head on his chest, with the feet-spread pose of a man needing such to maintain his upright position. The noise of arrival did slowly raise the head, so he was examined by bloodshot eyes, in an unshaven countenance, devoid of colour.

'You should be resting, sir,' he remarked, as he put aside the items he carried, before taking a lantern off a hook, this opened and lit by a taper applied to a tallow wad, one which was kept going throughout the day, replaced each morning from the embers of the fire or flints if they had gone out. 'No good will come to you of moving afore you are fit to do so.'

'Who are you?' was a rasp.

'It matters more who you are, sir. Just as it matters you having a musket ball in your shoulder and some knowledge of how it came to be there.'

'A name?' was to avoid answering the question.

'Zachary, sir.'

'There must be another?'

81

'Colton is how I'm known. Few use the one with which I was labelled, the name of the man who first bought me.'

'How do I come to be here?'

'By the Lord's good grace, sir, which you would do well to thank with a prayer.' The oil lamp now flaring, Zachary came close. 'Would you permit, sir, I examine the wound?'

Edward Brazier did nothing to acknowledge the request. As a wave of pain shot across his back, he dropped his head again, unable to stifle the slight moan which escaped through his lips.

'It saddens me, sir,' was imparted from above his lowered head, 'I have no more laudanum to gift you. I had some left, but it was a small amount and soon dispensed.'

The reply came through gritted teeth, 'I thank you for what you've done.'

Brazier could feel the fingers gently working their way round the seat of his pain, the lantern placed so close to his flesh he could feel the heat.

'Ugly, sir, for which I say sorry, but I think it is on the way to healing clean.'

'The musket ball?'

'Removed, sir.'

'By you?'

This got a wide smile and a look around the room. 'I live here alone.'

'Being black, added to what you said about your name, I wondered . . .' The obvious was left unsaid.

'My master is no longer with us and, since he brought me to a place where no man can be a slave, I give him the title out of habit. Now I will heat you some milk fresh from my cow and make you a posset. Then I suggest, sir, rest would be best.'

Brazier sat in head-bowed silence as his saviour went about the task of lighting the fire, which took some time to reach a decent flame. Zachary was moving around, doing what, the man to whom he administered had no idea, the latter's mind being very much elsewhere. He was back at Cottington Court, finding himself caught off guard, mentally reprising the sneers of Henry Tulkington, knowing as he listened and for the second time that he'd failed in his aim to get Elisabeth away from her brother's clutches.

The low groan emitted was not caused by physical pain but by the other thoughts which crowded in, producing many questions and no answers, not least how had Tulkington known of his plan? Was it because of it being altered from the original, due to Dan Spafford's insistence on trying to get his son back, and how had that worked out? He'd seen Daisy Trotter raise the pistol to point at Harry's face and had heard it go off, but to what effect? His aim had been to get clear, not to find out.

Would it have worked out any better had he and his crew been alone, as originally intended? Probably not was the conclusion, which was a bitter pill to swallow, made worse by the feeling he was at a stand in how matters could be altered. The bowl placed below his nose smelt strongly of cinnamon, while he offered little resistance as a tender hand lifted his chin so he could drink, tasting milk, which had been soured with ale and heavily spiced.

'Are you in need of food, sir?' A slow shake of the head. 'Then when this is gone, I say you should lie down.'

The sipping was slow, the feeling of internal warmth welcome, as were the large hands easing him back, to lie face down again with his mind full of whirling hopes and dashed dreams. Sleep soon followed.

Joe Lascelles stood across the road from the Old Playhouse, the ditty bag containing his few possessions slung over one shoulder, wondering if it would be wise to enter on his own. The faces of the two mean-faced toughs employed to guard the entrance did nothing to inspire. Stood under flaring torches, they were charged to prevent entry by those too drunk for peaceful enjoyment. Nor were they given to smiling on the sober; everyone passing got a glare, regardless of their condition.

In part, the caution was inspired by his background as a one-time slave; he had a caution regarding risk, which, having been bred into him as a boy, was never absent. To transgress was so simple and no slave was ever sure of what boundaries it would be unwise to cross; these lay at the whims of a master and his overseers, which took no account of the arbitrary impulses of the owner's family and even visiting friends. He'd escaped from the plantation in which he'd been a houseboy by swimming out to a ship dropping anchor not far offshore. He had no idea of the nature of the vessel he was trying to reach, only that it might provide salvation. It turned out to be HMS *Diomede*, fresh to the Jamaica Station, waiting for a tide before entering harbour, and commanded by Edward Brazier.

The captain, in his dark-blue coat with twin gold epaulettes, turned out to be a rare creature for a British naval officer, a fact this escapee only established later. He evinced no inclination to return Joe to his owner, more impressed with his courage than mindful of the property laws of the Sugar Islands, and the courage was real: the waters off Kingston Harbour were home to sharks. Added to the risk of being eaten, there existed a set of variable tides which ran strongly whatever the time of day; Joe had been lucky to find one helpful – a contrary tide and he would certainly have drowned.

Fetched out of the water by a ship's boat, given his colour and the desperate nature of the task he'd set himself, it was natural he'd be questioned as to why he'd run; there was no need to say he was a slave. Joe had declined to be open, to admit he had struck the son of the house in which he served, a fellow close to his own age, drawing blood. For such an offence he could expect to be lashed to a pulp and might even die.

'I got sick of seein' to the needs of others, sir. Fetchin' food and clearin' what they left.'

Brazier had asked, seemingly not put out by a garbled and

unconvincing explanation, 'Been at it long?' Joe had held out a low hand to indicate the height at which he'd begun his duties. 'Then it will serve if you attend upon me and, given this is a vessel of the Royal Navy, subject to the laws of the realm, no man aboard can be held in bondage.'

On *Diomede* he had stayed, mustered as a volunteer in the ship's logs, going on to prove the standards of domestic service in which he had been trained ran well ahead of anything provided by the navy. This got him prime place in the great cabin pantry, especially when he applied the knowledge he'd gained from being a constant pest to the plantation kitchen, not just wishing to endlessly pick at what they prepared, but keen to absorb the methods by which they went about their creations.

In time he found out why he'd been so readily taken aboard. He'd replaced a long-time servant from a previous Brazier command, one who'd decided, with peace coming after the American War, he was free to go ashore and stay there, declining to rejoin his captain when he was commissioned into a new frigate. He also heard Brazier was, due to his own experience, a man to abhor the trade in human flesh, from which sprang a happy association with only one restriction: Joe could never go ashore until he was paid off in Portsmouth.

Adjustment to such freedom had taken time; he was inclined to look over his shoulder for a looming threat, or see in the cast of an eye the desire to take him up and return him to bondage. What set him in motion now was the sight of a group of sober-looking Lascars being let through the door, men probably fresh off an incoming East Indiaman. Likewise steady in his walk, he drew little attention, so passed by easily. Once inside, Joe guessed instinctively the Card Room was not for him, nor did he feel he could ascend a staircase closed off by a chain.

So he made his way across the hallway to a set of double doors, which opened to reveal the main chamber: a large, packed and fug-filled space, with a stage at one end, on which an illusionist was performing sleight-of-hand magic. Finding a place to sit was far from easy, nor, when he'd done so, was it easy to think about a way to proceed, given the raucous din of catcalling and whistling as each trick was performed. Sat with his back to a wall, he peered through the clouds of pipe-driven smoke to observe the clientele. Sailors made up the bulk of the custom, while there to keep them company, as well as encourage their spending, were a matching number of females, well dressed and comely, with smiles which never slipped.

There was no sign of Saoirse Riorden and no way he could just sit there and wait to see if she came by. What did come his way was a buxom serving girl with tankards hooked at her waist, carrying a large jug of ale, only proffered when he declined to take either rum or brandy. Fishing out the means to pay, recalling how little he had in the way of coin, drove home just how much he would be on his uppers if Brazier wasn't found alive. He was halfway through his tankard, which had been well nursed, when Saoirse appeared, sweeping through the door to cast a roving eye on proceedings.

Any hope the gaze, alighting on his, might check with recognition was soon dashed. This left no option but an approach, held in check as she dealt with the many who wished to call upon her attention. Nor did his face seem to register when he finally caught her eye, forcing Joe to close and use the captain's name. This got no smile, merely a jerk of the head to make his way out the double doors, with her not following, leaving him to kick his heels until her round of the room was complete. Nor was he happily greeted when she emerged, which rendered Joe's explanation, even to his own ears, unconvincing.

'A High Sheriff, no less?' was her mystifying comment.

'So I was told, ma'am, so I reckoned it best not to hang about, which means . . .'

'You lack a place to lay your head.' Joe nodded as she added, 'And no word from your shipmates, who would be well advised any return to the Navy Yard might be unwise.'

'Their dunnage is there.'

'Which won't amount to much, to be sure.'

In this she was acknowledging what had been lost in the fire at Quebec House. If Edward Brazier had replaced necessities, he lacked the ability to do so for any kind of prized possessions. They'd lost everything barring what they stood up in and, if spare clothing could be provided once, it could be found again and at little cost in Deal: when visiting sailors began to run out of money, it was the first thing they sold.

'I'd say it's best you keep watch on the yard gate to make sure they don't just walk in.' Observing the face crease with uncertainty, she added, 'Not tonight, but come morning. As for now, pass up the stairs and tell my maid Dottie to find you a place to lay your head. Now go, for I have my affairs to attend to.'

'Can't help wonderin', ma'am, if Dutchy and the others have had any luck.'

'Wondering will do you no good. If they'd found anything they would have come back by now.'

What Dutchy had found was a mystery to him and the others. Following Hawker's party brought them to an isolated farmhouse. Given what he knew of the location – admittedly not much – he wondered whether it was the same one they'd visited the night before, home to Spafford and his gang. It was impossible to tell in the dark and they'd never clapped eyes on it in daylight at any time, but there was strong reason to see it as a possibility.

They watched, although it was far from clear even with the torches still lit, a party of five souls being harried indoors with musket butts, plus another half-carried, clearly unable to make his own way. More worrying was the sight, minutes later, of two sack-encased loads being lifted off the back of the van, likewise taken indoors, after which everyone disappeared and with them the torchlight, leaving them in darkness and with much uncertainty.

'What now, Dutchy?' asked Peddler.

'Don't rightly know, mate.'

'Could get close and ha' a gander through a winder.'

'Hawker and his men, Cocky? First sniff of us and they'll use those muskets they had slung.'

'Won't hold back, right enough,' Peddler added. 'Them bundles carried in looked a mite like bodies.'

'Think I saw that too, mate, but it don't tell me what to do about it.'

'Are we goin' to admit what we're all thinkin' it could be?'

'Could be the captain, right enough,' came reluctantly from Dutchy, 'but I'm half-guessing it might be from what happened last night. The Trotter cove couldn't miss, nor with what came about as we began to run would he have likely survived. Every musket was aimed at his back.'

'All but one,' Peddler added, gloomily.

'Tryin' to do owt in the dark is not a notion I'm fond of. Best we draw off and find a safe place to kindle a fire, which will serve as long as we have sight of the road. Can't see anybody leavin' till sunup. If they was, they'd be goin' by now.'

'So we have to be back watchin' by then.'

'An' fed,' Cocky insisted. 'Christ, that's the first time I've ken't you no tae go on aboot yer empty belly, Peddler.'

'If'n Jesus can go forty days and nights without, mate, then so can I.'

'Come on,' Dutchy ordered, as he began to inch backwards. 'Let's find a place for comfort.'

'Should've brought hammocks.'

* * *

John Cottin finished what was a good if solitary dinner at the Three Kings, amused by the way Garlick, who'd chosen to serve him personally, kept fashioning what he reckoned to be subtle enquiries as to what his guest had uncovered; they were about as delicate as a ton of bricks and amusing because of it. His guest's purpose was known to him and Garlick was probing to see what he'd uncovered.

Nursing a fine French brandy and picking at the last of his cheese, while idly watching the bobbing lights of the huge ships' lanterns which filled the anchorage, he was cogitating on what to do next. In truth he was also wondering if he had given himself such a wild goose chase it would be best to return to Westerham and leave the locals to stew in their own delinquency, thoughts distracted as Garlick came back into the private dining room.

'Can I offer you another drop of brandy, your honour?'

'No, Mr Garlick, though I must say it's a fine brew.'

'Kind of you to remark on it, sir, for I have a care on what I buy in.'

But not from where or whom you buy it was Cottin's silent conjecture: high quality and a far from excessive price hinted at contraband goods. Off on a boast, Garlick was content to leave matters there, going on to claim a superior standard to anyone else in Deal and all points of the compass as well.

'There's not a worthy soul who dines at the Three Kings who don't compliment me on my cellar, sir, and it goes double for the food I provide. Why, even the First Minister to King George himself takes his provender here for that very reason.' Cottin's obvious curiosity had Garlick continue, obviously delighted to be imparting superior knowledge instead of seeking to extract any. 'He does so when resident at Walmer Castle, which has poor kitchens and lacks anyone to produce what I serve.'

Enquiry from Cottin led to the boast Pitt was now a frequent visitor to Walmer Castle, given the occupant of the Cinque Ports sinecure whom he'd appointed, of which the fortress was the official residence, showed no desire himself to use it. The politician, he heard, had a love of sea air and gardens, which his occupation allowed him to indulge.

'This rumour of Captain Brazier being in league with Mr Pitt. What do you reckon to it?'

It was a sudden thought to ask, one which ran against the grain of his earlier resolution, in truth one brought on by a day of frustration. Amusement had to be contained on noting his host's abrupt change of expression, guarded rather than expansive. A touch of flattery was required to loosen his tongue.

'Come, Mr Garlick. I guess you to be a fellow fly enough to ensure nothing of note gets past you. Indeed, did you not intimate as much on my arrival?'

A whole gamut of emotions crossed the imbibed face in quick succession, discretion fighting with his desire to appear a repository of information not vouchsafed to all and sundry, the latter winning out when Cottin added,

'Be assured, anything you say to me will go no further.'

'Captain Brazier did dine in the company of Mr Pitt on more than one occasion, your honour, in this very room too, though what they talked of I don't know, nor would I make it my business to enquire.'

'Would you say their relations were cordial?'

'Seemed enough so, but as I say . . .'

'So who, apart from you, would know about these meetings?'

'Half Deal in a flash, your honour. There's no shortage of nosy folk around here and my doorway is in plain view to any seeking to know who's a coming and going. And Mr Pitt goes nowhere without a couple of armed soldiers, which is like a banner to say he's present.'

But not with whom he dined. It took no great leap to envisage Garlick boasting about his esteemed guest and with whom he shared a table, but gossip was no crime. Nor did he think any attempt to extract further revelations from his host would yield anything other than obfuscation. This accepted, what he had been told did lead to a possible way to proceed, though the half-formed thought required time to mature.

'On reflection, Mr Garlick, perhaps I can treat myself to another brandy.'

'Be back in a tick, your honour.'

Before the second glass was placed before him, John Cottin had come to a conclusion. He was damned if he was going to be side-lined by the scoundrels who ran this town. He'd write to William Pitt, ask for his help and, failing that, some indication of how to proceed in a way which would bring to justice one or more murderers, added to censure for those too lazy or implicit in the crime to pursue them. To do so had potent advantages, which had nothing to do with the case. Such a letter would bring to the attention of, next to the King himself, the most powerful man in the kingdom, both his name and his application, which could do no harm in the future and might even lead to greater things.

To write was the easy part, while the normal way once sanded and sealed would be to pass his correspondence to Garlick for despatch, which would never serve. He would have to find another location, one which had nothing to do with this hostelry or indeed Deal, given any missive given to the local postal franchise would be marked with the name and address of its recipient. Garlick could not be relied upon to keep his mouth shut but he was not alone. What was the alternative? Downing Street as the destination might set alarm bells ringing wherever it went from, enough for the letter to be passed to the quartet he'd met on arrival. He'd not put it past these villains to open and read what he said, so it needed to go from somewhere outside Deal. On his way to his room, he passed the proprietor's hatch, where he issued an instruction.

'I will require a horse tomorrow, Mr Garlick. I'm sure you know of someone who can provide me with something not too hard to control.'

'I shall send to Mr Flaherty first thing, sir, an' be assured, he keeps a capital stable. Also, with me to intercede for you, the price will not be excessive, cheating the unwary being the way with horse folk.'

'I wish you good night.'

He had the means to write the letter in his room, one being composed in his head as he ascended the stairs.

CHAPTER EIGHT

After what had been a trying day, Henry Tulkington returned home to a house in which matters still required to be resolved, without having taken the steps to investigate how it might be brought about. Meeting the doctor he'd hoped to question at the Deal Lodge, the fellow who'd supplied him with the potion which had so sedated Elisabeth, which had allowed him to see her married off to Harry Spafford, had been put aside while he dealt with more pressing matters. Much of this he'd mulled over on the way home with no resolution. Feeling far from well, he was sure he needed a good night's sleep just to reach any sort of equilibrium. This rendered unwelcome the information from Grady to say Joshua Moyle was waiting to see him and had been for some time.

'The Reverend Doctor is in your study, sir.'

'How long did you say?'

'He arrived just after luncheon, sir.'

'How much drink has he put away?' was delivered in a waspish tone.

Moyle was a fellow who normally amused Henry, he being the least divine person to ever wear the cloth. But the thought of dealing with him now, no doubt in his usual drunken state through having access to the well-stocked cellar, was best avoided. He was just about to order he be carried back to the vicarage when Grady replied.

'The reverend declined to take anything of that nature, sir. But he has asked for and been served with tea twice.'

The servant's expression was, as ever, devoid of expression, unlike his employer's, whose eyebrows shot up in surprise: the man was a true soak whose antics, after being at the bottle, rarely failed to make Henry snicker, as much for the depressing effect it had on the man's long-suffering wife as the embarrassment itself. Perhaps to take his mind off things the cleric was just the company he needed, so he said, in what he thought was a jocose tone, that brandy had better be served now.

'For myself as well,' was added as an afterthought.

Entering his study suppressed any feeling of humour. The man's ruddy, vinous face, once he stood to greet his host, left Henry in no doubt Moyle was in some way troubled. He was, as ever, an unprepossessing sight, his black waistcoat stretched over a substantial belly of strained buttons. Along with the lapels of his coat, it was covered with traces of snuff and food that had missed its target; above this and a worried countenance, the pepper-and-salt hair as unruly as ever. The only oddity was his sobriety. 'I've had a letter from the bishop, Henry.'

'Which surely must rank as a first.' He not being the type to correspond with high clerics, the attempt at wit did not go down well, very much the reverse, which prompted an obvious question. 'On the subject of what?'

'Surely you can guess?'

'Joshua, you're the second person today to require I deduce something from thin air. It failed to amuse on the first occasion.'

'It asks if there were any irregularities I wish to admit to, in the marriage of Spafford and Elisabeth.'

'I'm surprised he even knows it took place.'

'I told you, I had a visit from his secretary.'

Henry replied absent-mindedly as he went to stand before the fire.

'So you did, and now you've had a letter asking about irregularities, to which you can surely reply there were none.'

'When we both know it not to be the case?' came out as protest. 'No banns were called, added to which the ceremony took place in this very room, not as is required by law in a consecrated place.'

'To none of which you are required to admit.'

'Someone is putting about the truth, Henry.'

The door opened and Grady entered bearing a silver tray, the crystal of both glasses and the decanter catching the light of the candles and the flames of the fire, which covered the fact of Henry deducing the culprit, for there could only be one. Silently Grady laid the tray down and proceeded to pour the drinks, his presence rendering any further discussion impossible, minds not as restful as their tongues.

Moyle was in a true bind: he owed his living at Cottington to the Tulkington family, which meant his home and his stipend. The church lay in the grounds of the estate, so no authority could impose a priest. They could propose, but the final decision lay with the family, or to be more precise a man he dare not upset. But the diocese could remove him from clerical orders and oblige Henry to find another prelate. He would not have been reassured if he had known what Henry was thinking: Spafford was dead, so what did it matter? However, Moyle required to be reassured.

'Someone who would lack anyone to corroborate his gossip. No one in this house will say a word.'

'Except Elisabeth. The letter asks to be allowed the names of the assenting parties so the diocese can communicate with them.'

'In writing?'

'I assume so.'

Henry picked up one of the filled glasses and handed it to Moyle, knowing a reassuring fib was required to settle his concerns. 'I shall make sure all correspondence coming into this house is brought to me, regardless of the superscription. The servants and my aunt will say what they're told. Elisabeth? Best leave it to me, while you and I can say whatever is needed to see them off.'

Moyle took the glass of brandy, the only thing to ease Henry's state of mind. His worried guest had resurrected a concern which had lain dormant for most of the day, one the non-divine Moyle nailed right away.

'And what about Harry Spafford?'

'I shouldn't go concerning yourself about him, Joshua.'

Having sent the reverend home, under his own sail for once, Henry ordered a negus as a nightcap, prior to retiring. Sat in a chair watching the fire turn to ash, he set his mind to all the problems which assailed him, determined to examine them objectively, refusing to allow his frustrations to boil over into anger. What he'd just been told about ecclesiastical interference was added to the mound, another matter requiring attention, lest it grow from irritation into trouble, one telling factor being an alarmed Moyle could not be relied upon.

The earlier brandy had relaxed him while the sweet and spicy negus added to the mood. In such a state of mind, if solutions did not emerge, potential ways of proceeding did, first and foremost being how to deal with his sister. The twitch of his lips, which grew to a smile, convinced him he'd alighted on a clever ploy, though being a careful man it required to be thoroughly examined before being acted upon. If it failed to work, he could fall back on his previous notion of mental instability. Tested more than once, mentally argued, in which his views naturally carried the day, he went to his desk to take up his quill and pen a note. A ring of the servant bell ensured, when he made for the stairs and his bed, Grady was waiting for him, holding a five-branch candlestick.

'Oblige me by seeing my sister gets this first thing in the morning.'

'Certainly, sir.'

* * *

It was the loud crack of a burning log which woke up Edward Brazier, still in pain but nothing like that which he'd experienced before going to sleep. This tempted him to sit up, movement reminding him sharply of the wound, which had him gritting his teeth. But he refused to stop, albeit it was a slow and careful effort. Sat up, he looked around with a more focused eye than hitherto, noting the dwelling seemed to consist of only one room, sparsely furnished. All needed for existence was within.

His mind was now clear enough to think through what needed to be done, which brought into sharp focus the amount he didn't know, like what had happened to Dutchy and the rest after he had been sent away. They might be armed but they were also seriously outnumbered, which brought on the depressing notion he'd not only led them into a trap, they could possibly have paid a greater price than he.

Brazier soon refused to consider the thought: he knew them to be resourceful and bloody-minded fighters and had seen them in action. Mostly it had been in the boarding of American contraband runners seeking to access the British West Indian possessions in which they were not allowed to trade. As members of his barge crew, they went where he went, and a captain known by the soubriquet of 'The Turk' was not inclined to leave the task of taking an illegally trading vessel to a subordinate. Many of the contests had been hard fought. Even outnumbered, the Jonathans would not give up without a contest, though they declined to use guns on the very good grounds a 32-gun frigate had a lot more firepower at its disposal. Even cutlasses were rarely employed, which left clubs and fists. While interdicting them, their willingness to take on the King's Navy engendered a degree of admiration for people who never ducked making a stand.

Fretting on any number of possibilities would get him nowhere. It was necessary to assume them safe until it was established as true or false by contact. To stand up required a very straight-held back, made harder by the seeming weakness of his legs. Nor did he feel steady when upright, so taking a step came with the risk of a fall. If not quite a stagger to the fireplace it was close, while it needed a hand on the mantle to secure himself. His dark-blue coat, of good quality though bought second-hand in Deal, was hanging to one side. Lifting it told him the purse it contained was there, with it a decent sum in coin, soon confirmed as he fetched it out along with his Hunter case timepiece. Would the man who'd tended to him accept a reward for his endeavours and, if he would, what should it be? That could wait, right now anything to ease his pain was the primary concern.

He felt the heat from the flames licking around the logs, which told him this was a recently stoked-up fire. The same hand was used to keep him upright as he slowly turned to let the heat play on his back, which was welcome but too scorching to stay still for long. While he was contemplating moving to the sole chair in the room, his saviour entered, carrying a dead chicken and a basket of vegetables, frowning before smiling, which presented a fine set of teeth.

'I recall my late master and I tended to different types of people, sir – those who would lie still and beg attention and others who would never do what they were told, even for their own good. Odd the ones who died were often not the disobedient.'

'I need to get a message to some people, one I doubt I'm in a fit state to deliver.'

'In a day or two, perhaps.'

'Sooner.'

'To reassure them you're still alive?' Brazier nodded. 'And you wish me to take it?'

'All I require is you take the horse to a certain person, tell him of my condition, then bring it back again so I may use it when I'm fit enough to ride.'

'This tells me you think you have people to fear, sir.'

Forgetting his wound, Brazier shrugged and winced, which delayed his response. 'I have no idea if there are.'

'But you wish to be safe by thinking the worst.'

'I will go myself if you decline.'

'And where is it you would wish me to go, sir?'

'A livery stable outside Deal. I will give you directions.'

'The day is nearly gone.'

'At first light, then?'

The feathery and limp object in his hand was held up. 'After some food, sir.'

'And more sleep,' Brazier replied, not seeking to hide the fact he was still weak by moving to plonk himself on the battered sea chest. 'I think perhaps I should tell you my name. Edward Brazier.'

'Would it trouble you to tell me more, sir?'

'Perhaps when you tell me about yourself.' This got a chuckle so deep it sounded as if it was coming from his boots. 'You must admit to being rare in these parts.'

'A slave, you mean?'

'A free black man and seemingly a farmer.'

Tempted to tell him about Joe Lascelles, Brazier decided to hold back until he knew more of this man. Asked why, he could not have said but he felt it right. Anyway, Zachary was ready to oblige, plucking the bird as he spoke, first of a life of slavery on another farm, albeit a bigger one, where the work could be back-breaking.

'My master was not an unkind man, or it would be best to say he did not know when he was acting so, which made my sudden change of owner a blessing.' The curious look brought another low chuckle. 'I was lost in a game of cards, sir, or as the Good Lord no doubt intended, saved by a poor wager.'

Gentle questioning revealed more. The 3rd Regiment of Foot had bivouacked in his original master's fields in Pennsylvania, the officers billeted in the farmhouse over several days. This included the regimental surgeon, Mr Venables, to whom he'd come as winnings.

'And he brought you back to England when the war was over?'

Zachary, now gutting the bird, acknowledged the obvious, with Brazier tapping the chest on which he was sitting. 'And this is his?'

'Passed over into the hands of the Lord, two seasons past now. He left me all he owned, as well as livestock and this house, to hold and live by till I join him.'

'No other family?'

'None.'

'The crop?'

'Cherries first, and fine they are too. Pickings of them are over for this year, sir, but the trees still need lookin' after. Then hops in summer and apples in the autumn. Whatever I grow, God sees fit to try and inflict them with pestilence.'

'Perhaps it's the devil.'

A deep laugh. 'I'd take real pleasure in fightin' him, sir.'

'Can I say, you seem well educated?'

'I was taught to speak well, like a Yankee gentleman. I would only be educated if I could read and write.'

Zachary talked on as he cut up some vegetables, potatoes and carrots, finally filling the room with the sharp tang of onions, all his efforts going into a pot, which was hung on a hook above the fire, describing his early years as a slave boy, born in the New York colony, sold on when he began to reach maturity to work the plough, dig the plots and bring in the harvest. There was no resentment in his words, more a seeming acceptance the Almighty, often referred to, had decided how his life would be lived.

Listening, Brazier could not help but contrast it with what he'd seen of the fate of those violently dragged from their African homes, then packed into ships manned by sheer devils incarnate, chained below decks in vessels of which it was best not to be downwind, so great was the rancid smell. Having boarded one mid-Atlantic and seen the conditions in which the soon-to-be slaves were transported and abused, Brazier never wanted to experience it again. It had also affected his attitude to the institution of slavery: gone was the ignorance which allowed for complacency, to be replaced with deep repugnance, a feeling from which Joe Lascelles had benefited when he was brought aboard. This Zachary had enjoyed the same good fortune.

'You have been lucky.'

'I have been blessed, sir. Now, am I allowed to ask of you?'

Edward Brazier obliged, but it was a much-filleted explanation of his past and naval career, though he was open about his own father having been a naval surgeon.

'Then it may be we can see each other as brothers, sir, for I think of Mr Venables as a parent to me.' Seeing Brazier made curious, he pointed to the chest on which he was sitting. Looking closely, the name could be made out. 'You have no need to tell me of the wound, sir, if you do not choose to.'

'Oh, I shall, but it will make me sound like a fool.'

By the time he finished a severely edited version of events, which did not name people or places, the chicken was cooked and, as they ate, Zachary took the liberty of agreeing with him.

Dirley Tulkington went about his task with a growing sense of frustration. The way the candles, which illuminated his efforts, burnt down seemed to reflect the way his present standing was progressing. He only ever worked on these ledgers, related to the family business, when his chambers were closed and everyone else had gone home: they were for the eyes of only him and his nephew. His task was to ensure everything added up: income, expenditure, plus a list of goods outstanding, which required a good head for figures added to the acute memory of a successful King's Counsel.

While it was easy to seek certain items be despatched to the East Kent shore, it was not always possible for the French suppliers, due to the number of internal tariff borders in their country, to meet every order in a given time. Every region of France had its own tolls and taxes, which were jealously guarded. A number of these had to be circumvented, depending where the contraband was sourced. This often left much outstanding, which made achieving any kind of ongoing balance a formidable task.

His quill moved quickly despite his darkening mood, a sharp mind going about a task with which he was utterly familiar. In his head he had discreet and verbal orders for those with whom he had social contact in the capital, many people of wealth and position, even in government, who nevertheless felt disinclined to pay to the Exchequer the impost added as duty. Other outlets, such as hotels, gentlemen's clubs, dubious establishments from bagnios to brothels – and gender was not an issue – contacts built up over a long time, would drop off discreet coded notes at his home stating their requirements, plus the funds needed to secure delivery. A servant, one unable to read, was sent from Cottington Court to drop off at his chambers what was required in the areas served by his nephew, Kent and Sussex.

The source of his growing annoyance came from the way Henry had behaved on his most recent visit to London and it could not be explained away by his having too much to drink and a light head. When Dirley's half-brother Acton passed away, and it was sudden, his nephew, somewhat gauche and never having been fully briefed regarding the family business, lacked the skills necessary to oversee what was quite a complex enterprise. Thus, he'd relied on him for guidance, being properly respectful of the difference which existed between them in both age and experience.

This had been declining over some time, as Henry's confidence grew, which was only to be expected, acceptable until they came to what Dirley expected would be an equitable partnership. It was one in which the nephew naturally drew a higher proportion of the profits than the uncle, which to Dirley was only proper: the business had been the creation of his half-brother Acton, building on old Corley's rather rough efforts.

It was, however, incumbent on him, to his uncle's way of thinking, such a disparity remain unmentioned; they were in a partnership and good manners dictated it should be addressed as one of equals. Henry had breached the bounds by the way he'd behaved days past and it continued to rankle, issuing what very much sounded like instructions, if not downright demands, documents to be prepared within hours, as if his uncle had nothing else to do but meet his every whim.

This was in place of what they should and would have been in the recent past: appropriately submitted requests to which he would have been happy to accede. Other things troubled him, not least, the more he thought on it, the information that his niece, a widow still constrained by her period of mourning for Stephen Langridge, albeit said period was close to completion, had seemingly suffered a *coup de foudre*, entering into a sudden marriage with a handsome young fellow in a matter of weeks of their first meeting.

Dirley might be a bachelor, but he'd been witness to many idiocies in the matrimony line, some of which had required clients to be rescued from their own folly. What he was being told did not make sense. If he didn't know Elisabeth as well as he would like – his illegitimate birth had limited contact with those resident at Cottington Court – he found it hard to see someone he rated as eminently sensible act in such an untoward fashion.

Who was this Harry Spafford and why was he intent on handing over control of Elisabeth's Jamaica plantations to Henry, the documents to complete this required in such haste? In her previous correspondence, Elisabeth had stated her intention to sell them due to a dislike of their being worked by slaves. Could this Spafford fellow have so charmed her she would meekly change her mind?

It was, of course, no longer strictly her decision, there being no entail: on marriage her assets became the property of her husband

and he could dispose of them as he saw fit. Yet there had been something in the explanation provided by Henry which jarred. He maintained Spafford had no head for figures or any interest in matters of business, was fearful of the task of management, so was quite content to pass control of the plantations and the considerable income they produced to his brother-in-law, which would be passed on after expenses were deducted.

An admired legal brain, Dirley Tulkington was sure he could smoke anyone dissembling in a flash. Henry's throwaway manner, as he advanced this explanation, had set his hackles twitching. The letter of congratulation he'd sent to his niece was his way of making sure, by inviting her and her new spouse to visit him for two reasons. He wanted to cast an eye over Spafford to ensure he was no mere fortune-hunter; the other was to find out if what he was being told by Henry was the truth.

He'd not yet received a reply from Elisabeth, which was unlike her. A properly brought up young lady, who had taken assiduous care to regularly keep in touch from the West Indies, would surely reply – and indeed, had done so – from East Kent, his missives responded to by return from there in the past. So why not now? Given his troubled reflections, this decided him, after he'd finished his tasks and locked away the ledgers in his safe, to write to Elisabeth again.

CHAPTER NINE

Being up before first light presented no problem for a sailor in the King's Navy, it was habit given a man-o'-war stood to every morning at such an hour. In time of conflict a warship did so with its entire crew on deck and its guns run out, ready to fire, in case daylight revealed an enemy. Thus, the trio looking for their captain were within sight of the farmhouse as well as the covered van before the sun tipped over the horizon, very likely before anyone within its walls had opened their eyes. Not that it showed them much: all they could do was watch, wait and down the provisions they'd brought along.

The first sign of life was not from within. A bent-over fellow hauling a handcart stopped by the stoop to leave an urn as well as a basket, the contents unknown. There was no lingering or seeking to make contact with anyone inside; he moved on quickly with a cart heavy from what must be produce yet to be delivered.

'We need a ship's bell,' Peddler opined quietly.

'Well we havn'a got one,' was Logan's reply.

'Knowin' the hour don't matter much, Peddler,' Dutchy responded looking up at a sky going from pale grey to blue. 'But it looks like we're in for a warm 'un and sitting out here with the sun on our heads, with what we's got left of drink, don't appeal.'

'Idea tae move wi' the low sun in yonder sod's eyes. He'll hae a job seein' us.'

They waited as the sun rose, a bright orb so low in the sky it threw shadows which stretched into infinity. It also lit the red brick walls and thatched roof of the farmhouse, making the dwelling look more attractive than it probably was. Dutchy was up and moving first, heading for a large and ancient oak tree, with well-spread branches in full leaf, which would provide shade. If it was closer and more risky, the trunk was thick enough for the trio to hide behind if they were careful.

Once in place it was wait and see, again nothing to trouble an ex-tar; half of life aboard a ship was spent looking out at an endless ocean on which nothing happened, never a distraction from the daily tasks which needed to be carried out.

Dan Spafford passed away during the night without anyone noticing, nor was he mourned by the man who had fetched him there. Hawker had separated the badly wounded leader from his men, so it was Marker, left to guard the door of the room in which he lay, charged to take an occasional look, who told him the news. Rising from the bed, which had once been Dan's own, he threw open the shutters, blinking in the strong eastern light, which seemed to come straight at him. Before him lay a plate-flat landscape and, had he been able to see anything clearly, it would have shown very little, too much of it being marshland.

There was cultivation to the north, but such did not show outside the lines of trees and hedgerows, there to mark both the boundaries and tracks by which the farm folk made their way to their fields. The wind, being from the north-east, brought with it the unpleasant odour of the silage with which the farmed ground was being fertilised.

'Trotter and young Spafford are beginning to stink too,' said Marker when it was noted. 'So we won't be thinkin' silage for long.'

'Someone get my horse ready,' Hawker rasped. 'I need to get back to the slaughterhouse.'

Turning away from the window he noted the look of curiosity on Marker's face, though there was no desire to accommodate it or explain. He would have to be there when Tulkington showed up, as he was bound to, and it was moot what would come from such a meeting. With three bodies on his hands, two rotting, it seemed to Hawker the sooner they were disposed of the better. If the clear sky held it would presage a night with some moon, perfect for getting across to the long pebble strand fronting Sandwich Flats, on which the Spafford luggers were beached, without attracting attention.

He knew of old there were no others nearby; a smuggler, whoever he was, did not welcome close neighbours, folk able to observe his comings and goings, more importantly his unloading, unless they were known to be close-mouthed or paid helpers. Thus, Spafford had enjoyed much of the strand to himself, if you excluded small boats for fishing. Most preferred Deal Beach, with taverns close by for when work was slack. Not what Spafford had been about was any secret: everyone around Worth and Sandwich would know of his trade. Again, just like Deal and every town bordering the coast, the folk living had a bond of interest in saying nothing to authority. The benefits, and it behoved a smuggler to be generous to his locality, came from silence not squealing.

'Happen you'd best breakfast before setting out, John. One of Spafford's boys said they get eggs delivered fresh of a mornin'. Milk too.'

'Enough for all?'

'Enough for us,' got a rare chuckle from Hawker.

'A day without will not harm Spafford's lot, lazy buggers have got flesh to spare.'

Which exposed another problem; what if keeping them here went on? One day lacking food or water they'd have to stand but, if it lasted, they'd have to be fed, supplies would have to be fetched in.

Spafford had owned the farmhouse as well as the small fields around, but they were not used to cultivate anything. Likewise, the barns stored no food; they'd mostly been used to house contraband as well as ships' stores.

'Get our lads fed. I'll eat later.'

'Saddled horse has been led to the front door,' Peddler hissed.

This had the others, who'd been lying in the long, shaded grass, sit up. Taking care to keep the trunk of the oak between them and the farmhouse, they peered round to take a look.

'Has to be Hawker,' Dutchy said. 'He was the only one mounted last night.'

'Do we try tae take him?'

'Can't see how, Cocky. One sight of us and he'll spur off.'

Which left in the air a question already raised: what were they doing apart from keeping watch? Dutchy acknowledged they'd had a bit of unseen luck, though they could do no more than guess at what was within the farmhouse. It could be Brazier was one of the men they'd seen hustled inside; the possibility he could have been carried in might be in their minds but it was not mentioned. The only thing they could do was wait and hope for more good fortune.

'Be a notion to follow him,' Peddler Palmer suggested. 'An' if it don't show up owt, we can at least tell Joe what's happenin' out here. The Riordan woman an' all would want to know.'

'Good chance tae have a feed too.' Seeing Peddler take offence, Cocky added quickly, 'Just having a jest, mate, it's a good notion.'

'Right there, Cocky, but it'll have to be one of you two, Hawker knows my face.'

'An' uncommon tall too, Dutchy, one he'd spot.'

'Go on, Peddler,' Cocky added, knowing Dutchy would leave them to decide. 'Better than havin' you oot here all day moaning aboot an empty belly.'

'Hawker,' Dutchy spat.

And there he was, on the step getting ready to mount and talking, probably issuing orders to one of his men, who was then obliged to knee him up into the saddle. A few more words were imparted before he kicked his mount into motion, heading towards the Sandwich Road at a trot.

'He'll not be expectin' to be followed, Peddler, an' if he holds such a pace so can you. But if he kicks on, don't try to stay with him. An' take your beer, the sun is going to get hotter.'

Dressed in his customary black, John Hawker soon became aware of the sun's heat, which had him, once he was on the road and out of any shade, haul on the reins. Using the stirrups, he stood to remove his coat, which had him turn to lay it over the saddle. Peddler was quick to find a tree as soon as he hauled on the reins, so was now making out he was having a piss, looking idly this way and that like a man thus engaged. This showed others were on the road travelling in both directions, walking or in carts and, well to the rear, one big-looking dark-skinned cove riding towards Deal at no great pace. In what Peddler guessed to be less than half of the glass, they came within clear sight of the ramparts of Sandown Castle, dark and stark against the blue waters of the anchorage, while the roof of St George's Church rising above the surrounding buildings was visible, a Puritan construct lacking a steeple.

Little attention was paid by either man to the riders they passed, heading for Sandwich, and there were several, Peddler only noting one, who seemed to be as uncomfortable on a saddle as he was himself.

John Cottin had never been a true fan of horseflesh and was, at the moment he passed what appeared to be a sailor, on foot and grinning broadly, cursing himself for not ordering a hack to take him to his destination. But the reason not to do so was sound: a conveyance required a coachman, the hiring of which would never stay secret and, since he'd come to suspect the whole population of Deal as unreliable, it would not serve. His discomfort did have him deliberate on what bordered on a near aversion to horses and the constraints it had placed on how he was seen, which had extended through his schooldays and on into adulthood. He was studious, where his classmates were more unruly, bent on games not classroom work, which had not endeared him. In a society where a good seat was to be admired, a poor one was there to be derided and his had been denigrated often enough to render it a form of transport he did his best to avoid.

Nor did he hunt, which was a social barrier in the region of West Kent in which he lived. This also barred him from taking up a place in the local Volunteer Yeomanry, a desirable organisation to be part of when it came to social advancement; all the best families, fathers and sons, participated both in the training for action and the heavy drinking which subsequently took place. Cottin was of the opinion more effort went into the latter than the former, but it saw him once more tarred as a fellow wedded to the quill not the reins, in a society which appeared not to value such an asset.

The law had seemed the perfect place for a studious lad who showed no desire for an outdoor life, while he was content his younger brothers should take over the small family tenanted farm in which he'd been raised. Yet the profession had its own barriers to progress: too many elderly fellows with questionable legal ability blocking advancement. This he hoped to have sidestepped by applying for his present position, but it did mean he'd been obliged to leave the practice in which he had served his first pupillage, then become a partner, with the concomitant loss of prospects.

Destined for Sandwich – he'd told Garlick it was Dover – he would take dinner in the best hostelry, then ask for his letter to be taken to the local post franchisee by the proprietor, a common request to a host. To take his mind off an aching posterior he allowed himself, as he had the previous night, to speculate on where

110

the correspondence might lead. Proximity to power had real allure; would this provide a route out of a rural backwater into a situation where he would have the kind of standing he sought, not just in his county, but in his country?

An elderly black traveller was rare enough to distract him from his fanciful aspirations – one poorly clad, yet riding a fine-looking bay mare, even more so. When he looked with a degree of deep curiosity at this apparition, the response was a full smile showing snow-white teeth and a tip of the hat, followed by a deep-voiced greeting.

'Good day to you, sir.'

Cottin was obliged to reply. 'Of course, and the same to you.'

Had the fellow been singing before, the sheriff didn't know, being too preoccupied. But he was now: a low rhythmic refrain, which spoke of a deep religious faith.

Hawker entered the gate of the slaughterhouse when most of Deal was just risen and Peddler walked straight on, passing by the closed and shuttered Old Playhouse on his way to the Navy Yard. The gate of the base was guarded by a pair of marines, though the source of any further progress lay not with them, but the doorman on early duty, no doubt long-serving ex-navy, looked after by a well-connected officer. This would have got him the prized post, which came with pay, bed and board. He was long past his prime and gone was anything like a pigtail or wide-bottomed ducks. These had been swapped long ago for a blue jacket with brass anchor buttons, breeches, stockings and a tricorne hat.

'Ahoy there, matey,' was Peddler's opening gambit, preparatory to passing on through, as he had done before.

A hand went up to stop him. 'An' what would you be after, now you no longer berth here?'

'Who says I don't?'

'Well I do for one, an' I don't reckon to be alone.'

Tempted to argue, Peddler put it aside; the crabbed look in the old bugger's eye did not presage persuasion. All he could manage was a weak plea, not that what he mentioned amounted to much after Quebec House was burnt down.

'My dunnage is still here.'

The voice dropped as the doorman looked around to make sure there was no one in authority lurking, even the marines would struggle to hear. Peddler knew, by instinct, he was going to be given something that should not have been passed on by one old salt to another, which came through the brotherhood of the lower deck.

'If'n I was you, mate, I'd forget it. Bit of a to-do yesterday. That blackamoor mate of yours took off. Heard some sheriff cove was asking after him an' it never does to talk to such folk. Made the admiral's clerk look like a true arse, not that he ain't one, mind. But he was spittin' and spread the word about the lot of you, wanting to be told if any of you showed up. So 'less you want examined, what for I have no notion, I should show your heels sharpish.'

'No twice tellin' required, mate,' was Peddler's reply, delivered when he was already moving away. 'And beholden to you.'

'Keep yer head low, brother,' was sent after him.

Where would Joe go? There were only two possibilities and, since the Old Playhouse was closest, it was to there he went first to find a closed and locked door. The last time he'd been admitted, they'd been with Vincent Flaherty and, if the Riorden woman seemed to be on their side, there was no doubt the Irishman was, though it might just be he wanted his horse back. It was to there they'd gone yesterday morning after the fight at Cottington Court; if Dutchy reckoned it the place to get aid, then it was good enough for him. Flaherty could pass on to the lady what he thought best, which for all Peddler knew might be nothing at all.

'Christ, we're in a right stew here,' he moaned as he set off, which was a wrong thought to have on a rumbling stomach.

* * *

Vincent Flaherty was in a paddock lunging a young horse when Zachary Colton appeared, as much a strange apparition to him as he had been to everyone he'd passed on his way. The long, soft implement was dropped into the sand and Flaherty came to lean on the fence to stare, sure by the smile on the man's face there was no need for any kind of cautious reaction. Yet he admitted to an unpleasant feeling in his gut: Edward Brazier was not the man mounted and he should have been. What had this fellow come to tell him?

'I bid you good day, sir, and ask if you go by the name of Flaherty?'

'The very same, for sure. And who might you be?'

'Zachary Colton, sir, and I come to you with a message from Captain Brazier. Would you permit I dismount?'

'By Jesus, do so,' was the joyous reply.

The smile switched to a deep frown, one which looked about to precede a rebuke, but Zachary said nothing. Chastening folk for blaspheming was not in his nature: checking white men was constrained by his background for all his years of freedom. But the man he was addressing had seen the change.

'Have I troubled you in some way?'

'Only by your way of using the name of the son of God.'

'Then I beg your pardon for the offence. Please dismount and tell me of Edward.' Flaherty pulled a face, then exclaimed. 'I have no idea of how far you've come. Can I offer you anything? A drink, food?'

'I find my faith sustains me, sir,' was delivered as Zachary slid to the ground. 'But I would say your mare needs feed and water.'

Flaherty went to Bonnie, to put his cheek against hers and rub her neck. 'Then let us lead her to her stall. But first, am I allowed to enquire if the message is one of joy?'

'In blessings it is mixed, sir. Your friend is alive but bears a wound.'

'That I heard.'

The concerned look brought forth instant reassurance. 'The musket

113

ball that wounded him has been removed and I have good reason to hope for an untroubled recovery.'

They talked as Flaherty filled and strung up a hay net for Bonnie to munch at, which continued as, out of sight of the mare, he made up a feed of oats. By the time she'd consumed the contents of the bucket, the Irishman had taken Zachary indoors and, having laid out some food, soon knew everything he'd been asked to impart.

'He told you how it came about?'

The replay came with a slow headshake, which amply demonstrated his opinion. 'He did.'

'I see we think the same. So, what is it he wants?'

'Tell his companions he is alive and allow me to lead them to him. He also asks I take back your mare.'

'Is he fit to ride her?'

'Not yet.'

'Is who fit to ride her?' Peddler asked from the open door.

'I give you joy, Peddler, your old commander is safe.'

The smile and relief were genuine while the hearty shaking of hands was in order, but as this was taking place, Peddler could not avoid his eyes swinging to the food on the table.

'If you would oblige me, Mr Flaherty, I'm sharp set.'

CHAPTER TEN

Elisabeth was unsure what to make of the note from Henry, first of all his declaration things could not go on as they were. Did it hint at a weakening of his position? The assurance Harry Spafford was not within the house seemed even more curious. It was immediately open to question as to whether it was a trap, a prime example of the degree of distrust which had grown between them, one which would surely never be resolved. Should she join him for breakfast as he suggested, or send back a note to decline?

Elisabeth had always held herself to be more spirited than her brother. As a young man he had shied away from anything physical, the kind of manly pursuits common in her father's day, which saw crowds of visitors coming to Cottington Court. Riding to hounds and hare coursing, shooting game when the proper seasons came round, attendance at cockfights and bare-knuckle boxing contests held in the grounds, not that Elisabeth had been exposed to the latter.

To decline would smack of anxiety, more likely to encourage than discourage Henry, reasoning which got her out of her bedroom. The moment of entry into the dining room was one of pretend calm. Heart fluttering, she forced herself to act as if nothing was untoward, as if she was engaged in a daily activity in a normal household. Henry nodded but said nothing, while her Aunt Sarah, clearly surprised and not forewarned, kept her eyes firmly fixed on her plate. Having chosen what she required from the chafing dishes on the sideboard, Elisabeth sat down to pick up her knife and fork, though they poised over the plate, away from the food, frozen there by Henry speaking.

'It pleases me you've accepted my invitation.'

The silkiness of the tone was too much; despite prior strictures nothing should be allowed to irritate her, Elisabeth could not avoid her pithy response. 'It does not occur to you I might be here because it is my right to be?'

Expecting him to rise to anger, she was thrown by the even tone of the response. 'It shows what we've come to when you feel the need to say so.'

'This ham is particularly fine,' Sarah Lovell exclaimed with a sort of nervous trill, so obviously a ploy to ward off unpleasantness even Henry managed the ghost of a smile. 'Smoked to perfection, though I rate the pigeon a trifle tough.'

'Aunt Sarah, my sister and I have matters of a personal nature to discuss and, while I feel you to be as much a part of the family as either of us, I wonder if you could see your way to leaving so we can talk alone?'

The eating implements clattered on to her crockery as she pursed her lips, though no words followed. The first part of what had been said did not marry up with the rest; she was plainly being told, when it came to family, she was at best on the periphery. Henry had never lacked the ability to be insensitive, while to her niece, Sarah Lovell deserved whatever he cared to hand out. Yet did she want to be alone with him, even if she was intrigued?

'I have no objection to your remaining, Aunt,' Elisabeth said, her subjective reason being to say, if Henry wanted something, it was axiomatic she did not. 'I'm sure you're just as curious as I to find out what my brother sees as so personal you should not be free to participate.'

Lovell's face was like a mask: bloodless and rigidly set. Here was another example of her lowly standing in the household. Everyone knew it to be so, but it was something she declined to take on board unless it was thrown in her face, which of late had been too many times, by both nephew and niece. Knowing there was little alternative, she sought to cover her belittling with an excuse.

'As it happens, I have many things to attend to. You will be aware, Henry, this household does not run itself.'

Elisabeth had a vision then, of the servants below stairs, paying a price for what had just occurred. Sarah Lovell did indeed run the household, but was not loved for her haughty and impatient manner, which she required to maintain her dignity. Lovell described herself, to anyone who enquired, as a guest who'd sacrificed much, having come to Cottington to help her late sister look after the children. In truth, the arrival of her and her husband had been due to the complete collapse of his dubious business speculations, leading to the loss of both their Canterbury home and her prized social position.

Henry was all smooth appreciation for this apparent self-sacrifice. 'I'm sure you know how grateful I am, Aunt Sarah, and please let me know of anything you require to ease the burden you have so kindly taken on. Perhaps we can have tea together later.'

The tone of the reply failed to match the words as her napkin was folded slowly and deliberately before being, with excessive care, set down by the side of her cup.

'I look forward to it.'

'Was that necessary, Henry?' was asked once she'd left the room.

'I think it so.'

'For which there must be a reason.'

Henry pushed his chair back from the table, laboriously wiping his mouth with his napkin before speaking. 'I asked you to come here because this is a room the servants will not enter until it is time to clear things away. It is thus one of the only two rooms where I can guarantee we will not be overheard. I reckoned an invitation to come to the other, my study, would not have been accepted.'

Even if it was the truth, Elisabeth declined to agree. 'I go where I please.'

A slight gesture of frustration crept into his voice as he responded. 'Do you indeed?'

'Please get to the point, brother.'

'Very well. First let me say to you, on certain conditions being agreed, Harry Spafford will never again reside at Cottington Court. While I know you will be suspicious of any promise I make, this is one I see as being in my interest to keep.'

'Which implies there are others it would not trouble you to break.'

Such an obvious truth was neatly sidestepped. 'Have you ever stopped to ask yourself why I objected to your marrying this Brazier?'

'This Edward, you mean.' A shrug. 'I've sought a reason many times and can only conclude this. Anything which makes me happy has the opposite effect on you.'

'Which I can refute absolutely.'

'Really? I seem to recall you were the same when it came to my marrying Stephen Langridge, only to abruptly change your mind when you heard he'd inherited his uncle's plantations. Even seeing you as a misanthrope, the speed of the change perplexed me.'

'Misanthrope?' got a less tranquil look; it was not a description to please him at all.

'For all your faults, Henry, I did not have you down as a money-grubber.'

'Suggesting I saw Stephen as a burden on the family purse?'

'What else?'

'I admit to thinking him originally an unsuitable match and take leave to suggest our father, had he been alive, would have agreed. Stephen had no money to speak of, so could not have supported you, even given your very substantial dowry, without my help. You were brought up to expect an open purse.'

Much as he tried to disguise it, there was a trace of bitterness in the last remark. She had been the cossetted daughter, tutored at home by a pliable governess until her aunt arrived and took on the role, always able to twist an indulgent parent round her little finger, doubly so when her mother passed away. Henry was son to a stern father who expected much, sent away to be educated and, judging by what she knew from his visits home, hating every day of it. Their lives could not have been more in contrast and she was sure the resentments Henry felt for what she saw as her good fortune stemmed from this.

'*In loco parentis*, I was your guardian, so I had a duty to protect you.'

'So I'm right.'

'Partially so, but let me make plain to you it was not the value of the plantations Stephen inherited which changed my mind so quickly, but their location. In Jamaica you and he would be a long way off and in no position to probe into matters here and even, heaven forbid, give cause for worry.'

'What matters?'

'The same as those I cannot have looked into by someone like Brazier. You've been made aware by him of what they are, though I doubt the extent. Why seek to run off with him, if that's not the case?'

Henry's openness, even the manner in which it was being expressed, flew right in the face of his normal cautious and secretive behaviour, another trait he'd shown since childhood. It threw Elisabeth off balance, so what came next was expressed to give her time to think rather than to acknowledge what she knew.

'Do I understand you to be admitting to what you denied when I challenged you previously?'

'Obviously, but you need to understand my motives, so I concluded it is perhaps best if I tell you everything. Are you prepared to hear it, for I fear it may shock you?'

'I'm not a child.'

'We'll see.'

The food in the chafing dishes grew cold as he did as indicated, despite the tiny candles sat beneath. Eventually even they, one by one, spluttered and died. Henry went all the way back to grandfather Corley and the ruffian he'd been, a drinker and brawler by reputation, smuggler of repute, until he bought Cottington Court and set out to find respectability.

'I heard stories of his ways too, Henry, though our father, who never hid his pride, made them sound like amusing escapades.'

'Then it's probably a good thing you were not told everything. Such a description does not do justice to his antics, which in such a context has seen two words used which should not have been employed. Father was more open with me and it did not make easy listening. Our grandfather was a brutal rogue with the blood of others on his hands. But old Corley is long gone, so it's about our father we must speak. I know you were close to each other.'

'While you struggled to match it?'

'Our relationship was certainly very different, but I see now he treated me in a way he saw as necessary.'

'Which was?'

'That of his heir. The world he sought to prepare me for was a hard one, not of the kind you were expected to face.'

'What's the purpose of all this, Henry?'

'To find out if you're willing to see everything he and our family worked to create pulled down about our ears, to trash both our father's reputation and our prosperity.' A waved hand was used to encompass not just the room, but the estate in its entirety. 'To see this destroyed over an infatuation.'

'I'll let the last word pass.'

'Out of curiosity, no doubt,' Henry replied, with just a hint of gloat, 'for what I must tell you is a tale of parental genius. Our father took the trade of smuggling, which he inherited, to a level never before achieved. Are you willing to listen and find out what was vouchsafed to me and kept from you?'

Part of Elisabeth did not want to hear it, but it could not compete with a need to know. Henry described the way the enterprise had been set up and run, not the overt trade carried out by Corley, but as a cabinet of secrets kept in separate compartments so only he, like his father before him, had control of all the components. Of Dirley being another cog in the family enterprise, who corresponded with their suppliers through a regular courier service between London and France, it being impossible to trust to any kind of postal service. Dirley handled the account which paid for everything ordered, placed with Jewish bankers in the City, the sums forwarded to France and another consortium who oversaw both supply and transport, which meant they owned the ships so nothing could be traced back to the family.

'What kind of ships?'

'Proper merchant vessels carrying full cargoes and regularly, outside the high summer months. If intercepted by the Excise – always a risk, if not a high one – they can claim to be off course, which is a common enough occurrence. The captain carries the correct manifests to prove they are on legitimate business, as well as a false list of importers awaiting delivery. Again, nothing can be traced back to this house.'

'Uncle Dirley is surely exposed?'

'No. Being a lawyer, he can claim he is acting on behalf of a client fund with no knowledge of what any monies transferred are for; in addition he advises on the best use of the profits on the same basis. He's legally bound not to disclose any business or even conversations which take place between him and those who employ his services. But he too knows no more than is required. If you were to ask him where the contraband is landed, he could only guess, but he never enquires. If he did, he would not be told. Our father would have done likewise, and he trusted Dirley completely.'

'Which seems to imply you don't.'

'Let us say I've recently had cause to remind him of our respective positions, which would previously have been unnecessary. He was older and a mentor to our father when he was growing up, I do not have a similar connection. He was also a very good guide to what I needed to know, not everything being passed on before father died. Such is no longer the case. It will take him time to see things are not as they were, but I have no doubt he'll be content in time. Now, let us turn to matters closer to home.'

The role of Hawker was described, though both the name and his brutality were glossed over, as were the monies he and his gang of ruffians extracted from the traders of Deal, those who supplied the ever-changing merchant fleet, to ensure they could operate in peace. Hawker had legitimate well-rewarded jobs, both running the slaughterhouse and tax collecting; his men did not. What was paid by businesses to prevent trouble provided a good wage to such creatures, again cutting out any connection to the family, who had no need to supply funds, none of what was extracted being passed upwards.

Also unmentioned was Hawker's ability to either send the Excise running in the wrong direction or, should the occasion demand it, offer up a small-time smuggling operation on the beach to divert their attention from the Tulkington operations. The community there saw him as their best friend, the man they could tell of their plans, for he could warn them of Revenue activity, little knowing he was also the best source the government agents had for surprise arrests.

'Our father took this fellow under his wing at an early age and his loyalty is rock-solid. He collects government imposts on behalf of the family, which, being a well-rewarded sinecure means we never have to justify our prosperity. He's also in a position to find out, without arousing suspicion, what each outlet requires in the way of untaxed goods and they are numerous. Even to you, it will not be seen as strange there's a lively local need to be satisfied.'

This was seen as condescending: Elisabeth was not so naive.

'You cannot live in this part of the world, Henry, and not know about the running of contraband. We used to play Excisemen and smuggler games down by the lake as children. I had always assumed this household to be one of those doing the buying in.'

'Our fellow, who is a devil with figures, is also able to ensure no one makes stupid errors in their own accounts, which could raise questions under examination. This happens rarely but, when it does, it is always without warning. Their ledgers must marry up with the accounts and monies we submit to Whitehall and they do.'

Henry not only declined to mention John Hawker by name. He also left out how the goods were distributed, this the responsibility of one trusted business, paid in coin so it could not be traced. Tobias Sowerby provided the vans and one or more barges to take the contraband from where it was stored to where the customers were waiting; certain coaching inns where numerous conveyances would not appear unusual, likewise barges travelling up to London. This guaranteed no paperwork, as well as a collaborator who dare not have his activities face investigation.

Overall, the costs of operations were higher than the more commonplace forms of over-the-beach smuggling, but such open activity was riskier by far and could never have worked at the level and quantities employed. Over time, profits, plus the fact of being impervious to scrutiny, justified the complex arrangements. Henry now owned substantial properties in a capital city rapidly expanding westwards.

'Do you now see? I'm driven by my need to protect the family, which includes you. I admit my objection to Stephen Langridge was ill-judged. I know you were friends through childhood, but it seemed to me a foolish basis on which to marry, and I had always seen you both as immature in the extreme.'

The temptation to say they'd taken pleasure from their life when growing up, while he had not, stayed unspoken, not that she got much chance: he was in full flow.

'Recall our father had not long passed away. I claim to have been nervous, being fresh to the level of responsibility. It's just as likely, judging by what you've said about your games and, being local, he would have been no trouble at all, perhaps even an asset. Believe me when I say your loss saddens me.'

'But Edward?'

'He's not local, is he?'

'It's more than that, Henry.'

'He's a total stranger to this part of the world and this household and he's also a King's officer. I know the navy declines to allow its vessels to be used to stop smuggling, but it's very much a choice of individual commanders once at sea. How can anyone tell which one will act and which would turn a blind eye? You're happy to tell me he was assiduous, in the West Indies, in interdicting trade from the ex-colonies. This may come as a recommendation to some, but not to me. It suggests someone who would find it impossible to reconcile himself to what I do.'

Much as she'd wanted to object and question the whole explanation, what Henry was saying made sense: the family was rich, while Acton Tulkington had been known throughout the district as lavish in his disbursements. As a girl, how the family made its money was of no interest; she was just happy there was always enough to indulge her whims and fancies. Parties, ponies and horses, clothes and entertainments for her friends, taking them on trips to see curiosities and tableaux, as well as servants in abundance to oblige her every requirement.

Should she have been more inquisitive growing up? There was a realisation she'd never really managed to achieve such an estate here at Cottington. Maturity had come to her in the West Indies, along with the responsibility of running her own household. If there had been secrets, callers who came and went without being introduced, conferring with her father in his study, now Henry's, adding an air of conspiracy in their dealings: it was men's business and none of her concern.

Sometimes an atmosphere of dispute was apparent, raised voices behind closed doors and a strain in conversations when gathered for meals. There had been one uncomfortable period she could vaguely recall, when relations between her father and Aunt Sarah's husband seemed overwrought, but this too had washed over her. Such things could not draw her attention away from her own concerns, which, on reflection, now seemed even more trivial than she'd previously admitted them to be.

'Why was I not trusted to be told?'

'It would not be for lack of trust but an excess of protection, which devolved to me.' The memory produced a glare and had him add, 'What could have come about if I'd let you marry a serving naval officer and one of whom I have no knowledge; a potential fortune-hunter, who openly admitted to not owning a home of his own? I thought perhaps he saw himself living here.'

'He more than possessed the means to purchase a suitable home. He does not want for money.'

'His fortune in prize money, you mean? Of this I have yet to see evidence but that is by the by. I could not risk his living here and discovering things, which, should he choose to expose them, would destroy the family, which includes you.'

'Me?'

'Who would reckon you innocent, sister?'

'All of this shows you to be no judge of your fellow man. I can tell you Edward was willing to keep things to himself for my sake. He told me so and would have told you too if you'd bothered to enquire.'

'Then why was he in league with William Pitt?'

CHAPTER ELEVEN

Delighted by her surprised reaction, Henry drove home the point. 'Did he not tell you he'd met with the fiend, who must be the greatest enemy this coast has ever had, and I do not only mean to me? He even visited him at Walmer Castle.'

'Innocently, I'm sure.'

'Brazier dined with him more than once at the Three Kings. I earlier used the word "infatuation", Elisabeth. What if he's not the man you believe him to be, but is instead a danger to us both, as well as everything our father created? What if his promise was false? We're not talking about social disgrace here, but a rope round my neck in front of a baying crowd at Newgate Prison.'

Henry paused to let that hit home, his voice taking on a more urgent tone when he continued. 'Do you really think you'd escape the same fate? Would anyone believe you had no idea what was happening in the house in which you were raised? They would believe you were – even if not a party to it – complicit. Does it not occur to you now, you might have been planning to run away with an agent acting on behalf of the government?'

Combined with the astonishment of what had only been outlined by Edward Brazier came the shock as Henry's words hit home. It was too much to absorb and above everything she wanted to get off the subject, which meant changing it.

'So this was enough to drug me and marry me to a pig.'

'Whose attentions you may never have to suffer.'

'I recall you said on certain conditions.'

Henry declined to go there, going back to his main worries. 'I admit to taking a dislike to Brazier on first acquaintance, but my motive was to protect you from yourself and perhaps both of us from the fate just described. I hoped with sufficient pressure, he might be persuaded to go away.'

'To the point of employing violence.'

His hands went up as if in frustration, the lie following smoothly.

'An error. What I'd intended as a verbal warning got out of hand, though I am, of course, at fault for my instructions being a touch imprecise. Subsequent to that, he taunted me and set up a plan to snatch you away, so any guilt I feel has been moderated.'

'Snatched away, Henry? I was a willing party.'

The voice changed to one which was wheedling, a much more common tone for a brother who'd ever seen himself as put upon and misunderstood.

'What was I to think, especially when I heard a troubling tale, one of which I sought to tell you: the notion, and it is a strong one, he was party to the killing of his superior officer in Jamaica?'

'You seem to forget I was there. If Edward had been under suspicion, or anyone for that matter, it would have been the talk of the island. His name would have been on everyone's lips. I heard it only when we first met.'

'And those who say otherwise?'

'Are deluded. Admiral Hassall died from the venomous bite of a snake.'

'There is talk going the rounds of human agency.'

'Which I choose not to believe.'

'I fear it may turn out to be otherwise. If it does and it's him swinging not me, then I will know I saved you from the grave error of attaching yourself to a murderer.'

'How can you talk of criminality, when you live your life by it?'

'You hint at hypocrisy?'

This was delivered as if in response to a jest, an attitude not maintained. Henry was suddenly very serious in both manner and expression.

'I stand by my actions and we are where we are. You're now wedded to Harry Spafford, which precludes whatever was intended by Brazier. And, I have to tell you, Harry has signed over control of the Langridge plantations to me. So not only do you lack the independence you enjoyed as a widow, you are without any means of support, as is Spafford himself, lest I provide it.'

'He is so much your creature. And you wonder why I despise him.'

'Feel free to do so, but know this. He will do as I say and will not trouble you, as long as you agree to accept your situation.'

'It seems to be the same as our Aunt Sarah, who too has become your creature. When will I be required to polish the silver?'

'You are my sister and may call upon me for anything you require.'

'Except the freedom to choose my own course.'

'It is my hope, in time, you'll see it for the best. Then any restrictions can be removed.'

'And if I don't?'

'I cannot see such a possibility requires an answer.'

The increasing feeling of despair Elisabeth harboured, which had swept over her as Henry outlined her situation, had to be hidden. Nothing had changed: she was trapped, and the failures of the night before last underlined it. If she'd had to accept as true what she had been told about her family running contraband on an industrial scale, there was no requirement to take as read Henry's opinion, or scabrous tales about Edward Brazier being a spy or a murderer.

The man she had come to know was not devious in any way, nor, as already proven, was he the kind to give up. She'd been so drugged the night of her forced marriage, Elisabeth had only found out later he'd come to take her away, arriving too late, a fact gloatingly imparted by Henry. Surely he would make another attempt, but how would he contrive to rescue her? All she could do was hold her nerve and hope, but there was one concession she could extract and it was a vital one.

'I want the promise you'll keep Spafford away from the house and me. If not . . .'

The slightly enigmatic smile hardly registered, yet it did seem inappropriate to what was being asked. It didn't last: Henry's countenance set itself once more in the sententious, self-regarding cast, which was a reflection of his character.

'As long as you accede to my wishes, it will be so. Please do not, I beg you, give me cause to think otherwise. I will not have you challenge me and do nothing.'

'Given what you did to poor Upton, I believe you.'

The reply was abrupt. 'You would let a servant defy you?'

'You seem to forget he was seeking to help me.'

'To be what? I would point out, should you run from here, you will do so without a penny piece. And, before you tell me Brazier will support you, I ask you to imagine how it will be perceived, a married woman and a widow, running away with a lover. I shall have little choice but to spread the truth of your situation, so you will be ruined and so will Brazier. With such a reputation, as a debaucher, I doubt anyone with the power to do so will be inclined to advance his career. Socially you will both be as good as dead.'

Elisabeth rose to leave, knowing she had a great deal on which to think. Such sangfroid as she'd sought to project having been a performance, inwardly she was in turmoil.

Henry sat for some time contemplating the conversation. Had his ploy succeeded? Had he ensnared Elisabeth to the point where to act against his wishes would be seen as unwise? He had to doubt it, he knew her too well, something she might have scoffed at if said to her. Whatever, no harm had been done to a situation which had not truly altered. Spafford dead was as much a potent threat as he'd been alive and, at all costs, the manner of his passing must never come out.

The dining-room door opened and Grady's head came round, to mouth a quick apology before beginning to withdraw, which had Henry call for him to proceed, an order which saw a couple of the maids rush in to clear away the breakfast dishes. There was a great deal of food unconsumed; would they eat it even if it was now cold? He suspected it likely even if they were well looked after. The lower orders were like dogs, who would eat until they burst.

Exiting the room, Grady informed Henry he had been in receipt of post, adding the box of coin kept to pay for delivery required to be replenished, which engendered mild annoyance, it being the kind of domestic chore overseen by his aunt. It was important she kept abreast of her duties, which he would remind her of when they had tea. A small pile of letters, plus a copy of the *Daily Universal Register*, lay on a silver salver, scooped up to be taken to his study.

One letter dropped to the floor and, bending to pick it up, Henry saw it was addressed to Elisabeth. That in itself was not what led to a rush of angry blood. The handwriting he knew only too well, making it unnecessary to look at the return address: it was from his Uncle Dirley.

On re-entering her bedroom, with the door locked and the key left in, which assured no one could enter without permission, Elisabeth noticed right away the lack of quills in the leather vessel on her desk, normally prominent. Within a second it was obvious what else had been taken away: the box of writing paper, the well and the sand required to dry the ink. Gone too was her seal along with the tin of wax; not even the knife required to keep the quill sharp had survived.

Many times she'd sat down to write letters, obviously to Edward Brazier, others to Annabel Colpoys, even one to Stephen's mother, the

Widow Langridge, with whom she had what could best be described as a strained relationship, so much so they were the only missives which contained nothing about her present travails and so could be safely left lying about. The others, as much to get the thoughts that troubled her, not out of her mind, but in a sense shared, were composed in the certain knowledge they could not be sent. These went out with her on her walks to be disposed of in the lake, wrapped round a stone to ensure they sank to the bottom, it not being safe to leave them hidden in a room the servants would be sent in to clean in her absence.

She could easily envisage her Aunt Sarah alone in here once they'd finished, searching for any sign her niece was seeking to communicate with anyone outside the grounds, the only question being, was she driven by her own desire to discover or acting on the instructions of Henry – not that it made any difference. This must have been a deliberate instruction and to her mind it was crass, petty and stupid, just another indication of how much he controlled everything. If he had, for a very brief moment, dented her resolve in the dining room, such an act completely demolished any notion she would comply with his wishes. Why was it he thought himself clever, when so often he acted like a spoilt child?

Anger at such a move sustained her for a while, but it wasn't long before a wave of despair began to take over. Writing plans and concocting stratagems, even knowing it was pointless, had helped sustain her and now such release was gone. Her determination not to succumb to tears held for a while, but broke eventually and left her sobbing, while wondering how her life could have, in so short a time, come to this.

The Reverend Joshua Moyle was in the process of actually trying to write a letter, a reply to the bishop in Canterbury, in truth the incumbent in Dover, who undertook the pastoral duties of the premier diocese to cover for the archbishop. He, besides a few major religious festivals, which obliged him to take services in his seat, stayed in London for the very simple reason it was where the things which mattered took place.

The quill was not moving with anything approaching fluency, for the way his confidence had been boosted by Henry Tulkington the night before had not survived his slumbers. He'd woken long before his normal hour – a lack of drink contributing – to face the possibility of further investigation into his activities. How had something which should have stayed within the confines of the Cottington Estate come to the attention of his ecclesiastical superiors?

The bishop's secretary had already paid a visit to examine the parish register, making no comment on the entry relating to the marriage of Spafford and Elisabeth, yet leaving Moyle with a feeling he was suspicious. The communication which had so alarmed him underlined the supposition had been correct. It was not a night or a situation he recalled with much pleasure. Why had he not had the courage to point out what was suggested was sinful, in reality a forced marriage of the kind Acts of Parliament had been promulgated to stop?

He could recall working himself up to do so more than once, but the courage to speak never surfaced. Even fortified by too much brandy, it was obvious Elisabeth had been given some kind of drug. Her intended had put away more brandy than he, while Henry, sober, had masterminded the whole affair, even to the point of forcing his tearful aunt to act as witness. How many times in private had he resolved to tell Henry his duties to his ministry took precedence over his responsibilities to the man who controlled his appointment?

Such determination never survived being in his presence and it had been the same with Acton Tulkington, the person who'd chosen him to fill the vacancy, which had come as a godsend to a cleric with a wife to support and in desperate pursuit of a place. Moyle knew he was unfitted to his office. If he'd been the priest he set out to be, the man Mrs Moyle had been happy to wed, this is not where he would have ended up. Somewhere along the way he had lost his faith, something he supposed was kept private but was in fact no mystery among those to whom he ministered. Often he was the worse for wear due to drink taken, which, he convinced himself, was to bolster his confidence.

This in itself said much of the level to which he'd sunk. His congregation consisted almost exclusively of the workers on the estate, added to labouring folk, servants, farm workers, woodcutters and charcoal makers disinclined to crowd outside the much busier church of St Leonard's, often in the rain or buffeted by the wind. There was no room inside for the commonality: pews were reserved for people of quality, who could be relied upon not to let the collection plate pass without donating silver, the kind of folk he'd dreamt himself administering to as a young man.

A glance at the open parish register demonstrated the difference: not there the long list of births, weddings and funerals, which would have been inscribed in any normal parish; his was singular in the paucity of entries. However he calculated a reply, Moyle knew to say anything which could rebound on Henry was impossible, for the very simple reason he would suffer equally, if not more.

The prospect of being moved was terrifying, for there would be no likelihood of another living. This meant no home, no stipend to pay for food to eat, which would oblige him to seek charity from one or more of his fellow clerics. The notion of such an impoverished existence was not to be borne, so the quill, which had stayed poised too long, began to scratch across the paper.

Your Grace,
It troubles me to find rumours are being spread of events and ceremonies taking place in Cottington Parish which do not adhere to the tenets of the Holy Church. Let me assure you in the matter of the recent nuptials between the widow Mrs Langridge and Harold Spafford Esq. all proper steps and obligations required for the ceremony were met . . .

134

Of the dangers Moyle faced, Henry Tulkington was by far the greatest. Lying to a bishop was a risk but, in comparison, one much less threatening.

Henry was not writing, but mentally composing a reply to what had not been addressed to him. Dirley's previous communication had been irritating enough, added to which it had been opened to be first read by his Aunt Sarah, something which still rankled. At least she'd passed it to him, not Elisabeth, so his sister knew nothing of its existence, or the invitation issued for her and Spafford to visit him in London so he could both cosset and congratulate them.

This follow-up was even more disingenuous; it assured her he, Henry, would be a sound custodian of the affairs of the new couple, which was seen as questionable for, if it was not, why mention it? Dirley took leave to assume they'd put aside any notion of returning to Jamaica to oversee the management of the plantations themselves, a possibly wise choice given the fate which had befallen poor Stephen. But it was the last paragraph that really raised his hackles.

I'm aware I've been a distant presence in your life, even more now than when your father was alive and for reasons upon which I do not have to elaborate. Yet I hope you know from our correspondence these last few years, and the advice I have proffered to be taken or declined as you see fit, I hold your interests as dear to my heart as those of your brother. Being at one remove does not mitigate what I see as my duty to my family.

I extend again the invitation to you and your new husband to come to London, where I can entertain you and, I must also say, show off to the elevated society in which I move, the charms of my most beautiful niece, as well as the no doubt outstanding attributes of your new husband.

On the other hand, perhaps a visit to Cottington Court would be in order, where it has to be admitted tranquillity in the article of appreciation of your new-found status is likely to be more speedily achieved than in our teeming capital city.

It was signed off with the kind of flowery tributes, mixed with self-effacement, which had never been present in any letter Dirley had addressed to Henry. This caused him to swear out loud on first reading, with a statement as accurate as it was heartfelt.

'You devious old bastard!'

CHAPTER TWELVE

Prior to departure, Zachary Colton had seen Edward Brazier fed, re-dressed his wound and informed his surprise guest the sun was shining, on what was looking to be a fine day.

'There are times, sir, when my labours permit, I sit out on my bench and praise the Lord for the life I now live and the bounty his grace bestows upon me. I would suggest, while I'm absent, it might suit you to feel the warmth of the sun and the purity of the air.'

'The last of which, as a sailor, I'm well accustomed to.'

The point drew another of Zachary's humorous and chest-heaving rumbles.

'How anyone goes voluntarily to sea! I recall the crossing to England, sir, and my terror at the sight and activity of the ocean, for which nothing prepares a man raised on the land. But for my faith, I could have succumbed to despair.'

'How did you come by such a deep faith?'

'My first master was a God-fearing man and he helped me to become the same, though he was too fond of the entries on chastisement.'

He went to the chest and, kneeling to open it, took out some books, given the size of his hand quite a number. The one he drew on particularly was a well-thumbed Bible, which he held out like a trophy.

'Mr Venables likewise, sir. This is the Good Book from which he would read to me each evening. Then we would pray together.'

'He never married?'

'No, sir,' was a reply without the addition of any reason; with Zachary so quick to move on, Brazier suspected there might be a motive he had no desire to discuss. 'The pity is, I was never taught to read so I could carry on after he died.'

'Would you like me to do so now?'

His expression showed the notion appealed. 'Perhaps on my return, sir. Your mare is saddled and the sun is well up now. Best I go upon my way.'

'The message?'

This got a tap on the forehead to indicate it was locked in there. From the still open chest he produced a blanket. 'For your shoulders, sir, should you take the air, as I suggest.'

The lid was closed, with the books placed on top and, following the smile, which seemed his habitual expression, Zachary was gone. Brazier listened to the sound of Bonnie's hooves as she was ridden away, dull on what was soft ground, feeling at a loss as to what to do. He'd asked if there were any tasks he could undertake in Zachary's absence, only to have it pointed out any such would involve the kind of labour more likely to reopen his wound than help the stitching to hold.

So he went outside, to look at the neat lines of cherry trees, in leaf now but well shorn of their crop, the apples on others yet to fully ripen. Walking with one arm holding the upper part of the other, he took in the domain: a small paddock with a donkey in a field, a sty with an old sow and, in a byre, the cow whose milk he'd drunk that morning. Dominating the whole was a double line of hop poles, part of the crops which would provide income for the whole year.

The bench, facing south and hard by the circular well, was half of a tree trunk, backed by interleaved branches set on a pair of stumps.

Onto this he settled gingerly, to ensure his good shoulder took any pressure, finding Zachary had been right about the sun, which shone on and warmed him. As far as he could, he leant back and lifted his face to sit, eyes tight shut as his mind wandered.

What else could fill it but the same thoughts which had troubled him from the moment he came back to consciousness? Yet he did not want to go to a place where there could be no resolution until things presently beyond his control were sorted. Eyes open once more, with a hand to keep the sun out of his eyes, he drew a comparison, not a flattering one, with what Zachary had and the house and farm in which he'd grown up. Not a wattle-and-timber construct, which looked as if a gale might blow it down, but a four-square brick building of the type common to prosperous farmers and clergy.

It hadn't occurred to him, till many years later, when he'd grown to manhood, to question his home's size and comfort, to see it was an establishment beyond the means of a mere naval surgeon. Being in the service himself, the pay such a position produced was no mystery. Added to which, being in southern Hampshire, just south of the village of Anmore, it was an area of valuable farmland and stout houses, much settled by the families of naval officers, senior captains included, and thus of high value. The Brazier property was not shamed by any comparisons with neighbours.

'Sold now,' he whispered, wondering at what he felt now was a mistake. With him at sea and his parents gone, it was too much trouble to keep, but the thought would not go away. 'We could have been happy there, Betsey.'

This was done head back and eyes closed once more, as he conjured up a picture of the house in his mind, indeed much more than the building. There had been two substantial barns, orchards and fields, as well as farm workers in numbers, which assured no member of the family must toil; indoor servants in rank and duties matched the best of their neighbours.

'Or perhaps you would hanker after something grander.'

The image of Cottington Court had brought on the thought, for it was an imposing edifice, aged in style to show intricate and mellow red brick, topped with lead cupolas, while those inside gazed out through numerous and mullioned windows, regardless of the taxes they drew. The neat parterre just inside the inner gates lay at the end of a long carriage drive to the outer gateway and the road to Canterbury and Ramsgate. He'd recently sat on Bonnie there, guying the keeper and his dog by his presence, well aware it would be reported to and infuriate Henry Tulkington, who was the last person he wanted to be thinking about.

With no notion of time, thirst eventually took hold and led him the few steps to the well, to loosen the rope holding the bucket. It slid through his hand as he let it down till he heard a splash. The stones weighting the bottom took it below the level of the water and, after a few moments, he made to haul it back up, the first movement inducing a severe enough pain to stop him cold. To get the bucket up and tie it off, so he could cup out a drink, took a long time and was not without hurt. This done, he needed to sit down again to let it subside back to a dull ache.

Much as he sought to distract himself by thinking of other matters, he could not prevent troubled thoughts intruding. Everything – home, the navy, some of the many places he'd been, even the battles in which he'd fought – whatever he tried, his mind came back to gnaw on the problem of Tulkington and his actions. He had little doubt who had set the riot in motion, which saw him burnt out, not that the deed would have been done by his own hand: it would have been left to Hawker. A cheering image of him on the receiving end of the beating he deserved was a short but pleasant distraction. Mostly he was assailed by a mixture of anger and hopelessness, returning constantly to Betsey and how he could bring about her rescue.

Eventually, having enough of this circular gnawing, he went back inside to look at the books Zachary had left on top of the chest: surely here was distraction. The Bible he ignored, knowing it too well for, as a ship's captain and lacking a parson on board, he'd been obliged at sea to take divine service an endless number of times of a Sunday morning. The others were a mix, one on treating ailments in horses, a Smollett he'd read, the largest Johnson's dictionary, a copy of which he had left, along with many other things, books and bits of personal property, with his prize agent in London.

Two of the others looked the same, bound in tooled leather with no indication of what lay within. Flicking one open and seeing fine handwriting, with the page dated, he realised it was a diary, his first instinct to put it down. Yet these surely were the property of Zachary's rescuer, journals which spoke of the life of a man now dead. If they'd been written and left, it was to be read. The newest-looking one being opened at the very back page, he saw the writing was far from neat and he carried on to realise he was reading the words of a man who knew he was dying.

There was the plea to the Almighty for forgiveness of a life of sin, the details no doubt previously listed. Venables had scrawled a wish his good servant Zachary be preserved, the desire he should live in comfort on the land about to be left to him, with an additional inscription to say who had possession of his will and testament, presumably a local solicitor. Taking both diaries back to the bench, Brazier, having gingerly lowered himself down once more, went back to the beginning and the perfect, if small, copperplate.

This, dated in 1777, described what Venables found on taking up a surgeon's position with the 3rd Regiment of Foot. It stated for whoever was to read it, this was the local East Kent Regiment known as the Buffs, bound for the Americas to bring back into the royal fold the troublesome colonials. There was a curious one-line declaration.

Asked why I must do this, I say there is no choice. Life, as lived prior to the loss of Samuel, is no longer possible.

Following on it was not a daily record, but a list of things which took the diarist's fancy, interspersed with uplifting quotations from the psalms. The oddity of regimental routine, the personality of the officers, a goodly number not highly thought of. Then the crossing, with descriptions of Lisbon, the Azores and the vastness of the ocean as they made for the West Indies on the trade winds before heading north to disembarkation at Sandy Hook in the colony of New Jersey.

First impressions of colonial life followed, towns with buildings which replicated the shapes found in England, both in brick and wood, churches too. In a New Jersey town called Wethersfield, he'd found and worshipped in a church, which was of the exact same design as St George's in Deal. Outside habitations there were vast and endless forests, which impressed, few roads and poor-looking dwellings in which they were billeted, which did not. Nor was he much impressed by the Yankees, inclined to be grasping, seeking to make as much profit as possible from the troops.

There was a great deal about the picking out of mounts for the officers, as well as sturdy animals for the transport of kit and supplies. Camp life, which applied to the troops, was tedious, as were the various ailments to be dealt with, seemingly more to do with horses than humans. In time came battle and the wounds sustained, men patched up or buried, the horses put down as well as those he'd sewn up because of sabre cuts or pike thrusts, others from which it had been necessary to extract musket balls, with too many having to be put down due to broken or fractured bones.

Flicking through he found the day when Zachary had been won in the card game and the doubts Venables had about the value of the prize. Yet, a few pages on, it was all praise for a man he saw, despite his colour and the way he'd been raised, as a mirror to his own soul. He'd found an assistant of good humour, empathy and ability when it came to treating the ailments with which he had to deal. No one, on an amputation, could match Zachary for the way he sliced flesh at speed, warding off what was common by any hint of sluggishness: death by shock.

It seemed he also had a rare affinity with horses, the way he could calm them by whispering some kind of chant in their ears, which made tending to them so much easier. There was an aside regarding the callous nature of the actual riders, military officers who could not see how a close relationship with a mount, one required to take them into conflict and danger, was something to be fostered.

Turning to the other book, which preceded the one he'd been reading, Brazier discovered, in the early pages where he recounted his youth, Venables had begun life as a barber before learning, from an older practitioner to whom he'd been apprenticed, the art of cutting human flesh. There was no surprise in this progression: the title of surgeon as a singular denomination was a recent one, even more so in the armed services than civilian life, where it had more commonly been barber/surgeon, given similar instruments would be employed for both.

Venables proudly wrote how he'd begun to forge a more lucrative career tending to animals, horses a speciality, which at least, judging by his words, he had taken the trouble to study. This was a highly valuable skill in a county of farms and studs, though his work extended to cattle and sheep. Dogs figured too, seemingly so much more loved by their owners, the well-being of the canine taking precedence over that of their family. Several years of such activity was relative and held little of interest, which led to a high degree of skipping.

The entry which stopped him dead was dated 3rd Feb., 1775 and read: *Called to Cottington Court today, required to attend to the pony of the daughter of the house. Unable to save the poor animal; much distress.*

A few pages on and he was called back to Cottington, answering a request to put his services to the expanding Tulkington stud, to which he'd readily agreed, given the generosity of the fee on offer. Brazier leafed on through many weeks to come, to another page, which imposed concentration: Venables being invited to join Mr

Acton Tulkington in a fox hunt setting out from Cottington, a mount provided. It was a new experience, given he lacked the social standing or the income for such pursuits. He described the thrill of chasing Tulkington's pack of hounds, with vignettes of some of those taking part, Acton first of all.

Curiosity regarding Betsey's father had him read these passages with some absorption: his height, which was above the norm and with it came a muscular frame, a hearty laugh added to a deep determination to be in at the kill. Two of the other names Brazier recognised: Mr Colpoys, described as a wild and undisciplined rider, and a Mr Lovell, more sedate by far, but a strikingly handsome fellow with a good seat and enchanting wit.

Further pages revealed Venables became a regular caller at Cottington Court and not just for his occupation. The flicking stopped when Brazier came to another paean of praise for Acton Tulkington: his good humour, despite his recent widower status, his open-handedness and generous hospitality. Betsey, properly called Elisabeth, was named as a charming child, praised for her love of anything equine, as well as her willingness to undertake those tasks she could easily have left to servants. And there was Upton, recently raised to the position of head groom, ever eager to learn from the wise Mr Venables, words smacking of vanity.

Listed in the pages and frequently, indeed more than Acton, was Samuel Lovell, husband to the Aunt Sarah who had so taken against Brazier in the West Indies, much replicated since his arrival in East Kent. The former was written of very warmly, his wife barely mentioned at all and when she was, always with a tone of icy and polite correctness, which hinted at a person difficult to like, an opinion with which the reader could only concur.

More entries revealed the entertainments to which Venables had been invited, seeming to become something of an intimate with the family over the space of a couple of years. Yet it was obvious, while he respected Acton Tulkington, he had become a firm and close friend of Samuel Lovell, soon only referred to as 'Dearest Sam'. His name cropped up more and more, with endless references to his fine manners and enchanting presence, added to his sympathy and wisdom, praised to the point of being somewhat disconcerting in its effusiveness.

It was clear they'd spent much time together and not always in the company of others, with hints of the days spent riding out to seek places of solitude, each one named and described in flowing bucolic terms. There was a hint of worship about his references to his 'special friend' which Brazier found strange, but there was nothing on which to pin a conclusion. Henry got one mention only, as being unlike his sire in nature or physique, in no way robust as was Acton, but a fine young man, with good if rather reserved manners.

'How little you were able to see,' Brazier spat, turning page after page, all in much the same vein about his Dear Sam, with most other events reduced into the background until he came across an entry which again stopped him abruptly, for it looked to be near the last.

Called at Cottington today to go riding, as arranged, with Dear Sam, only to be told he had departed the evening before, went off without saying where he was going and had not yet returned. Most strange! Mrs Lovell in a state of frenzy, which would be appropriate if she had shown Samuel any regard or comfort in their marriage, the lack of which was vouchsafed to me in intimate conversation.

His absence was doubly odd, since the day was supposed to be special. On our last outing, he hinted at a forthcoming change of circumstances, which would see his near total dependence on his brother-in-law curtailed, which intrigued me. Oblique asides intimated he soon might hold a better position at Cottington Court than hitherto, indeed such riding out to seek solitude with me would no longer be necessary. I would be accommodated within the house as an honoured guest, a blissful prospect.

The next date was over a week later and was enigmatic.

I find I must sever any connection with Cottington Court and all who reside there. It is said my Dearest Sam has run away from his wife, whom, it is true, I found shrewish. But so upright a friend had many times insisted he would never abandon his vows any more than he could contemplate abandoning me. In the last two years, it would be correct to say, we have become the closest of friends, to the point where I'm sure, if such an act had been contemplated, some hint of it would have surfaced and I would have been party to any plan.

Not only is Dear Sam missing, but so is the stallion on which he rode away, and no sign of this creature has emerged. The reaction of Acton, when I asked for an explanation, was so out of character with the man I've come to know, it shocked me, while his son suggested, in a very cold manner, it would benefit me to mind my own business.

Dearest Sam had said on more than one occasion the family were not as upright as they appeared. He insisted the house harboured a secret which, exposed, would bring into disrepute the whole Tulkington tribe. A pity he never told me of it, for I should certainly have taken his part.

He is in my nightly prayers. I so do hope he has no need to be.

The rest of the book, and it had many more pages, was blank. A check on the dates established the next entry to be in the second of the Venables diaries already perused, his joining the 3rd Foot and contemplating America. It was as if he'd abandoned the previous one by entering a line under it, indicating an alteration in his circumstances. The little Betsey had told him about her aunt's husband was exactly in the vein described in Venable's scribblings, a bit full of himself and not in the least constrained in his conceits, despite his being a dependant.

146

He'd been cock o' the walk when resident in Canterbury but speculation in funds – there was a hint of underhand trades – had seen him brought low. As to the leaving of Cottington, there had been no hint of anything other than a fellow running off from a tiresome spouse, which was far from unique. Yet here it seemed to imply another reason and, if he allowed his imagination free rein, a dark one.

Venables's references to Lovell were odd, almost too explicit in their warmth. Was there anything untoward there? He recalled the way Zachary had reacted when asked the simple question about his master's marital status, only to then conclude he was fishing in the dark and looking for something, anything, which might provide leverage in his quest to free Betsey. Any theories conjured up could not be expanded upon; he would get no information from Cottington and the only man who could explain the diary entries was long gone.

Going back inside, he put the journals back on the chest and took up the Smollett. At least *Roderick Random* had humour as well as pathos within its covers, much about a poor benighted Roderick blundering his way through a series of misadventures, including becoming a pressed seaman. There was of course a happy conclusion, in which the hero married the woman of his dreams, without the consent of her brother and guardian.

As of now, this was the kind of encouragement he could do with.

CHAPTER THIRTEEN

Brazier was well short of his happy marital conclusion when, well into the afternoon, the sound of horse's hooves had him carefully turn toward the entrance to the smallholding. It was a stiff ex-commander who stood to greet the party of four, two of his old crew, all mounted, even Peddler Palmer, though the common expression he ever wore on a horse, one of acute discomfort, was there. Zachary Colton was in the lead, riding Bonnie, the usual wide smile on his face, which was matched by Joe Lascelles. Only Vincent Flaherty wore a frown, no doubt wishing to impart that a man he considered a friend might also be short on sense.

Once dismounted, Peddler and Joe were at a loss to know how to greet him, outside an enquiry to his being well; the barrier of rank prevented what might have been an embrace of the kind automatic for a shipmate. Yet he was content by their obvious pleasure at seeing him whole, as well as the sympathy for his wound.

Vincent took and shook his hand without vigour, while Zachary began to remove the tackle from the mare, a sure indication Brazier was going to keep her; hardly surprising as he'd paid a long-term rental in advance. Zachary led her away, heading for the tiny paddock and a braying donkey eager for company, which allowed for open talk.

'I'd been after wondering if you're sound in the head, Edward,' Vincent remarked, 'after it was told to me the rashness of what you've been about.'

'Failure rates things rash, Vincent. Nothing successful is so described.'

'But carrying muskets and barging into Tulkington's lair . . .'

'I did not barge,' was a sharp response.

Vincent held up his hand to ward off what might come next, for the face before him was far from composed. Unbeknown to the Irishman, such a reaction stemmed from the word rash, added to the feeling Vincent might be right. Yet he felt the need to defend his actions as being brought about by necessity.

'There's no other way to get Betsey free,' he said, easing himself slowly back onto the bench.

'I don't sense a past tense there, brother.'

'Where are Dutchy and Cocky?'

Brazier asked this to divert; he did not want to contemplate where the last remark from Vincent was inviting him to go, not that he had any idea. It was Peddler who replied to the question, leaning over the well and drinking from the lashed-off bucket, water dripping from his chin as he spoke.

'They be watching the house where Hawker's men are holed up and, we reckon, some of Spafford's lads, the ones who went with us t'other night.'

He went on to describe what they'd been about, how they'd been searching for him and had had the luck to stumble across Hawker and his men, along with what looked like wrapped bodies. He told how they had followed them to a farmhouse and decided to watch the place and see if anything turned up, meaning Brazier. Peddler also left out the thought they'd discussed, the notion one of the bodies could have been his.

'Dutchy reckons it could be the place we was a'callin at afore the fight.'

'They're still there?'

'Not all. Hawker left this mornin', an' I tailed him to a slaughterhouse on the edge of the town. Tannery as well, by the stink.'

'Any sign of Tulkington?'

'Since I's never clapped eyes on the sod, outside the light of a lantern and for no more than seconds, I'd struggle to know.'

'Do they know I'm alive?'

'Not yet, Capt'n,' was delivered with the kind of look which implied he was daft. 'We'll not go near them till the light fades, less they be spotted from the house.'

'Do we have any notion of why Hawker's lot are there?'

'I'd be guessing.'

A look towards Joe got from him the information he'd stayed at the Navy Yard, as well as the reason why, and the manner in which he'd left. The presence of a high sheriff visiting Admiral Braddock – according to the clerk, asking about Quebec House – surprised his captain, who was left for a moment to consider the ramifications. He couldn't reprimand Joe for ducking being questioned, but he did see the need to point out something obvious.

'When it comes to what happened there, we are the innocent parties.'

'Are you saying you'll be seeking him out?' asked Vincent.

The question threw Brazier back on to his conundrum. It was one he'd gnawed on since the probable nature of Tulkington's business had been outlined to him by Saoirse Riorden: how would exposure of Henry affect Betsey? His desire to bring about the bastard's downfall was strong, but there was no way he was going to put her at risk and, besides, he had given her his promise. If he'd been prepared to do so, he would have been in touch with William Pitt, a vastly more effective man than any county official.

The return of Zachary put an end to speculation, his enquiry as to who'd be staying met with looks at Brazier, though Vincent was quick to say he would not.

'Never had this many mouths to feed, sir, since the army days.'

'We need to get to our mates, either to haul them off or take them some grub so they can stay.' Peddler looked at the still blue sky. 'And drink, which they will need, havin' been out all day. Tongues must be hangin' out by now.'

'Zachary, what can you provide, for which I will pay?' Seeing the face move to an expression presaging refusal, Brazier added, 'And do not say you will not accept. You will find my purse in my outer coat, take what you need.'

Apples and cheese were offered and accepted, as well as an old army canteen, which had been used to carry water when Zachary was assistant to Venables.

'I now must ask if it's possible for all of us to convene here and possibly overnight. You will have five mouths to cater for.'

'No notion they should stay watchin'?' Joe asked.

'They've been out one night already, Joe. If there's watching to be done, and it will be for Dutchy to advise, it will be you and Peddler.'

'What happens then?'

'I don't know. There could be any number of possibilities, but one thing is certain. I need to be fit enough to look at matters myself.'

'We won't be givin' up, then?' Vincent asked.

'It's not my habit to do so.'

'Do I tell Saoirse you're safe?'

'She knows what happened?'

'I took the boyos there as soon as I heard the tale.'

'How did she take it?'

'Calmly I would say, she's not a woman for display. Never asked why Joe was wanted when I sent Peddler to fetch him.'

'Neither a woman for display or for a lack of discretion. Please let her know I'm alive and well.'

'She's bound to ask what you intend to do next.'

'Did you not hear what I just said, Vincent?'

'Sure, I did an' all, but hearing is easier than believing. I don't suppose any advice I give to let matters rest will get much attention.'

'Thanks for what you've done so far. Next time we split a bottle of wine, it will be on my bill and a damn good one.'

'I'll say good day to you, then.'

A hand was held out by Brazier to be shaken once more. It was, but Vincent Flaherty was more taken by the look of determination in the eyes.

'It was no joy to hear you might be dead, Edward. Nor is it you might be risking it come true.'

'How many falls did you have as a jockey?'

'Lots, and puff went the purse with it.'

'And you got right back on, I'll wager.'

'I did when my bones healed.'

'Bones, wounds? Same thing.'

John Cottin could be reasonably satisfied with his day, the events of which he was running over in his mind as he made his way back to Deal. His letter had gone off through the Sandwich franchise, he'd enjoyed a splendid lunch, while a note to the mayor had brought him to the Crispin Inn to take wine and enthusiastically damn the villains of Deal. Cottin's supposition Sandwich was just as criminal when it came to smuggling was put aside for the mayor knew the men of whom he spoke.

In living memory, Deal had been under the jurisdiction of the ancient Cinque Port, according to his guest the breaking of which and the granting of a town charter to Deal being a grave error. Cottin now knew something of the personal failings of the men with whom he had dealt, not one, according to his informant, having anything which qualified them for office. Recollecting this polemic, he could smile at what was obviously rivalry from a much more sedate neighbour to one raucous in the extreme. Added to which, and this had been the real source of complaint, the income from the Downs anchorage, which had once filled the coffers of Sandwich, now provided the main revenue of Deal.

Even ruminating on these thoughts, he could not help but wonder how long Pitt would take to respond. Would he even read the letter, for in the office he held he must receive dozens every day? Cottin couldn't just hang about forever: he had duties to attend to and matters coming in to his own office, which might be of more vital import in terms of reputation than the death he was now investigating. He too would be in receipt of much correspondence from Westerham and if it was sufficient to call him away, he would just have to go.

Back in Zachary's sparsely furnished abode, with his host fussing over the grate and the food cooking therein, Brazier was wondering about the presence of this lawman. Not knowing any better, he took it as commonplace such an untoward death as Lionel Upton's should draw such a personage to investigate. As he had no doubt who was the likely suspect, he was wondering how to play matters so the culprit faced justice, but without involving Betsey.

Already deduced, there would be no sign of Tulkington's hand in the torching, but what about Hawker, who was cut from the same mould? Even if Henry set matters in motion, he was too wily to have his own actions visible. It was idly taking in Zachary's back, added to his lack of alternatives, which prompted him to pose the question. He knew immediately it was one unwelcome as his normally smiling host spun round: he wasn't smiling now.

'Cottington Court is unknown to me.'

This had to be a lie, merely by the nature of the reaction. From such a deeply religious and cheerful soul, it had to be serious enough to warrant him breaking his faith. He had to remind himself the things he'd read about had happened long before Venables had won the services of Zachary. Added to which, the man lacked letters, so would not know what was in the journals. What he'd read had raised suspicions and, the more he thought on it, perhaps something objectionable, though he was no prude. Life in the King's Navy inured you to much, while relations between men which transcended mere friendship were far from uncommon. One of the first lessons a new naval officer learnt was when to apply the 'blind eye', given no ship of war was free of activities forbidden by the Articles of War.

HMS *Diomede* had carried a crew of over three hundred men, the total varying but not by much. Some of the first rates in which Edward Brazier had served as a rising lieutenant mustered crews of over eight hundred. They were made up of young men from any number of backgrounds, usually several nationalities, and would number a few women, those never enough for the crew numbers. The gunner's wife excepted, women were technically barred from being aboard.

The Articles of War stood as the bible by which navy discipline operated, formidable in the number of offences it prohibited, the most common requiring a loud step, the warning of approach, being gambling. No matter what the admiralty said, it could not be stopped; Jack tar would always find a way and a place discreet enough for a bit of wagering, cards and dice, though the latter were noisy, with men to warn of the coming of authority.

The purpose of a man-o'-war was to fight and defeat the nation's enemies. Discipline had to be tight but not taut; a crew too heavily weighed upon by the ship's officers were likely to become sullen. It was necessary to trust the petty officers, who would bring to the attention of their superiors if certain activities were getting out of hand, things which might harm the fighting efficiency of the ship. But they would not report or see everything as long as it was kept within acceptable bounds.

They too would turn the 'blind eye', sometimes even to acts bordering on indecency. Such men had to live close to the crew, while it was an axiom well known in the service someone seen as a bully or a sneak could, too easily, disappear on a dark and windy night in the middle of an endless sea.

If Venables had been inclined to anything untoward, could he have hidden it from a man with whom he lived so hugger-mugger, given there was not much more than room to swing a cat in this abode? In addition, Zachary had claimed an association with Venables which transcended one of pure master and servant. If the former had spent so much time at Cottington prior to serving with the army, could it have passed without mention in the time they'd spent here?

'I thought you would know of it,' was imparted with an ingenuous look.

'And why would that be, sir?'

Zachary asked this over a bent shoulder, he having returned to his cooking, a pot in which he was boiling a pair of rabbits. So as I can't see his face, was Brazier's thought, but how to proceed? Nothing would come without being open. Was what he suspected true and who did it involve? He would need to be bold and take a risk of causing offence.

'I took the liberty, since you left them out, of casting an eye over the diaries left by Mr Venables.' The growl in the throat was low but audible. Was it anger or just seen as natural curiosity? 'A quick glance, I do assure you. The name of the place was mentioned often and, since I know something of it myself, I wondered at the connection.'

'It was a house and grounds my master took great pains to avoid.'

'Why?'

'He must have had his reasons, sir, but they were not told to me.' The smile reappeared, but with a quality unlike before: it seemed forced. Soon he was looking at the man's back again. 'You too, sir, have a former slave as a servant and like me a freed man.'

'I do, and he is here by invitation.'

'Joe told me on the way how he came into your service and why. It's a tale which elevates you for what was a truly Christian act. He claims

155

to know you well, but I doubt he knows everything about your past.'

Was it just a change of subject or both, an attempt to deflect the line Brazier was taking by introducing talk of Joe? It mattered not, it was time to get things out in the open and it had to start with Zachary.

'Cottington Court is a place I have good reasons to avoid.' The turn was slow, the whites of the eyes very obvious in his dark-skinned face. 'In relating how I got my wound, I didn't tell you where I was shot, by whom I do not know, but it would have been on the instructions of a fellow named Tulkington, who owns Cottington Court, both of which frequently crop up in the first of the journals. There's another name, Samuel Lovell, who seems to have been a particularly close friend of Mr Venables.'

'If you say it is so, sir.'

'A man who, it is implied, disappeared without explanation, this being the cause of some grief.' No reaction. 'Zachary, I'm going to tell you the full story of how I got my wound, so desist from stirring a pot, which scarcely needs it, and come and listen.'

There was reluctance: he didn't want to hear what Brazier had to say, which only increased his suppositions. To ensure nothing was missed out on this occasion, he began at the beginning, telling how he met Betsey in Jamaica and what he took to be mutual attraction, not forgetting to add the disapproval of her Aunt Sarah.

'Whose name, incidentally, is Mrs Samuel Lovell.'

The face didn't move, which had Brazier think such an ability to avoid reaction must be natural to anyone who'd been a slave, put in a situation where even a lifted eyebrow showing a hint of doubt could qualify you for the whip. In any event it told him nothing, so there was no choice but to carry on with his arrival in Deal, the mystery of Tulkington's objections to his pursuit of his sister, the beating he'd suffered and subsequent events, partly already related. The only one which got a serious reaction was the sham wedding, while the tale of the groom from Cottington turning up at his door, needing to be accommodated, got another of Zachary's bromides about being a good Christian.

'Was it Christian? It would have been best if I'd turned him away for he'd still be alive.' The carapace of indifference Zachary had worn broke down then, surprise being the cause. 'A mob was set upon the house to burn out me and my companions. Luckily, we were not present, but Upton was. For reasons I cannot fathom he failed to wake to the clamour, nor the heat and smoke, one of which took his life. His body, unidentifiable, was found in the embers. So someone committed murder.'

Zachary crossed himself.

'You do not enquire as to why I'm giving you all this detail?' A very slow headshake. 'You see, having been open with you, I'm hoping you'll be open with me.'

'I best see to them rabbits, sir.'

Wanting to press home his point, Brazier was thrown by the noisy approach of his old barge crew. It was not a subject to pursue in such company.

'By all means.'

CHAPTER FOURTEEN

Brazier was extremely sensitive to the behaviour of Zachary Colton: outwardly normal, he felt there was an undercurrent in his manner which hinted at disquiet. The noisy arrival of Dutchy and the others, which had curtailed his interrogation, had not abated, each being eager to talk and voice an opinion regarding what Hawker was up to, which seemed to increase in bloody conclusion the more they went on. Various bits of furniture put together – from both inside and out – provided a board off which they could eat. To this was added a stone flagon of cider, which had been fetched out from an underground store. Made by Zachary himself from his own apples, cloudy in appearance, it was tart in taste and suspected to be of ferocious strength.

When it came to easing tongues, nothing could have served better, so a great deal of reminiscing was in the air. If their old captain took little part in recalling their joint adventures, references to him were frequent and not always wholly complimentary. The lads spoke in a way they could never have done aboard ship, treating him as one they could gently guy, not the godlike creature a naval captain was supposed to be.

It was something to enjoy, the feeling of camaraderie, and was a mood not to be missed, even if this had not previously been the case with his barge crew or servant. More common among lieutenants, with the shared accommodation of the wardroom, it was rare with captains who occupied a solitary cabin at sea; the lack of company was not always compensated for by the amount of extra space or entertaining. It did happen ashore, mixing with officers of similar rank and above, though care had to be taken with tetchy admirals.

For Dutchy and the others it had not, in the past, manifested itself so openly, but there had been such a sense of shared sentiment aboard HMS *Diomede*. She had been a happy ship in the main, in which each man went about their duties with seeming satisfaction. There was, of course, the odd transgressor, usually an endemic offender, requiring to be hauled up and punished for some offence, almost always to do with drink. Edward Brazier had made sure to look carefully into the faces of his crew on such occasions: it was necessary they should approve what was being administered to the miscreant, to assure him it was deserved.

Harsh it might be, but as long as it was seen as fair it would never excite disquiet. Various actions were recalled and described to a seemingly attentive host, until the question arose as to Brazier's soubriquet. If he was known as the Turk, it required explanation, which only he could provide.

'It came to me first as a younker in the midshipman's berth.'

'Hellhole by all accounts,' Dutchy interjected. 'Not that I'd go near the place.'

'I sense your colouring, sir, may have been part of the naming.'

'Havn'a seen you with a growth afore, Capt'n,' Cocky added, regardless of a mouth full of rabbit. Brazier rubbed his chin, feeling the thick stubble, which he knew would be as black as his hair. Cocky went on chewing and talking. 'If yon Frenchie has seen you wi' a beard like yon, you wouldn'a have had to fire a gun.'

'Scary, right enough,' came from Peddler.

'Used to shave you, Captain,' said Joe. 'Couldn't let you on deck, lest your chin was shining.'

'I had a good look into your eyes, Joe,' Brazier growled, with mock seriousness. 'When you had the razor by my neck, I knew never to complain about the soup.'

A joke, it was readily taken as such, with many a reason advanced as to why Joe might have done all a favour by a quick bit of untoward pressure. The offer to shave him now or come morning was declined: Brazier was unsure if he might need a beard to move around without attracting attention, so it was best left to grow. Then it was back to recollection and on they went, describing the destruction of the Frenchman Cocky had mentioned. He'd called himself a privateer but was, in truth, no more than a pirate, one who'd been in league with the commanding admiral on the Jamaica Station. Both had set out to cheat the rest of the squadron of their rightful due in prize money.

Such talk had Brazier retreat into his own thoughts as the conversation flowed around him. The fact of Admiral Hassall's actions, using the intelligence he received to alert his French partner to potential prizes, thus making many times more money than would come to him through his position of command – not an eighth but a half or more. He recalled the furious exchange when he challenged him, full of denials, which did nothing to convince, but vehement in the face of possible disgrace. Then there was Hassall's demise, the strong supposition there had been foul play, as well as the knowledge that, despite he being entirely innocent of involvement, it was an act which might come to haunt him.

'Blew the bugger to bits,' Dutchy exclaimed, finishing his tale, before going on to tell Zachary of the treasure taken out of the Spanish vessel the Frenchman had captured. 'A mint of money when valued.'

Even thinking about Hassall, Brazier had been aware Zachary

was not wholly engaged in the talk. There was no adding tales of his own, usual in such conversations, which he must have had from his past, if not in bondage then as part of a regiment of foot caught up in fighting the Americans. What he did notice was the glances the man sent in his direction when he thought Brazier wasn't looking, penetrating and fleeting, jerking his head away if he thought it had been noticed.

What was he thinking about? Those journals, what I asked, what I told him? Brazier could speculate endlessly and did so, rendering him semi-detached, which was easy since, having been involved in the events described, he knew most of what was being related. If it tended towards the boast, along with praise for him as captain, it came with good humour and many a mishap related, but more often the high points of sailing in a crack frigate in the West Indies, under blissful blue skies, which could change in a blink to fearful hurricanes.

'Sleep,' Brazier said eventually: the food was finished, the flagon empty and he was weary. 'A pair of you have to be off at first light.'

'Not much space to offer your friends,' came as an apology.

'Ye've never been aboard a man-o'-war, Zachary,' Cocky hooted. 'Then ye'd ken what nae space is like.'

'You will occupy the cot, of course, sir.' A look at a set of determined faces meant no postulating anything other was possible. 'And I think it best we say prayers now, at this board.'

Everyone complied, even if Brazier doubted any of his old barge crew, or even Joe Lascelles, were deeply religious.

Up at cockcrow, Peddler and Dutchy were on their way to take cover behind the oak tree, with Joe and Cocky, the least conspicuous pair, making their way back to Deal, with instructions to seek accommodation from Saoirse Riordan, keep an ear to the ground and watch the slaughterhouse for signs of any untoward activity, only departing if they sensed a danger which would threaten their shipmates. Brazier was thus alone once more with Zachary, or would have been if his host had not said plain he had much work to do and left. The diaries had not been put away, just shifted so they could eat. There was no compunction in taking them up again, no thought he was prying.

The temptation to look over again what he read the day before he put aside, going right back to the very beginning of Venables's entries, which he had too readily skipped through. Perhaps there he would find more telling clues to the man and his dealings with the Tulkingtons.

Up at a more normal hour, Henry went through his morning ritual of early coffee, being shaved by Grady and then breakfasting with his Aunt Sarah in attendance, the mood less frosty than the day before, albeit there was little conversation until Henry broached the subject of Harry Spafford.

'I think the lack of his presence will help,' Sarah Lovell concurred, when Henry made the point of his being barred from staying at Cottington. 'He was a far from suitable guest, never mind a . . .'

The word husband died in the face of Henry's expression, not angry as such but more a look to dare her to say it. In truth it was performance; she had accepted his explanation for the sod's absence and this was all that mattered.

'I daresay the servants are wondering what has become of him.'

'They will be relieved not to be the subject of his outrageous demands.'

'Then you may ease their minds.'

His thinking moved on to the letter from his uncle and the possibility of what his aunt might be able to bring to the problem. She was vocal in her dislike of his presence as being something which, if his illegitimacy required to be explained, would bring disapproval on the family. Wondering if she might in some way deflect Dirley, the door opened so Grady could deliver the message his coach was ready.

It was a subject kept in mind all the way into Deal. The first question Henry asked himself was this: could he dispense with his uncle's services? The conclusion was negative, at least in the immediate future, which led to speculation on doing so over time and the drawbacks were manifest. All the work carried out by Dirley could only be taken over by himself, there being no one else he could trust, while it would take a great deal of time, and indeed might be impossible, to find a replacement. The burden this would place upon his comfortable way of life was not something to contemplate with much happy anticipation.

His father had foreseen the possibility of Dirley no longer being able to function: an older half-brother could be expected to die ahead of himself, the shock being it had turned out to be the reverse. Henry found the documents put in place for what had been expected. These passed total control of the law chambers, which Dirley ran, back to the Tulkington family, who'd financed their creation. This ensured any evidence of illegal activity would remain secret. Acton's last will and testament, the one which subsequently mattered, bequeathed the same to Henry.

It was a thought to which he had given consideration, but not in a pressing sense. Yet it was being thrown into stark relief now: at some time in the future it might devolve upon him and suddenly. If his father had expired of a seizure, in what looked like rude good health, who was to say it was not possible for those who shared his bloodline to fall victim to the same malaise? It was a mirror image of the problem with John Hawker and highlighted something he'd known but declined to act upon because everything seemed to be progressing so smoothly: he was running his affairs on a legacy at both ends, which – long term and present glitches notwithstanding – could not continue. At some time there would have to be in place new people and they would be far from easy to find.

It was a fact, even if it was not something he hankered after, he would eventually have to take a wife and perhaps contemplate producing a family of his own, children to whom he could pass on what had been left to him. Yet when such a notion surfaced it brought forth in abundance the complications. Any woman who became his wife would have to be blessed with one of two qualities: either the ability to work with him or to be the type so self-possessed they took no interest in the activities of their spouse.

Although he could not be sure, it seemed as if his own mother had been of the latter variety, although she had pronounced views on manners as well as interests of her own, which she pursued. If his father could find a suitable bride, surely so could he, the only problem being his social contacts did not often include meeting the opposite sex.

Lost in these thoughts, he realised the coach was no longer moving: it was outside the Lodge and stationary, with him having no idea of how long this had lasted. Annoyance at his own lack of awareness was naturally taken out on his coachmen for failing to alert him, remonstrations taken stoically by a pair who would see no alternative. There was no desire to surrender, through pride, a far from arduous and well-remunerated position, even if their master was given to irascibility.

Henry was in just such a state now and thus, on entry, in the wrong mood for the encounter he had arranged. His irritation was conveyed to the club servants who disrobed him, likewise the cast of his features when he was spotted by the man he'd come to meet. The look of unease, allied to the guarded wording with which he was greeted, obliged him to both compose himself and apologise.

'I have had a trying morning, Rudd.' A flat hand tapped his chest.

'I fear a temporary weakness in the lungs from being out in the chill air the night before last.'

This brought a concerned look to the physician's face, immediately followed by words of commiseration and an offer of his services, waved away as unnecessary.

'Let us find a place to sit and talk.'

'Might I suggest a tot of brandy, Henry, it can be most efficacious to the chest.'

'As ever, your advice is sound.'

A corner of the room was occupied, quiet at this time of day, the drink ordered for both, given Rudd was not one to pass up on the opportunity and, once served, it was possible to have a discreet conversation, the first point being Henry was not here on his own behalf.

'As you know, my sister is of a nervous disposition.'

'As you described it the last time we met, it is certainly so. I must ask if the means to calm her more extreme moods was effective. The apothecary assured me it would be so.'

'The apothecary?' Henry asked, unable to keep surprise out of his tone. Responded to by an 'Of course' did nothing to ease his discomfort.

'I was under the impression you mixed for yourself.'

Rudd uttered a humourless laugh. 'Good Lord, no. Each to his own, I say. While I see to the problem, if there's remedies to be provided, outside a good bleed, then they are prepared by the apothecary.'

'The recipient named?'

'Not always. Why do you ask?'

'Is it not obvious? I would not want it getting around Elisabeth is, how may I put it, unsound?'

'You gave the impression her problem was temporary, to do with an extreme reaction to the regular female affliction.' Sage nods were exchanged on a subject it would be improper to speak of in any detail. 'Are you saying it is more?'

'I fear it may be, which is why I asked you to meet me today. I'm wondering what to do if a thing, which seemed momentary, turns out to be . . .'

'A cause for ongoing concern,' Rudd pronounced in a grave tone, finishing Henry's sentence, then his own brandy.

'It troubles me to even mention such a possibility, but to deny it would fly in the face of what I see from day to day.'

'Perhaps if I were to attend upon her.'

'This I suggested, only to send her into a frenzy. She will not hear of it.'

'Then I suggest a repeat of what sufficed previously, discretely acquired of course.'

'Most grateful. But I do wonder if her affliction might become enduring and, if it should be so, what to do about it.'

'A matter of grave concern.'

'My sister's welfare guides my every act. I'm led to believe, properly cared for, patients may recover their equilibrium. But the obvious question arises, will this be possible in our home setting?'

'I'm obliged to enquire as to what you think may have brought this about. I doubt the original given reasons would explain it.'

'I suspect the loss of her husband to be the root cause.' Sensing doubt, given the lapse in time, Henry was quick to add, 'They were so very close, Dr Rudd, enamoured of each other since childhood. It could be said they strolled into their nuptials, so inevitable it would be they should marry. They had my heartfelt blessing, of course.'

'No sign previously?'

'It has only manifested itself on coming home. I enquired of my Aunt Sarah, whom I asked to go out and bring Elisabeth home, if she could recall any incident which would point to what we are dealing with now and her answer was an emphatic no. I suspect, while still in Jamaica, Elisabeth would have been surrounded by memories of their shared existence as husband and wife. Here, in the grounds of our estate, she recalls not such things, but does the games they played as children.'

Rudd made a cathedral of his hands, then tucked them under his chin. The 'Hmm', he uttered, like the pose, Henry saw as affectation. The man had no idea but must pretend otherwise.

'Elisabeth walks every day,' Henry added, 'for in excess of two hours.'

'Surely this is a good thing?'

'One would think so, but her perambulations take her past the very places where they cavorted as children, most often by the lake. I, of course, pray this to be a passing affair. What I want to know is, what can be done if it's not? More tellingly, what would be the solution if her condition deteriorates?'

The response was slow in coming; Rudd was taking the matter seriously, which pleased Henry: there was no question of him failing to convince. 'There are places where people in mental distress can be accommodated.'

'A fount of horror stories.'

'Not all are bad. I agree there are mere holding pens for the tormented and terrible they are. But some of those are licensed to provide care and counselling, the aim being to seek to return their patients to a normal state of mind and discharge them back to their homes.' The keen look Henry was giving Rudd was an invitation to continue. 'The nearest house operating in this way, so I'm told, is in our own county of Kent, at West Malling.'

'You do not know of it?'

'I have had no occasion to.'

'There must be cases locally who require such treatment?'

Rudd actually laughed, which plainly did not please Henry and had him try and cover it with an unconvincing cough.

'I apologise, but this is Deal. A walk along the strand and contact with the beach folk would have you wonder if there is sanity at all in the town. In amongst such a community anything of a mental disability would be hard to discern. The common sign of disorder manifests itself in drunkenness and violence. How could you note disorder with the boatmen or fishwives? They live by bestial behaviour and riot.'

'I assume their being poor has a bearing?'

Henry posited this in a wry tone. He carried no great affection for the denizens of the beach, the men who worked the hoys and wherries, the cutters and hovelling boats, who lived a precarious life. But Rudd was being conceited, which was not a trait he ever applied to himself.

'It may be so,' was a guarded medical admission. 'But the parish officers have the right to take up people for confinement.'

'And they can send them to this institution in West Malling?'

'Only should it prove necessary. For the assurance of acceptance, the opinion of two physicians would be helpful, though only one is required. I assume you would be prepared to provide the funds to secure the best of treatment, plus the avoidance of common accommodation, but I must alert you to the fact of its expense.'

'No expense would be too great to see Elisabeth restored, Dr Rudd.' Henry declared as he stood up. 'Let us hope my concerns are overstated and my sister returns to settled behaviour.'

'Of course,' Rudd said, rising likewise.

'But the remedy with which you armed me before. I would wish to have it to hand, in case of need.'

'I will have it made up. Would you wish me to send it over to Cottington?'

'No. I don't sense any need to rush. I will pick it up from you here, at your convenience, if it suits.'

The Henry Tulkington who emerged was not the irascible fellow who'd entered the Lodge. For one thing, he was smiling, as well as indicating he would walk. The Three Kings was not very far off and that was where this Cottin fellow was staying. It would be a good idea to get a look at him, to put a face to the office, but not to engage in conversation. It came as a disappointment to find him out. Garlick, however, was very forthcoming to a caller as prominent as he about the nature of the fellow and what he got up to.

CHAPTER FIFTEEN

Henry's good mood, which lasted all the way to the slaughterhouse, was lifted even more by the news of the successful and discreet transfer of the Spafford gang to their farmhouse. The eventual demise of Dan Spafford was even better, it being a solution to a niggling problem, though he was required to insist Hawker be patient in the matter of rotting cadavers.

'The lads will be askin' to bury the bodies if'n we don't act quick.'

'Surely they're inured to the smell, John?' was the less than satisfying reply, as Tulkington took a shot at being humorous. 'Lord knows how they'd be troubled, given they can be more than ripe themselves.'

There was no point in Hawker even hinting at what he thought. Tulkington was ignorant of the men he was denigrating, another mark against him compared to his pa. Acton, though happy to let Hawker command them, had taken the trouble to get to know those who, at one remove, did his bidding. As for the bodies, his employer was never going to be near enough to the smell to be troubled by it.

'I still want to be sure the way is clear.'

'This sheriff is one sod on his own, not the Excise and them we make dance to our will.'

'Then why did he depart Deal by horse yesterday and ride to Dover?'

'Did he so?' was all Hawker could say in response.

'Does it occur to you he could be visiting them to seek out information?'

'I's at a loss to know what they could tell him.'

'We must wait till we're sure he's gone. He can't stay forever but it would be an idea to know of his movements while he's here.'

'I can have him trailed, just like Brazier.'

'Make it so, John.'

Hawker used the local waifs as his eyes and ears, lads who would readily do his bidding, with no shortage willing. Living in an anchorage, with hundreds of vessels coming and going, Deal had dozens of brats living on the streets, while the girls who matched their way of life made their living by selling their bodies. Stunted in growth, immoral to the core, the boys were tenacious survivors, the offspring of uncaring parents, local whores brought to childbirth by visiting sailors or runaways from the countryside around.

Sleeping in doorways or the cemetery of St George's, they spent most of the day grubbing for or stealing food, trying to pick the pockets of sailors just discharged and drinking gin, if they could filch the means to buy it. There lay the means by which Hawker could employ them, the task of late to keep an eye on a certain naval captain, reporting back on who visited Quebec House, to where he went and to whom he spoke, all for a flask of their chosen spirit. Adding Cottin presented little difficulty, as long as he was in the confines of the town.

'Now what of Brazier?'

'Far as I know, there's been no sign for the last two days.'

'Is there a way he could avoid being spotted?'

'Not from the buggers I have on his tail. They're like rats, everywhere but not seen. Reckon he's either gone to meet his maker or you've seen him off at last.'

Tulkington departed, cheered by what he'd heard, leaving John Hawker in a very different mood. He'd been obliged to lie, though it was not the telling which rankled, but the reminder of having been let down by those very same lot of filthy tykes he'd just been praising. One of them, a bit of a ringleader called Danny, probably full of gin, had failed to see Brazier leaving Quebec House on the evening of the riot. Hawker was still to catch hold of Danny, but a few of his mates had got the clouts he deserved in lieu, which did little to moderate his fury.

The way he had been dragged from Cottington in the dark still festered like an itch he couldn't scratch, so the desire to avenge it was more than just strong. He could recall every fall, feel every bruise from the rocks he'd been hauled over and hear in his mind each taunt from Brazier's tars, voices in the dark with no faces clear. Even in distress he had resolved they would pay with their lives and said so, only to be barred from his revenge by Henry Tulkington.

The men he led were of no consequence, but Edward Brazier was a post captain in the King's Navy. The murder of such a worthy would not pass without stirring up real trouble, maybe even an incursion by the military. It would certainly cause concern amongst those who turned a blind eye to the smuggling trade. They would rush to cover their own backs and who knew what they'd be prepared to sacrifice?

Hawker had ignored him. Just ahead of the mob he'd helped to stir up, with four of his most trusted men armed with clubs, he'd broken into Quebec House only to find the place empty, barring one cove asleep on the top floor, who'd been clubbed unconscious. If Brazier was gone, unless he was dead, it was, for John Hawker, unfinished business and hatred did not blind him to the nature of his enemy: the bastard had proved hard to shift before, so it had to be concluded he was not one to give up in seeking to get to Tulkington's sister if he still had breath in his body.

On his rounds of the town, he made a point of finding his sewer rats, dispensing the coins needed to provide a flask of gin, telling them to keep a sharp eye out for Brazier still and Cottin now. Then it was on to his real tasks, dropping into various places to confirm orders and hint they'd soon be fulfilled, examine a whole raft of accounts and calculate what was owed to the government, with a quick check to ensure the sums added up.

In his travels John Hawker was ever accosted by locals who wanted him to be aware of their respect. There was also the fact he was a fount of knowledge regarding what was going on in the town, though he was generally guarded in what he passed on, mostly hints which would work to his advantage. He had a good ear too, being trusted, for any hints some folk might be planning a run to France for contraband. Later in the day, he was going to have to go back to Spafford's farmhouse and ensure things were in order, taking food as well, which required to be bought and part of it would have to go to the captives.

'Name of Christ,' he swore. 'Feedin' the sods instead of stopping their gobs with brine.'

Edward Brazier was moving better. There was still pain, but a good measure of the stiffness, which had made it difficult, had eased and was continuing to do so. Many times he rose to walk about, stretching a left arm till it hurt until sense caused him to cease and make his way back to the sunlit bench. There he took up the earlier diary, to reread the Cottington passages, which produced little to enlighten him: nothing more could be gleaned than had been extracted from the first time.

This drove him to look for earlier clues regarding Venables' character, there being entries dating from the time he could begin to write in a clear hand. He was not a robust type, given there was much on youthful ailments. Then there was school, intermittently attended for two reasons: money being available to pay for lessons and the needs of the family when it came to getting in crops for subsequent sale. When he was able to partake of lessons, he wrote of his enjoyment when learning and his misery when dealing with his classmates, from which Brazier deduced he was not popular.

That said and reading on, local friends and events were mentioned, games of cricket on the green, the various fairs which coincided with religious festivals and the fun to be had with bear-baiting and cockfighting. The rumbustious nature of elections were described with sheer enjoyment, though there was never much doubt about who would win the Cinque Port of Sandwich: always a senior naval officer, but such a sure candidate was still required to spend on food and drink, to entertain even those who lacked a vote, with a band provided too. It was the life of a class of folk on the rung below yeoman, but above the common labourer.

There was mention of his father who was, by nature, reported as tyrannical and roundly condemned as a brute. Much kinder were his comments on his Dear Mother, who'd suffered, like her son, from violence in the home, stoically borne, which took him back to the passages already twice read. The second journal told him she'd been left to run the smallholding when he went off to America, the father no longer being alive. On return from the war, the workload had fallen to Zachary, especially after his Dear Mother passed away, this being the cause of much written lamentation. Later entries spoke of the contentment he found both in his religion as well as the company of Zachary, who shared his faith. Then it was failing health.

Journals finished, he considered joining Zachary in his labours, pruning his apple trees of any produce which had been attacked by the numerous pests attracted to growing fruit. But the way he'd acted indoors in the morning did not encourage Brazier to think he'd be more forthcoming in the fresh air, not that he had given up any hope of extracting information. He turned his mind once more to ways of reversing matters with Henry Tulkington, the first conclusion not hard to reach: rescuing Elisabeth could not now be done, in any way he could fathom, without violence. The next fact was equally obvious:

without Hawker and his men, Tulkington was vulnerable and, in reality, it was the leader not the followers who provided the protection. Take Hawker out of action and many things might be possible.

Deduction was easy, acting upon it much more problematic. It was an axiom of warfare, be it on land or sea, you did not attack your enemy where he was strongest and he could call on numbers, which precluded Hawker's own backyard of Deal. This led to thoughts of the farmhouse to which he'd taken . . . what? His own men and maybe Dan Spafford and his crew? There was no way of telling from where he was sitting, but he did know he had little time for them. Whichever way he turned in search of a solution, one fact always intruded, his shortage of the kind of strength he needed. Spafford was Tulkington's enemy, which should have meant anyone so inclined was a potential ally, but it was the same lot he'd been forced to take with him to Cottington and nothing he'd observed hinted at trust.

Dutchy had insisted no approach could be made in daylight without being seen a goodly distance away, so surprise would be impossible, which left the night. Given the failures of his previous excursions, it was not a notion to readily appeal except in one sense: there was no alternative, the other choice being to do nothing, which meant going to see for himself how the land lay, in pain or not. Anything attempted would have to set off from Zachary's. Should he tell his host or leave him in the dark, a thought which caused Brazier to wonder at himself: he was proposing to seek information from him, while at the same time contemplating concealment of what he might be about to do.

Seeing his Good Samaritan coming in from the orchard, tellingly without the habitual smile, he picked up the relevant book so as to have it open at what was now a well-thumbed page. There was, once more, a lack of eye contact, which would not serve, obliging him to press. Either information would be provided or he would receive a blank refusal.

'Zachary.'

He was reluctant to respond but he did stop. 'Sir?'

'I need your help.' The eyes went to the journal, open in Brazier's hand, the point obvious. 'I have to rescue someone and I'm not sure it can be done without I know more of the late Mr Venables and his relationship with a certain person residing at Cottington Court.'

'And if I say I cannot talk of him, sir?'

'I would find it hard to believe.' The diary was lifted up to eye height. 'Perhaps if I was to read to you some of the entries, it might help.'

'I'd prefer readings from the Bible, sir,' came with a hint of forward movement.

Brazier ignored it, challenging Zachary to walk on past, which he could not do, his curiosity overcoming his disinclination to engage. He listened as the first meetings, then the growing friendship were described, the days spent together on country rides, added to the deepening affection, looking Zachary in the eye when he finished.

'They were extremely close and it's chronicled here. Yet Dear Sam went off without a word of farewell. Let me read the passage to you.'

Which he did, pausing to look up at the end of each sentence, finishing with the last word of Venables about saying prayers, while hoping there was no need.

'What do you take from such an entry?' Nothing, not even a shrug, which had Brazier think he was a man to avoid playing cards with. 'I will tell you what was vouchsafed to me by the lady I'm intent on marrying. Samuel Lovell's wife says no more than her husband rode out one day, seemingly in good spirits, never to return. This was on the very same day he arranged to meet his friend for some kind of special outing. Then the final entry. What was it that Mr Venables feared?'

'Look to the date, sir. How would I know?'

'I don't say you were around when these events took place. What I wonder is this. Did the man with whom you shared this place ever speak to you of it, the man who had no desire to go near Cottington Court, the very place where I was shot?'

'He named it as the devil's lair, the home of Beelzebub. Knowing such a thing, no man would risk his soul by going close.'

'He never gave you the real reason?'

'Is Satan not real enough, sir?'

'To some but not to me. Did he add something more?'

'He did, on the understanding I would speak of it to no one. And sir, much as I respect you, I will not break such an oath.'

'Which in normal circumstances I would admire.'

'Not now?'

'I shall ask no more, Zachary, and forgive me for pressing you, not least because I have a deep suspicion I owe you my life.'

A glance to the heavens, with the sun going down, was enough to lay the praise where Zachary was sure it lay. 'Your companions should return soon. I'll go and bank up the fire.'

It was not an admission but a mistake and one Henry should have seen as possible. He had failed to note the person who took in the post was Grady. Since letters had to be paid for on receipt, money would only be forthcoming if the addressee was resident at the house. Thus, he knew of the two letters addressed to his master's sister, including the most recent, but had no idea they had been kept from her. Therefore, his remark, delivered to Elisabeth while helping her to disrobe when she came in from her morning walk, was entirely innocent in wondering if Mr Dirley, whom he remembered fondly from her father's day, was in good health. The reply threw him slightly.

'Why are you asking me?'

The servant knew immediately he had misspoken. Despite his years of service and innate discretion, he could not avoid a cast of the eyes, which indicated his discomfort. This caused Elisabeth to look in rapid succession towards both the staircase and the doors off the hallway. Seeing no one, her voice dropped to a whisper.

'Is there something you're trying to tell me?'

'No, Miss Elisabeth.'

Yet he pointedly glanced towards the hall table on which post would be left for later distribution. Holding Grady's eye was difficult when he was busy avoiding hers, but there was some residual spark in the man, a touch of rebellion surfacing, which had him say in a sonorous tone,

'I would be grateful if you would send him my best wishes, when you reply.'

The combination allowed her to make the connection. A reply clearly meant there had to be incoming correspondence, obviously something she'd never seen. Elisabeth had never collected her own mail, waiting for it to be brought to her and besides, it had not been a regular daily occurrence, though it occurred to her now she'd had none for some time.

Heart beating like a kettle drum, Elisabeth replied, 'I most certainly shall.'

'Shall what?' Sarah Lovell enquired as she came down the stairs, not in any demanding way, more a general query.

'Keep an eye on the weather, Aunt Sarah,' was desperate and sounded feeble to her niece, yet it needed to be carried through. 'This spell of good weather is not going to last.'

'Will there be anything else, Miss Elisabeth?'

'Nothing, Grady. And thank you for your concern.'

Sarah Lovell was frowning, the look which went with it aimed at Grady, not her. This was followed by a hand held up, indicating she should wait, which lasted until he went through the door to the servant quarters.

'My dear,' was very quiet. 'I think you should say to Grady to have a care how he addresses you. Indeed, it should be made plain to all the servants.'

'Whatever for?'

'I think Henry would not wish to see you spoken of in such a manner.' Eyes were raised towards the ceiling, so what was implied was obvious. 'After all, you have not been Miss Elisabeth for a very long time.'

If the reply was mischievous, and it was, there was nothing in Elisabeth's expression to hint at levity. 'Are you suggesting he addresses me as Mrs Langridge?'

'You know I don't mean anything of the sort.'

'Then if you refer to whom I suspect, you tell them. I'm sure it will do wonders for the esteem in which you're held.'

Elisabeth didn't wait to enjoy her aunt's discomfort; the servants disliked her and she knew it, though it had to be said, in her world, being popular with those below stairs did not come as a recommendation, quite the reverse. Even if she'd wanted to drive the point home, the need to be alone took precedence, to wonder if there had indeed been a letter from her Uncle Dirley and if there had, what it contained. If it was being kept from her it could only be for one reason: Henry's desire to cut her off from outside contact. Not that realisation solved the dilemma of what to do about it.

She would have been even more concerned if she'd been looking over her brother's shoulders later in the day, reading the letter he was writing to Dirley, informing him Elisabeth and her new husband had decided to visit Paris and had taken the Dover cartel to Calais . . .

As of this moment I have no idea of their itinerary, for there was much talk of hiring a coach and visiting various places of interest on the way, for it turns out Mr Spafford has a bent for the history of battles, the sites of which litter northern France and the Low Countries. No doubt they will write to me when they finally reach Paris and advise me of where they've decided to stay. Until then, Uncle Dirley, I shall hold on to your letter, to forward it when the time comes.

I am, as ever, your loving nephew,

Henry, as he signed it, knew it would only hold Dirley for a while, but hold him off he must. The time would come for the truth, but not just yet. Then it would be fitting he be reminded of his place in the scheme of things and made aware of who was in charge.

CHAPTER SIXTEEN

Dutchy made himself small when he saw Hawker approaching along the road from Deal, riding at no great pace, mounted himself and pulling along a pair of laden packhorses. He had to hope Peddler, no longer with him, caught sight of him too. He'd gone to get a closer look at the farmhouse by merely strolling past it, showing no particular interest, acting as if he was heading somewhere else, and, for once, he was not to be dissuaded or told to desist by his one-time coxswain.

'The cove you say dropped off milk and eggs didn't set off any bells, so I won't either. If I make bold, it should serve, an' 'part from that, I'm sick of sitting still and owt going off.'

It produced no alarms: there had been no men guarding an approach outside and it seemed those inside were content to stay there. Yet if he came back the same way, then he'd walk smack into the bugger. Would Hawker mark him if he did? Dutchy couldn't be sure and he had no idea what to do about it. The notion he might come out from his cover and take on Hawker was not to be considered: as he got closer the butt of the pistol sticking out of a saddle holster was plain to see.

Heart in mouth he watched Hawker all the way to the farmhouse door, saw him haul out his pistol and dismount, to then rap loudly for entry. When it swung open, he disappeared inside, a couple of his men soon sent out to unload the pack animals. This done, they led all three away to he knew not where, somewhere out of his field of vision. They returned a short while later, going back indoors, with as yet no sign of Peddler, which made the worry greater. A look at the sky didn't tell Dutchy the actual time, but the long shadow running from his oak tree hiding place towards the shoreline was proof enough: the day was close to ending. It also told him, with a clear sky, there was going to be a moon, but probably not till he was well clear.

The smell hit Hawker's nostrils even before he entered the farmhouse. Doors and windows having been closed all day and no one venturing out, with the sun playing on the thatched roof and red-brick walls, had made the interior warm and stuffy. Thus, the odour of rotting humanity had built up to a powerful stench, one less noticed by those left behind. The next thing observed by Dutchy was a procession of three sackcloth bundles being brought out and carried off by half a dozen men, again these taken out of his eye line.

It was Peddler, hidden in some trees on the far side, who saw them being taken to one of the barns, old and in need of repair, the faces of those carrying them screwed up with disgust. They were not out of sight for long, soon heading back to the house. Impulse made him move while they were still in the open with their backs to him. He skipped silently across the long uncut grass to get behind the barn, only creeping round to slip through one of the double doors when Hawker's men were back inside, which was pulled to just enough to let in some light.

The smell had the same effect on him as it had on Hawker, bringing on a curse, while the trio of horses were a surprise. For a moment he stood stock-still lest they react, which proved unnecessary since they were too busy munching hay to give him even a look. Coming closer he saw a saddle on a rail, with the tack for all three hanging on a hook. One mount, the largest, turned her head to look at him but not for long; she was back to feeding.

Gingerly, having approached the piles of sackcloth, he uncovered his first bundle, to reveal the waxy, stiff face of Harry Spafford, previously only seen briefly in lantern light. But there could be no mistaking the fair hair as well as the round hole surrounded by black powder trace on his forehead. The other two were easier to identify as Trotter and old man Spafford. The thud, as one of the horses kicked the wood of the barn wall, nearly had Peddler jumping out of his skin.

Hurriedly he recovered the faces, sidled back to the door and opening it a shade more, peered out to see the way was clear. Making 'bold' as he would call it, ignoring the fact the previously closed windows were now wide open, he strode out like a man without a care in the world to retrace his earlier footsteps. What Dutchy saw nearly brought on an apoplexy, Peddler passing the front door with lips pursed, as though he was whistling a tune.

There was true admiration as he kept going, past the tree behind which he knew his mate was hiding, the call to say he was making for Zachary's place loud enough for him to hear but no one else. By the time the light had faded enough to allow Dutchy to move, Peddler was back with his old captain and telling his tale.

'Had me shitting roundshot,' was Dutchy's response, when he finally joined them, a remark which got a chuckle from Zachary, once more preparing food. After being told what Peddler had found, Dutchy gave an account of his day, which did not amount to anything. No one had come out of the farmhouse and there was only Hawker's arrival to cause comment.

'Can we find our way back there in the moonlight?' Brazier asked.

'Why would we want to?'

'The way I see it, we've been gifted a chance to give Hawker a scare. More than that, something to worry about.'

Clearly previously mooted to Peddler, Dutchy was of the opinion enough risks had been taken for one day.

'You don't know what I have in mind.'

'I can guess, Capt'n, an' am I allowed to say, you ain't fully fit?'

'I won't be doing any lifting, I promise.'

'Lifting?'

Brazier's smile, through his thickening stubble, did little to reassure Dutchy. 'I'm guessing one of the horses in the barn Peddler found is Hawker's.'

This being confirmed, as well as the nature of the other pair, led to the obvious question: what does it mean? It turned out to be rhetorical as Brazier answered himself.

'If Hawker was going back to Deal, he would not have had his mount unsaddled, so he's staying the night and returning come morning. All day, you tell me, his men have been indoors with no lookouts posted.' A slow nod. 'So, I think we can assume there'll be none at night either.'

'And if he wakes up on the morrow and his horses are gone?'

'Not just the horses, Dutchy, I want to steal the bodies too.'

'There's some who'd say yon musket ball ain't done much for your brains, your honour.'

'I'm not surprised the dead have been carted away from Cottington, but why bring them to where they are now? Why not bury them?'

'Don't make sense to me, right enough.'

'Nor to me, Dutchy, but there's a reason and, even if it's a mystery, they're something they want to hang on to. So I say let's pinch them, because I reckon, and don't go asking me why, it will cause trouble, not just for Hawker but for Tulkington.'

Dutchy looked at Peddler. 'What do you reckon on this?'

'I'm game for a look-see. That be when to decide.'

'Be best you stay here, Capt'n.'

'Never. All I'll be doing is leading a horse. Zachary, we need to ask you for a lantern and some flints.'

'Would you wish, sir, I come with you?'

'No. It is all very well for us to court danger, but not you.'

'Then you go with my prayers.'

'Keep sayin' 'em,' was Peddler's heartfelt plea, Dutchy concurring.

Food was served and eaten in silence, each man with his own thoughts until the time came to depart, Brazier donning his uniform coat, which being dark blue was perfect for night work. This he did after he and the others had examined the neat hole, high on the shoulder, producing a sobering thought. Six inches lower and who knew how much damage it would have done?

Once outdoors they could see the moon as a creamy orb, which at the time of year rose slowly over the French coast, turning pure white as it cleared the dust of its low trajectory. The starlight around it was rendered faint by its orb, though the rest of the sky was carpeted with pinpoints, some twinkling, others not, a sight to make Zachary cross himself as he saw the three men move away. For to him it represented the presence of God. Edward Brazier saw a celestial map by which he had often navigated.

Moon and stars created enough light to move, albeit with care, an excess needed if the tree canopy closed overhead. Yet even then, a landscape bathed by light usually showed the way to proceed. There was no talking and neither was there an audible reaction to the pain Brazier was feeling. Once out on the open marsh it could have been daylight, which had the worry of their being seen, though with a sighing wind there was little danger of being heard.

'We can't go walking past the door, Capt'n,' Dutchy whispered when the farmhouse, no more than a black silhouette with bits of leaking light, was in sight. 'Slightest sound and we'll be staring at a musket.'

'I'll fix on Ursa Minor, which will allow us a detour.'

The arc of the constellation, with the Pole Star the brightest, stayed visible as they moved, their way also rendered possible by human-made paths through trees. It took time to cover the progress needed, but Brazier wasn't worried about time. They had one job to do and all the hours of darkness in which to accomplish it. One false choice of path took them to the wrong place, but by backtracking and moving to the north, it brought them to the point where Peddler had first spotted the barns. The farmhouse roof was silhouetted against the starlit sky.

'Best stay here while I see what's what.'

Peddler got no argument or any hint Brazier was narked at being told what to do: Peddler was the right man for the task. He was like a black ghost as he slid away, with Brazier realising, with the clear sky and much time gone already, there was bound to be a substantial overnight dew, so dawn would show a human track through the grass, never mind three, plus, if what he wanted came to pass, a trio of laden horses.

Was it a problem to be dealt with or a good reason to abandon what they were about? This had to be examined – he could not allow his determination to get at Tulkington to dictate how they would proceed. The answer was to use more of the tree cover on the return, indeed to wait, once they'd gone some distance, till the sky was grey enough to allow them so see their way. Then they could pick a route which would leave no trace at all, lest, and this was unlikely, one of Hawker's ruffians was an experienced tracker.

Peddler did a mean owl-like hoot, the signal for him and Dutchy to move forward, never taking their eye off the outline of the farmhouse. They were unarmed, so the slightest sign of life and it was run and pray. The bulk of the barn rose up quickly, with Peddler's disembodied voice whispering, he being invisible against the wooden wall. The door creaked as it was opened, a fact not recalled by Peddler, who cursed under his breath at the sound, but having come this far, stopping was not an option. Knowing the noise would come with movement, he hauled it open to shorten the time it could be a threat. It made the same scary sound when closed, a crack left open so they could be sure no one had been alerted.

A decent wait was called for before Brazier asked for the lantern to be lit, the sparking flints giving him flashes of three pairs of equine eyes, luckily not disturbed. Once the tallow had taken it was possible to see them in the flesh, Brazier approaching, with Dutchy standing off slightly, lantern held high. Noses were rubbed and muzzles touched, with one – the best and sleekest stallion, which had to be Hawker's – taking a snap at a hastily removed hand. A glance at the walls showed various things to do with boats either leaning against the walls or hanging on hooks: oars and rowlocks, ropes and marked barrels, whatever within being too indistinct to pick out with any clarity.

'Let's get the pack animals rigged.'

The lantern now high on a hook and this being one of the tasks physically beyond him, Brazier went over to look at the barely visible bundles. He thought of posting himself as a lookout, but it would mean being outside, with the risk of opening and shutting the door, which would send out light, which would be spotted from the farmhouse. Hearing cursing, he went to help Peddler, struggling with the leather rigs.

'Never had cause to doubt you on knots.'

'And, I thank you, no barky is rigged in leather.'

Having been raised on a farm, Brazier knew what to do and softly instructed Peddler, turning to observe Dutchy either had the knowledge or had figured it out for himself. Next it came to saddling Hawker's horse, which went without fuss, it being an animal accustomed to the ritual.

'Why d'ye want the saddle, Capt'n?' Dutchy enquired, as he tightened the girth.

'Only because it will make Hawker spit when he finds it's gone. Let's get loading.'

The first packhorse was led over to the bundles, Dutchy and Peddler at foot and shoulders, each producing a retch in the throat as the stink rose up.

'Worse'n bilge,' Dutchy spat.

'Not Cocky's breath,' was a gasp from Peddler, mixed with laughter.

Brazier held the horse's head while the others lifted the first body across its back, needing to take a tight and painful grip as the animal reacted. Again he instructed Peddler on the tying of the pack straps, the animal lashed by its reins while the task was repeated. Hawker's horse was not going to cooperate, dragging itself back from having a load on its back with such force Brazier, given the pain, couldn't hold it. The task fell to Dutchy until it calmed down, no doubt because it had become used to the putrefaction. Once the last body was loaded, the lantern was killed and a single barn door, with its creaking screech, pulled slightly open, the still dark walls of the farmhouse examined closely.

'One at a time, back to the trees. If a light shows or anybody appears, slap the horse hard and run. I reckon they'll want the bodies more than us.'

Both doors creaked as they were opened wide, the animals slowly led out to be taken towards the trees, with their bulk between them and the risk of a musket ball. On the way out it had been far from smooth going, but it was much worse seeking a way through thicket-bound paths on the way back. Finally, they came back out on to the moon-blessed marshland and could move with reasonable speed.

'Capt'n, you'll forgive my enquiring, but have you thought on what we're going to do with these buggers?'

Not wanting to say he had no idea, the answer was a bit inexact. 'I think they'll be safe enough for a while by Zachary's pile of cow manure. The horses we'll maybe set free, but for now let's find a place to tie them off so we can rest until first light.'

'Downwind, for the love of Christ,' Dutchy insisted.

Brazier would not have cared: all he wanted was relief. He was in real pain and worried the fear Zachary had voiced, that his stitches would work loose, could have come to pass. Even using only his good hand, the tugging involved in making progress was agony, which had to be borne silently; he could not have his companions concerned by it.

Finding somewhere to hitch in the dark proved too difficult, so they merely sank down and held onto the reins, wrapped round a hand, with grass tall enough for the horses to munch on, which at least kept them passive enough to allow for Dutchy and Peddler a snooze, while he, who would struggle to sleep, kept watch. The moon was well to the south-west now but still high enough to illuminate the landscape and, if Brazier closed his eyes, which he did often, he could imagine himself at sea, albeit there was no swell, nor the creaking of timber and rigging.

Would he ever be granted another ship and get back to sea? William Pitt had as good as told him it would be challenging, he being in bad odour at court, this due to the spat he'd had in the West Indies with Prince William. They called him the 'Sailor Prince', which had a jolly ring to it. The reality was a spoilt martinet who treated his inferiors with disdain, or at least those prepared to question his more dubious commands. Those who fawned on his royal rank were favoured.

William also drank too much, becoming over free with what he saw as dalliance. Others, husbands especially, observing their wives being subjected to vulgar and overt attempts at seduction, saw it as salacious as well as uncouth, their wives naming it scandalous. One planter had to be dissuaded from calling the Prince out, which would have been a fine imbroglio for those like Edward Brazier, set to watch over him, especially if William had been wounded or, the Lord forgive, killed.

But the real nub was his behaviour as a captain, he being choleric by nature as well as embedded in his privilege. His Premier, the man attached to the ship by the Admiralty to ensure the royal sibling, not the most competent of seaman, did nothing stupid, had been roundly and publicly abused by his commanding officer when querying a plainly incorrect instruction. Lieutenant Schomberg had, as was his right, demanded a court martial to clear his name and it fell to the senior captain on station to adjudicate and, on the evidence, Brazier had been left with no choice but to find for Schomberg. The rights and wrongs of his decision were not relevant, but he'd dented the pride of King George's son and His Majesty was far from pleased, a fact the monarch had seemingly made known to their lordships of the Admiralty.

Which might pale beside an accusation he'd had a hand in the murder of Admiral Hassall, for he had no doubt of it being a crime, even if he was innocent of the actual deed. Justified? How could any man deny the killing of a treacherous criminal, who'd stolen from his own subordinates, was unjustified? The worry was his own legitimate fury, loudly expressed, on uncovering what Hassall was up to. Had it been used as a spur to act by others?

He could see their faces now in his mind's eye as, having only just anchored off Kingston, they'd come out to gather in his cabin to tell him the news, the eager young faces of the masters and commanders to whom he was now the senior officer. He knew, without being told, the reported death was not natural, but he could not pick out a culprit. Nor would anyone else, which left him seeing it as a collective act, one he took steps to ensure could not be properly investigated.

'You have a rare ability, Edward Brazier, to drop yourself in the steep tub.'

'What'd ye say, your honour?'

'Time to get going, Peddler, sky's showing a bit of grey.'

'We should run out the guns,' Dutchy joked.

'Believe me, Dutchy, if I had them I would. And I'd use them too.'

CHAPTER SEVENTEEN

The expression 'hit the roof' was one common enough, but the thatch above Hawker's head would have seen him through to the open sky, given the level of his fury. The main person to suffer was the poor sod who'd gone to fetch the horses, he being treated as if the whole thing was his fault alone. It didn't last: every one of the men Hawker led was roundly abused and, since he went into exact detail of what had occurred with a carrying shout, those locked up in the room, which once accommodated Harry Spafford, were given full knowledge of what had happened.

Listening at the door up till now had been frustrating, with only rare snatches of conversation loud enough to be clearly overheard and none of it suggesting what was to become of them. This Hawker outburst brought forth smiles but also a fear: in danger already, they might pay the price for what had been spirited away. It was Dolphin Morgan, obviously not as dense as he was held to be, who pointed out the use of the word three when shouting about bodies, which allowed it to dawn on his mates what he'd figured out: Dan Spafford was no more.

'Means we're buggered, whatever happens,' was one opinion. 'Without Dan we'll whistle for a crust.'

'Worse than what you say, mate, happen,' was Dolphin's gloomy response. 'Killin' has taken place. Who's to say where it will rest?'

The voice had moderated enough now to become indistinct, partly because John Hawker had realised several obvious facts, the first being he was as much at fault as anyone. The second was really worrying. This could not be kept from Henry Tulkington. But it was the third which was the most concerning. The only person he could think of with a reason to steal three dead bodies, the horses included, as well as own the means to carry them off, had to be Brazier. The sod was not only still alive, but in a fit state to bring off such a sting.

'What do we do now, John?'

This question brought Hawker back to the present. It was posed by Marker, who it could be said acted as a bit of a leader, he being well trusted. But the same query was in every face and there was no doubt what was being asked. Do we see off the rest of the Spafford gang now or better still, set them free and damn quick? If the name Brazier would mean nothing to them, somebody had done the dirty. This pointed towards what they were about being known where it should not be.

'We stay as we are,' came after a degree of consideration.

He was not going to say it was down to his employer, but it was the case. No great wit was required to see how disposal had now become too risky. There was no knowing what Brazier would do, or how he would use what he had, but there was one certainty: it would not be to anyone's advantage but his own.

'I need to get moving, so you lot stay here and for the love of Christ, post lookouts.'

There was no choice but to walk, the pistol he would carry tucked into his belt. He would have it primed and made ready for use, with wary eyes searching ahead on the road. If three bodies could be lifted, so could he. Hawker could not avoid running over and over in his mind not only what he was going to have to explain but how it had come about, for which he would also have to produce a reason. Somehow, he, or even the whole party two nights' past, had been followed, which failed to explain how Brazier had known about the barn.

'You lot, get your muskets and spread out noisy all around.' The look of confusion had him shout as loud as he had previously. 'We're being watched, which means whoever is doing it will be out there now, so go and flush the bastard.'

'Do we shoot?'

'To wing, Marker, nothing more. I need someone to tell me where to find a certain party.'

Hawker stood in the doorway while his orders were carried out, praying whoever was doing the spying would have to show themselves by trying to get away. Frustration grew as nothing happened, until a shout took him down the track to a large oak tree and the crushed grass at the back. When he got back to the farmhouse door, seething, he went to take a look at the barn, both doors wide open. There, in more trampled grass, lay the route Brazier and whoever had been with him had taken. At least he could send some of his lads to track it into the woods, which would allow him to say to Henry Tulkington the matter had a chance of being resolved.

It was an exhausted Edward Brazier who led his men, in full daylight, back to Zachary Colton's smallholding. Already up and about his daily tasks, he put them aside to come and wonder at what was loaded on the horses. Close up, the drawn face of his patient told him how trying a night it had been, but this was not his first voiced concern.

'These poor souls deserve a Christian burial.'

Brazier was tempted to disagree: Zachary knew nothing of the lives these men had led or the crimes to which they were a party, only to then realise he would probably have forgiven their sins.

'All in good time. Let's get them off the horses and laid in a place where the smell does not offend. Also, the horses need to be fed and watered.'

'Us too,' said Peddler, with true feeling.

If he got a grin it soon disappeared: it was back to the horses and what had been asked. 'For which I lack the means, sir.'

'I supposed as much. Can I suggest I give you some money and you go to where you can buy feed?'

'And my work?'

'I can only ask you to set it aside for the day.'

'And what of you, sir?' The direction of his look left no doubt to what he was referring. 'It may be best if I take a look.'

'Of course.'

The examination was carried out while Dutchy and Peddler unloaded the bodies, as Brazier had suggested, laying them out near the piled-up manure Zachary used as fertiliser. The horses, free of tack, were put into what was now, for its size, a crowded paddock. Indoors, shirt off, Brazier was lying face down as Zachary bathed his back, first with water and then an application of extract of witch hazel, which was cool and soothing on the skin, but not much use for the seat of his now throbbing and constant pain.

'If I take enough coin, sir, I can acquire more laudanum from the apothecary.'

Brazier nodded towards his coat, back on the hook by the fireplace. 'Take what you need.'

'Can I say, sir, you need to sleep as well.'

Which he did throughout the morning – four hours in duration, familiar from watch-keeping at sea – along with Dutchy and Peddler, once they'd had some food.

John Hawker was dressed for riding, wearing the kind of thigh-high boots which made walking uncomfortable, not least for their weight. This caused strained hams and aching calves well before he caught sight of the buildings of Deal. The ground was dry from days of good weather too, throwing up dust at every step, more when a rider of a cart passed by, not much noticed by a mind concerned with a multitude of thoughts. He had, in his imagination, done for Brazier in a dozen different ways, the most satisfying a vision of strangling him with his bare hands.

But with the town coming close he had to concentrate, to go over and hone his excuses to the point where they made, at least to him, some kind of sense. The sight of Tulkington's armed coachmen, standing by the conveyance, added to their lifted eyebrows and wry smiles, had him wonder at what so amused them. He was under the equally curious gaze of Cocky Logan, watching the slaughterhouse from the corner of a nearby building, equally mystified as to why, having been seen by Joe Lascelles to depart on horseback the day before, leading a pair of pack horses, he was now on foot and covered in dust. Having thudded up the stairs, Hawker found his employer seated, legs crossed, he too adopting an expression of amused curiosity as he came in view, which deepened after an up and down look.

'I find you covered in filth, John. Have you been wrestling your horse, perhaps?'

As an attempt at humour it fell flat. With a dry-throated voice Hawker croaked, 'If your honour don't mind, I need to get these damn boots off. An' I need a wet too, so if you could spare me a moment . . .'

'I have been waiting for some time and I do have other matters to attend to.'

It wasn't a no, but it might as well have been. In addition, Tulkington was sitting in the chair he would have dearly liked to occupy. As Hawker admitted he had a problem to relate, the slightly amused look remaining on Tulkington's face evaporated, to be replaced by one of disbelief. Nor did he remain sitting in a relaxed way, soon changed to one of outright anger.

'I'm struggling to believe what you're telling me.'

'Has to be Brazier.'

'You think this sufficient as an explanation? Why did you take no precautions?'

'Did we not both reckon him out of it, happen even dead?'

'I seem to recall you did so. I do not remember my being quite so sanguine.'

There was a slight struggle with the word but no doubting its meaning. If Hawker felt aggrieved for what was, he thought, a piece of downright dishonesty, there was no point in saying so. He moved on to describe how it had been carried out, finishing on a more confident note.

'I've sent my lads out to search, but you've got to ask yourself, Mr Tulkington, what can be his game.'

The response was weedy complaint. 'You know very well what his game is: to discomfit me. And if he succeeds, you will not be far behind. What am I saying, he has already humbugged you!'

Suddenly on his feet, Tulkington spoke with calm fury. 'I suggest you find a horse and join in the search. And John, bring those bodies back, at your peril should you fail.'

'Peril!'

For all his meek acceptance of what was a justified rebuke, this was a word taking matters to the different dimension of a serious threat. He was not going to let it pass and, given his feelings were manifest in his infuriated countenance, Henry knew he'd gone too far: what he had said was clearly seen as presaging menace.

'I meant our peril,' came with the kind of feeble arm waving, which suggested an error. It didn't wash and Hawker was so incensed he lost his normal self-control. He had been humiliated by Brazier as far as he could work out. This, added to what his employer was implying, broke a dam, one which had been building for weeks.

'Peril we would not be suffering if'n you'd let me see to Spafford first off. Likewise the lot of 'em. Dealt with proper, an' we wouldn't have had this now.'

It wasn't just the words used, but the passion behind them, which rattled Henry. It was a direct challenge to his position, a statement he, as the man with whom rested the decisions, had made not just a bad choice but one the end of which it was not possible to foresee. Having broken a boundary of how he dealt with his employer, and his temper high from everything which had occurred, including his sore legs and feet, Hawker was not about to stop.

'You can't duck, dive and play the gent, which is your way. You has to come down hard and quick on any sod who crosses you. Soon as we knew the Spaffords had filched those two cargoes, Dan should have been found with his throat slit in the Lower Valley Road, a message plain to all.'

'Are you mad? A body in the street? How many times have I told you, we cannot act with impunity?'

'Fancy words don't serve, an' I take leave to say plain, your pa would not have stood off from what was needed, and he was man enough to see to it hisself if need be.'

He might as well have slapped Henry Tulkington across the face. In total silence he walked past Hawker and thumped his way down the stairs, as if using his footwear to send a message. He left an employee breathing deep and far from calm, one well aware of the bridge crossed and far from unhappy it had finally taken place. Too many times he'd kept his mouth shut when he should have spoken plain. If Tulkington was too lily-livered to take what was the truth, so be it.

The coachmen were on the box in a flash, having seen the face of their master, who instructed them to take him home, a journey in which he fumed. Once there, he called for his horse, riding out as soon as it was ready. There was only one place he could go to gain relief from the mood he was suffering and it was taken at a fast canter, an unusual pace for him, so keen was he to get to where he needed to be.

It was a more relaxed Henry Tulkington who, two hours later and at a slow trot, rode home. This new mood came from much physical and mental humiliation, followed by a wonderful gush of carnal release, left behind in the cottage where the whip had been applied, the insults to his inadequacies spat at him, followed by gobbets of actual fluid, until finally he had been granted, after a crying plea and a golden guinea proffered on bended knee, the right to gratify his lust on the disdainful whore's body.

He had much to ponder on, but then he always had. Should he require to make changes, the time was not propitious. There was a cargo due, the last before the short nights of high summer made smuggling too risky and for that he needed John Hawker. But there would be a gap of two months to follow, in which he must find a way to alter matters so he never had to face a repeat of what had happened at the slaughterhouse. He also needed to take full control of the family enterprise. Those who deferred to him, Hawker included, must do so absolutely and, if they did harbour any dissatisfaction, they must keep it to themselves and simply do as they were ordered.

The first thing he did on returning home was to sit down and write to his Uncle Dirley once more, telling him, in no uncertain terms, when it came to Elisabeth, there were matters of which he had no knowledge and he was to cease to interfere.

It was obvious to her, if Henry had intercepted her letters, always assuming he hadn't destroyed them, they would be somewhere in his study, a place he held to be sacrosanct. No one was welcome to enter when he was out of the house, a stricture Elisabeth had broken once before, not long after Edward, making a surprise visit to Cottington Court, had told her the real nature of her brother's affairs, as well as his recourse to violence when thwarted.

She blushed now to recall how she'd reacted, coming close to accusing him of lying, intimating he was no longer welcome to call on her, also any hint of matrimony was no longer to be pursued. It was in defence of her father, of course, for he'd been included in the disclosure of what was a family trade and this she could not abide. She had resolved to challenge Henry directly, to see if there was any truth in the allegations, his denials far from convincing. Hence her visit to his study, spontaneous and opportunistic, her aim, to find if anything existed that would prove the contention true or false. It had proved fruitless: she was confronted with shelves full of ledgers, too many to examine, while his desk drawers were locked.

Discovered as she exited, Elisabeth had tried to convince Henry of her innocent intentions, but by one slight and physical movement, she established not only had she failed to carry off the deception but there had to be substance in Edward's accusation. From this came the decision to elope. This effort to get to his inner sanctum was brought on by desperation: doing nothing was driving her mad and opportunity was there. It was easy to tell when Henry was out of the house, much harder to make her way to the study without being observed by either her aunt or a servant. As well as Grady, Cottington Court had four maids, two of whom were really skivvies to do the cleaning, plus a pair of footmen, while the kitchen boasted the cook and her two scullery girls, with a dozen more outside caring for the garden and the stables.

She chose a time when Grady would be on duty, which was most of the day, since he held his position to be one he had no desire to delegate. If he saw her heading down the side of the staircase to the study he might turn a blind eye: he'd already shown he would help where he could. Provided there was no sudden return by Henry, as had happened before, she trusted him not to tell. The risk was not just discovery; there was still the threat of Harry Spafford, given no promise of Henry's was worth the breath employed to utter it. Get caught and this could become a certainty, with the fate she so dreaded, which could descend upon her and no one would lift a finger to help.

Stood on the landing, listening out for movement, she felt like a foolish child, especially after a few downward steps were taken, to be quickly retracted when she heard a noise, this happening twice and with opportunity slipping away. Heart beating, Elisabeth resolved to be bold, making her way to the hall without guile, to skip down the passage when she found it empty. On tiptoe she approached the study door, which swung open silently. Once through she closed it with care.

On the north side of the house, even with wide and high windows, it was a room cut off from much of the daylight by high trees. For once there was no fire in the grate, not even embers, this an indication her brother was to be out for some time. Sadly, the same factors which had defeated her previously did so once more. Too many ledgers to study, those she did all relating to domestic matters; the desk drawers again locked, nothing on the desk of interest except . . .

Half a dozen quills sat in a pot alongside writing paper in a box, bits of sealing wax in a tray along with a shaker of sand. The idea she could take the means to write foundered on the inkwell, heavy and sure to be missed, so there was no alternative but to sit down and pen something here. There was no doubt as to what needed to be imparted, her sham marriage and being close to a prisoner, albeit she was required to be brief, which eschewed any chance to polish her composition.

Addressing it presented no problem – she'd corresponded extensively with Dirley from the West Indies – but there was no way to seal the letter once folded, due to a lack of anything to heat the wax. There being several half-used sticks, Elisabeth simply took one and, once she had, with great care, blown the sand off the letter and into the fireplace, slipped out. There would be candles tonight, so sealing the letter would present no difficulty. The problem was how to get it out of the house and sent on its way, and she could only pray Dirley would act upon it.

Having just got her hand on the lower newel post, spinning to take the first riser, the door to the servant's quarters opened and Grady came out. A short stare ended when he spun round and went back the way he had come, which had her run up the stairs. Back in her bedroom, door locked, the means of sending it occupied her thoughts, a task seemingly insurmountable. Yet it cheered her that a step had been taken; she was fighting back and nothing could be better for her spirits.

Unbeknown to Elisabeth, Grady had appeared in the hall having been alerted to the imminent arrival of his master. Henry thus came very close to catching his sister for a second time. Once indoors and disrobed he went straight to his study. Irritated at the lack of a fire, he nevertheless sat down to write the letter to Dirley Tulkington he'd been composing in his head on the way home.

Brazier awoke before the others, half his upper body so stiff he experienced difficulty in getting up, quick to note Zachary had yet to return. There was no need of a mirror to tell him he was filthy, added to which he had any number of scratches where he had caught brambles and bits of tree in the dark. Going outside to relieve himself, the position of the sun had him reckon it to be midday. Something to drink and a wash came first: raising the well bucket was even harder than it had been the day before, but at least he assuaged a thirst, before splashing a face he suspected was covered in grime, wincing as the water stung his minor abrasions.

Making for the bench, he sat down to plot a course of action. No doubt Dutchy and Peddler thought there was a plan, but they were mistaken. There had been no point in forming one until the overnight action had worked out, which had been a long shot from the outset. Looking confident, as he had before they'd set out, was a habit, one honed by every naval officer needing respect from the crew: for the captain of a warship, a show of certainty was paramount, especially when going into action.

Now he had three bodies and the need to work out the best way to employ them. The aim was to ward off any more attempts on his life as well as to get Betsey free of her brother's clutches. A straight trade he put aside: he had no trust any arrangement would be adhered to and, once Tulkington had regained possession of the corpses, they would just disappear. Badly played, he himself might do so as well. As he weighed possibilities, it occurred to him how much Henry Tulkington must care for his reputation. For all his nefarious activities, it seemed to Brazier he played the part of the successful country gentleman. Could what he now had be used to dent such a carapace of respectability? He was weighing the notion when the call came out, a shout from Zachary to say he and his now loaded donkey were back.

The horses were excited by the prospect of being fed; he was more taken by the small bottle he was given. Cap off, a goodly drop of the laudanum was taken and, by the time the oats had been mixed and consumed, Edward Brazier was in a blissful pain-free state, though one making any form of communication futile.

Not too far distant, maybe not more than half a mile, a group of Hawker's men were combing the woodland through which the villains who robbed them had made their way, the horses leaving a trail obvious to even the worst tracker, and circuitous it was. In time this took them out onto the open grass-covered marshland, where the trail disappeared. John Hawker, on a borrowed horse, found them as well as their lack of success, which allowed him to take some of his still boiling anger out on those who could not reply.

CHAPTER EIGHTEEN

Sitting twiddling his thumbs all day was not John Cottin's way. He had paid for and dealt with the correspondence from his Westerham office, letters which had arrived early, mostly enquiries from other districts of Kent, none of which were serious enough to require his presence, but as yet nothing from William Pitt. Allowances had to be made, since it was to be routed through his office and sent on under a new cover to avoid his making contact becoming public. Garlick served him luncheon, in his usual way, probing to see if anything had occurred worth tucking away, only to lay out the last course of cheese visibly disappointed; Cottin refused to respond to his enquiries about the mail he'd received or to relate anything regarding his supposed trip to Dover.

Feeling the need for air, he decided on a walk, first along Beach Street, which was just as named, a twin row of weather-battered stone houses either side of a narrow roadway, those on the west side containing a surprising number of taverns: every corner seemed to house a drinking den. Anything else, on both sides, seemed tumbledown constructs, with bits of wooden extensions added in a random fashion to an original building, the whole showing signs of dilapidation. These clearly provided living space for multiple families, being full to the brim with noisy human occupation, seeming more akin to crowded rookeries. This spoke to a man like John Cottin of as much criminality here as in the similar slum dwellings he'd been taken to see on a short visit to London.

Between each building backing on to the shore, a narrow alleyway provided access to the strand so he, more than once, strolled down to stand on the sloping pebbles, there to marvel at the sheer quantity of folk involved in the activities necessary to serve the massed vessels in the anchorage. Drying fishing nets, lobster pots and crab creels told of another occupation, no doubt catches sold from the tables heaving with produce on the street behind. These were manned by a particular breed: thick-armed and broad-beamed women, generally toothless, with raucous voices, spouting foul language, who looked tougher than their menfolk.

Further wandering took him back down to the Lower Valley Road and, in moving to pass the Old Playhouse, he observed it was open. Curious, he wandered past the two club-bearing toughs guarding the entrance, neither of whom spared him a glance. The room just inside and to the left contained numerous tables, at which a few men were playing cards, others merely drinking and talking. He took a seat intent on just sitting and observing, quickly approached by a serving girl, who took his order for a flagon of wine.

There was much pleasure to be had for a man like Cottin in examining his fellow humans in such a setting, the game being to seek to place something of their nature and occupations, also perhaps to try and discern what could be their secrets. Sea captains (he assumed their rank) were easy and numerous – there was an archaic quality to their dress, as if they feared not to be identified: long waistcoats and wigs, oversized hats, heavily cuffed coats of various blues and reds, with many a highly polished brass button to hint at prosperity. Others he took to be local tradesfolk and it was diverting to seek to place their trade by the sobriety or showiness of their garb.

Such examination ceased as Saoirse appeared in the doorway, looking, if anything, more beautiful than she had in her own parlour. She was popular, which came as no surprise, nor did the number of her customers willing to engage her in conversation. But before entering, she'd seen him in her survey of the room; when it came to moving around, would he be subjected, as others were, to her undoubted charms, or deliberately ignored?

After his interview, Cottin had left her with a feeling of disquiet, sure of there being things she was not willing to divulge, not that he could pin down anything definite. If the proprietor passed him by now, the truth of the supposition would be confirmed. If she did stop to exchange a few words, it would give him a chance to question her in a more informal setting, which might reveal something of interest. So without seeking to catch her eye, he kept her location marked as he slowly sipped his wine until she approached his table.

'Mr Cottin, you do the Old Playhouse great honour.'

'I'm sure you say the same to all your guests.'

The smile was engaging, the Irish lilt of her voice enchanting. 'Sure, only to those making their first call.'

For a man not at ease in the company of the fair sex – he had a tendency to stutter – Cottin surprised himself in the articulacy of what came from him next. 'I don't suppose this extends to sharing a glass of wine with them?'

He was not to know the agreement, as well as her taking a chair, was driven by curiosity: Saoirse was as eager to pump him as he was to examine and compare their previous encounter. Cottin's problem was what to say next, this leading to a hiatus accompanied by a near blush. The words which emerged, when he broke it, were singularly inappropriate.

'Heard from Captain Brazier at all?'

'I have not,' came with a disarming smile.

Having chosen the wrong avenue, there was no choice but to

continue and, in truth, it was proper he should: duty came first. 'I nearly managed to get hold of one of the men who occupied your property. He was staying at the Navy Yard along with Captain Brazier and a trio of others, but he was the only one left there. A blackamoor, according to Admiral Braddock's clerk.'

The response had an air of vague memory. 'I seem to recall he had such a fellow as a servant.'

'Well he was a slippery cove. Ran off before I could question him.'

'A strange thing to do.'

'Is it, Miss Riorden? It seems everyone is avoiding me, including Brazier himself, which is a pity, as I feel it is he, and he alone, who can properly advance my enquiries, and perhaps he should do so for his own well-being.'

'I fail to see your meaning?'

'Really? What if I were to say to you, given the rumours regarding an association with William Pitt, that he was surely the intended victim of the riot?'

No reply, just a small sideways tilt of the head as if to say, 'You may be right.'

'Then, is it not also the case, his speaking to me may offer some protection? Anyone wishing him harm will know we have spoken but not what was said.'

The fellow, short of stature and slim, who appeared in the doorway, stopped dead, filling the space and staring hard at Cottin. This obliged the sheriff to look in his direction, in turn causing Saoirse to turn round. Much to his annoyance, she immediately stood up, bestowing on him another smile, one hinting at regret.

'I have matters to attend to, Mr Cottin. Enjoy your wine.'

She went to the door and the fellow still framed there. After a quick verbal exchange of some kind, what came next was pealing laughter before, with linked arms, they disappeared.

* * *

206

Vincent Flaherty was mightily thrown when he found out who Saoirse had been sitting with. His face must have given away his feelings, for Saoirse laughed at both him and what she knew to be misplaced jealousy. Yet he felt he had cause, in seeing the same fellow who'd been an early morning visitor, not named but immediately taken upstairs just days past. On another occasion he might have got a wigging for his suspicions, just before being shown the way out to the street, but not this day. Instead he was led to the same private quarters, though any hopes raised of the familiarity he craved were soon dashed when up came the subject of Edward Brazier.

'This Cottin has got the right of it.'

'He's safe where he is, Saoirse, well away from Deal and no one knowing but us.'

The response was larded with irony. 'Sure, you'll be telling me he'll be stayin' there and letting bygones be bygones.'

'You're right; soon as he's fit enough, he'll go after his lady again. He as good as told me so.'

'Which means it might be an advantage if it's known he's talked to the sheriff.'

Flaherty could see immediately what she was driving at: if Edward wouldn't give up and appeared back in Deal, it was highly likely Tulkington would try even harder to either drive him to leave or to find another way to have him killed. But throw such a highly placed law officer into the mix and anybody seeking to act would have to be damned careful.

'I think he should be told what we're thinking. Then he can make up his own mind.'

'You seem very concerned for him.'

This was as much a question as a statement of the obvious and it came with a look that failed to disguise its true purpose: what are you feeling for Brazier? Saoirse knew Vincent carried a torch for her, one which no amount of amused refutation seemed to dent. In part it was her own fault he persisted in what was futile.

'I think of Edward as a friend and one in need of help. I think you should go to him and recommend he make contact.'

'I'm to be your messenger?' was uttered with a degree of pique.

'Are you suggesting I go in your place? You have the time for this, I do not.'

He would agree, Saoirse knew it, and she wondered if she was abusing what should be no more than another friendship. But how could she help how Vincent felt?

'And I would say soonest would be best.' Saoirse faked a sudden thought. 'It might be a notion to take his men, Joe and Cocky, with you.'

And for this she had a strong motive. Logan was no problem, but blackamoors were few and far between in Deal. Joe Lascelles, coming and going from the Old Playhouse, was too obviously risky for him, but also for her.

When he came back to full consciousness, a drowsy Edward Brazier put aside any temptation to indulge himself with another drop of tincture of laudanum: he knew too well it was addictive, having been warned off it by his father. He'd also met many, both at sea and ashore, who were slave to the opiate. He recalled the balm his father concocted, one which the Navy Yard surgeon had also administered after his beating, a wonderful salve for pain, though the notion of acquiring some was akin to asking for the moon.

Zachary had got Dutchy and Peddler chopping wood, probably the sound which had roused him. Stiffly upright, he took a deep drink of water, necessary with a drug-induced thirst. This slaked, he went to exchange a few words with the woodcutters, before passing on to where Zachary was mending the netting round his vegetable plot, set up to keep out rabbits. Idle conversation about cultivation established he had rigged snares on the route the creatures took from their burrow to his patch, which provided food as well as security, while some old cracked crockery filled with ale served to keep at bay the slugs.

It was mid-afternoon and warm, with the buzz and sight of insect life pleasurable. Zachary was easy to converse with, as long as a certain subject was avoided. Given Brazier's background, and the parental possession of a kitchen garden, there was a great deal which could be shared regarding planting, growing and protecting. Yet, with the way his mind was working, he was unable to stay off the sensitive topic entirely.

'Was Mr Venables a gardener?' The shoulders stiffened at the name, no immediate reply being forthcoming. 'There's no hint in his diaries.'

'The plot was kept by his mother. I took it on after she passed away.'

'You had a good life together, I take it, with reasonable comfort?'

'We were favoured by God's abundance most years and wondered at our sins in those less fruitful.'

'I cannot help wondering what Mr Venables would say, if I'd been able to tell him what I told you. Surely it would have confirmed what he thought of Cottington Court. It might even have caused him to tell me everything he knew, everything I think he told you.'

'I swore an oath on the Good Book.'

'I wonder if the God we worship would want us to use what we know to fight evil, which would make any oath, however sworn, worthy of breaking.' A grunt. 'I also wonder, given my own experience, if Samuel Lovell didn't just ride off one day and not return. The journals suggest something bad happened. I think it may be the case he was disposed of, for what reason I do not know, but I'm prepared to guess.'

Zachary stood up to stretch but he would not look at Brazier.

'The Lord will judge those who commit such sins.'

Brazier was not going to say his own conviction did not extend to such a belief. There was much about the Anglican faith to which he happily subscribed, the major festivals especially. But his father had been a sceptic on religion, if not rabid, one who took exception to some of the more fanciful notions advanced by the clergy, and

Brazier had inherited this scepticism, having, among others, a limited credence in the notion of Judgement Day.

'You do not think those who sin should pay in life. Let me tell you what I came across once at sea, Zachary: a ship full of people of your race, kept in appalling conditions, deprived of food, water and enough space to lie down, lying in their own excrement, men and women together, the latter no doubt playthings for the slavers.'

'I have heard of this and thank God I was born into slavery, not transported as my forbearers must have been.'

'What of those doing the transporting, does your deep faith run to forgiveness of such people, leaving retribution to God? What of the man who was master to my man Joe, who was so afraid of what he would face for drawing white blood, he risked swimming in waters where he had more chance of drowning than surviving?'

It had been a whole two years before Joe told Brazier his story, when HMS *Diomede* was on her way home and he was sure he was safe.

'If we had not had a boat in the water, there to observe the trim of the ship as we shifted stores, Joe would have died, a victim as much as those I found aboard the slave ship. I wanted to string up the crew and release the slaves. How would God judge such an act?'

There was no joy in making Zachary uncomfortable, but there was a need.

'Would you, if you could smite them, not do so? If I was to tell you I can get justice for myself and perhaps even for the man Mr Venables so revered, would you not see your oath as breakable?'

Zachary straightened up again to look Brazier right in the eye, this followed by a glance over his shoulder. 'Rider coming, sir.'

And there was Vincent Flaherty, on his heels Cocky and Joe, enough to bring the probing to an end. Yet it had not been entirely wasted, there being things Zachary, in his bodily reactions, had not denied. There was something odd about the relationship between Lovell and Venables, one not too hard to take a stab at, which was the truth he thought Zachary was protecting. So be it: that was something to which Brazier was indifferent.

He moved away to close with Vincent, who once dismounted, took from his saddlebag a mahogany writing case and handed it over, with the information it had come from Saoirse. Also passed on was the fact she'd been talking to the High Sheriff again and what their thinking was.

'Hence the means to write. He's lodged at the Three Kings and neither of us reckoned it a good place to talk. But if you drop him a note for a meeting somewhere else, say my yard, then it lessens the risk of it getting about.'

'How little you know Garlick.'

'For all love, no one's saying you should put your name on it. Leave it blank and I'll see it delivered.'

'Perhaps. Come with me, I want to show you something.'

There was no waiting for agreement, Brazier was striding towards the byre and behind it the pile of manure. Once there, the three bundles were pointed out, who they were and how he had come by them, in the middle of which Vincent called down divine intervention and crossed himself.

'The question now is what to do with them. You coming here has helped me to see a possibility.'

'Which is?'

'Dump them in St George's churchyard tonight, to be found in the morning. Let's see what your sheriff makes of that.'

'What makes you think it will aid you?'

'I told you, one of the corpses is Harry Spafford. The last time Deal saw him alive he was being dragged off by John Hawker, witnessed by Dutchy and half the town. Harry's father and Trotter were known to be Hawker's rivals in smuggling, so who will be held to account for them being murdered if not Hawker?'

'Whatever is implied will be denied without proof.'

211

'Even if I add the name of Upton?'

'And where he came to you from, surely?'

'I'll hold back on that, for use later. You may be right about the lack of proof, and there's no doubt Tulkington has the town in his pocket. But there's a saying you will have heard of, Vincent, which is this. If you want to wake a beast, you must first rattle the cage.'

'The letter to the sheriff?'

'Bring the case indoors and I shall pen it now, but I shan't meet with him yet, that will come later. What he wants is a name and this I can give him, added to how Upton happened to be in Quebec House: my extending charity to a dismissed servant, but no more.'

'I don't perceive the purpose.'

'You will in time, Vincent, but for now think on this. Tulkington will soon find out I've revealed Upton's name and I am guessing he'll think the sheriff knows from where he was dismissed. What if he tries to find out?'

This was greeted with a mystified shake of the head and Flaherty was not really enlightened when Brazier added. 'In battle at sea, Vincent, it is vital to gain the weather gauge, to have the wind in your favour, which gives the power of decision, when to attack. That's what I seek now because Tulkington has been making all the running and is comfortable. Let's see how he behaves when the shoe is on the other foot.'

'The risk?'

'Is there one? He would happily see me dead. Now let us find Zachary – I need to know where I can get hold of a flatbed cart and I'm hoping he has a neighbour who can provide one.'

CHAPTER NINETEEN

In so many ways Cottington Court was self-sufficient and, given Henry's misanthropy, there were few visitors outside one regular caller, a stranger who did no more than enter the house and leave with no indication of his purpose. Wood for the fires came readily with annual thinning and pollarding; there were vegetables from the kitchen garden and game from the woods, while the home farms not only provided fowl, they reared cattle and pigs, which, through the use of the Tulkington slaughterhouse, ensured a ready supply of meat. Likewise, flour from Henry's mills was delivered by carters he directly employed, with there being only one exception: the supply of coal.

This was something Sarah Lovell insisted be used in the communal rooms, her complaint being wood created too much mess, one always made as though she had any hand in the clearing away of it. Henry, who liked the wood fire in his study, didn't even notice; as long as there was a blaze in any grate by which he took up a stand, it was fine. Rare were the days, even in the summer months, when none were lit anywhere in the house, if for no other reason than to keep at bay any chance of encroaching damp. It also ensured and warded off complaints by Henry, ever in fear of a chill.

The fuel used was sea coal, lumps garnered from what was washed up on the beach, in what was one of the lowest local occupations. The poorest inhabitants of the East Kent coast collected what they required for their own use to heat their hovels in winter. But, as was common, where a coin was to be made, there were those who sent out women, children and those unable to find other employment, to gather up what was in abundance along an eight-mile strand, this bagged and sold to those too grand to undertake their own collecting, both within the town and the surrounding countryside.

The crunching sound of wheels on an open cart alerted Elisabeth to its presence as she was coming in from her morning walk. It was heading up the drive, loaded with filthy sacks, being driven by a fellow covered in black dust. This was of enough interest for her to stay on the parterre, seemingly examining the formal patterns of flowers, which, at this time of year, were coming in to full bloom. The cart turned away from the ornamental gates to go round the side of the house where, she was vaguely aware, lay a shed in which the coal was stored.

She suddenly found herself contemplating what was the longest of shots, a truly desperate throw, yet there was a lack of alternatives, every other avenue having been considered and dismissed. No one going off the estate, and there were few, given the lack of necessity, would risk taking the letter she'd written and now had tucked into her pinafore pocket, along with the money she likewise dare not leave in her room. Discovery would not only be instant dismissal, but word would be spread in the district of the miscreant being an unreliable employee, with foreseeable consequences.

The idea of approaching the carter herself was risible: not only was it beneath her social station, the sight of her and the suggestion of any request would be likely to scare the man rigid. Nor did he have dealings with Grady, which took away the only person known to be in sympathy.

'Happy to cut a bouquet for your room, ma'am.'

Lifting her head from these thoughts and the flowers, she realised the man addressing her was Creevy, a fellow of unprepossessing features with whom she'd never had any kind of relationship. She'd seen him with Henry, in the kind of hunched pose of the groveler, so had him down as her brother's man, but he sparked a train of thought: coal, as well as wood, was used in the kitchens. If the division socially between employers and servants was absolute in terms of exchange, neither held the other to be mysterious. Below stairs, they knew what was going on in the better parts of the house, while those to whom they tended also had a good notion of their lives and relationships, none more than one who had grown up in their orbit.

Creevy, in his obsequious offer, reminded her of how different he was and always had been from Lionel Upton, the man discharged for seeking to aid her. If Upton thought it a secret, Elisabeth knew, indeed the whole house probably knew, he'd had a sort of arrangement with the cook. To call it romantic would have fallen foul of the reticence with which they both approached anything like mutual attraction. Yet she was sure the pair had an understanding, one never quite taken to nuptials, because to do so would require the permission of their master. Her father would surely have bestowed his blessing, but they left it too late to ask. She could understand any reluctance to approach Henry.

'Which would be most kind, Creevy. If you could have them sent to my room.'

There was a cast in the man's eyes, added to a twitch of the lips, an expression which said he knew what was what in said room. Elisabeth wondered what images he was conjuring up in his mind – uncomfortable ones for her, surely – which had her move away quickly. As usual, Grady was waiting, even on a warm day in which she'd worn only a shawl, but there was no sign of her Aunt Sarah. She no longer automatically appeared on her return, done previously with a searching stare, as if she could discern anything untoward which might have taken place in the time her niece had been out of sight, misdemeanours to be reported to

Henry. Habit had rendered it an imposition to be often skipped so, after a smiling exchange with Grady, she was free to go to her room.

At the base of what she was about to attempt was the feeling the Cottington servants didn't just feel uncomfortable under the thumb of their master, but they actively disliked him. It was an impression, no more; the way Grady was acting now and what Upton had done before his dismissal gave it credence. If it truly was the case, how far would they go to thwart him, one in particular who had just cause?

'Would it be in order for me to have a word with Cook?'

He was surprised: the woman he called 'The Loveless' was the one who oversaw the arrangements for what was supplied by the kitchen, yet any member of the family was free to go wherever they wished. The fact Elisabeth had not done so, content to leave what was a chore to her aunt, might raise a question, but this gave him no reason to discourage her.

'If you wish to do so, Miss Elisabeth, I'm sure she'd be pleased to see you. Bunty often talks of how you were in and out of the kitchen when you were young.'

'If my aunt asks, would you tell her I'm in my room?' Smiling eyes went glassy as his gaze was lifted to a spot above her head, the voice sonorous. 'Of course.'

Still avoiding her eye, he stood aside to let her pass to the door behind which lay his domain and that of the cook. Moving swiftly, Elisabeth, once through, skipped to the kitchen, to enter a place she was ashamed to admit not having visited since her return from Jamaica. It spoke to her of bad manners but entering in apology would not do. She uttered a loud greeting and added a beaming smile.

'Bunty, how long is it since I have come here?' The surprised cook never got a chance to reply, her scullery maids half-curtsying in greeting. 'Shame on me for not doing so before.'

'Miss Elisabeth,' was uttered with surprise, bordering on shocked delight.

216

A woman of short stature and considerable width, with a lot more flesh now than Elisabeth recalled, she was even more surprised to be kissed on both cheeks, the second peck, on an ear unseen by the maids, coming with a whisper, part covered by the sound of sacks being emptied into the coal shed close by.

'I have a letter regarding Lionel.'

The mere fact of her using his given name caused astonishment, which had Bunty put her hands to her ample rosy cheeks, to see a throw of the eyes, indicating the maids should be sent out so they could talk. Elisabeth knew her hopes depended on one thing: had Upton confided in Bunty in regard to his intention to help her? If he had not, then this ploy would struggle.

'You two,' Bunty warbled. 'There's plenty to do in tidying the pantry, so away with you. Miss Elisabeth and I have much to catch up on.'

Another dip of the knees and they were gone, with Elisabeth taking Bunty by the shoulders, her head forward and close. 'You know what he sought to do for me?'

'I know the price he paid, Miss Elisabeth.'

'Did he tell you our arrangement?' A mystified look was enough and, there being no time for lengthy explanation, she took the letter from her pinafore pocket. 'I sent him to the home of Captain Brazier, who I knew would take him in. He will also look after him, for my sake. I have here a letter for the captain to make sure he knows I wish Lionel to be treated as he would a servant of his own.'

Shoving it into Bunty's hand, it was inevitable she would look at it but, since she lacked the ability to read, a fact known to Elisabeth from childhood, it would mean nothing. The shame she felt at the deceit had to be measured against the need, and besides, the last and most risky part was yet to be proposed.

'The coalman is delivering – do you know the man?' A nod. 'Well?'

A more emphatic nod. 'He'll be in for a bite when he's done, allas does, an' we chat about this an' that.'

'I want you to give him this half a guinea.' Sensing hesitation she added, 'I'm in danger, Bunty, great danger.' A plump hand came out to affectionately and caringly take hers, making her feel even worse. 'The letter must somehow be posted. I dare not try to have it delivered in case the captain's house is being watched. If I can get away from here, perhaps you and Lionel . . .' Her intense look told Bunty they might be reunited, this followed by a manufactured snuffle. 'Will you help me, please?'

The held hand was tightly squeezed. 'Best go, Miss Elisabeth, case anyone comes through the door. Leave the coalman to me, an' bless you for your care of my Lionel.'

Elisabeth kissed her cheeks again, as much to hide her expression as to confer agreement. Then she was gone, getting to her room without being seen, there to sit and wonder, with wet eyes, at what kind of person circumstances had made her become.

Cottin was far from pleased to receive Edward Brazier's note: it did not run to the description of a letter, being short and to the point. But it told him the name he was after, as well as the occupation of the corpse, but not much more other than he was an innocent victim of a crime, aimed in Brazier's direction, by certain parties not identified.

'Damn you, man, if you know the culprits, why don't you say so!'

It was a reasonable outburst to make, but it did leave Garlick wondering at the meaning. He had taken delivery from Vincent Flaherty and handed over to Cottin the folded and sealed paper, as always the exterior examined closely for clues, usually the identity of the sender; those he drank with liked to know these things. This one had none, and a good stare was not enough to see through to what was inside. He had to move sharpish as he heard his guest approaching the door on creaking floorboards, getting out of sight on tiptoe, to be back in his hutch before Cottin made the hallway.

Without any acknowledgement, the sheriff stomped out the door, making for the business premises of the coroner, who owned a sail loft and rope-walk behind the Navy Yard, which provided commodities much required by departing ships, as well as – very likely – a good income. Cavell's office looked out on the making of the ropes, with great coils of all thicknesses, from whip lines to anchor cables, stored and available for sale, as well as the pair of machines, counter-twisting the hemp.

'Cheaper to buy them here than in London docks, sir, much cheaper.'

Cottin was not in the least interested in ropes or their use, even less in their price, nor was he impressed by Cavell's reluctance to close his office door so they could talk over the noise of manufacture, obliging him to employ a near shout.

'I have the name of the poor soul found in Quebec House.'

'Indeed,' came with no excessive interest nor much volume.

'His name is Lionel Upton.' Raised eyebrows rendered it unnecessary for Cavell to plead ignorance. 'Accommodated by Captain Brazier as an act of charity.'

'Not always a kindness, too often a waste and, in this case, certainly not so.'

'I was wondering if we could institute some enquiries to find out more about him.'

'Man's dead, Mr Cottin. Good to have his identity, but what does it do but serve to put a name to the plot in which he will be interred?'

'What about relatives?'

'Ah yes,' Cavell sighed, as if such things were unknown to him.

'I suggest some printed posters asking for information.'

'On the town's expense?' hinted at reluctance. Seeing his visitor was determined, he added, 'If you think it necessary.'

219

'Mr Cavell, can I remind you this poor fellow died as the result of a crime? Someone is responsible for his death and the person or persons should be found.'

'You know, Mr Cottin, there's no need to shout.'

Edward Brazier was writing another letter, this time to Sarah Lovell, in which he enquired anonymously if she recalled a particular friend of her husband's, a man called Venables, now deceased. He related he was in possession of the man's diaries and was drawn to certain entries with dates provided, to then enquire whether the suggestion something untoward had befallen Samuel met with her recollection. The exact date of his disappearance was then referred to with the mention of the definite and binding arrangement he had made but didn't meet, added to the fact she knew: no sight nor sound of him had been heard of since.

He concluded with the promise further letters would follow, giving a more complete explanation of what he had come to suspect, with the final declaration of sympathy for the fact she was obliged to reside in the same house as one of the persons probably responsible for her husband's disappearance, as well as whatever fate had befallen him.

The day, for his barge crew, had been spent waiting for Zachary while carrying out a list of tasks he had left behind to be completed, the owner off to borrow a cart from a neighbour and willingly so, taking with him a packhorse to do the pulling; if he couldn't bury the dead, getting them off his property, to a place unspecified, was the next best thing.

There was a degree of fretting about time: Brazier wanted to be much closer to Deal so he could choose his moment to act, which would be in darkness when all was shuttered, and a cart would take time to cover the distance. When Zachary returned, the unpleasant task of lifting on the bodies was carried out. An old tarpaulin, also borrowed, was then used to conceal them but not before they were liberally scattered with dozens of rosemary stalks from an old and gnarled bush to mitigate the smell. Peddler drove the cart with Brazier at his side while the others rode.

As a matter of course Sidney Cavell had sent round to his fellow members of the town council, those who'd met with the High Sheriff on arrival, the news of Cottin's discovery and his request for posters. The work of the day was far from finished when he was visited by Tobias Sowerby, who insisted they speak with the office door closed.

'There's an Upton at Cottington Court, John. Henry Tulkington's head groom – met him any number of times in Acton's day, when there was a regular hunt.'

'A long time ago, Tobias. Might not still be there.'

'He was hale the last time I saw him, which was when Henry's sister came back from Jamaica and had her fete, not so long past.'

'Related, d'ye reckon?' was calmly posed.

'No idea, but it's possible. These posters Cottin wants, that's not a direction to send folks in, himself in particular.'

Cavell pondered for a bit, which left his visitor wondering how much he knew about Henry's affairs, not a subject of general discussion, more of knowing looks and avoidance of comment. Not as much as Sowerby, certainly, who was commercially involved, but it would be close to impossible, in a society as interconnected as theirs, not to have some inkling.

'Haven't done anything yet, Tobias. Happen it would be best to keep it that way.'

'Thought the bugger would be well gone by now.'

Cavell finally showed some passion. 'Should be, too. It don't make sense him hanging about.'

The thought was not voiced by either man, but it was there. What if Cottin knew more than he was telling, information that had given him a reason to come to Deal as well as to stay? Neither man had any certainty about who'd set the riot in motion, but they'd picked up the William Pitt rumour, which narrowed the field to a name no one wished to mention.

There was no guarantee the coal delivery man would take Elisabeth's letter, and going back to the kitchen to enquire right away was out of the question: she had been lucky once and it was tempting fate to try again too soon. Even if Bunty, who had intimated she knew him well, had paid him her money, was he honest? He could just pocket it, do nothing and it need never be known. Did he have the wit to post it, which was likely not something he was accustomed to?

All these possibilities rattled around, mixed in with the promises Elisabeth made to herself as a penance for her deceit: should she get free of Henry and marry Edward, when they set up home, there would be places for both Upton and Bunty where they would happily bless their union.

CHAPTER TWENTY

The jostle of the cart, on less than smooth surfaces, common to the kind of country tracks avoided by too much human contact, did nothing for Brazier's shoulder, though even the pain caused could do nothing to dent his mood. He was acting not reacting, producing the same feelings he'd experienced in the service when a fight was in the offing. A tingling of anticipation, with none of the prior concern he'd previously felt as, in common with everyone else aboard ship who could write, he penned a farewell to his still living loved ones, in case he should not survive.

It was possible, given the lack of conversation from Peddler, to reflect on a career in which he was well aware he'd been lucky. Many naval officers went through their entire service without being given the opportunity to distinguish themselves in battle; others granted such good fortune failed miserably to shine where he had succeeded. He'd taken part in the battle off Porto Praya in the Azores, this followed by the successful cutting out of half a dozen Dutch merchantmen at the Cape of Good Hope. The campaign was topped for him by his being promoted to post captain for his part in the capture of the forts at Trincomalee.

He was feeling confident, yet it was tempered, as it always must be, with the knowledge things could so very easily go wrong. The need to be able to respond and adjust was paramount, so his tendency towards recollection faded the nearer the party got to Deal and this took him back to a critical examination of his intentions. It wasn't just Tulkington who was too comfortable in his existence, it was the whole town, or at least the prosperous citizens who turned a blind eye to nefarious practices, not that the lower orders would be exempt from blame. If the rumours and the riot had been set in motion by Tulkington, they had been too willing and likely too drunk to act as his useful idiots.

He wanted to throw so much grit into their works so everyone, high and low, would be affected. If the demise of poor Upton could bring down on them a high sheriff, what would result from the discovery of a trio of murdered bodies? It should let in daylight where it was needed but, more importantly, and Cottin was right in this, any more attempts on his person would become too dangerous to contemplate. Even if he could evade involvement in any enquiries, Betsey's brother would need to show great care or risk attracting attention.

It would also, given he had knowledge of the truth, put him in a position to pressurise Betsey's brother and force him to free her, given he had no deep interest in the suppression of smuggling. Perhaps heads would roll for the deaths of Trotter and the Spaffords, which would be a good thing and, if he could help bring people to justice, he would do so. But his primary aim of getting Betsey away from Cottington Court came before anything.

It was easy to toy with the notion of taking revenge and he had done so sitting on Zachary's sunlit bench – if not on Tulkington, then on Hawker. Betsey, even if she might now despise him, would hardly take to her brother being slain and he would have to be, there being no way such a lily-livered stick of misery would face up to him in a proper duel. With Hawker, the act of killing would be much harder, given what would have to be overcome in terms of numbers: involving his old shipmates he could not contemplate.

To do it alone, without drawing down on his head the very law he was hoping to use for his own ends, would be near to impossible. When cogitating on this, he'd acknowledged his thinking lacked the kind of nobility common in many of the books he'd read, but this was flesh and blood not pen and ink. He declined to be a knight in shining armour, taking down evil; let the likes of William Pitt take on the role for which he had been elected.

'Getting near too dark to see the road clear, your honour.'

It being lined with trees in leaf, Peddler's observation was acknowledged, but he reckoned on there being not far to go, while the horse pulling the cart had keener eyesight than any human. They'd come by a circuitous route, aiming for the fields to the west of the town, where root vegetables were the crop, still grown in feudal strips. Visibility would be restored when they emerged to clear and moonlit skies. At twilight, those tending their patch would cease to work and head back to their hearths. Out of the arc of activity centred on the Lower Valley Road, they would be left with a view of the lights of the town, sat in darkness, only moving to act when those lights were extinguished.

Given the number of places dispensing drink and carnal gratification, added to the endless supply of visiting merchant seaman, not to forget inhabitants who were great topers themselves, Deal was a town to stay up later than most. Having got to where Brazier wanted them to be, he and Peddler got off the box, the others dismounted and they sat away from the cart, for the rosemary was only so effective in countering the smell. His old barge crew once more talked of old times and adventures or, more often of misadventures, three of them being footloose. Dutchy had a wife and family in a house on the Fal Estuary at Restronguet Point and had taken to boat repairing once he was paid off from HMS *Diomede*. All had come home with a decent sum from the recapture of the Spanish plate ship, taken back from the French villain who'd been in league with Admiral Hassall.

It was money spent on pleasure by Peddler and Cocky, while Dutchy's had been spread over an extended and needy family. Joe Lascelles, in a strange land, with an even odder climate, had husbanded his until, settled enough, he could seek employment. There was a degree of embarrassment for Brazier when the subject came up: a naval captain made many multiples of what was paid to common seamen in prize money, in his case enough to never have to be concerned about being out of funds again, a comparison not mentioned. He was paying them to be here now, which, with his day-to-day coin getting low, would need to be addressed.

To the question of another ship, which came up eventually and was gently pursued, their old commander could only demur, at the same time wondering what they knew of the circumstances surrounding the death of Admiral Hassall. It was a truth well acknowledged nothing could be kept secret from the lower deck: they could hear a whisper through six inches of oak. It was also true they'd have a care with whom they shared anything, and it would certainly not be raised in Brazier's presence. Cheering was the reassurance, as soon as he had another command, they would seek to join him.

'If you'd have us, your honour,' Peddler suggested, only half-joking.

'How could I expect to manage without you?'

'Ye'd hae a struggle, right enough,' Cocky hooted.

In time the lights began to dim, first those in the houses, obliged by the municipality to keep going a candle in a first-floor window to illuminate the street below. Unheard would be a watchman doing his rounds, telling the citizens the duty was no longer required. This left the glow of other lights, torches and the much bigger ship-sized lanterns at the entrances to the various places of entertainment. In time they too were extinguished as Deal went to bed and the visiting sailors either returned to their vessel, passed out in a doorway, or bedded a whore.

The cart was slowly manoeuvred round the growing strips to get as close to St George's churchyard as possible, in silence because there were several free-standing and substantial houses on the town periphery, each with dogs set to warn of intruders. An occasional bark was soon taken up by other canines, to crescendo and then die down, the common sound of the night which should cause no alarm.

The first task was to clear the graveyard of those who used it as a place to sleep, the gin-addicted urchins. Brazier wanted them rousted out with threats of violence, though he was hoping none would be required: the waifs were there through circumstances not choice. Also, it had to be carried out without too much noise: shouting and yelling would alert those on the nearside of the Lower Valley Road, though most were places of business not dwellings.

Bandanas were used to hide faces, even Joe's, with rough staves from Zachary's woodpile employed to threaten a group of ragamuffins quite used to being harried. They also had a grapevine which warned of trouble, so youngsters in their dozens fled at the first sign of disturbance; in such a precarious existence it was a group always at risk from people sick of their activities, who would take up cudgels from time to time in an attempt to curb what they brought to the town: petty thieving and the dipping of pockets.

Some could not be stirred, too intoxicated on brain-rotting home-made gin, bought from the naval widows of Middle Street, to react to the whispers of alarm rippling through the graveyard, or even a sharp kick from the more alert. Given they lay against tombstones, in the dark and unseen, and with only the sound of their snuffling or snoring placing their presence, it was held they could safely be left to their slumbers so the unloading of the cart could proceed without disturbance.

Heavy work on a mild night, it left Brazier's tars sweating as the three bodies were placed in a circle, with much effort given their rigidity, as if sat down for a conflab. Care was taken to ensure they stayed upright and didn't fall over. Hawker's horse, tack removed, and one of the pack animals he'd led to the Spafford farmhouse, were to be let loose to graze on the way back, only Bonnie and the one pulling the cart being taken all the way, the latter to be freed once the loaned cart was returned.

Once clear of the vegetable plots, it was best to wait for the dawn: Brazier, with cart now empty, reckoned it safe to get going again in daylight. Waiting naturally engendered speculation of what would happen on the discovery of the bodies, unaware it had already taken place. The urchins, creeping back to the graveyard had followed their noses to discover what had been left. Accustomed to being accused of every crime in creation, they did not linger and nor did they abandon their comatose fellows. Well before cockcrow they were all long gone, seeking shelter elsewhere so, come the day, they could plead ignorance.

Brazier and his party returned to Zachary's smallholding mid-morning, after a second night out, to take a breakfast of oats and milk before finding a spot in which to sleep. The last to close his eyes was Edward Brazier, he having too active a mind for immediate slumber, with two things on which to ponder: what would be the result of his night-time deeds and to think on was to follow. When he did go under, it was while wondering how Betsey was faring, mixed with images of their shared future.

She too had encountered trouble getting to sleep, imagining, or was it hoping, the post-chaise, which would depart Dover in the morning to come through for a pickup in Deal, would be carrying her letter to Dirley, while wondering how he would react.

Given the graveyard provided a route through to the various vegetable strips, discovery came as soon as it was light enough to see and by more than one person, not that any alert was immediately forthcoming. A town steeped in wrongdoing, with an inbuilt distrust of the magistracy, no citizen, like the urchins who'd crept back only to flee again, wished to be the one to let it be known they were even in the vicinity. It took one upright fellow, making a very early morning visit to lay flowers on the grave of his recently deceased wife, a duty regularly carried out prior to his working day, to react to the sight of the first body. Harry Spafford had been sat up against a headstone, his eyes wide and staring and the hole in his forehead obvious as the cause of death.

Within an hour the verdant green space, dotted with granite sarcophagi and headstones, was full of the curious, come to gaze at what was held to be a rare phenomenon, one not to be missed, with the town watchmen seeking to keep them from touching the bloated bodies or seeking to take souvenirs. For every expression of horror, there was another kind of attendee, ghouls who revelled in the sight and smell of death. Identification took no time at all in the case of the Spaffords, both being well known: Harry for his debaucheries, the father for his foolish and costly attempts at filial reform.

Fewer were sure about Daisy Trotter, as unlovely in death as he had been in life, an object of much interest for the number of wounds, each having wept blood to stain his clothing. Yet there were some who knew him well: the denizens of Basil the Bulgar's Molly-house, which had been his place of choice when in Deal, who may have wished to cry at the sight if discretion in the face of the mass of citizenry had not prevented them.

Soon lining up to gaze were the leading citizens of the town, the foremost being Sidney Cavell, who was at a total loss as to what to do next. Death was not uncommon in the world he inhabited, violent ones included, but a trio of obvious murders lying in plain sight was beyond his ability to process. Phineas Tooke was in a state of utter flap, a nosegay pressed against his face, fussing about how Deal would be perceived when this atrocity became widely known, which it must.

Tobias Sowerby was steadier and he was also silent, even if his thoughts were in turmoil. Dan Spafford had robbed one of his carters of Henry Tulkington's contraband tea. Harry had last been seen, and this by half the town, pleading and disappearing into the slaughterhouse with John Hawker's grip on his collar. The third corpse he knew nothing of, but given the company in which it had been left, it had to be connected to the very same robbery. He had no illusions about Henry Tulkington and his propensity for action against those who threatened his interests, but this went beyond anything he could countenance. Sowerby didn't have to be told of the need to keep the operations in which he was involved low-key. Now, looking around the faces of those who ran the municipality, all of whom knew something, he was wondering at what connections were being made behind their worried frowns.

Added to this was the buzz of conversation amongst those who'd been pushed back by the watchmen. They speculated on how many had either seen or heard what Hawker had done with young Spafford, who, when marched through the town by Hawker, must have wondered why he was still in one piece and not dead from a gunshot, given the reputation of the man who'd collared him. He surely should have been cut up and stuck in a barrel marked pork.

'Has the undertaker been sent for?' Cavell demanded.

'I was wondering if a physician should be called first,' Tooke flustered. 'Surely it is proper to certify death first?'

'What certification do we need?' Cavell cried, his exasperation obvious. 'Even you can see they're dead. Somebody call an undertaker, we must get them out of sight.'

'And not killed here,' Sowerby added. Cavell spun to look at him, his face showing this obvious fact had not occurred. 'There's no blood on the ground and, by the smell, they have been dead for days.'

'What are you saying, Tobias?'

'Just that, Sidney, but I suggest they are put somewhere away from the common gaze, before every resident of the town has come to look. As to certification, it can be done later.'

The silence which fell was unnerving, the cause soon appearing. John Hawker strode into the graveyard in a manner to tell all he expected the crowd to part like the Red Sea, and they did. A nod was given to the worthies, but nothing was said as he stood in the middle of the circle of death and examined what lay before him while it was telling no one asked him for an opinion. To appear indifferent while inwardly seething took every ounce of his self-control. He alone knew who'd done this and why but to say anything was out of the question. Eventually it was Sowerby who asked him for his thoughts, which got a slow turn and a steady, slightly unnerving look.

'A dispute among smugglers ain't unusual, Mr Sowerby. It be obvious to me there's been one and this be the result.'

'But why dump them here?' Tooke demanded.

'Put you off the scent, Mr Tooke. I reckon this didn't happen here.'

'A point already made,' Cavell said.

'So whoever did the deed does not want it known where.' Hawker knew he was taking a huge risk when he added, 'Find the spot and you'll find the culprits.'

'Aside there,' came from the back of the assembled crowd, who saw no reason to part for the unknown John Cottin.

He was obliged to elbow his way through. The trio whom he'd met previously exchanged concerned glances before he emerged and, once in plain view of the sight, he stood shocked. He'd seen a dead body in his life before; who had not stood over the open coffin of a relative to pay their last respects? But even as a high sheriff, and having taken a look at the charred body from Quebec House, this was his first sight of death by such obvious violence and it stopped him cold, struggling to find words to articulate what he was feeling. He looked at the faces closest to him, the three he knew and the one a stranger, he now the subject of the cold and unnerving stare.

'What happened here?' Even loudly expressed, it was feeble and treated as such.

'Nowt unusual,' shouted a wit from the crowd. 'Happens every day.'

'Fewer mouths to feed,' added another.

'Mr Cottin,' said Cavell, 'this is my concern until I have drawn certain conclusions. Then and only then do you have an interest.'

'I beg to differ, sir.'

'Differ as much as you care to,' Sowerby snapped. This pest must be kept out of matters if at all possible. 'But if you do not stand back and allow us to perform our duties, I will have you removed.'

'And if you interfere with me in the performance of my duties, sir, you will find yourself under lock and key. As High Sheriff of Kent, I represent the authority of both the county and the nation and I will not be treated as a person of no account.'

Naming his office, Cottin had set up a buzz amongst the gathering, the majority of whom had no idea who he was. Having, he felt, silenced Sowerby, he went to stand before the body of Harry Spafford, hands on hips and gaze fixed, trying to give the impression of being in command of his thoughts. In truth they were all over the place. A lawyer by trade, his appointment was political, nothing but a link to higher authority as usually carried out; he had not come to it with any ability in the investigation of crime. Sage nods covered his ignorance as he stood over the unknown trio.

'Do we know who they are?'

'Not all,' Cavell responded, without adding names.

'No need to establish the cause of death, Mr Cavell, so your duty as coroner is straightforward. This is murder, plain and simple. Let us hope nailing a culprit will be easier than your efforts over Quebec House.'

Sowerby was sure John Hawker's actions then were plain wrong, for he visibly jerked at the mention, to spin on his heel and make for the throng, which again parted to let him pass, proof of the concern felt immediate.

'Who's that fellow?' Cottin demanded, to receive no answer.

CHAPTER TWENTY-ONE

Heading into Deal, later than normal and after a good night's sleep, Henry Tulkington mulled over things as they were. His first task was to meet with Rudd and collect from him the potion he would need to render, in an emergency, his sister comatose. It was now the time to lay before Rudd the proposition of committing her to West Malling, should it become necessary, with himself as the sole consulting physician. Once within the confines of such an institution, he was sure he could contrive to keep her there, by the provision of excess fees if required, though it might be in order to pay a visit and survey the way they operated; should it prove to be unsuitable, another home for the mentally troubled would have to be found.

With Hawker, it would be necessary to act with caution, given a cargo was imminent: the weather looking set to be perfect in the coming nights, he needed to see it safely landed. His feathers were ruffled and required a degree of soothing, given their last exchange had been uncomfortable. But surely, allowing those bodies, as well as his horses, to be stolen must dent any arrogance he still possessed about who was in control. His last problem, Dirley, he saw as easy to resolve. His uncle had never come across to him as willing to dispute, and besides, he had little choice but to comply.

Being mid-morning, the Freemason's Lodge was quiet, but Rudd wasn't present as arranged, which was irritating if not seriously so. It was not long before Henry realised quiet was too mild a description, the place was deserted, which had him ask the steward for an explanation, which brought no enlightenment. Having no one to take coffee with, he decided it would be a good time to visit Garlick again and keep abreast of what that damned sheriff was up to.

'At the graveyard? Why, in the name of all that's holy, has he gone there?'

'You don't know, your honour?'

'Obviously not.'

'They've found three bodies there. Murdered fer certain. Word is it's the two Spaffords and Dan's mate Trotter.'

To avoid reacting was impossible and Henry could in no way manage it. But what was visible to Garlick was taken for astonishment, not shock, and the 'My God' fell into the same category.

'Whole town's gone to look. I went down on being told but couldn't get close for the crowd.'

'I would be remiss if I didn't join them. Good day, Mr Garlick.'

It was a relief to get away from the gaze of the man, though it allowed for nothing in the way of relaxation. There was a moment when he wondered if what he'd been told was true, only to then castigate himself for being a fool. He knew those bodies had disappeared, now he knew the purpose, albeit such knowledge did not bring much comfort.

Head down, thinking and walking, he paid no heed to those tipping their hat in respect because he couldn't see them. His first instinct was to make straight for the slaughterhouse, but it was quickly put aside. Best stay away from Hawker until he knew more, so it was back to the empty Lodge, to have brandy with his coffee and think things through. Doing so eased his pulse somewhat: if you excluded the sods held at the farmhouse, the only people who could connect him with those bodies had been involved, so could not speak, while he would do his best to ensure any enquiries were limited. Easy with those who looked into such matters locally, but would it work on Cottin?

Tobias Sowerby's words came back to him, about throwing the sod a bone like Dan Spafford to cover the riot; more difficult to use such a line now, but could it present a way to keep his name clear of any involvement? Yet this raised Sowerby's gaffe about Spafford being a thorn in his side. It mattered not he was wrong, he'd believed it to be so, which raised the question, did this apply to others? Suddenly the discretion of his fellow worthies, which he relied upon to operate, looked less secure, given he was the last person to whom they would talk to regarding what they did and didn't know.

It took time to calm himself and take a rational look at where he stood. The events which led to those deaths happened on his property, but his contact with the names involved was minimal and he certainly hadn't fired any shots; he hadn't even been armed. John Hawker had taken them first to the slaughterhouse, next to the Spafford farmhouse; again, he'd had no actual involvement.

'Henry?' He lifted his face to see Doctor Rudd, thinking at this moment he did not want to deal with the man, yet he was obliged to, Rudd holding out a hand. 'The potion you asked for.'

'Thank you,' was grudgingly given as he took the small bottle.

'Afraid I can't stop. I'm needed to sign some death certificates.' A pause. 'I take it you've heard?'

'Rum business,' was as non-committal as he could manage.

'Is that. Perhaps we could meet later.'

'Perhaps,' Henry said, then added, 'Actually, I'll come with you if you don't mind. If everyone else has gazed up this raree-show, it would be wrong of me if I did not.'

'Then I suggest you buy a nosegay on the way. Been dead a few days, I'm told, so they'll be a bit ripe.'

'Fear not, I have a strong constitution.'

This raised an eyebrow with Rudd. Here was a man who was ever complaining of the exact opposite.

If Tulkington had been rattled it was nothing compared to John Hawker, convinced what Brazier had done was aimed squarely at him. He could see it would have an effect on his employer, but the same process by which Tulkington had eliminated himself from guilt left Hawker in a very different place, especially with Harry Spafford. It was hard to admit in the case of that sod, Henry Tulkington had been right. Furious at the theft of part of his cargo, and right under his very nose, he'd allowed his anger to get the better of his judgement, made doubly enraged by the taking of the cart of tea a day or two later.

Those who'd seen him drag Harry Spafford down the Lower Valley Road, even those who'd heard of it, could set a line between the son and the father; given how close Jaleel Trotter was to Dan, having practically raised the wastrel son after his mother fled, it would rope him in too. The conclusion people would draw was easy to imagine. He collaring Harry sends Dan, a laughing stock for his attempts to redeem the little sod, raving mad. He sets out armed, with Daisy in tow, to get his boy free and who should he run up against? A fight ensues, weapons are employed and blood flows.

There was no need to go further and the fact it wasn't true counted for naught. If he could make such a case so could everyone else and it would match his reputation, which in another case might have been a good thing. If anyone pushed the story too far, like the law enforcer he'd eyeballed in the graveyard, it might not be.

'Where the hell is Tulkington?' he shouted out loud.

Hard as it was to admit, he reckoned he needed him now.

He was being sick, the smell of the bodies in the undertaker's parlour being one powerful reason but, with Rudd present and his examination complete, the undertaker had punctured the bloated stomachs of the corpses to produce an odour which nearly had Henry faint. His pallor was not improved when he recalled the look Tobias Sowerby had given him when he arrived, one which said plain he must have had a hand in their deaths. Back outside the parlour and face to face with him and the others, there was a period of contemplative and collective silence, which he could not bear.

'I hear this Cottin pest has got involved.'

'Can't stop him, Henry,' Cavell replied, with a concerned expression. 'He has the power to call in help from outside, even the military.'

A still flustered Phineas Tooke added, 'And who can doubt, with the wounds, it was murder? Rudd tells me Trotter was more than once shot in the back.'

'I think I'll return to the Lodge.'

Cavell indicated himself and Tooke. 'We'd better stay till Cottin returns.'

'Where is he?'

'Questioning people who passed through the graveyard early morning. Good luck to him with that.'

'Tobias, are you free?' A cautious nod. 'Then why not walk with me.'

They were not far away before Henry said, 'This has to be stopped.'

'You heard Sidney.'

'Damn Sidney.' There was a long pause before he added, 'I'm going to tell you what happened.'

'Henry, I'm not sure I want to know.'

'You will have to, given you're the only one I can trust.'

It looked innocent enough, two well-dressed gents walking slowly along the Lower Valley Road, heads bent, one talking, the other listening, as Henry told his tale. This was subject to frequent pauses, meant to give the impression he could not quite believe what had occurred himself. First, he changed the location of the incident away from the grounds of Cottington Court, without specifying exactly where.

'You will have heard about Harry Spafford being dragged to the slaughterhouse?'

'Who has not?' was a guarded reply, Sowerby wondering where this was going.

'Well, it produced the proof we needed. It was his father who robbed your cart.'

Tempted to mention the cargo stolen from under John Hawker's nose, Henry thought it best not to for now. Maybe it would be needed later.

'Once he had the information, Hawker kicked him out, only for Harry to come to me. He was pleading for protection from his father, whom I was told was threatening to horsewhip the boy, frightened into thinking he and his actions were betrayed.'

There was a longer pause and Tulkington sucked on the notion, only to think an alternative might serve better.

'Or perhaps he thought him still confined and held by me, so sought to rescue Harry – who is now to know? Whatever the reason, he came after him armed to the teeth. What do you now know of Edward Brazier?'

'The name and his rank since the fire, before then nothing.'

'He has designs on my sister Elisabeth.'

'Really?' was all that could be said in reply.

'She entertained the notion originally but has now set her mind against his advances. But the sod will not take no for an answer and it fell to me to tell him, which was not taken well, obviously seeing me as a barrier to his hopes, refusing to believe Elisabeth had changed her mind. I think he thought to elope with her and roped in some of his old crew to help him.'

Another gap, this time to allow passage to a handcart, allowed Henry to add something which pleased him.

'Typical naval type, of course, not long on either brains or manners.' This was taken with a wry smile. 'Upshot of it all, Tobias,

238

I set out to thwart Brazier and Spafford's appearance coincided with his, he and his gang also carrying weapons. Two headstrong individuals carrying guns, clashing in the pitch-dark, each seeing their intentions as of vital importance and the result was inevitable, with myself unable to intervene.'

There followed a hiatus and a slow long shake of the head, the action of a man wondering at the folly of his fellow humans.

'They ended up shooting at each other and that's how poor Harry got a ball in the forehead. I myself was lucky, given he was close by me, but do you know Tobias, the lad, and many have named him useless, knocked me to the ground and may have saved my life.'

'A lucky escape, then?'

'Won't hear a word said against his memory, let me tell you.'

Acceptance of this assertion merely engendered a grunt – Sowerby had no illusions about Harry Spafford, no one in the town did – as Henry took up his story again.

'You will have observed, as I did, Trotter was riddled and Harry's father clearly ended up with one in his gut. So you see, the whole thing can be laid at the door of two headstrong individuals, Dan Spafford and this Brazier fellow, with his deluded designs on my sister.' There was a moment he thought to add how it had affected Elisabeth's mind, but Henry decided it would merely complicate matters. 'I'm sure it was never supposed to be as it turned out. It was, in short, a terrible accident.'

'And the bodies in the graveyard?'

'Clearly an attempt to shift the blame, possibly to me. I told Brazier I was not at fault, he was responsible, advising him to contact Sidney and explain it as an unforeseen accident. He obviously feared he would not be believed, especially after Dan Spafford passed away from his wound. I thought he was taking him to a physician, clearly he either did not, or it was too late.'

On concluding, Henry was quite pleased with his construction, though he knew it required refinement; no mention of Hawker and the blame for everything shifted to Brazier, who would of course deny the story being true. Yet, even if certain parties were questioned, namely John Hawker and his men, he could rely on his version being confirmed. So it would be the word of an upstanding local citizen, who had the power to put pressure on the magistrates, against that of a stranger to the town, the two other principles being bodies in the undertaker's parlour. There was the number of shots fired, but it could be laid at the door of both men's support, Brazier naturally exonerating his men. Spaffords's lot were out of sight and would soon be out of mind.

'I see it as very much a local matter, to be dealt with by those charged with keeping the peace in Deal. If they feel it warrants the involvement of a high sheriff, it is for them to decide, do you not agree?'

If the necessary answer was forthcoming, it was hard for Tobias Sowerby to disguise the fact he didn't believe a word of it, just as he would never accept Henry had no hand in the torching of Quebec House. He felt as if he was being used as a sounding board, Henry testing the account, practising it on someone he knew dare not act against him. It was partly to get off the subject and this pack of dishonesties he said,

'By the way, not having seen you, there's a bit of a coincidence I need to pass on. The body discovered in the embers of Quebec House was identified as a fellow called Upton. Any relation to the man running your stables?'

The reaction was abrupt, as Henry stopped dead. 'Actually, Tobias, I've just recalled some pressing business I need to attend to. What we've just been discussing has addled my brain. If you will forgive me.'

And he was gone, leaving Sowerby confused, but not for long when he realised it was the name which had led to his sudden recollection, this examined as he continued on his way. The two well-dressed individuals might be heading in opposite directions now, one for the slaughterhouse, the other for the Lodge, but both were equal in the depth of their concerns.

As Henry was wondering how Upton had ended up in Quebec House alive, never mind dead, it soon became obvious as being something arranged for him by Elisabeth, a safeguard against their conspiracy being uncovered. If he could curse her for such devilish plotting, part of Henry was obliged, albeit grudgingly, to acknowledge her foresight. It still remained true what he'd intended, and Hawker had overseen, had got out of hand. The mob converging on Quebec House, made passionate by rumour, had been there to inflict pain on Brazier and his men, enough to convince them their presence in Deal was not just unwelcome but unsafe. It had never been his intention the house should be set fire to, and certainly he'd made it plain to Hawker, who'd seemed set on the notion, anyone being killed was out of the question.

Again, further worried reflection established he was in the clear. It had been his idea to set the riot in motion, but the only two people to whom he had spoken about it were Hawker and Dan Spafford, the latter promised freedom for him and his men for driving Brazier away, so silence was assured. But it still begged the question regarding the result and there was only one person he could even discuss it with.

John Hawker was made angry by his employer's preoccupation with Quebec House. To him it was done business, if you excluded the fact Brazier and his men had survived. He certainly was not about to admit he was responsible for the fire and, since Spafford was the one to whom he'd given the instructions to set the place alight, which ran counter to those given to him, he was safe.

As Henry Tulkington reprised the sequence of events, from the first time the Spafford gang had been humbugged and captured, Hawker was reflecting on his own actions, not in a critical way, but in frustration at the lack of a desired outcome. He had no doubt of

241

his responsibility for the death of Upton, not that he felt an ounce of remorse. Dan Spafford, leading the torch-carrying mob, could be counted on to do what was required and, if blame was sought, he was the one who'd carry it.

'Do you think Spafford was trying to get even with us, John?'

It took a second for Hawker to drag himself away from his reflections and respond. 'In what way?'

'He was a devious old sod, was he not? Look at the way he tried to seduce me into an alliance, with his talk of imminent death.'

'Which you did not feel obliged to tell me about, I recall.'

'I've explained my reasons,' Tulkington snapped. 'And I do wish you would stop referring to it. What we are dealing with now is more serious.'

'I'll say, your honour. Won't take much imaginin' to lay those bodies at my door, least of all Harry Spafford.'

'You can say you set him free and get your men to swear it to be true. I am working on a tale which will support such a contention and it will be a brave magistrate who goes against it.'

The image of Cottin – a false one, given he'd never seen the man – rose up, only to be shaken away, as was any notion of discussing him with Hawker.

'What we're concerned with now, John, is any connection being made between any of the four dead and Cottington Court, which drags in my name. How many people in town know Upton was an employee of mine?'

'No way of tellin', is there? Could be dozens, could be none. Name meant nowt to me, an' I know ten times more'n most.'

'It registered with one person I know. There may be more than you think.'

Henry had an image then, of Cottin turning up to question him. Was it inevitable? Would it lead anywhere? If it could, should he seek to pre-empt such a visit or did such a course have its own dangers? All required to be thought on. Henry would have struggled to recall the mood in which he'd set out this very day and, as was ever the case, the alteration lay solidly at the door of Edward Brazier, the one person whose actions he felt unable to control. The likes of Cavell and Tooke were looking less than utterly reliable, but they and their kind had yet to feel the force of his displeasure and he had good grounds to believe, once applied, he could count on them to accept his version of events. This articulated, Hawker's opinion was a dampener.

'Exceptin' Brazier might have another surprise to send our way.'

'Can we find him?'

'Can't see how, when we've no idea where to look, but I don't reckon he'd hang about round Worth, seeing he's got what he wanted and there's nowt more to gain. Asides, with this weather an' what we're waiting for, I ain't got time. We need to get a boat out to signal our ship, which could well be in the offing any day now. If it is, I can't have my men stuck out at Spafford's place when they're needed at the bay.'

'We can hardly now say Spafford is away on a smuggling trip.'

'A rumour I've already set goin', sad to say, as was last decided. An' those who manned his luggers, who're supposed to be with him, are Deal men and you must know what that means.'

'Some will be wondering where they are,' was reluctantly acknowledged. 'While you, John, I suspect, still want to take them out and drown them.'

'Might have to think of another way, right enough. If we can keep 'em quiet till our cargo's landed, they can be dealt with after.'

'Surely a couple of men are all we need to keep them quiet?'

'But it'll leave me short at St Margaret's. Each one has a task and place to look out for trouble.'

'Then you must contrive to make sure the Excise are somewhere else.'

'Can't say I know of any other plans afoot.'

'Then make one up.' Seeing doubt, Tulkington pressed his case. 'One time for the Excise to be misdirected should not affect the way they see you. Let's get on with what is important, then we can fully concentrate on finding and eliminating Brazier.'

'You see it as the way?'

'I do now, John, there's no choice. He knows too much so he will need to disappear.'

For all his concerns, and they were numerous, John Hawker was pleased: they were now pursuing the same goal. Taking his men away from Spafford's place represented a risk, but for Brazier at his mercy he would take it.

CHAPTER TWENTY-TWO

Sarah Lovell did not receive much in the way of post, only the occasional letter from the few people in Canterbury who still saw her as a worthy person with whom to correspond. Most of her old acquaintances, those who'd previously seen her as a doyenne of local society as well as an arbiter of acceptable behaviour, had cut her dead, even before leaving for Cottington Court. She and her husband had been obliged to depart their fine house and comfortable life due to his failures in speculation, a subject never discussed. Apart from the odd middle of the night tearful recollection, it stayed buried at the very back of her mind.

Henry had issued the instruction all mail was to pass through him, she assuming this applied to Elisabeth, not her. Anyway, it was on the salver on the hall table, a plate she could not resist looking at on a daily basis once the post had been delivered, and there was her name. Had it said whom it was from, it's doubtful she would have broken the seal: it did puzzle her whoever had sent it had not bothered to put their return address, which hinted at parsimony. Failure of delivery meant a return to sender, with them having to pay the price of both postings. Still, the cost fell to the household so, like whosoever had penned it, she was not going to be subject to any charge.

With Henry gone to Deal and Elisabeth out walking, she was free to read it at her leisure. Having ordered tea, which involved the staff asking Grady to unlock the caddy, she took a seat in the drawing room and opened it while waiting for the beverage. The maid who delivered it found her sitting with the letter open on her lap, face white and expression rigid as she stared out of the window, the tray being put at the table by her side receiving no acknowledgement.

'Would ma'am be requiring anything else?'

The lack of a reply sent the girl out, to immediately discuss this phenomenon with every member of staff she met who shared her menial level, so they could speculate on what news Sarah Lovell had received to render her so distraught. *Bad, I hope*, was the general opinion. Had anyone gone back to look, they would have been pleased to see her in tears. By the time the tray was retrieved, she had left the room, it being noted the cup was unused and the pot still full.

For Edward Brazier, having set two hares running, the question was what to do next. With no idea of how his graveyard ruse would work, the notion of just sitting around was not one to appeal. Feeling better as each day went by, he craved some kind of action, yet was at a loss to know what would tweak Tulkington's nose more than the things already put in place.

'All we can do is look for opportunity, which means keeping an eye on Hawker.'

'Who will be on full alert after what's happened.'

Dutchy's point did not require elaboration: up to the stealing of the bodies, they'd been an unknown presence and threat, able, within limits, to move freely and, two of them excluded, take up places of observation without arousing suspicion. No more; the farmhouse must now have watchmen out, while any observation on the slaughterhouse would be risky.

'Which leaves the route between,' Brazier concluded. 'Hawker is in Deal, his men out here, along with how many others we don't know. Seems to me not much can happen to act as a threat to us unless they're back as a whole. As to what's happening in town, Vincent will keep us informed and he will be coming here today.'

It would be with money. He had an arrangement to draw regular funds with a lawyer in Deal, the one who'd acted for Saoirse in the matter of his rent, who in turn would indent his prize agent in London for the sum plus a small fee. Vincent had been sent with a written and sealed instruction, authorised to collect twenty guineas in mixed coin on behalf of Captain Brazier. No money in quantity was required out here, but not knowing what was going to happen next, he wanted a full purse just in case.

'So we keep an eye on the Sandwich Road afore it splits to the farmhouse, easy to find a spot where we can't be seen.'

'In pairs, Peddler. One to come back here if anything sets bells ringing.'

With Cocky and Peddler off on first watch, and the others once more assisting Zachary, Brazier sat down with the Venables journals to copy out certain entries on the relationship between him and Dear Sam. He had no idea what the effect would be; it was a ploy with unreadable consequences and perhaps none. But anything which affected the equilibrium of the Tulkington household had to be tried. He was still occupied in his copying when Vincent appeared on horseback, bearing a bag of coins and some welcome news about how the town had reacted.

'Sure, the whole damn place is throbbing with rumour.'

'Blaming John Hawker, I hope.'

'If they are, it's with care. His is not a name to bandy about in such a situation.'

'The magistrates?'

'Probably trying to find a way to do nothing. Get the bodies in the ground then set up an inquest going nowhere. I talked it over with Saoirse and she's of a mind they will do as little as they can, and they'll certainly do their best to avoid anything touching Tulkington.'

'Cottin?'

'Asking for facts and getting not very far, I should think.'

'Then he needs a bit of assistance. Can I impose on you to drop off another note?'

'Course you can.'

Brazier reached into the bag Vincent had brought and pulled out a couple of guineas, to see the Irishman pull a face, to which he paid no heed.

'I'm taking you away from your own affairs, Vincent. And I will remind you, I felt the need to reward you for your efforts when we were searching for the mysterious Daisy creature, before we knew it to be Trotter. Now is no different, and if you decline I will ride into Deal myself and make delivery.'

Acknowledgement came with a swerve. 'Garlick will be pulling at his whiskers trying to work out who these notes are coming from.'

Laughter brought a twinge of pain, but it was less troublesome by the day so he could reply without wincing. 'He'll make something up if he fails to find out and very likely have to. I've yet to meet this Cottin, but common sense should tell him to avoid giving Garlick anything to chew on. Perhaps best if you invent something.'

The note was quickly written, for it contained few words, to be folded and sealed with no named sender added.

'Next time you come, Vincent, fetch some wine, will you? Zachary's cider is a good brew, but too strong for my head.'

John Cottin was indeed struggling to get anywhere once again: no one tending their vegetables admitted seeing anything in the graveyard on their way past. When he referred to the smell, it was pointed out to him what they used to fertilise their strips – cow dung and excrement – which meant no one could smell anything else. At least he'd been given the names, added to the information they might be involved in smuggling. When pressed to be more definite, Cavell and Tooke had become quite arch and offended, as if people such as they would know anything about such illegality. When challenged, they claimed the information had come from those in the crowd.

Having left early, he came back to his correspondence; quite a pile and not of much interest, although every one would command a reply, until he opened one letter to find another inside. This being franked with a government stamp set his pulse racing for he had, to keep his identity secret, suggested anything sent to him should come through Westerham and a clerk alerted to what was required. It was indeed from Pitt, he first deploring the contraband trade, then thanking Cottin for his efforts to curtail it, which seemed to be stretching somewhat his own original communication. At the end, just before his felicitations, came the news he was planning to come down to Walmer within the week, which when Cottin examined the franking really meant, at most, five days.

'Damn me if that doesn't shake this damned town up.'

Down below in the hallway, Vincent Flaherty was handing over Edward's second note, like the first examined by Garlick for the addressee in a way he thought surreptitious. It was a sort of cocked eye sideways affair, with the paper held way from him.

'Getting a lot o' these,' Garlick said eventually, when he realised he'd been spotted, not hard since Vincent was visibly amused. He was, nevertheless, in search of enlightenment.

'From a lady,' Vincent whispered, which caused the proprietor's eyes to open wide.

'A lady?' was mouthed, not spoken.

'One who does not want her name to be known.'

'As if I'd let on to anyone, Mr Flaherty.'

'A married lady, who has lost her heart to your Mr Cottin. To be exposed could bring on ruin.'

'He ain't been here long for such a thing. Any roads, I don't have him down as the type for dalliance.'

'More than dalliance, Mr Garlick. We're talking seduction.'

'Well I never.'

'Sure, its deep waters when it comes to lawyer types. We must not rely on appearances.'

He didn't laugh out loud till he passed through the door. Invent a tale, Edward had suggested. This one would be all over Deal before the day was out.

At the Spafford farmhouse, Dolphin Morgan, who surprisingly had assumed a sort of leadership, was standing with his ear to the part of the door where age and movement of an old building had created a slight gap, for there was no 'easy to hear' shouting going on. In amongst the odd clearly stated words, he could hear nothing but a buzz of conversation and much movement. He knew, from his earlier eavesdropping, his captors were coming and going, unlike the first day, when they'd all been present and talking across each other and the noise had been consequently greater.

When he could hear clearly, it was to register a moan at their present situation, which came as no surprise. The people holding them, from Hawker downwards, were not strangers to any of Dan Spafford's crew. They were very far from friends but, in a close community like the one in which they spent their days, both parties knew of each other and, in the case of Dolphin and his mates, with regard to their counterparts, caution was mixed with envy.

While they had recently needed to scrape for a crust – Dan Spafford's profitability had been badly affected by the coming of peace – Hawker's lot lived high on the hog and were arrogant with it, the kind to strut through the streets and expect way to be given. If they were involved in the same game, they didn't rely on what could be got across the Channel and were never short of money.

John Hawker's gang lived off and spent 'gifts', monies handed over to them by the traders of Deal, which split evenly acted as a wage, allowing for food, drink and women in a quantity for which others could only wish. For entertainment, the odd workshop or emporium smashed up, or a boat holed, acted as a reminder to others of the cost of reluctance to pay. It was also true, when they did resort to violence, nothing was ever done about it – none would bear witness for fear of being the next to suffer.

It could hardly be said Spafford's lot were angels. While cautious of Hawker's crew, even more of the man himself, they were not beyond a bit of unruly behaviour when in funds, as they had been during the American war, and downright mayhem from time to time; like most of the tribe who happily went under the banner of the beach community, adherence to a set of laws and obligations, set for them by their betters, were there to be ignored.

'Marker's telling them to stop moaning.'

Dolphin passed this on to his mates in a whisper as he took a break to poke a finger into an itchy ear.

'Hawker would just fetch them a clout,' was the single response from Eastry Sam, so called for the village from which he'd originally hailed.

'They ain't happy, brother, fer certain. Not their normal way to spend the day lookin' after us lot. Cock o' the Walk is their game.'

'Least we're bein' fed, Dolphin, an' by Christ I hope we get some more grub soon.'

'Scarce enough to keep a mouse,' was a remark followed by a wistful look from a man whose frame was bigger than most. 'Got to hand it to old Daisy, God rest 'im, he did look after our belly.'

This, as it had before, brought on memories of better times, when a contraband cargo had been run and would be sold on, with coin in abundance for each of the men who manned Dan Spafford's luggers. After landing and storing their goods, there would be a feast prepared for them by Daisy Trotter, this prior to departing for Deal and its fleshpots, to blow their gains with credit on which they knew they could make good. Seen as ill-gotten gains to the upright, it was a just reward to a smuggler.

As was common, it was all a bit rose-tinted, with no recollection of the times the sea state had nearly seen them sent to the bottom, or the occasion when a Revenue cutter had appeared and they'd had to run from gunfire, but not before ditching their cargo. It also took them, in time, to a place most were reluctant to go. What was going to be their fate? The deaths of Daisy, Dan and his boy could not have been foreseen, but there was no feeling the likes of Hawker would hesitate to see them gone too. Being fed was one thing to give hope.

Itchy ear seen to, Dolphin went back to his listening, to hear what sounded, by their exchanges, like some coming in and others going out and he had the right of it. The farmhouse was covered front and back by armed men, with another one sent out to the oak tree to keep an eye out over the flat landscape, looking for people in the distance acting odd. If anyone was coming to cause mischief, they wanted to be well warned.

Even if he wasn't entirely happy with them, John Hawker had his instructions and they had to be carried out. So he was on his way to the farmhouse, back on his own horse, which had been found and brought to him, for a reward, by a couple of the ragamuffins, identified by dint of the JH brand on its flank. There was no sign of his saddle, and his accusation the boys had stolen it produced the kind of furious denial which made it not worth pursuing. So he'd been obliged to persuade the local tack merchant to supply him one as a gift, at the risk of being shut off from the produce of the tannery if he declined.

Peddler spotted him and gestured with a hiss to Cocky, unnecessary given how far off Hawker was. The Scot was up and beside his mate, well concealed by bushes, as they watched him ride by, pulling another loaded packhorse, eyes right ahead. A quick discussion established neither thought it worth rushing to tell Brazier: best to stay and see what happened after, like him going back to Deal.

Hawker was deep in thought, wondering which of his men to leave as guards, deciding Marker – close enough to be one he would occasionally confide in and was a man he could trust – with one other to help him, whom he could choose. Both would be missed in what was coming and it was to such matters he turned his mind. Regardless of how many times he'd seen a cargo landed, Hawker always went over the arrangements to ensure all the possible measures were covered. They would not be this time, he being two men short, which had him wondering where he could allow a gap. He decided the clifftop path from the fishing village of Kingsdown could be left unguarded, since no threat was likely to come from the north.

The men he employed were not along to act as porters: those people, and they were numerous, given the quantity being landed, came from round and about as word went out through a long-established grapevine. It told the people who lived in the vicinity there was a bit of coin to be made, pennies to folk and especially families, who lived with constant insufficiency; if they had jobs they were badly rewarded and many lacked even this, so there was a strong reason to spare a night of labour, then to keep their mouths shut.

Deep cliffs surrounded the bay and, if you talked of a track, there was one, which presented the sole way in and out to get you to the beach, which would leave any Excisemen exposed. But there were narrow paths down to the shore and these had to be covered, a single gunshot enough to alert everyone if danger threatened. The others on guard and the porters would disperse, while the ship would haul off the shingle shore, long before any authority could get close enough for an arrest. The chalk cliffs being riddled with tunnels, those getting away would do so unseen.

Long a location for the landing of contraband, Corley Tulkington had ruthlessly driven off other smugglers seeking to use St Margaret's. It had, since his time, been the family's to exploit, with anyone else going near it spotted and warned off, one gang from the Alkham Valley who'd failed to listen never heard of again. There was a permanent presence to ensure no repeat, a cottage at the top of the bay permanently occupied by a fellow on Hawker's payroll, there to warn of encroachment, but with another vital task. He was required to show one of the two shaded signal lanterns to the offshore vessel, to guide it safely in to the middle of the strand, avoiding the rocks on both promontories. John Hawker manned the other and was very much in charge. He gave the signal the approach was clear.

It would also be necessary for Hawker to send a couple of his lads into Dover, as a precaution, to sniff for any impending activity. This was where the Revenue men were based, though the White Horse Tavern was the place to listen in on their talk and even buy them a pot of ale. As a group they were poorly paid and far from energetic in carrying out their task, while rarely being supported with the funds to maintain their cutter.

The politician at the top of the chain, an aristocrat already rich, held the sinecure for the county, one valuable for the length of its coastline and its proximity to France. Most of the money paid to him for this sinecure stuck to his own fingers, little of it passed on to those doing the work. A sour joke was oft repeated: the man who held the office called The Riding Officer for Kent Customs was too old and infirm to get on a horse.

CHAPTER TWENTY-THREE

The Spaffords, or to be exact Dolphin and his eavesdropping, knew Hawker had arrived, first by a burst of activity, followed by the loud issuing of what sounded like instructions, none of which he could clearly make out. He had to jump away as the lock on the door clicked. It swung open to reveal John Hawker holding a pair of pistols, the look in his eye enough to have even those who'd not been inside a church since baptism crossing themselves, by which time they were, to a man, pressed against the far wall.

'Don't know why I don't take you outside, one by one, and put a ball in your brain.'

A voice came from over his shoulder, recognisably Marker's. 'Skull, John, there's can't be much brain to stop a ball.'

'You have the right of it,' was said over his shoulder before the look fixed on the Spaffords again. 'But know this, you lot, Dan has gone to meet his maker and if you don't want to join him, then do what I say. When you hear two knocks on the door, you'se got a couple of seconds to get to where you is standing now. Anyone not with their back right to the wall gets shot and no askin', do you get me?'

'We do, John,' Dolphin murmured.

'Mr Hawker to you,' got an immediate nod. 'Food, Marker.'

He moved aside to let Marker kick in a tray piled with bread and cheese, a full bucket of water placed just inside the door. About to close it again, Dolphin issued a quick plea, nodding towards a corner.

'T'other bucket needs emptying, Mr Hawker, close to overflowing it is.'

The reply was not instant but eventually he nodded, so Dolphin edged over to pick up the receptacle which had been given to them for waste, to then be forced to squeeze by Hawker, careful not to spill the contents, thinking if it hit his riding boots with the piss and shit he was carrying, a pistol ball would follow before a second had passed.

Marker, also armed, led him to the kitchen door, which came out the back of the farmhouse, to a spot which looked as if it had once been a sty. Filth emptied, Dolphin was led back in, to be afforded a fleeting glance at the main parlour, enough to register all of Hawker's men were dressed for outdoors and holding their weapons, powder horns over their shoulders. Back inside the room Hawker, holding the handle and preparing to shut the door, growled and thrust forward the pistol.

'Recall what I said. No second chances.'

As Eastry Sam looked set to speak, Dolphin held up his hand for silence, to then tiptoe over to the door and press his ear to the crack. A whole minute passed before he turned round to tell his mates that, by the sound of it and what he'd seen, Hawker's lot were pulling out.

'What does that mean for us?'

Looking around the whitewashed walls, then up at the two slim, dirt-encrusted windows close to the ceiling, which gave them all the light they had, though neither could be opened, Dolphin mumbled, 'Nowt I can see, we's still locked in.'

It was Cocky on watch when Hawker was spotted for the second time, the men behind his mount and packhorse a gaggle of boots kicking up dust. By the time they passed, two pairs of eyes were counting to ten, while reckoning them to be a grim-looking bunch. When they'd moved away from any chance of hearing or seeing, to the watchers, one question was obvious.

'D'ye reckon it be the lot, Cocky?'

'Only one way tae find oot. Go take a gander at yon farmhoose.'

'Capt'n first,' Peddler insisted, 'it'll be his choice.'

'One of us?'

'No point, Cocky. Reckon we've seen all we're goin' to be gifted this day.'

Back at Zachary's smallholding, they gathered for a talk to decide what to do. Told of Hawker being on his own the first time he was spotted, Brazier wondered if he'd missed a trick, passed up a chance to get the sod on his own, which he so wanted to do. But he reasoned trying to take him in the open would be too risky, lest he just wanted to shoot him, not the real aim.

There had to be a reason for Hawker removing his men, not a conclusion to get him very far: it could be any number of things, while he was in no position to look for possibilities. He needed eyes and ears in Deal, which meant asking the likes of Vincent and, more importantly, Saoirse Riorden what they knew or could find out. Again, he had no idea of how many men Hawker could muster. Probably dozens from Deal beach with a click of his fingers, but it was just possible what had been observed mustered as his core strength.

'Don't suppose you counted them on the way to the farmhouse, Dutchy?'

'Never occurred, Capt'n, my eye was on Hawker. What chance them they had as captives are still breathin' is what my mind's on.'

'Yer no alone, Dutchy.'

'If they'd shot 'em, Cocky, we'd have heard,' Peddler suggested.

'Might have cut their throats.' The looks Brazier got made him add, 'And don't go thinking they're not capable of it, which means we need to go and look.'

'Not this night, your honour,' Dutchy proposed, glancing at the sky, now the deep blue colour of a sun on its way to sinking. 'I's got enough scrapes from the last time.'

Brazier ran a hand over his face, which had the same kind of scratches. 'Trouble is, it's the best time to tell. If there's lights on it means the Spaffords are still breathing. If the house is dark, they're dead. It only needs one to see, so I'll go.'

'Not on your own you won't.'

As Dutchy stood so did everyone else. 'I could make it an order.'

'Might not be obeyed, us having been paid off.'

In the end it was he, Dutchy and Joe, Cocky and Peddler having done their stint. There was enough twilight to allow for a direct route and they had a lantern for the return, while it was reckoned if any of Hawker's men were left at the farmhouse, they would not be in the numbers necessary to mount a proper watch. By the time they reached the trees at the back of the place, in the approaching darkness the spill of lights emanating from the shuttered windows told them it was occupied, which for Brazier was enough to turn back.

The smell of cooking came from Zachary's shack and, on entry, there he was, bent over the grate, this time roasting on a spit a leg of pork he'd bought in Sandwich, paid for from the funds Brazier was now providing. So it was another round of tale-telling, good food and enough cider drunk to ensure, after prayers, sound sleep.

At the farmhouse Marker and Isaac Tombs, who'd been left with him, ate a lot less well, while contemplating a night in which they'd have to take turns staying awake. In Deal, John Hawker treated the bulk of his men to a good meal and ale at the Ship Inn – not too much of the latter for, as he made plain, there was work to be done on the morrow.

* * *

258

At the Lodge, Tobias Sowerby was dining with Cavell, Tooke and Gould, another magistrate and the fourth person, the silent and nodding one, who'd been at the Three Kings when Cottin arrived. They were, inevitably, discussing what to do about the events of the day and going round in circles, without getting close to naming a culprit. Sowerby had barely engaged in the conversation, instead trying to work out what to do with the tale he'd been told by Henry Tulkington.

The hours since had convinced him, even if it was likely claptrap, the story contained insinuations it might be in his interest to pass on. Even if he suspected him to be the guilty party, he was a dependant of Tulkington, so protecting him, even from his own too vivid imagination, came down to self-interest. So he cut in, when a gap in the conversation presented an opportunity.

'It occurs to me, the fellow we should be looking to pin the blame on is this Brazier.'

'Why?' Cavell asked, with the others just as inquisitive.

'Motive, Sidney.'

At the Three Kings, August Garlick was wondering what had been in the note Cottin had sent, by the hand of his stable boy, to Mr Tulkington, but his guest was not saying. Nor was he letting on about the reply he'd received by return, though an indication came from his ordering of a hack for the morning, enquiries about his destination rebuffed. It was, of course, Cottington Court, where Henry was at dinner, having decided on the tale he would tell the High Sheriff, while wondering why he was getting such odd looks, close to glares, from his Aunt Sarah.

Elisabeth, eating in her room, could not help wondering what was happening outside the walls of her family home, hoping for actions which might aid her plight.

* * *

Up with the lark, albeit with a thick tongue, Edward Brazier decided it was time he was shaved, with Joe obliging, using Zachary's strop and razor to cut through his thick growth. As the blade moved, he was thinking about his plans for the day, the first being to find out how many men Hawker had left behind at the Spafford farmhouse and what was he up to in taking the others away? Could a clue have been left behind? For any other inkling he'd have to press Vincent Flaherty, and hopefully Saoirse as well, to act as his eyes and ears in Deal, a request passed on to the Irishman when he turned up for what had fast become a daily call.

'I told you before, Edward, Deal is not a place to go about enquiring, and on the likes of Hawker it's damned deadly.'

'Saoirse has an ear to the ground.'

'She has feet on the ground too, brother.'

'You'll ask her, though? I can't stay out here forever, but when I move I want it to be with a purpose. Hawker has to be confronted and hopefully put out of the picture so I can deal with Tulkington.'

'There's only one way to put a bastard like that out of the picture.'

'Which is what I will do if I have to, but not at the price of a rope round my neck. Another thing – can you bring from the stables the muskets, which Dutchy tells me were left there? I also need a pair of pistols, as well as powder and balls.' This got a jaundiced look, to which Brazier responded, 'To threaten with, not to use.'

'Holy Mary, there's a notion that worked well the last time, did it not?'

'I'll get you some more money,' was said to avoid admitting he was right.

In Deal, a cutter, supplied with small beer and food, was being rolled down pebbles and into the water, where the pair manning it raised a single sail. Their task was to take station out to sea, off St Margaret's, apparently fishing but with an eye out for the vessel carrying the expected contraband, easy to recognise by a singular non-national flag. Once spotted, the captain could be advised it was safe, weather permitting, to make a landing the following night and they would speed back to set in motion everything on land.

The rest of Hawker's men left Deal in pairs to scout out the ground and approaches to the bay, looking for any signs of unusual activity. They would also alert the people who would port the cargo to an imminent arrival. One pair hitched a lift on one of Sowerby's vans, on its way to Dover, to drink in the White Horse, there to spread a bit of charity and listen in to gossip.

By ten of the clock, Dirley Tulkington was entering his chambers to begin the day's business, in consultation with his partners and juniors to discuss what cases, mostly commercial not criminal, were still in progress, those coming up and the line of approach which would be taken, as well as the size of any offers of settlement in those where the client had a poor chance of winning. As usual, following on from the morning conference, he took coffee in his own office to open his freshly delivered mail, leaving those he knew to be of a personal nature till last.

The rush of blood to his face was strongly felt as he read the pair from Henry, one he suspected a lie, the other telling him to stay out of Elisabeth's affairs. What had him worried was the scribble from her – even the addressing did not correspond to her usual tidy hand – but it was the contents which left Dirley in shock, wondering what had got into his nephew to have visited such cruelties on his sister. It took a real effort to calm himself and allow the barrister to take over from the agitated relative.

It was plain Henry had lied to him about the marriage, which in terms of motive now looked to be an underhand manoeuvre to get his hands on the income from Elisabeth's plantations. Given his own wealth, this seemed ridiculously avaricious, but the task now was to

261

invalidate the papers he'd been obliged to prepare at Henry's request. There was a slight hope they'd not been signed.

What had occurred, as described by Elisabeth, was a crime, pure and simple, one sufficient to put Henry on the ship about to sail for what the government hoped would be a penal colony in Australasia. Somehow, this had to be avoided; none of what he'd read must come to light but, at the same time, it required to be put right. An Ecclesiastical Court must annul the marriage, but how to keep this from becoming public?

Also a consideration was the notion Henry might be insane, so Dirley dragged the root of his memory of their last meeting for clues. He'd been insufferable, yes, but mad? One fact was obvious: this could not be resolved by correspondence, so the bell was rung to summon his chief clerk.

'Get someone along to Charing Cross and book me on the next available post-chaise to Dover. And send another round to my residence and have my servants pack a valise as well as my pistol case. All my commitments for the next few days will need to be handled by others.'

Saoirse Riorden was a well-known figure in the town and well respected, if you excluded the religious and those in the kind of social order, certainly the women, who thought the whole of Deal a sink of iniquity; their menfolk held to a fine line in downright hypocrisy, equally ready to condemn, while availing themselves of whatever suited their tastes, with a strong line in virgins. But it had to be admitted, compared to some of the places in the town, where every vice would be met, the Old Playhouse could have qualified for near consecration.

Sharing a type of business with many others, which would loosely be described as hospitality, it was a necessary requirement to keep in touch with others in the trade, a freemasonry every bit as solid as those who frequented the Lodge. In addition, there were those who supplied her emporium with the means to feed her customers and, in the case of beer, drink as well.

So on her rounds she would call in on the tradesfolk, as well as various places which provided accommodation for visitors, people who made up a slice of her clientele, one of them being the Three Kings. Garlick was always happy to greet another proprietor whom he saw as having an ear to the ground.

There, as in other places she visited, it would have been unnatural to have avoided what was now being called 'The Graveyard Slayings', this having occupied much talk and endless speculation with the baker, the butcher, the brewer and the candle maker, Saoirse agreeing to the general opinion the town was going to the dogs, with criminality rife and no one safe, even in their beds.

'Sure, it was ever thus was it not, Mister Garlick?'

'A war would cheer their mood, Miss Saoirse. There's not a soul who does not prosper when the French dander is up. I only need to look at my ordering in to see how my trade is down since the last peace.'

Saoirse agreed. The American fight dragged in the French, which in turn brought on the need for convoys. With Deal being the place in which they assembled, it had been very good for business.

'Mind, I sense a mood, don't you, these last weeks?'

'One that has cost you dear.' Sensing her expression demanded more, Garlick added. 'And at least one poor soul his life.'

Anyone watching would have seen it as performance, though they would also have been obliged to note the quality. Saoirse lent forward, in her mind working on the principle if you wanted something, it was wise to offer an inducement first.

'Can I trust you with a bit of news?' Garlick's lugubrious countenance became animated as he closed to near nothing the gap between them. 'I have been told the fellow's name.'

'You have? By whom?'

Equally theatrical was the sideways looks to ensure no eavesdroppers. 'Best I not name the source. Called Upton, he was, and he had just been given his marching orders from – you'll never guess where – the stables at Cottington Court.'

'Holy Christ, if you'll pardon the expression.'

'Not that I sense a connection, mind.'

'Heaven forfend,' was a hasty agreement; he would be careful with anything to do with the Tulkingtons.

'But it has set things disturbed, Mr Garlick, have you not noticed? There's agitation about.'

'I heard a rumour this morning.' Interest from Saoirse invited further disclosure. 'Hot off the beach.'

It was a satisfied lady proprietor who departed the Three Kings.

John Cottin was impressed, but so would be anyone of their first sight of Cottington Court. Built in the time of the second Charles, it was more elaborate in design than the modern taste for clean square lines, having intricate red brickwork and numerous leaded windows. The sheer length of the drive attested to the extent of the estate, while the house itself was enclosed within a high and extensive wall, which ran far enough to be out of sight.

Once through the ornamental gates, the hack swung on the gravel to stop outside the pillared portico, where stood a tall slim fellow, slightly hollow-chested, whom he took to be the owner, behind him a soberly clad servant, the latter stepping forward to open the hack door.

'Mr Cottin.'

'Mr Tulkington?'

'The same – allow me to invite you in. I think it best we talk privately in my study, for reasons I will explain.'

'Of course.'

'Coffee or tea? Perhaps you would like something stronger?'

'Coffee would be most pleasant.' This got the servant a nod and Cottin was ushered indoors, to find it as impressive as the exterior. A spacious, light hall with a round table in the centre, this bearing a very substantial solid silver punchbowl. Satin-covered settles sat against the art-lined walls, pictures extending up the wide staircase. The study, when he was shown in, came as something of a disappointment, being, thanks to high trees, without the level of daylight outside. There was also a fire in the large grate, which seemed singularly inappropriate on what was a mild day.

'Please be seated, Mr Cottin,' Henry said, taking up station with his back to the fire. 'It's not every day this house plays host to such an elevated official as the High Sheriff of Kent.'

'The purpose of my calling, sir—'

Henry held up a hand. 'Which I know of.'

'You do?' was said without any attempt to hide disappointment.

'I had a message from Mr Sowerby this very morning, advising me of the name of the poor fellow who perished in Quebec House.' The question was in Cottin's expression. 'Sowerby has been a frequent visitor to Cottington, many times in the days when we hosted a hunt, and naturally he got to know those who staffed my stables. He wondered if the victim was a relative.'

'Is he?'

'I fear it is one and the same person. Upton was my head groom. I'm afraid I had to dismiss him.'

'For?'

'He ran my stud, Mr Cottin, and was selling foals I had no idea had even been born. When it came to my attention, I had no choice but to immediately show him the gate.'

'Of course.'

'Ah, coffee,' cried Henry as Grady entered, this followed by a look warning for Cottin to say nothing while he was present, speaking again as soon as, coffee poured, he exited. 'He and Grady were friends and I have kept from all of my servants why Upton was dismissed. It is out of embarrassment I have to tell you, for it shames me to have been such a dupe.'

'Quite,' was necessary in order to be polite, but it seemed a strange way to act.

'How did he come to end up at the house of Captain Brazier?'

'I have no idea.'

'The dismissal took place when?'

'I would put it at a couple of days before the terrible fire.'

'Which indicated he went straight from here to there.'

Henry pulled a face of enquiry. 'Perhaps Captain Brazier is the one to tell you.'

'I've yet to find or question him.'

'Really? How odd.'

'What is odd, Mr Tulkington, is the reluctance of anyone to talk to me, so Captain Brazier is not singular in that regard.'

'I do hope you're not including me in such a statement.'

'Of course not, and I'm grateful you agreed to see me so swiftly.'

'It would be a bold fellow who put off a man in your position, sir.'

Cottin took the flattery with a serious look. 'Perhaps your servants will know why he went from here to Quebec House, or even family members?'

'You have a point, and you have the right of it, but I have a favour to ask, which I will of course understand if you cannot grant.' Cottin looked questioning. 'Upton was in the family employ for many years and my sister grew up with a love of horses, so saw him as a very special servitor, indeed they had a firm bond. I have so far kept it from her that he is no more and I'm looking for a good time to tell her the news, if there is such a thing. She will be heartbroken, as she was when she found out I'd had to send him away. Before you question her, I would appreciate being allowed to inform her.'

'Do you mean now?'

'She's not in the house at the moment, and I have to also say she's not of completely sound mind, a fact you may check with Doctor Rudd. He would advise you not to cause her upset, indeed we are considering if her staying here is wise. What I can say is she is too fragile to have a person utterly unknown to her asking pressing questions. Maybe in a day or two.'

'The servants, then?'

'It strikes me, Mr Cottin, I would be the best person to undertake such a thing.'

Seeing him about to object, Henry spoke quickly. 'I fear they will not tell you anything, in fact, they may go as far as blatant lies in what they see as a need to cover up for a man who was one of their own. I, on the other hand, can demand answers in a way you would struggle to match. Let me undertake this and, if I find anything relevant to your enquiries, you will be the first to know.'

'I really think it would be best—'

'I fear, Mr Cottin, I must insist. Unless you have any proof Upton's presence in Quebec House was in any way connected to wrongdoing, which it may well have been, then you would require some form of warrant to interrogate them. For myself, the tranquillity of my domestic arrangements takes precedence over anything to do with the man, who has done enough harm already. And really, surely, you must find the fellow who could answer any questions you have, namely Captain Brazier.'

'How well do you know him, sir?'

'Passing acquaintance and perhaps even such an expression is naming it high. More coffee?'

CHAPTER TWENTY-FOUR

Not much watching was required to establish what they faced: two men guarding the Spaffords, assumed to be still living, both armed, who never came out of the farmhouse without a weapon, even to fetch water from the well at the back.

When Vincent Flaherty turned up the following morning, he had brought along an extra mount, having done as asked in the article of weapons, though he had no great opinion of their use when it came to the muskets.

'Where in the name of Christ did you get them?'

'Dover. I didn't want to buy in Deal because it would be bound to spread.'

'Well the fellow who sold them to you saw you coming a mile off and had a good laugh when you departed. Having got your powder and balls I had a try with them last evening by putting a bottle on a post and I can tell you, Edward, it's still sitting there. Not one shot went straight, because the barrels are near to worn away, so I'd be looking for a barn door to hit if you're seeking for a target.'

'As it happens, I have a choice of two.' Having confused the Irishman he asked, 'Anything to tell me?'

'Far as we know, Hawker is going about his business, though most of his men are moving in and out of the town.'

'Most?'

'Can't keep an eye on them all, Edward, but Saoirse picked up a rumour there might be a cargo coming in.'

'When?'

Vincent was a bit put out by the abrupt questioning but answered anyway. 'Days, but you're the sailor, so you'll know it depends on weather and God knows what else besides.'

'Which is holding fine.'

'More than that I cannot say and neither could Saoirse. If she hears any more, well . . .'

'I will thank her when I see her.'

'Which I will happily do for you,' sounded a touch waspish. Going to his saddlebags, Vincent fetched out a couple of bottles of red wine.

'Not the best but will still need a day at least to settle. Wine was never meant to travel by horse.'

'I'll save it for your next visit.'

There was much to chat about, centred mainly on the fact there had been no apparent action over Edward's trio of dead bodies, with the High Sheriff seemingly tearing his hair out.

'But I must be away, Edward, I have a mare in foal and close to term.'

With Vincent gone, Brazier made his way to join Dutchy who was doing his four hours on, to stare at a building in which nothing was happening. The only way to get close was in darkness: moving in daylight when you had no idea who was behind those windows would never work.

'We've got the muskets now, Dutchy, we'll have a stab tonight, after we've been fed.'

He did not mention inaccuracy or worn barrels.

'We have asked till we're blue, Mr Cottin, and not just in our own bailiwick, but we can neither find out who is responsible for those deaths or where they took place. I fear it may be a mystery impossible to solve.'

Tobias Sowerby explained he'd used his own carters, busy delivering or collecting goods around the district, to probe for any rumour of violence since there had been gunshots and they could be heard for miles, with nothing to report. Cavell, who had accompanied him to the Three Kings, was nodding vigorously.

On the desk in his room the sheriff had a letter just delivered from Henry Tulkington. This told him close questioning of his servants had established none of them knew any reason why Upton had ended up at Quebec House, the only logical explanation being he'd been employed as a servant by Captain Brazier. This made no sense, given he already had one, and besides, what would a man in a town house and no stables want with a groom?

'Have you had any word of Brazier yet?' Cavell asked.

'None.'

'Then does this not suggest,' the coroner proposed, with a glance at Sowerby, 'if anyone is possibly to blame, it could be he? If not, why is he hiding away?'

'I seem to recall, Mr Cavell, you thought he might have left Deal altogether.'

'Another reason for suspicion, surely?'

'I'm bound to ask – whether he has or has not – on what grounds?'

'What if the three dead men were involved in the riot?' Sowerby asked.

'You're suggesting revenge?' came after a pause.

'Obviously.'

'Yet one thing we do know, for it was in your report, Mr Cavell. Captain Brazier was absent from Quebec House when it was set alight and it is my impression, again from what you sent me, most of the mob had disappeared by the time he reappeared and tried to help put out the blaze. How would he have known whom to pursue if he was not there to observe the crime taking place?'

'Perhaps he has better sources of information than any of us.'

This got Sowerby a glare, which reflected Cottin's conviction of his abilities, but he could bear such a look. The seed had been planted: if Brazier did show up it should be to a frosty welcome. If he did not, which all had agreed over dinner was most likely, the lack of his presence would get shot of Cottin, even if he failed to buy the proposition. There was no point in him hanging around if he could not examine the man who was the prime witness in the first matter and who might be the prime suspect in the second.

Unknown to his visitors, Cottin had already come to the conclusion he was wasting his time. He had no faith in the men just departed or their colleagues, was distrustful of Tulkington, sure Mrs Riorden knew more than she was saying and had no idea from whom he was receiving clues by cryptic note. Someone was seeking to point him in the right direction, but who?

He would have departed this very day if William Pitt had not intimated he was coming to Walmer. The facts of an as yet unsolved case in this hotbed of smuggling, to which it was surely connected, added to his seeming determination to solve it, could be used to raise him in the King's First Minister's opinion. Who knew what could flow from being seen by him as zealous in the search for truth? All it required was an interview.

The note to bring this about was already written and only required delivery. It being a not very long walk to the castle, he would, for the sake of discretion, deliver it himself. Within the hour he set off to do so, unaware he was being followed, as Edward Brazier had been before him. The ragged urchins of Deal were so ubiquitous they drew no attention.

Dirley Tulkington was too old to be coaching on such a journey. Even over one of the best maintained roads in the country, it was still bone-jarring, he the sole passenger in the two-seater conveyance, pistols loaded in the case beside him in fear of highwaymen, said to plague the country. He had been placed with a typically rude and utterly unsympathetic post boy on the reins, 'boy' being a misnomer: he was old, if not older than Dirley, a man who saw his first task, as the horses were being changed and mail was being transferred, to satisfy his thirst with ale and damn his passenger.

Nothing about what he'd read made any more sense when fretted upon than it had originally, which made it a mental as well as a physical strain. So, on arrival in Dover, he resolved to rest overnight, even if he thought time of the essence. He could not bring himself to face Henry without he felt fresh for what was going to be a very troubling interview.

If his nephew was going to behave in the fashion as reported by Elisabeth, and could not be brought back to reason, Dirley would have no choice but to break all contact, given his next task would be to drag him through the courts in order to get Elisabeth's property back, which he saw as a higher duty to the much-loved daughter of Acton. How different matters had been in partnership with him, two fine minds applied to a problem of setting up an enterprise which could not be penetrated. He was aware his half-brother sometimes resolved problems in questionable ways, but he had been assured this only occurred when absolutely necessary.

Given his exhaustion it was remarkable sleep would not come as he rehearsed what he would say. But when he returned to recalling happier times, he finally went under.

Brazier and his crew were in the dark, spread out in the trees at the back of the Spafford farmhouse, weapons at the ready. Luckily the wind had got up to rustle the treetops and cover any noise of approach, coming from the south-west, reckoned by salts used to sniffing for it to presage rain. Hopefully, this would not be before the muskets were needed. The firing pans would have to be covered if their weapons were to be of use.

Again the first hint of grey in the east was the signal to think of moving, still dark on the ground but an indication of the time. Peddler and Cocky acted on his signal, to make their way to the coastal side of the farmhouse and take up station, backs to the wall. Joe and Dutchy crossed the patch of grass to the nearest barn to the well, which would be visited at some time, hopefully not long after it was fully light.

A good hour passed as the daylight came under cloudy skies, with Brazier, pistols out and cocked, leaning against a tree, trying to will some movement. A sound to his rear had him spin round and take aim, which induced terror in the old fellow with straggly hair hauling a cart. The handles were dropped with what had been holding them shooting into the air, which made his loose smock flap in the wind. At another time and another place Brazier might have burst out laughing, but this was not it. Coming closer he reassured him he could put his hands down, to which he only agreed when the pistol muzzles did likewise.

A glance into the cart showed straw-filled baskets containing eggs, loaves of bread still fresh enough to smell of yeast, blocks of cheese, fruit and half-filled pitchers of fresh milk. Gentle enquiry established he had a regular round and the farmhouse was one of his daily stops.

'Every morn to deliver. Daisy's allas seen me right, he bein' a decent cove, but not recent. Won't leave owt agin if they don't pay.'

'And after?'

'Why, I gocs on my way,' this delivered as if he was talking to a bonehead.

Brazier reached into a waistcoat pocket to find some coin. 'Give them what you normally deliver today and tell me what it costs.'

'Eight pence would be the bill.'

'Here's a shilling. Drop your goods off and move on.'

'I'm minded to ask what's afoot here.'

'Do you know what the occupants in this house do?' The sly avoidance of eye contact was enough of an answer. 'Then you don't need to know what I do and nor what will crossing me bring on your head.'

The shilling was bitten before it disappeared into his poke, the cart handles taken up and he moved on, to do exactly as asked. The rest of his round was spent telling the folks he supplied to have a care with what they had stored, cos the Excise was about.

Marker, not that the name was known, came out the front door after a while, bucket in one hand, pistol in the other, to look long and hard in all directions, his eye then caught by the delivered food, which seemed to induce even more caution. Brazier heard a faint call, which brought out his companion as well as his musket, he too eyeing the food and milk. As Marker made for the well, his companion moved away from the door into clear space, opening up an angle by which he could cover him.

The move was slow and cautious, but there was no way to hold a pistol and work the rope lowering and raising the bucket, so it was stuffed in his belt, at which point Brazier stepped away from the tree. Hoping what he was firing was better than the duff muskets he'd bought, he put a ball over the man's head, then jumped behind the tree again as the man with the musket swung it onto him to pull the trigger, the ball cracking past his ear to strike another trunk.

At the well, the pistol was out and the musket was in the process of being reloaded, when Dutchy and Joe appeared, weapons levelled and aimed at the pistol holder's back. At the same time Cocky and Peddler shot out to cover the fellow in the middle of cramming a ball into his muzzle, a call to both telling them to drop their guns. There was a moment when one had a target in Brazier, who'd stepped out again, his second pistol raised so it looked an even contest. The shout from Dutchy and a glance over his shoulder was enough to see the muzzle dropped; to fire was madness.

Cocky took the musket and Joe stepped in to retrieve the pistol, Brazier coming forward to indicate they should head back inside, where a quick check was made to ensure no other weapons were available, which turned up another musket. The pair sat down and, well covered, were asked for their names, these sullenly provided.

'But by Jesus, you will pay for this,' Marker spat.

'I note you don't ask who I am.'

'Don't take much guessing, do it?'

'Maybe you've seen me before.' No reply. 'In the grounds of Cottington Court?'

'Happen I've seen your back.'

Dolphin Morgan was at a stand trying to work out what was going on. The sounds he was hearing made little sense, but the rattle of the lock had him jumping away, while gesturing to the others to get against the back wall. The door opened to reveal Dutchy Holland but, since he was not familiar, he was armed and he wasn't smiling, no one moved. They even stayed still, just looking at each other as, door left open, he moved backwards.

'I've seen that bugger before, and here too,' hissed Eastry Sam. 'He was with the navy cove.'

Dutchy grinned. 'Don't you lot know when you'se free for Christ's sake? Capt'n wants you outside.'

As they shuffled out, a bedraggled-looking lot, a few sobs could be heard: these men, sure they were for the chop, were thanking God for their deliverance. They were also afire to know not only who'd set them free, but why, something Brazier was about to explain. Having left Marker and Tombs under guard, he came out to address them, shutting the door so he couldn't be heard inside, the sight of Spafford's lot underscoring his original thought: he had no use for them. There had been doubt in the eyes of Peddler and Cocky as he'd outlined this, they having seen the number they'd had to contest with before, but Dutchy understood Spafford's lot couldn't be relied on.

'They be local and smugglers, an' not one of 'em would stand up to Hawker if they came face to face. More likely ask to join him and ditch us,' eyeing the men up and down as he spoke.

'And,' Brazier added, 'if you've yet to work out who it is I'm after, then now you know.'

He had to put into practice what had been agreed and, having confirmed the death of Dan Spafford, he asked, 'Is there anybody you call a leader?'

A couple elbowed Dolphin Morgan forward, which was not easy: he was both bulky and reluctant, but it mattered not if they acted as a group or on their own.

'What do you reckon will happen if you run across John Hawker?' The glum looks were a sure sign they didn't expect to survive. 'Well I can tell you, he's in Deal, so if you go back there, it will be to have your throat cut.'

'So what's we to do?' asked Eastry Sam, hastily adding, 'your honour.'

'I want you to stay here.'

'He'll be back,' Dolphin insisted. 'You don't know the bugger.'

'Maybe not as well as you, but know him I do and I intend to remove him from your life and mine.' The looks exchanged were as good as a communal scoff. 'Until that's done, you stay here. After I've seen to him, you're free to do as you wish.'

'Not much, with Dan gone.'

'An honest crust would be one way,' Dutchy sneered.

'Which tells me, mate,' Dolphin retorted, 'you ain't had to make a living on Deal Beach.'

'What do you know about the torching of Quebec House?' came from Brazier. Here for once were people who might tell him how it happened.

'It were Dan,' Sam bleated. 'He roused us out when we was set free from the slaughterhouse . . .'

'Set free? Who set you free and why were you confined?'

A demand to tell got a jumbled story, with too many talking over each other, but facts did emerge. After being captured on the night of Elisabeth's sham marriage they, ambushed in the grounds of

Cottington by Hawker's mob, had been taken to Deal and locked up in the slaughterhouse.

'Dan was kept in t' other shed,' Sam confessed, 'but when he joined us, he said we's got a job to do. It would see us free an' back to doing the French run regular, with Tulkington's blessing too.'

Dolphin took over having called for quiet. 'We joined a mob on Beach Street and Dan said to get to the front an' grab some torches. Never thought it was to set light to owt, but it's what befell.'

''T'were Daisy,' Sam admitted, as the first of the expected rain began to fall, 'who told us after, it was where you berthed.'

'Did he tell you someone died?'

'Sad to say, he did. Had to believe your place was empty. Winder were smashed in and Dan chucked a lit torch. We was told later, that was the deal with Hawker: get the place well alight or kiss goodbye to smugglin' for all time.'

As he listened to a litany of admissions, one thought was uppermost in Brazier's mind. Had Hawker acted alone, or had the whole thing been ordered by Tulkington? It was likely he would never know.

'Well, you've gone from being captives to gaolers. I need Marker and Tombs kept here and you're going to do the keeping. But first I have to question them, so go back inside and stay there for a bit, door shut.' The look this got had him add, 'But not locked.'

As they filed in, Dutchy whispered to Brazier, 'They'll likely leg it as soon as we's out of sight.'

'Not all, Dutchy, and none of them will go Deal way.'

'Capt'n, they could just be daft enough.'

CHAPTER TWENTY-FIVE

Marker and Tombs obviously reckoned fierce glares would serve them best. It was an attitude which brought a smile to Brazier's lips, as he began to ask them a series of questions, in a deliberately even tone of voice, none of which they were prepared to answer.

'Why has Hawker taken his men away?'

'Is a shipment of contraband on the way?'

'Where is it landed?'

'What signs are there to say when it's due?'

'What's John Hawker's role?'

'Not much in the talkative line, Capt'n, is they?'

'Doesn't seem so, Dutchy. Any ideas?'

His musket was lowered and pressed against the back of Marker's neck, which had his look change, the same with Tombs when Cocky copied his shipmate.

'If they're no going tae talk, they're nae bloody use.'

'Bit messy,' Brazier decided. 'Blood and brains everywhere.'

'Wouldn't matter out o' outdoors,' was Peddler's opinion.

'Quick too,' Joe Lascelles said. 'And Captain, I'd like to be on the trigger. Have these sods pay for every slave beaten by their kind.'

'Too quick, Joe, there's no suffering, for God only knows how many crimes they've had a hand in. Before a man meets his maker, he should have time to show repentance. Dutchy, there's ropes hanging on the walls of the barn we were in the other night. Oblige me by fetching a couple of a good length.'

The attitude of Hawker's men had changed from arrogant to fearful, even if the muskets had been pulled away, their eyes following Dutchy as he went out the door. But their faces froze again as Brazier repeated the same questions, to no avail, he smiling all the while, as though their not answering suited his purpose. Dutchy didn't re-enter, he just called from the doorway to say he was carrying what was needed. This brought forth a gesture to tell the pair they should get up and go outside, all following until Brazier said,

'Joe, tell Spafford's men they can come out and there's food on the stoop. They can feed themselves, but on no account are they to leave the house.' He looked at Peddler, who had a questioning look on his face. 'If any of them are going to run, now would seem a good time.'

It didn't need saying, there was no way of keeping them here and guarded if they were determined to get away, while at the same time being able to take any action, whatever it turned out to be. They were five-strong and this was not enough to take on Hawker, without they were lucky.

The rain had been a shower, enough to wet the ground and the grass, but it had stopped, not for long by the look of the sky. Once outdoors Brazier pointed to the solitary oak tree standing proud in the middle of the marshland.

'Is that the one you hid behind, Dutchy?'

'Can't see no other, your honour.'

'Perfect for our purpose too.' A nod got Marker and Tombs moving, aided by a musket shove in the back, Brazier alongside them talking in a friendly way as they made their way towards it. 'I think I must tell you about how we treat people who do murder or mutiny in the navy.'

'We string the buggers up,' Cocky gloated, moving to look the pair in the eye. 'An' a fine sight it is tae see a man dangle.'

279

'Did you know, Marker, in public hangings, if you or your relatives have the funds, you can pay the man in charge to attach weights to your lower legs, so when you drop, it breaks your neck and a quick death ensues? But we don't have trapdoors in the service, we have only yardarms set high in the rigging.'

'We ain't killed no one,' Tombs pleaded.

'That I find hard to believe. If you work for a bastard like Hawker, I'd say it was almost the first thing he'd have you do, to prove your loyalty and also bind you to staying with him. There are tales of this being the pirate way. Capture a merchant ship and have any new recruits cut the throats of the crew.'

'Ever cut a man's throat?' Peddler asked, in a matter-of-fact tone, to a pair of furiously shaking heads.

'As I was saying,' Brazier continued, his voice betraying no emotion at all, 'we run a rope through a block on the yardarm of a first rate. Generally, these affairs take place on the flagship, a vessel of ninety to a hundred guns, but on the deck are members from the same ship as the fellow about to pay for his crimes, thus justice is served by his own crew. All the usual rites are observed, sentence is read, with the chance to confess and show remorse given, a chaplain to read a homily for a man about to look his God in the face. A final word is allowed before the command to stamp and go, which has the hanging party run along the deck, the sinner's body taken into the air, to kick as the noose chokes the life out of him.'

'Got to add, Capt'n, body's over the water, so when he shits himself it don't stain the deck.'

'Good point, Dutchy, but not one to concern these fine fellows.'

'And there he stays,' Peddler added, 'lashed off to a cleat. If'n the gulls want to peck at his eyes, well he's not goin' to note it, is he?'

'Crows mair likely here, Peddler, though there's gulls an' aw,' Cocky added, looking skywards.

They were now beneath the oak, with Brazier making a great play of examining the branches to pick out something suitable, still keeping Marker and Tombs aware of his thinking.

'Trouble with a tree at this time of year is to find a branch that is both strong enough and clear enough of leaf growth to cast a rope over without it getting snagged.'

'We don't know owt,' Marker gasped, 'we goes where we's sent.'

The response was delivered in a jocose tone. 'Well, perdition will do just as well as anywhere, will it not? Only it won't be Hawker doing the sending for a change.'

'Happen he won't be far behind,' called Joe, who'd caught up with them.

'Dutchy,' Brazier said, gesturing to a suitable branch. The ex-coxswain stepped forward to throw the coiled end of the rope so it went over the branch and unravelled, with his one-time captain, having taken the end, to then address the proposed victims.

'I daresay, being Deal people you've done some time on boats and will be handy with a knot.' The end was pushed forward. 'You'll be able to knock up a noose in a trice. I see a certain amount of nobility in a man having a hand in his own departure, a sort of confession of his sins requiring no words.'

'No?' Brazier enquired, as Marker violently shook his head.

'Bit unfair, Capt'n,' came a call, 'one of these poor souls having to watch the other swing.'

'Spoken like a Christian, Dutchy, so let us do them together.' As the second rope was thrown, Cocky took the first and began to swiftly fashion a noose, the second rope taken by Peddler to do likewise as Brazier mused, 'Let's hope we have enough muscle to get you aloft at some speed, with only two men per whip. Lacking a block, the rope will not run smooth and this could prove your ordeal slow and painful. Still, nothing we can do about it, so let's have you in place, shall we?'

The pair were shuffled forward to stand under a thick branch they could not avoid looking up at, a sound escaping both throats as the nooses were placed round their necks and adjusted. Dutchy and Joe took the end of one, Cocky and Peddler the other, to walk slowly away and take up the slack, so the nooses were pulled up under the chins, with Brazier assuming a position in front of them.

'What you have to understand is this. If you're not going to provide me with the information I need then, in common with the rest of existence, I have no use for you. In fact, you become a burden I have neither time nor the manpower to deal with. This, I fear, is my only solution.'

Their looks changed; was this a chance of salvation?

'St Margaret's Bay,' Tombs shouted, adding, when Brazier's expression changed, and ignoring Marker's demand to shut up, 'It's where the cargo comes in.'

'Well, well,' was the calm response. 'And how do you know when it comes in?'

Tombs, having started talking, was not going to stop and it all tumbled out, though in no real order. The ship in the offing, how it was guided into the bay, who unloaded it and the chambers in which it was stored, everything until his final outburst.

'An' I ain't takin' the blame for what Marker done, neither.'

'Tombs, for the love of Christ, stop your gob.'

'Not for you, Marker, always up Hawker's arse, crawling for favour.'

'What is it he did, which he fears I should be told about?'

'He was with Hawker when they broke into your abode in Middle Street and boasted of it. Happen he's the cause of yon poor soul bein' burnt to a crisp.'

It was almost as if Brazier was silently communicating with Dutchy, for the rope tensed and the noose tightened, the tugging continuing till Marker's heels were being lifted off the ground.

'I didn't whack the bugger on the top floor,' he croaked. 'It were another.'

'Perhaps best you tell me everything.'

This was accompanied by a sharp tug, as if to say and damned quick. Brazier had to work hard to keep his expression blank as he heard how Hawker and his men had gone to Quebec House, just before the riot got going, and why, looking to find him and the four on the ropes.

'So we were all intended to die in the fire?'

'Dan Spafford would set the place alight, with no idea you was inside and knocked out. Hawker left him a broken winder to chuck his torch through. John hinted it was summat to do with what you did to him after you took him away from Cottington when he were groggy.'

'Did Tulkington know?'

'Can't tell you,' Marker moaned, as he felt another jerk on the noose. For good measure Cocky and Peddler tightened their line, which had Tombs cry out desperately.

'Marker knows more'n me 'bout what happens at St Margaret's. He can do chapter and verse, bein' close to Hawker's right hand.'

'Lyin' bastard.'

'Too late, I think.' Brazier looked past the pair to give a nod and they pulled in tandem, with Marker wheezing, 'I'll tell, I'll tell.'

'Then do so,' came with a sign to ease the rope tension.

So Brazier heard about the identifying flag on the contraband ship, not only how it was guided into the bay, but who did the guiding and from where, how men were spread out to make sure no Excisemen were seeking to sneak up on the operation and the signal for trouble.

'A single shot?'

'Then everyone runs.'

When Marker finished talking, claiming there was no more to tell, Brazier had him go over it all again to make sure he'd missed nothing out. It had started to rain again and with the two bareheaded, their hair was soon plastered to their foreheads with water dripping off their chins – some of it, Brazier suspected, might be tears. Their tormentors

283

were getting wet too, but hats and coats make it easier to bear. It was in an almost jocular tone he said,

'You could have told me all this indoors, which would have spared you a soaking.' He looked past them once more, to add, 'I think the game has played out, don't you lads?'

'Game?' Marker cried as the nooses fell off both chins, this to the sound of laughter.

'Played it well, Capt'n, an' no error,' Dutchy chortled, which came with 'Hear him' from the other.

This got a slow bow, his smiling response, 'I'd say we all deserve applause.'

But this evaporated as he put his face close between Marker and Tombs. For the first time Brazier allowed his true feeling to show. Gone was the urbanity, his voice was close to a snarl. 'Do not bracket us with the likes of you, who will kill for a pot of ale, or do the bidding of a creature like John Hawker while grovelling for his attention.'

Isaac Tombs actually asked for forgiveness.

'I'm in no position to provide it, but one day you'll answer for your crimes. Let's get these swine back inside, before I change my mind.'

There was no pride left in either man as they were led back to the farmhouse; they didn't walk, they stumbled until they were back indoors. Spafford's men were gathered in the kitchen, having fed themselves on the bread and eggs, with not much left.

'See what you can rustle up, Joe.'

'Not a lot after these greedy buggers have been at it.'

'Don't suppose they were fed much. In truth, I'm surprised Hawker fed them at all. But he must have left supplies for Marker and Tombs.'

Pointed towards a pantry this proved to be the case. There was dried and salted fish and smoked meats. Brazier told Dolphin Morgan to lock the pair in the room he and his mates had just vacated, into which they were pushed. But a look in a corner told Dolphin a task needed to be seen to. He pointed to the shit and piss bucket he had helped to fill and had been obliged to dispose of the day before.

'Get hold of yonder pail, Marker, and take it out. An' don't go spilling any, or I'll have you and Tombs lickin' it off the floor.'

Once back indoors he found it was him under interrogation from Brazier, who wanted to know about everything which had happened in the time since he arrived in Deal, and he found many eager to oblige. How Harry Spafford had run his pa ragged, he never forfeiting trying to get the lad to change.

'Wasted,' Eastry Sam announced to general agreement. 'He was a bad 'un from the day he was born.'

'Which is what you were doing when you were taken.'

'Aye, seekin' to get him out of Tulkington's clutches, an' look how it turned out. They say shit floats an' Harry was proof.'

'That's not how it started,' Dolphin said. 'You need to hear 'bout it all.'

Morgan referred to there being a meeting between Spafford and Tulkington, just the two of them in a closed carriage. 'Never happened afore an' didn't look as if it went well, with Dan spittin' bile later. So he decided we should do a bit of thieving by carryin' off some of Hawker's contraband.'

Which did surprise Brazier: to him it bordered on suicide.

'Took it from right under his nose,' sniggered Sam. 'Rowed round Leathercote Point, into the bay an' lifted as much as we could bear away.'

Next came the interception of the cargo of tea, which was admitted may have been a step too far. It had probably caused Hawker to grab Harry and take him to the slaughterhouse.

'Sold us down the river in no time, the bastard. Hawker told Dan so, but he still wanted to get him back. There was no gettin' him to see sense. Not even Daisy could get through and he and Dan been hugger since they were lads.'

'How close were they really?'

'Not that close.' There was a pause before Dolphin added, 'We had a word 'mongst ourselves, your honour, an' if you're looking to do the dirty on Hawker, we would be willin' to give you a hand.'

'I thank you and I'll hold it in mind.'

He had no intention of involving them. It was easy to say they'd help and just as easy, having turned once, to turn again. But he had another question, having recalled what he'd seen in the barn the night they stole the bodies.

'You say you rowed into the bay when you robbed Hawker, so where's the boat?'

'Two, your honours, cutters in a boathouse down on the flats.' Seeing confusion Morgan added, 'Sandwich Flats, on the strand right from here, with an old cove and his dogs set to go by regular and make sure no one breaks the padlock.'

Morgan went to a hook above the fireplace and took down a key, which was held up. 'Oars and rowlocks are in the barn.'

It was moot if Morgan understood why the key was taken. Brazier had no idea if he would use it, but he was certain he didn't want anyone else to. All eyes were on him, his old barge crew included, waiting for him to pronounce his intentions, something he would not have done, even if he'd had a set plan. What he had was information and it was not yet complete, the point made.

'But I have people who are looking out for things in Deal. When I know more, then I – perhaps even we – can act. Until then, keep those two locked away and yourselves in readiness until we return.'

Once outside, Dutchy asked, 'What now, Capt'n?'

'I'm thinking on it,' was all he got.

Brazier made for the barn to have a proper look at what was stored there. More ropes, which would have been for rigging repairs, barrels of tar and turpentine, odds and sods of blocks and tackle as well as a small keg of gunpowder, with a date chalked on top, probably the last day it had been turned to ensure the mix stayed right. Having taken all this in, it provided even more to think about.

'Let's go back to Zachary's.'

Out at sea, the men Hawker had sent in the cutter spotted the flag for which they were looking, a set of fleurs-de-lys surrounding a heraldic key. Closing with the vessel, they were able to board and assure the master, who spoke broken English, a landing was possible the following night, and a check on the system of signals was carried out. There would be a single flashing lamp to the south of the bay to say it was safe to enter, followed by the deployment of the two guiding lanterns either side to ensure they steered clear of the rocks.

The porters would be on the beach with a gangway, waiting to begin immediate unloading, while it was confirmed an anchor would be dropped offshore, paid out on a cable, so the vessel could haul off without the need to raise sail. It was also a guarantee this could be carried out at speed, in the highly unlikely event danger threatened.

All matters agreed, the pair took to the cutter to sail back to Deal, coming ashore late in the afternoon. They were able to alert John Hawker, who in turn could get orders out to his men to prepare to get to their various stations on the morrow. There was no requirement to alert Henry Tulkington: he had nothing to do with this part of the operation, quite the reverse. It was essential he stayed well clear.

CHAPTER TWENTY-SIX

Dirley Tulkington, being, since the death of his brother, a very infrequent visitor to Cottington Court, ran into an immediate problem on turning up in a hired hack the following morning: Tanner, who manned the gate, would not let him in. At least, given he was dealing with a gentleman of a decent age and some presence, he was polite, which had his dog, endemic when it came to snarling, sit quietly by his side.

'I don't take leave to doubt you have right of entry, your honour, but my instructions is clear. No one to pass without I've been told afore of their comin' to the house.'

'And when was this instituted? I was once part of the household and Acton imposed no such restriction.'

The name struck home. One of the ironies beyond comprehension to the likes of Elisabeth, all of Henry's servants were long-serving and went back to their father's day. This led her to conclude, given it could not be brought about by affection, it had to do with the difficulty of finding another suitable place, added to the fact he would probably never provide a recommendation.

'You're Mister Acton's brother, sir?' came with a deeply inquisitive look.

'I most certainly am and you, my man, have seen me before, though I grant it is some years past. I seem to recall your name as Tanner.'

Which left the gatekeeper on the horns of a dilemma: he had his instructions as he said, but could they be extended to a visitor like this one? From such a mercurial employer he was just as likely to get a rocket for obedience as employing discretion and, since there was a vague recollection of seeing this gent before, he unlocked the gate and waved the hack through.

Years rolled away as the conveyance made its way up the long drive, of a place he knew well, though many of the trees in the park were beginning to look mature now, not the saplings he recalled from the day the family moved in. It had been a run-down estate the first time he'd clapped eyes on Cottington and, in his time here, a place of constant works in both the house and grounds as Corley spent lavishly on improvements, sums of money, which came from his years of running contraband. He could remember the parterre as freshly dug and laid out in its formal way, designed to be, as his father had said, a miniature Versailles, albeit without the fountains. Likewise, the ornamental gates; he'd watched those being installed. At least they were opened without any discussion, the crush of the gravel on the drive having him steel himself for a meeting with Henry.

Grady was in the portico and, if he was wondering who was calling at such an early hour, likewise how they'd got past Tanner and his mutt, nothing showed in his stoical demeanour. Elisabeth, finishing her breakfast prior to going out on her morning walk, looked out with some hope to see who'd arrived, blessed with nothing more than the top of a black-hatted head and a heavy-shouldered body, which quickly disappeared, so assumed it was someone come to do business.

'Mr Dirley,' Grady exclaimed, when the black hat was raised to reveal thick grey hair.

'The very same, Grady, and I hope I find you hale.'

'Kind of you to enquire, sir.'

'My nephew?'

'Is preparing himself for the day.'

This got a frown from a person born and brought up in an age when men did not undertake what the French called a toilette. Fine as applied to ladies, it seemed somewhat questionable when applied to his own sex. As the exchange was taking place, Henry was descending the stairs, on his way to the dining room to take breakfast. There before him was the open front door.

'Grady?'

The servant appeared in the doorway. 'You have a visitor, sir.'

'Damned if I have at this hour.'

Asperity died as Dirley came through the doorway, his face sternly set.

'Uncle Dirley,' came from shock, the next words came from rising anger, mixed with anxiety. 'What the devil are you doing here?'

'I'm responding, nephew, to the letters you sent me, which I must tell you entirely lacked respect and, in the first instance, even a modicum of truth. But more importantly I've come to find out if what Elisabeth has informed me of is true.'

'Elisabeth, informed you. How?'

'Her letter made some very alarming accusations, which I can scarcely credit.'

Henry's response was somewhat panicked. 'You may discredit them from being the truth.'

The sound of loud voices brought Elisabeth out of her room, the sight which greeted her as she came down a few stairs making her heart swell. Here was salvation, looking up at her in a kindly, avuncular way and smiling. His broad, somewhat sallow jowly face, not much altered since she'd last seen him, if perhaps the heavy bags below his eyes looked darker and more bulging than she recalled.

'My dear. It gives me great joy to see you looking as comely as ever. Your letter had me deeply concerned.'

'It's none of your concern,' Henry snapped, glaring at Grady, stood erect and silent at the front door, his eyes, as usual, making

290

contact with no one. 'And can we stop having this family quarrel in the hallway?'

'Is it a quarrel, nephew?'

'It will most certainly become one if you choose to interfere in matters that are none of your business. I am about to have my breakfast and refuse to be troubled on an empty stomach.'

'Then I shall join you,' Dirley said, looking at his niece before saying, 'Grady, my coat, if you don't mind.'

Tempted to go to the dining room as well, Elisabeth thought it might be best to leave her uncle alone to speak with her brother. All of Henry's machinations were falling apart and there was bound to be a time when she could refute any assertions he made.

'I go for a long daily walk in the morning, Uncle Dirley, and shall do so now. I hope by the time I return, certain matters will have been resolved.'

'It is my wish also. But I would like to speak to you alone.'

'For which I can barely wait.'

'Am I mistaken or is this my property or the abode of someone else?'

'It was my home once, Henry. Surely you would not deny me repast when I've come all the way from London especially to see you?'

'You may go to the dining room, if you wish, but I shall not. Grady, make me up a tray and bring it to my study.' Henry turned on his heel and departed, with Dirley calling after him, 'Later, then.'

Unbeknown to all, Sarah Lovell had been witness to this, having, on the sound of those raised voices, slightly opened the dining-room door. Henry's departure saw it opened fully, she emerging to glare at the new arrival.

'You'll forgive me if I vacate as well, sir. I have care with whom I share any room.'

'The only thing I have known you share, Madame,' was delivered in a splendidly suave, metropolitan manner, 'is toxic venom.'

With an imperious snap of the head, Sarah Lovell passed Dirley to make for the drawing room, the door shut with some force.

'Elisabeth, it seems I'm so unwelcome, I have no choice but to walk with you.'

'Then I would be obliged, Grady, if you would return my uncle's coat.'

When they departed, they left behind two people whose mood could not be said to be sanguine. Henry was punching his left hand with his right and contemplating one murder if not two. His aunt was running through her mind the implications of a second letter she'd managed to spirit off the hall table without anyone knowing, one which hinted at an unnatural relationship in the first instance and pointed towards criminality in the second.

Dirley had helped himself to a cane from the stand in the hall and the way this was employed as he walked seemed to indicate his mood: the more disturbed he was, the more violently it struck the ground. He said little, unbeknown to Elisabeth mentally steeling himself to behave in a professional manner, a barrister hearing a deposition from a client, without emotion, sure he was doing so and unaware of what the stick was giving away.

The background to her relationship with Edward Brazier was taken with nodding equanimity, Henry's reaction to it less so, but it passed without comment, though he did swipe a bush when he was told in great detail of how the marriage had been conducted, albeit maintaining the apparent composure of his features.

He was only once really troubled enough to cry out, information causing him palpable alarm, this when Elisabeth outlined how she had been brought to challenge Henry in the first place on the family's involvement in smuggling, from which everything else had followed. In recalling the day and the circumstances in which Edward Brazier had relayed to her these truths, she also had to recall the way she'd behaved, refusing to believe a word of it.

He'd come once more to a clandestine assignation, accessing Cottington Court through their secret gate, to meet a woman full of anticipation, though far from absolutely sure the feelings she harboured were mired in certainty. Surely this would be the day to disperse her doubts. Then, instead of a heart-warming declaration of deep affection came his bombshell and her dismissive reaction. Edward's pained expression, as she told him his marital intentions were no longer welcome, brought a blush to her cheeks.

Dirley didn't notice, too thrown by the notion of the family's affairs being gossiped about in Lower Deal, and seemingly with some knowledge of the details, which led to an immediate enquiry about the man who'd brought this to her attention and his sources.

'I have no idea from whom Edward got his information. And to think I damned it as untruthful at first, especially when he sought to implicate my father. I now know it all to be fact.'

'All?' saw the cane aimed at a bush.

'Henry told me everything, your part included.'

This had Dirley stop, head down to look at the ground, the voice concerned. 'His reason? I assume he gave you one.'

'He seeks to imply I'm complicit or, to be more truthful, will be seen to be and will thus suffer whatever is visited upon the family as retribution. He claims the marriage to Spafford was to protect me, which, if he truly believes it, will demonstrate how far he has drifted from any sense of reality. I suggest he is mentally unstable and requires treatment.'

Dirley obviously had no desire to go there, so changed his angle of questioning. 'You say he's not here, this Spafford creature, so where is he?'

'Only Henry knows, but he's using the cur as a threat to me. Abide by his wishes and he will be kept away. Challenge them and I will be left at his mercy, of which, I must tell, I doubt he's over endowed.'

'Did Henry tell you he has complete control of your assets?' Following a description of what this entailed, there was a slight hint of embarrassment as Dirley added, 'I'm afraid I had the papers drawn up.'

'He made it plain that if I wanted anything, only he could provide it.'

'That must, of course, be reversed.'

'Like the marriage, Uncle Dirley, and then I can unite with Edward.'

'I must tell you, Captain Brazier was brought to my attention by Henry. He asked me to look into certain rumours about his actions on the Jamaica Station.'

'The death of Admiral Hassall, no doubt?'

'Then you know?' came with genuine surprise.

'I know it is nonsense.'

'What if I were to tell you it may not be entirely so?'

'Then I would refuse to believe you.'

'In such a case, are you not acting just like your brother?'

'As I told Henry, if there'd been any truth in the rumour, I would have heard it. You know I was there, and you'd find not a word in the letters I wrote you regarding Edward Brazier, which would hardly be the case if there was any truth in the story. Who could resist speculating on such a juicy tale?'

'Then I must tell you the government are being prodded by Lady Hassall, as well as some old shipmates of her husband, admirals all, to send a commissioner out to investigate.'

'None of which is germane to my present difficulties.'

'I know.'

'Surely now you're aware of what has happened, it can be reversed?'

It alarmed Elisabeth the way he seemed to hedge, she being unaware of a lawyer's aversion to certainty. 'Let me talk with Henry . . .'

'From what I saw before we left, he has no desire to do so.'

'He will have to, unless he wants to have me forcibly removed from Cottington. Be thankful such a right does not fall to your Aunt Sarah or I'd be gone by now.'

Henry was cogitating on this very act and trying to see the complications outside those he'd already considered. In the end, all he had was the threat to take away his part of the enterprise and the substantial sums Dirley earned and control them himself. Not that he would be rendered poor: his chambers were highly profitable and he was one of the founding partners.

Then he recalled the legacy, which said they were ultimately the property of the Tulkington family. Could they too be wrested from him? The only way to find out was to examine the documents – but who had them in his possession, none other than his uncle! Which left getting the old sod to see sense, to make him see the risk of having the likes of Brazier connected to Cottington Court in any way was one which could not be accepted.

So no to seeking an annulment, which would be what his sister would be after. Yet what if it became known Harry Spafford was dead? It could not be kept a secret forever. If the marriage stood as legitimate, who was the heir? None other than Elisabeth, who could not be trusted now, even less if she had her plantations back and her own funds. In the final analysis, Henry reasoned, it might be necessary to create the circumstances where the aforementioned legacy on Dirley's chambers had to be brought into force.

The bottle containing Rudd's concoction was sat on his desk and, when all things were boiled down to essentials, Henry decided he had to stick with his original intentions. If Dirley would not go along with him then extreme measures, of the kind his father had employed, would have to come into play: there was no choice when the family affairs stood at risk.

For once in his life Henry did not delude himself he was up to what might be required if persuasion failed. He needed John Hawker here and posing as a potent threat. Dirley must know he would pay the same price as had been paid by others and, since he knew of them, no explanation would be required. He rang the bell, which would see his breakfast tray taken away, ordering his coach to be made ready at once. There was no avoiding what was going to be a difficult interview, but if he was not here, it could not happen. When it did, he wanted Hawker close by.

Who could she ask? There was no one. If the letters she was receiving genuinely came from the diaries of such a creepy character, then the implication was plain, as were, etched in her memory, the days before her husband rode off and failed to return. There had been some prior meetings with Acton, which could not have been pleasant, regardless of how much both he and Samuel sought to keep up the appearance of cordial relations. Not that she'd been aware of any other truth, which made it galling Samuel – if as reported – had confided in his 'friend'.

'Dear Sam, indeed! How dare the upstart use a diminutive?'

She'd never much cared for Venables. He was, to her, very much mutton dressed as lamb at best, for all Acton treated him with what she saw as inappropriate indulgence. To Sarah Lovell, such behaviour just exposed the parvenu status of the family her sister had married into, a tribe she knew to be not long off the beach, having manners, which, to her mind and her standards, no amount of money could burnish.

Venables had been even lower in her estimation, a simpering nobody whose only skill lay with the curation of the ailments afflicting horses or dogs, as if that amounted to anything. Who cared about such creatures anyway? If they fell ill it was easy to buy another one, a thought to hit her hard on consideration. It was a long time since she'd had money of her own to replace anything.

It was no surprise her mind turned to the other hint, one she was partially ready to embrace. Samuel had not deserted her for another woman, as she'd supposed at the time and agonised over for near ten years. He had been the victim of a foul deed, while she was resident in the very house of those who had carried it out. Henry had apparently told Venables it would be best to mind his own business. What 'business' was he referring to?

The notion of challenging her nephew barely got a moment's consideration. He disliked being asked about matters mundane, things to do with the running of the house, so he was unlikely to enlighten her about something as serious as what was being implied. But Dirley Tulkington had been around some of the time and heavily engaged with his half-brother. This was something of which she'd mightily disapproved at the time. In her world, it was risking social disgrace to be known to possess an illegitimate relative; to have him under your roof was an abomination, a fact she hoped she'd made plain to Dirley on the few occasions he had visited after Acton passed away.

She had cut him dead at Elisabeth's wedding and, when enquired of as to his name and situation, had fobbed people off with a display of ignorance. Could she ask him now what he knew? Certainly there was a lack of cordiality in their relationship, just demonstrated in her abandoning the dining room, but could he be charmed into seeing her as less of an enemy – even, in time, a friend?

More importantly, could she put aside her aversion to his status and engage with him? Who would know outside these four walls? No one and, if she could extract from him anything about the disappearance of her husband, it would allow her to challenge Henry with some hope of disclosure. Once she had what she sought, there was no need to keep up any pretence of holding him in any regard. A smile crossed her lips as she recalled what she'd overheard. Somehow Elisabeth had got a letter out of Cottington, only the Good Lord knew how and no doubt she would get the blame.

Was that the key to breaking the ice, for if he'd come at Elisabeth's request, he must know of recent happenings, while she was in a position to back up anything her niece said, albeit such would have to be imparted without Henry knowing. It took no genius to see Elisabeth would be asking for help to get an annulment. She could pretend to be an ally, could tell what happened on the night of the sham betrothal and say, truthfully, how upset she'd been, could infer she was willing to act as a witness to help prove Elisabeth's case.

There was no need, should it come to an action to dissolve the marriage, to stand by what had been imparted in private. In short, she could not take an oath to bear witness in public against Henry, could not contemplate being slung out of Cottington Court and on to the cold, unforgiving street. Sarah Lovell resolved to go up to her room and get out a better dress than the one she was wearing, while a bit of powder and rouge would also not go amiss. Knowing she was not, in any strict sense, a beauty, she had other attributes to make an impression. She was possessed of exquisite manners and had a certain amount of breeding, enough surely to work her wiles on a parvenu bachelor in his sixth decade.

CHAPTER TWENTY-SEVEN

Henry Tulkington spent the remainder of the day, as well as the night, at the Lodge in Deal, gnawing on his troubles. In the morning he made his way to the slaughterhouse to alert John Hawker, to tell him his presence was required at Cottington Court and, in a much-filleted way, why.

'Can't do it,' was the reply he got, which did not go down well.

'What do you mean "can't"!'

'I've got our cargo comin' tonight an' arrangements to make.'

'Then we have the whole day.'

'Which I need to be sure it's safe.'

It was with close to childish pique Henry said, 'Then it will need to be put off.'

'There ain't no way to do it,' Hawker insisted. 'You stay well away from this, your honour, which is the right way, so you wouldn't know.'

Which was not strictly true. It was not impossible, but it would require good fortune. He could send the cutter back out to delay the landing until the next night, but there was no assurance they would find the vessel before it got dark and they'd never spot it afterwards. No captain running contraband would hang about off St Margaret's Bay. In order to maintain the appearance of innocence, he would up his helm and head out to sea as if on the way to another destination, only coming about when necessary to make his landfall at the right time.

'There has to be, surely?' got a firm shake of the head.

Henry began pacing up and down, audibly cursing under his breath, finally stopping to turn and face Hawker. 'At what time will the landing be complete?'

'Well afore sunup.'

'And I assume then your task is finished?' A slow suspicious nod. 'Then come from there to Cottington as soon as you're done. And John, come armed, for there could be work to do of the kind of which my father would mightily approve.'

The look inviting enlightenment was ignored. Henry Tulkington stomped down the stairs, knowing he'd have to return home now. A whole day and night alone had given him his arguments and his conclusions, but they would have to be modified to gain time. He would seem to bend to what he was bound to be asked for, which would hold till Hawker arrived.

Then he could put his proper plan into action and force acceptance of his authority. Back at the Lodge he wrote a note to be sent round to Doctor Rudd, requesting he attend on him at Cottington Court mid-morning the next day, a summons he was sure he'd obey. Then it was back in his coach and heading out of Deal, his first question being to Tanner when he arrived outside, to ensure the instructions he'd issued on the way out the day before. No one was to be allowed to leave and it had been obeyed. The gateman reassured him it was so, without adding no one had tried.

The signs were there, but neither Vincent Flaherty nor Saoirse Riorden had been looking and besides, they could not be classed as street or beach people, having a higher or different calling; likewise those who frequented the Lodge, much of what happened in the town being too far beneath their noses to attract attention. This debarred them from much of the rippling gossip which fed the endemic inquisitiveness of a population, whose day, or the toil this entailed, rarely varied unless the weather was dead foul and stopped it altogether.

Living on the strand, the state of the wind and water dictated their ability to earn and was thus closely studied. Thus, over centuries of scrutiny, what lay in the offing was rarely a mystery. They knew the tides, could read the formation of the clouds, extract warnings from the run of the sea and sniff the wind for signs of bad weather long before it arrived. Likewise a period of calm could be forecast, when the running of contraband would be possible without the danger of drowning.

The long pebble beach was a community with its own hierarchy, connections and internal dissensions, all in a constant state of flux. It was also a place of blether and a dearth of secrecy on who was doing what and why, some of it accurate, much of it not. Everyone had an opinion and were ever ready to share it.

Certain parties had a sharper eye even than those on the beach, one group being the crossing sweepers, paid to keep certain points free of the filth of hundreds of horses, each of which seemed to traverse the central parts of the town dozens of times in a day. They could see and note everything, merely for the places in which they were positioned. So the presence or absence of certain parties, in the three streets forming the parish of Lower Deal, was easily noted.

Far from the least of these was John Hawker, who, just for his imperious manner, daily strode the streets in a way which drew attention. Even with a fixed expression, there were those who claimed to be able to discern a mood, either darker or different, merely from his gait or level of condescension. It took acute observation and a constant presence in one place to mark Hawker as a man of habit. His routes were regular to those who occupied the same places every day of the week.

Likewise the fellows he led, a tight-lipped bunch but liberal and noisy spenders in certain locations, most notably the couple of taverns they frequented. So when they were not to be seen at all, it set tongues wagging. There had been speculation two days past about what was afoot when none of them could be seen anywhere in the town, not least a query from the owners of the establishments in which they spent money. Traders and merchants with property and business to run and protect noted their 'gifts' were not being collected on the day they fell due. This died when they reappeared to take up their habits.

Yet it represented an unforeseen crack in the security of the Tulkington operations. By laying so much on John Hawker, it created a lightning rod for what lay outside his twin occupations of tax and slaughter. There was no doubt he was the major source of contraband in Deal, the man who supplied near every business as well as a large number of private citizens.

He had also come to be seen as a protector to the beach people. Over time, it was seen as sensible for any group of boatmen, contemplating a run to France, to alert Hawker of their intentions. They believed he possessed inside knowledge of the Revenue and their activities, for they were far from inactive. Within their limited means, they did as much as possible to interdict smuggling and could notch up the odd success.

John Hawker, advised in advance, could say if the notion of a crossing was wise and, if it went ahead and the landing spot was threatened, he was the man to issue an alert to have it changed, which would put the Revenue men in the wrong place. His other trait, of occasionally alerting the very same authorities to keep them happy with arrests, was not known. But it did mean he was a man to look out for, if only just to attract his attention and have it acknowledged.

Vincent Flaherty had taken to riding into town as soon as his morning tasks were complete, at least this was his excuse. It also allowed him to call upon Saoirse when the Old Playhouse was shut and he could be with her alone. The only impediment to the propinquity he sought lay in the number of people occupied in cleaning and restocking in preparation for a new trading day.

It was better when she occupied her office on the ground floor, small enough in itself, made more cramped by the bundles of paperwork and ledgers, which went with her business affairs. Able to take a chair and sit very close, it was perfect as far as Vincent was concerned. Not so Saoirse. In order to keep his flights of romantic innuendo at bay, very obvious in such a confined space, she'd taken to undertaking errands she could claim went with her trade, while he would wait for her to return.

If it was remarked upon she was seen more frequently than normal of a morning, it was positive to some, not least the crossing sweeper who had the post at the front of St George's Church, one of the busiest in town and not very far from her front door.

'Good day to you, Jack.'

'Miss Riorden,' came as he looked for a gap in the traffic, by which he could brush the road clear of dung for her and others to cross. 'Happy as ever to see you.'

'And a nice day it is.'

'Good weather for a while is the word.'

The coin slipped into his hand disappeared into a leather pouch, without any acknowledgement by look or deed to say it was silver, not the normal small copper.

Jack, for he had no other name, was a sad-looking creature, as befitted his occupation, clad in clothing close to rags, with a face where grime surpassed flesh. With drawn features he lacked a single tooth, this giving a wheeze to his voice. But he had good if watery eyes, peepers which observed everything.

'So what's goin' on in the world this fine day?'

Jack's lips compressed into a gurning smile, his eyes taking on a sly look. 'Saw certain parties heading south, first thing.'

'Anyone I know?' was quietly put.

'I'd say if you was awaiting owt delivered, then it'll be over by the morrow.'

'Hawker?'

'None other, an' his lads as well.'

Jack dashed between the twin lines of carts, which gave way, allowing enough time to employ his brush, his progress followed by those needing to cross. It was only when he was on the other side, leaning on said brush, he realised Saoirse Riorden had not done so. She was hurrying back to the Old Playhouse.

Vincent put his horse to a gallop in order to let Brazier know the landing seemed imminent. He found him using a stick as a pretend sword, thrusting, cutting and parrying in the way he'd been taught and had practised since his days as a young midshipman. It caused him pain, but this he accepted: it had to be borne, given his intention to confront John Hawker – to do so without he could employ his sword would be foolish. The others were, as normal, being ordered about by Zachary in any number of tasks. Presented with a chance to mend his fences and see to his hop poles for free, Zachary was not going to pass up the chance.

'How sure can we be?' was Brazier's first question.

'Does it not tell you how progress is marked? His men being out of Deal two days was all the talk? I can't be certain and neither can Saoirse, but the signs are there for a landing this very night.'

'Then we must trust them.'

'You have, I hope, a plan?'

'Not one fully formed yet. So let us sit and share a glass of the wine you fetched while I think on it.'

'Whatever you intend needs a clear head, Edward.'

'Then I will be abstemious, I promise.'

Sat side by side on the bench, Brazier told Flaherty of how he'd freed Spafford's men then humbugged the pair of guards Hawker had left behind, a tale to provoke much amusement.

'The thing is, Vincent, I said not a word to Dutchy and the others of what I intended. Yet they took up the notion so quickly and with such conviction, even I was astonished. Mind, I know from experience how eager a tar is to guy anyone gullible, lubbers especially.'

What followed was a few of the tricks the hands of his first ship had visited upon him as a midshipman, like being sent aloft to find a sky block or being encouraged to piss into the wind, with obvious results.

'The pair were convinced they were going to hang if silent, so spilt everything I needed to know about the landing.'

'Everything?'

This point had Brazier acknowledge to himself certain problems. Much as they would insist on accompanying him, he could not involve the men who'd come at his request to provide protection. With the risk of serious harm or even death very high, it had to be for him and him alone to bring about what was needed, none of which was vouchsafed to Flaherty. The Irishman sat silently sipping as he watched his companion in deep thought, ruminating on the difficulties of securing several outcomes. The ultimate aim was still to get Betsey free of her brother. To do that he had to remove from the equation John Hawker without forfeiting his own life, while at the same time ensuring damage to the whole smuggling operation. Did he have everything? The conclusion was, he had a great deal, but not quite enough.

'Vincent, I thank you for what you've done on my behalf. Be assured I will find a way to do so properly.'

'Sure, you're staying whole will suffice.'

Sensing the finality of this, the Irishman downed his wine and stood to shake hands, masking his concern at the way Brazier's face reacted as he pumped his hand, an indication of how much the wound was still troubling him.

'It's my fond wish to see you on the morrow, Vincent and with a resolution. Take my regards to Saoirse as well as my gratitude for what she's done.'

Flaherty mounted to then look down at Brazier, with an expression which carried the look of a last farewell. The response to this was a confident grin.

'There are some people, my friend, who have no idea of the trouble they're in.'

'May God go with you?'

A nod and he was gone, with Brazier heading indoors to fetch out the writing case. He then headed for the paddock, to take out Bonnie and saddle her, waving to those working to carry on as they looked to see if he wanted their help. At a trot he made his way to the Spafford farmhouse and once there, asked to be left alone with Marker, door closed, which had Dolphin and his mates confined to the kitchen, not one willing to wait outside.

'Never know who might be watchin', your honour,' was the excuse.

Marker, sullen as he had been originally, was brought to sit opposite Brazier at the large table, the writing case between them. Opened, a quill was taken out, as well as a sheet of paper, the case then turned round once the inkwell was opened.

'I can't write, if it be what you'se after.'

The quill was handed over. 'I want you to draw me a map.'

'Of what?'

'Not even you can be so dense. Everything you know about St Margaret's Bay. The location of any tunnels' entrances and an outline of the system as far as you know them, where the signal lanterns are positioned and how the men working them get there and back, the places for those set to lookout for approaching trouble.'

'Why should I?'

'What do you think would happen if I handed you over to the men you kept prisoner, to do with whatever they like?' Seeing the face pale, Brazier added, 'Being of the same ilk as you, they would have a real interest in ensuring you could never exact retribution and there's only one way to guarantee such a thing. The same would then be visited on

Tombs, as long as I allowed it. A map, as detailed as you can make it.'

'An' if I don't believe you after what went yesterday?'

Brazier stood and went to the door. 'Beyond this point, I will not be responsible.'

Marker gave in as soon as his hand was on the knob, so Brazier returned to the table and sat in silence as the quill was taken and employed, the only sound the scratching of the nib, he resisting the temptation to go and look over the man's shoulder. When Marker was done, the paper was slid over to be examined, this followed by a number of questions, which had Brazier making notations of his own.

'Right, back to your confinement. With luck you'll be free tomorrow.'

On the ride back there was much thinking and refining of what was yet an outline plan. But there was one obvious fact which struck him: he could not be in two places at once, or at least in the time frame he envisaged. He came back to find everyone sitting outdoors eating and talking; Bonnie was taken to the paddock, where he espied Hawker's pair of packhorses, yet to be set free.

With these in his mind he turned to other possibilities, which had him, once he too had eaten, arranging to send Dutchy and Peddler to the farmhouse, more specifically to the barn with a list of items he wanted to be brought back. The requests that followed were comprehensive and detailed. A list of certain items which he required, as well as the means to transport them, finally the place they should meet later in the day.

'And now I will go and make contact with a man desperate to meet with me.'

'No too many o' them in the world, your honour,' said Cocky, with a grin.

'Not even a bawd,' was Peddler's opinion.

The reception Henry received on entering his own house was frosty. There was no sign of Elisabeth or his aunt, but Dirley was waiting to talk. With a huge effort, he set out to be emollient, to give him the impression all matters were up for discussion and agreement. Yet knowing he would scarce be believed if he just gave way, it was necessary also to be firm on certain points.

'Under no circumstances, and you, Uncle, should see what I'm driving at, can I agree to Elisabeth marrying Edward Brazier. And I can't see how this can be prevented, if she is free to come and go as she pleases, while having use of the assets which were signed over to me.'

'A fact she knew nothing about.'

'Why would she, it's her husband's business?'

'A marriage she wants annulled and to a fellow I have yet to meet. Where is this Spafford?'

In a moment of pure inspiration, Henry replied, 'I've sent for him to be here tomorrow. You will be able be to cast your eyes over him and see the qualities I spotted on first acquaintance. Then we can sit and sort out the whole business.'

'I look forward to it, Henry. Now, if you don't mind, I'll go and talk to your sister.'

CHAPTER TWENTY-EIGHT

Edward Brazier's first port of call was the Navy Yard, which got him, as he rode through, a very jaundiced look from the hat-tipping gatekeeper. His first stop was the stables, to get Bonnie unsaddled and fed, then he went to the office of the captain who carried out the work for which Admiral Sir Clifton Braddock took the credit, he being the man who actually ran the Navy Yard establishment. There he examined one of several charts affixed to the wall, which showed the depth of water in the Channel between France and Kent, as well as the coastal features all the way round to the heights of Capel. Those germane to his intentions he took the trouble to memorise.

He requested and was given the local tide and timetables, which, when taken over the hours, indicated a vessel coming in as soon as it was dark, to beach at a near low tide, which would keep it stable for unloading. This complete, which must take many hours, if what he had been told was true, she could then float off on a tide now rising.

His next task, given what he had in mind, was to change his working uniform coat for his best, plus clean breeches, linen, stockings and best hat, the clothes he'd been wearing the night of the fire, thoroughly cleaned by Joe Lascelles and no longer smelling of smoke. So he made his way to the guest quarters he'd been allotted and, with a degree of care, prepared himself, which included the strapping on of the sword he'd rarely been without, prior to the fire and after his beating.

Thus, it was a post captain, in the full panoply of the rank, who emerged on foot to head for the Three Kings to find, for once, Garlick was not at his hatch. It took some time for him to respond to the ringing bell and, with eyes on stalks, he showed amazement at who was calling. He was even more thrown when Brazier, as hale as he'd ever seen him, ordered a room for himself as well as a message to be sent up to Mr Cottin's room to ask if he was available.

'Can I say it's a sight to see you whole, your honour?'

'And why would I not be, Mr Garlick?'

'After Quebec House, and things,' was suitably nebulous.

'Mr Cottin, please. Ask him if it's convenient to call.'

A maid was sent upstairs with the message, to quickly return and ask he proceed immediately. A look at the proprietor elicited the information it was the one he'd previously occupied.

'I wish the room I have booked to have flowers, Mr Garlick, lots of them.'

He left Garlick wondering at how long it would be before the whole town knew Brazier had resurfaced and what would be the consequences. Another riot could see torches outside the Three Kings with no knowing how it would end.

The steps were taken two at a time and Brazier knocked on Cottin's door, swiftly opened by a man who'd clearly been waiting for the sound, the pair standing looking at each other, as if it was inconceivable they should actually meet.

'You are, I believe, the High Sheriff of Kent.'

'While you, sir, are the most elusive fellow in creation.'

'I don't get your drift, sir.'

'Don't you? I have been seeking to meet with you and have some questions answered since I arrived in Deal.'

'Am I to be invited to enter or am I required to converse on the landing?'

Cottin stood back and allowed Brazier in, the naval scraper being swept off his head as soon as he was through the door. 'Can I ask to see your seals of office? I have only your word for who you say you are.'

'One would hardly pretend to occupy such a position.'

'Nevertheless.'

Cottin went to a small trunk and opened it, to reach in and produce a highly polished square wooden box with an engraved brass plaque. Opened, it revealed said seals, bearing the Invicta device of the county, surmounted by the royal coat of arms. There was a second, smaller version for the sealing of documents plus several scrolls, which no doubt also attested to his status.

'You are the first person here to ask to see them.'

'Be assured I have my reasons, sir. I'm told you've been enquiring into the death of poor Upton.'

This got Brazier a queer look: Cottin was wondering if he was the source of those cryptic notes but this had to be put aside. 'Indeed I have.'

'And you have uncovered?'

'Enough,' Cottin flustered, 'to justify further enquiries.'

Brazier waited for elucidation but none was forthcoming, which told him exactly how far the man had got.

'There is also the matter of three dead men left in the cemetery of St George's churchyard, all with wounds caused, I'm reliably told, by musket fire. Which prompts me to ask this, Captain Brazier. Can you fully account for your movements these last nine days?'

'I'm at a loss to know why this would be of any interest.'

'Surely the answer is obvious. There is a very strong chance the trio of men murdered were involved in setting fire to your house. It was a blaze in which you and your companions – and by the way where are your companions – could just as easily have perished.'

'Am I to understand you would want to lay these deaths at my door?'

'It has occurred to me.'

'Then I wish you joy in seeking to establish it. As to my whereabouts, I have been investigating the extent of smuggling on this coast, which necessitated remaining out of sight.'

'On behalf of the government, I daresay,' was smugly delivered.

'I cannot fathom what prompts you to say such a thing. It is criminality pure and simple.'

Then Brazier threw up his hat and pretended enlightenment, an emotion replicated on his face. 'You refer to the rumour, which was being maliciously spread, intimating I was acting as a clandestine agent for Mr William Pitt.'

'One I have heard expressed, Captain.'

'One which is a totally false calumny, which I believe was responsible for the riot in which Upton lost his life. I have good reason to trust I have uncovered those who might have been the scoundrels to set the disturbance in motion, the same people who intend to land a cargo as soon as this very night, though this is yet to be established as a certainty.'

Cottin could hardly dispute the first part of the assertion, it being his own original opinion, while he was more than intrigued by the second and said so.

'The reason I have come here today, sir, is to find out if you are willing to aid me in the apprehension of these villains.'

'You think it possible, sir?'

'I think it certain, if the correct steps are taken.'

'Captain Brazier, it is remiss of me not to offer you to sit.' This was accepted, with the host's mind working overtime. 'You will permit me some time to consider what you're saying.'

'Of course.'

'Meanwhile can I offer refreshments?'

Coffee was requested and a bell rung to order it, with Cottin going to look out of the window and think. Brazier had agreed the riot had been sparked to prevent any discovery of smuggling. It was too early

312

to say if he was innocent of those bodies in the graveyard, but what if he spoke the truth? Was it possible the trio, identified as carrying out the very trade, had fallen foul of the people who initiated the riot in order to cover their tracks?

It then occurred to him, the way Cavell and Sowerby had suggested Brazier must be the guilty party came over as damn convenient when looked at objectively. It could be an attempt to cover up for one or several of their own, by pinning the blame for everything on a stranger; if this was truly the case, he would hardly turn up and risk exposure. The possibility of Brazier's guilt could not be put aside completely but, surely the way to proceed was to treat him as innocent and, if he was not, hope his arrogance, fully on display now, would trip him up.

Should he bring up once more the name of the aforementioned William Pitt? He had on his desk a letter from Walmer Castle acknowledging his correspondence and informing Cottin of his intention to take luncheon at the Three Kings on the morrow. The invitation to join him, if he felt so inclined, had set the Cottin blood racing. On balance he thought this a matter better kept to himself.

'This smuggling of which you speak?'

Brazier put a finger to his lips to command silence. The creaking of the landing floorboards had alerted him to the presence of someone outside the door and so it proved. With the talk having ceased, the knock and request to enter produced none other than August Garlick himself, tray in hand, trying to look ingenuous and, as ever, creating more suspicion, not less.

'Personal service, Mr Garlick?' Brazier exclaimed, with an arch expression.

'Only for guests I hold as valuable, Captain.'

'Thank you, Mr Garlick,' Cottin said, with a trace of astringency. 'On the table, if you please.'

The tray was put down with the proprietor acting as if he had no idea what to do next. It took him some time added to a degree of hesitation to withdraw, with much smiling and nodding.

'Insufferable man,' Cottin whispered.

Brazier had to supress a smile. This one remark put the meeting and their conversation on an entirely different footing, the one he hoped would meet his needs.

'Smuggling?' was a little louder from Cottin, but not much.

Brazier stood, went to the door and hauled it open at speed. Garlick was too quick for him; forewarned by creaking floorboards he was out of sight. The door closed, Brazier moved to the table and poured himself some coffee, his enquiring look getting a nod from the owner of the room.

'You imply you require my help,' this said as he took and balanced the cup and saucer.

'Please do not take it amiss when I say it's your position which brings me to your door.'

'I am proud of my office, sir.'

'And so you should be. So let us sit and I will inform you of what I have uncovered up till now.'

As he spoke, he confirmed the very thoughts Cottin had harboured since he arrived in Deal: the whole town was steeped in criminality and he'd probably been face to face with it on the day he'd arrived. No names were vouchsafed to him, but the scale of the operation was outlined in detail, added to the knowledge he had of the likely landing place.

'Then, sir, surely this information should go to the Excise, not to me?'

'If you can guarantee, Mr Cottin, not one of their number is complicit in the trade, I will happily do so.'

'You think them corrupt?'

'It only takes one to be less than honest and with the profits at stake, the temptation is great.'

There was no need to add more, for Cottin nodded. 'Any landings would be aborted.'

'Or shifted to another location, of which I have no knowledge. The whole eight miles of coast could serve, it being so open.'

'You said information you'd gleaned up till now, Captain Brazier?'

'Sir, I am certain it is imminent, I know it will take place at night, my only area of ignorance revolves around which one. But my guess, given the tides, it will be tonight or tomorrow.'

He then went into detail, Cottin nodding sagely, with Brazier reckoning what he knew about tides could be scrawled on the back of a lottery ticket.

'The only way to be sure is by observation, which presents for me a dilemma. My aim is the Excise should be told only once the landings are in progress, so even if they are penetrated, it will be too late for the alarm to be raised by anyone who might be untrustworthy. It is my intention to be the eyewitness.'

There was a pause for effect. 'I must also say, sir, relations between the Excise and the navy are far from cordial. They see us as unhelpful in the execution of their duties.'

'How so?'

'We have many more vessels and a hundred times more men, not one of whom the admiralty will offer as a way to interdict the contraband trade. I cannot be in two places at once, seeking to ensure the landing is happening, then reporting it. I fear, even if I could get to Dover and the Excise in time for them to act, as a naval officer I'm far from sure they would shift on my word. But you, sir, with your seals of office to hand, could activate not only the Revenue, but perhaps the Dover garrison as well. In essence, you can guarantee what I can only hope for.'

Cottin was thinking a King's First Minister would shift such bodies faster than he, unaware of how much trouble Pitt had experienced in getting any soldiers to do his bidding three years past. Nor did Brazier believe for a moment anyone would stir the Dover garrison to aid the Excise, but the ability to deploy such power must sound tempting.

'I wish to engage you, sir, to act with me and clap a stopper on this trade for good and all.'

There was a moment when Brazier wondered if he was overdoing the outraged citizen performance, only to have it laid to rest as Cottin responded with commendable *gravitas*.

'What is it you would have me do?'

'You asked where my companions are. They are spread out between here and the heights above the village of Kingsdown, there to act as my signallers. You, I hope, will be sat in a carriage, ready to speed to Dover when the landing is confirmed. On your authority, you can instruct them to make for St Margaret's Bay as fast as their feet will bear them, so able to catch the smugglers in the act and effect a mass arrest.'

Cottin was struggling to contain and keep hidden his growing excitement, even harder when Brazier added,

'And who knows, in the taking up of these villains, it may reveal who commands such activity, even who was responsible for the death of Lionel Upton. Of the other bodies you mentioned, I have too little information to speculate, but there could be a connection.'

Cottin was glad he'd made no mention of William Pitt; even if the contraband was not landed tonight, he could, when he met with him, hint at knowledge of it happening soon. He could also put himself forward as the person who'd uncovered the whole conspiracy. Brazier might baulk at the claim, but Cottin knew one thing: he who got in first garnered the greatest credit. As a post captain Brazier was elevated enough not to require any further assistance. Survival alone would have him an admiral, whereas he had one year in office to make his mark and here was an opportunity, surely one never to be repeated.

'You must go over the details again, Captain Brazier, so I know I have them right.'

'You will first have to acquire a chaise and someone to drive it.'

'I shall.'

'The distance you must cover is just over four miles and will have to be undertaken before nightfall. The customs house is hard by the admiralty pier and there should be someone on duty who can rouse out the required strength, while you alert the Dover garrison. If not, they gather in the White Horse tavern to await any news of there being contraband run.'

'You have thought on this carefully, sir.'

'As I must.' In fact, it was Marker who'd told him. 'We have one chance, Mr Cottin. I doubt, if we fail, it will ever occur again. Do you wish to make some notes?'

Cottin acknowledged the wisdom of this, immediately seating himself at the desk to take up his quill.

Half an hour later Edward Brazier exited the Three Kings to return to the Navy Yard, where Admiral Braddock, advised of his reappearance, requested he attend upon him at his convenience. A quick glance at his Hunter reassured him he had time, though word was sent to the stables to have Bonnie saddled for a quick departure.

'Damn me, Brazier, we were all afire to know where you were.'

'I went to visit Admiral Pollock, sir, at Adisham. I had no desire to abuse your hospitality.'

'You're singular in that, sir, every other sod here seems content to feed off my personal stores.'

There was a bit of quiet contemplation as Clifton Braddock considered his fellow flag officer, Eustace Pollock, who'd been Brazier's first commander on joining the service. Braddock, with a full ruddy sailor's face and wily eyes, had a post for which Pollock would have given his right arm, for all the man before him damned Deal as a backwater. Sir Eustace was a yellow admiral, a senior officer without benefit of flag, which meant unemployment, albeit with pay. Expecting Braddock to talk of his old shipmate, which could go on forever, he quickly asked to be excused.

'Before you go, Brazier, had a fellow asking after you, low lawyerly type, even if he does style himself High Sheriff. Wanted to question you but I did my best to divert of course. Can't have a civilian seeking to lord it over we sailors.'

'I assume you refer to Mr Cottin, sir?'

'That's the fellow. Didn't take to him, snarky sort.'

'I have just been with him.' The eyebrows asked for more. 'Matters to do with the body found in the embers of Quebec House.'

'Nasty business.'

'Indeed. But I have satisfied him on those matters he wished cleared up.'

'So, what are your plans? Staying in Deal?'

'I doubt it very much, sir. One or two loose ends need to be cleared up and then I will set myself to acquiring another ship, which I would suggest is better pursued in London.'

This statement broke any eye contact, telling Brazier this wily old bird was aware of the rumours regarding the West Indies.

'Then I can only wish you good fortune,' came out with a fair dig at sincerity. In truth, his visitor knew Braddock couldn't care less: when it came to a career, there was only one the admiral cared about. 'But do let's split a bottle before you finally depart.'

'It will be a pleasure, sir.'

The last thing Brazier did was to change back into the clothes in which he'd arrived. Where he was going was no place for display, but it was for his sword. Passing the Three Kings he was pleased to see outside a single-seat chaise, with a driver hunched over on the box. Cottin had done what was required. He just hoped he had given Garlick no hint of the use to which it was to be put.

He had no doubt the man would seek to do his part. If he'd tried to hide the gleam of ambition in his eye, it was too obvious for an acute observer to miss. There was amusement too: he was humbugging Cottin just as much as he had done to Marker and Tombs, the kind of games he had not played for years. Command militated against such levity.

CHAPTER TWENTY-NINE

The next stop was Vincent Flaherty's paddock, where he found, as arranged, Dutchy, Peddler, Cocky and Joe, all anxious to know what they were to do next, eager to get on with it. They were also curious as to why he'd had one of the packhorses rigged to carry a couple of barrels – one of gunpowder, the other of turpentine – both from the Spafford barn, though it was open to a good guess, with only Flaherty voicing concern.

'There's enough to set goin' a war, Edward.'

'Wars have to end sometime. This might be one of those occasions.'

There were a couple of lanterns, as well as coils of rope hanging off the strapping, along with Zachary's old army canteen, filled with water.

'My pistols?' he asked.

'Primed and loaded,' Dutchy said, handing them over, as well as a long sheathed knife, which was attached to his belt.

Instead of putting the pistols in the same place, Brazier stuck one each side of the horse, jammed into the straps holding the barrels, likewise his sword, which did nothing to diminish the desire to know what he intended. When he told them, it was not well received. Even the Irishman thought it rash.

'You're going up against known killers. Jesus, you should have with you all the help you can get.'

'All the help won't get to where I need to be, Vincent, it will do the exact opposite. I have been told Hawker will have men all around the bay. Somehow, I've got to get close to the cliffs overlooking it without being either spotted or sent away and it can only be done alone. But there are things which must be carried out, the first to get to where I need to set off from and, with time running out, we have to get moving.'

'I'd wish you God speed, but somehow I think Old Nick might be more what you need.'

Brazier grinned. 'Don't let Zachary hear you say that. One more thing, I'll be coming by in the morning and I would want you to have Canasta ready saddled.'

'I won't go asking who it's for.'

'You don't have to. And fix me a price, a true one, not what you'd do for a friend. I intend the pony to be a present.'

He remounted, the others following suit, to be led out of the stables and on to a path which would take them south. Brazier had an eye on the heavens, on this day a mix of billowing cloud and blue-grey, both of which, if it stayed this way, were going to be helpful at different times and a damned nuisance at others. What he feared was either becoming fully established; he neither wanted pitch-blackness or a clear sky.

He could sense the mood of those following, just by the utter lack of banter. There was no moaning from Peddler either, which would have Cocky joshing. This was something he'd experienced from time to time at sea, though never on one of his own vessels, the discontent of a crew so real you could touch it.

He was not about to explain, this being another maxim a naval officer required to keep in the forefront of his mind. There were occasions when a captain could take his men into his confidence, but it was something to be rationed carefully. There was no time in battle for elucidation; each man had to do that for which he'd been trained, then he had to obey without question any orders he was given, even if it looked to make no sense. The man in command had to have the sole power of decision or confusion would sink them all.

Vincent had spoken nothing but the plain truth: for all his manoeuvring and devious ploys, the chances of things going wrong was well past high and the price, if it happened, could be mortal. Going into battle in war was different: everyone aboard ship knew the risks and, with a few exceptions, they accepted the chance of death or wounds. If he asked his old barge crew, they would volunteer to a man to go where he went and so would Joe. But he'd risked their lives already the night he was shot and he was determined never to abuse their loyalty again.

So it was a silent group who came to the cliffs overlooking the fishing huts of Kingsdown, dotted along the beach, with the boats the locals used hauled up on the strand. From where they sat, it was possible to see the stretch of seashore running many miles north, where, with the mudflats of the Stour estuary hidden, it appeared to meet the snow-white cliffs which ran round to the North Foreland.

To a smuggler it was as if God had chosen it to favour them in the fight against the Excise. One of their number sat here might see the distant lanterns waving on a dark night as a cargo was landed but they could do precious little about it. By the time they closed the distance, their quarry would be long gone, and even their cutter would struggle to intercept a lugger, crewed by men who knew the water and the shore like the back of their hand.

'Who would want to be a Revenue man with this to battle against?' he asked, to get no reply. 'Am I to be sent off with gloom?'

It was Dutchy who replied. 'No sense in pretendin' to be happy when we ain't.' He added more, acting as a spokesman for them all. 'We came when you asked for help, Capt'n, an' it weren't just for the promise of pay.'

Peddler pitched in. 'Well said, Dutchy.'

'Only the Lord can count the number of times we's been at your back an' in many a scrap. Never did we ask for even a nod of thanks.'

'For which I'm grateful.'

'You don't know how down we were after you was shot, with the notion you might have snuffed it.'

'I'm a hard man to kill, Dutchy, and it will be as true of tonight as any other.'

Silence descended again, which made uncomfortable the wait for Cottin, this relieved when Brazier saw the twin lamps either side of a chaise, making its way along the coastal track. This had him kick Bonnie into a trot, taking them downhill to meet it at a point where the track came to a natural halt against the bluff. This marked the end of the beach, beyond which there lay only a rock-strewn path along the bottom of the cliffs and even this ran out when the tide was full.

By the time he made this spot, Cottin had arrived and had got down from his seat to look at the approaching party, one brought to a halt by Brazier well away from contact. He dismounted to issue a greeting, then took an arm to lead the fellow well away from his coachman.

'You asked about my men, Mr Cottin – come and meet them.'

Cottin was introduced name by name, not one of which elicited a smile, which had him place them in the same category as the worthies of Deal, which was miserable. He was then pointed to the way they'd come down to meet him.

'It's a steep climb and not the best of tracks, but it will take you directly to the road to Dover. The signal to do so will come from one of my men, swinging a lantern from the heights above us. As soon as you see it, you will know this is the night of the landing and can proceed with the alert.'

'And where will you be?'

'Further along the cliffs, for it is I who will have to signal to him. He cannot see the bay and I must to be sure.'

Cottin pulled out his pocket watch. 'And when do you anticipate this taking place?'

'Hopefully I will have a sign before it is fully dark. I'm glad to see you have the coach lamps already lit. They will surely be required.'

'I insisted upon it, Captain Brazier. The fellow might say he had the flints he needs, but I have known coachmen who refused to light the candles unless an extra payment was met. This man has his fee and will get no more.'

'Can I suggest you retire a hundred yards or so? It will be easier to see the light from a position further back. Is there any doubt in your mind regarding what needs to be done?'

'None.'

'Then we have come to the point of action. May I express a wish all goes well for both of us?'

Brazier took the violent handshake well, but it did hurt a bit. He went back to where the others waited and remounted, to lead them up the track Cottin's chaise would take, swinging left on to the leas, where they dismounted. Closing with Dutchy, after he pulled the lanterns off the packhorse, he asked they be lit and, once aflame, for the shades on both to be closed. Out came his Hunter next, flicked open, obliged to ask a question to which he felt he should know the answer.

'Can you read a clock, Dutchy?'

'I can,' came without a smile.

'The fellow I was talking to requires from you a signal, sent by a waved lantern. I want it sent to him a quarter shy of nine, which should be when the sun is down and only the afterglow remains.'

'Do I need to know the purpose?'

A glance at the piece said there was time, but it was not a wide-ranging explanation, just the bare bones. 'I calculate he can be in Dover at a fast trot in not much over an hour, though it will depend on the time it takes him to get from rough track to road.'

'What if he can't rouse out what he needs?'

'If you'd met him properly, you would have seen determination. Soldiers no, but I think he will light a fire under the Excise. I hope it matters not if this takes some time, even if they fail to arrive till after dawn.'

'Don't take much of a brain to see a lot goin' wrong.'

'If it does, it does. All I can do is make a plan and hope it works, and this goes at sea or on land.' He took up the second lantern. 'Now, I must be on my way. It would cheer me to be wished good luck.'

'Goes without sayin', Capt'n, an' for all of us.'

Tempted to shake their hands, it was put aside for a pat on each shoulder, which was less painful. Then he was gone, leading the packhorse along a well-worn track, used by many people to get from Deal to Dover, but only when the light was good. Late in the day, it was deserted.

Brazier would make no attempt at subterfuge till he was much closer to St Margaret's Bay, and he was never to know how luck favoured him, for this was the approach where, short of his regular body of men, Hawker had decided to leave uncovered. His whole body was tingling with anticipation, ready when challenged to either bluff his way past or use his sword, a pistol being too loud and only employed to get away.

As the light began to fade he realised he must hurry; this was no path to be on in darkness and, if the cloud covered the starlight, he would be a fool not to stop and wait till it cleared, for he risked going off the cliff edge. As it was, he got close enough to the point where the grass-covered sward sloped sharply downwards, which had to be the southern edge of the bay. There he stopped, crouched down and allowed the packhorse to graze, while he soothed a very dry mouth with a drink of Zachary's well water.

According to Marker's rough map, there was a route round the bay along the heights, which would take him to the south side and his real destination. But first he would have to clear the way, which had him consider if he needed to be closer to what would be going on below. Did he need to see the ship beached, which was the only way he could be sure the operation was in progress? Anything else would be guesswork, which might not serve. He decided it was too risky.

To the west the sky was now home to a bank of orange cloud, with a clear strip of gold, while it was clear overhead and still now pale grey, his vision aided by the light of a dying sun reflected on the clouds overhead. Still in the arc of its beam and, having been fortunate so far, he decided on a recce. The packhorse's reins he tied to a bush, his sword pulled out and unsheathed. Moving cautiously along the slope, the sound of snoring stopped him dead, for he could not believe his ears. Given where he was, it had to be one of Hawker's men, who would have been keelhauled or worse if the bastard knew.

The temptation to get closer and silence him he dare not risk. He could possibly clout the sod, but what if he heard him approach? It would end in noise, for all he had to do with a loaded musket was pull the trigger. So he made his way round to stop again at the sound of much shuffling. Creeping forward on his belly, he saw through bushes vague outlines, a line of people making their way downhill, a few exchanging quiet words, no doubt the folk who would unload and port the cargo.

This pathway told him he'd gone as far as he could on this side of the bay, and besides, he had come across something which would totally suit his purpose. It was another slow crawl back to where the packhorse was tied off, where he removed his pistols, to stick them in his belt, before loosening the straps holding the barrels. These he carried, one at a time, to where he needed them and, once placed, he unwound the long length of slow match, which had been lashed round the turpentine. The protruding bung in the powder barrel he removed, then the turpentine lid, which had been fitted through the wood with a knotted rope. This he turned and soaked before replacing it.

Lifted and tipped, he emptied a quantity of powder on to the turps barrel, then pushed the slow match in to the powder itself, jammed by the very same bung. There was a small amount of spill, but it didn't matter. Another length of slow match was buried in the pile of gunpowder on top of the turpentine.

By the time he was finished the light was near gone, so, after coiling a rope around his shoulders, it was sit down and wait, knowing what was going to happen below him could not be utterly silent. When full darkness came, which it did without a bit of cloud cover, Brazier used the time to imagine the next day and what it would bring: nothing if tonight did not go as planned, possibly everything if it did.

The flash of a light out at sea had him sit up. What he could not see was the response, a double unshaking of a lantern in a southern cliff side tunnel to say it was safe to enter the bay. From his position he could only imagine what Marker said would happen next: two lanterns would be fully opened as guides. The temptation to crawl closer to the cliff edge to try and see what was happening he had to fight, patience not being a virtue of which he was excessively endowed.

But he could use his ears. Within what he took to be half a glass came the unmistakable sound of a keel grinding on pebbles, this followed by, not shouts, but indistinct voices, just loud enough to carry. He took them as faint indicators of the vessel being secured to berthing posts, and from then on it was imagination or a recalling of pleading words from Marker and Tombs – made flowing by occasional jerks on the ropes round their necks – which had him picturing what was happening.

A cable would be used to haul it side-on to the shore, this followed by the setting up of a gangplank to carry a line of people on to the deck and down below, there to grab bolts, crates and barrels. These they would then bear up the steep pebbles to the ladder below the main tunnel entry point and, once up the rungs, would make for the chambers hollowed out of stable chalk. These acted as storerooms, where the contraband would stay until the people tasked with distribution came to take it away.

Brazier waited intentionally: he wanted the operation to be well in progress before he acted, but it was a tense time, his body itching until the point came when a fired musket would do more to aid his purpose than interfere with it. Under a sky showing a mass of stars, mixed with broken clouds, he took off his sword, which interfered with his movement, to slowly and carefully move both barrels to the edge of the now deserted path.

By its side a gorse bush was used to hide both him and the ends of the slow match. With the minimum of light spill, he unshaded his lantern, using the flickering tallow to set the flammable cord fizzing. A boot was then used to kick the powder barrel onto the path, where he prayed it would roll down: the other barrel he intended should stay where it was. The length of match he had calculated gave him time to get away and, lantern in hand, he moved quickly, running uphill, hoping his feet would find flat ground.

He didn't find any before the gunpowder exploded, a huge flash of orange flame, which went up to the sky above and surely reflected off the few clouds close to passing over, also sending out a shockwave which came close to knocking him over. Next, the powder atop the turpentine went up, a lesser flash but it set light to the highly combustible liquid. In quantity, it too was explosive, if not as much as gunpowder, but it sprayed out to cover and set alight the surrounding gorse.

Brazier, moving as fast as the light would allow thought, if that did not panic everyone into fleeing, he could not think of what would. But uppermost was something Marker had said about John Hawker: he would be the last to leave the tunnel system, because he would not do so until he was sure all the entry points and exits were sealed off. And Brazier also knew, from the same source, where he would finally emerge.

CHAPTER THIRTY

The fires he'd set going were not going to last and, if anything, the slight glow made it harder to see than previously as they rendered less effective the starlight. The moon, up now, was still too low to provide much illumination, forcing him to progress slowly, it being wise to do so, in case there were still some of Hawker's men around. With only the vaguest idea as to where his destination lay, his headway was carried out with many a stumble and one fall to bark his knees. He had the details of Marker's map fixed in his mind, but the actual terrain he had dared not reconnoitre would never quite match up to what had been written down.

It was Hawker's horse, saddled and waiting, tied to a stunted tree, which saved him from going past the place he was seeking. Away from the fires, which were now no more than distant glowing pinpricks, opening the lantern was a risk, not least because it required he use both his hands, which meant no pistols. But it was one which had to be accepted, because it showed the path by which Hawker had made his way to the cliff side house, within which lay the entrance to the tunnel he used, it taking him to the point on the face where his signal and guiding lantern could be seen offshore.

There was no trace of any light coming from within, it was just marginally blacker than its surrounding so it took another flash of lantern light to find the door and the latch by which it could be opened, not that it was any better inside. He could only allow a couple of seconds of illumination to orientate himself before the lantern, flap shut off, was placed on the floor. This allowed him to take out his pistols and cock one in readiness.

The open trapdoor he'd seen briefly established Hawker was still here, yet this in itself was strange. If he had been the Excise and they were presumably swarming over the area, how could Hawker feel safe? Mounted or on foot, he was in the wrong place to avoid danger, just another of those things Brazier had to accept he would probably never know. Right now, with the time seeming to be interminable, he was damning the man and wondering where the hell he was.

The first hint of light, showing the outline of the trapdoor, had Brazier stiffen and reverse the uncocked right-hand pistol, lifting it high as the glow increased. Then came the sound of boots on a hard surface, the light rising up from below to bounce off the ceiling, refracted just enough to give Brazier an indistinct sight of his surroundings, the bare walls and exposed beams, also allowing him to move into the position he required. Those boots hit the wooden risers of the ladder, making a sound which seemed to echo.

The lantern came out before the hat-covered head and there was one hand on the trapdoor edge to aid him up, as the unmistakable black-clad shape appeared. Brazier waited till the body was nearly out, one boot on the floor, before the butt of his pistol was used to hit Hawker as hard as he could, a blow which sent him crashing to the floor, his lantern dropped but still functioning. Brazier stepped forward and gave him another kick to the crown, which sent his hat spinning away.

'Move and you'll die.'

Just like the gun pressed to his neck, this was a precaution in case he was still conscious. With no sign of movement, Brazier righted Hawker's lantern and unshaded his own, which lit up the room. There

331

was a groan to say if he was down, Hawker was not completely out, but he was in no state to fight, so Brazier could put his pistols away and uncoil the rope he had looped over his shoulders.

Dragging his hands to behind Hawker's back, one end was used to tie them, which allowed Brazier to ponder what to do next for from here on it was all improvisation. He realised how heavily he was breathing, not from effort but from the strain he'd been under for hours now and, since there was a chair handy, as well as a table, he sat down to both look at his victim and examine his options, both pistols laid on the table and handy. There being no rush he was there some time, until a way of proceeding emerged, one which would do what was required.

He was also scolding himself for not bringing the canteen of water, first because he was thirsty, but secondly, he would have been able to dash water into Hawker's face and start to bring him round.

Elisabeth had been unable to sleep, so rose from her bed to pace the room and wonder at what the day would bring. Release, hopefully, but there was no certainty and the way her uncle had seemed to hedge when they were walking – and later talking – was worrying. They'd had dinner together, Henry declining to join them, but with Aunt Sarah in attendance, her behaviour not only precluding any intimate discussion, but also because she had dominated the occasion.

She had also gone to some trouble with her appearance, wearing a dress Elisabeth knew was kept for special occasions, like the Easter services at St Leonard's and the May Day fete on the Mill Hill, which saw her under public scrutiny. She'd also sought by the use of powder and rouge to enhance her features.

More remarkable was her behaviour with Dirley, whom she'd made plain in the past she despised; indeed, she could hardly allow herself to acknowledge his existence. Not this night, where she had been simpering and flattering, referring to his immense charm and obvious intelligence, while insisting he regale her with tales of his court appearances and successes. Despite the response being an exercise in commendable modesty, the conclusion of each anecdote was greeted with the enthusiastic clapping of her hands.

It got more serious when she asked how well Dirley had known her husband, the first of many questions which created an atmosphere, even if Sarah Lovell sought to make it sound like normal dinner table conversation. The clue for Elisabeth, able to watch the enquiries without being in eye contact, lay in the creased upper lip, which seemed to contract as each query was posed.

'Did you find Samuel *simpatico*?'

'I'm sure, dear Dirley, you were impressed by his wit and charm?'

'As I saw it, he was an asset to the household, wouldn't you agree?'

All were answered politely and in the affirmative, but his niece could also see it was merely Dirley avoiding anything confrontational. Then his face stiffened when she asked him,

'How would you say were Samuel's relations with Acton?'

'You must understand, Mrs Lovell, my main occupation was the law, which takes place in my London chambers. I did visit here many times, but not enough to provide you with an answer.'

'So Acton never mentioned to you there was any difference between them?'

'Not that I can recall.'

'Yet you,' she simpered, 'with your fine legal brain, would surely have been sensitive to the atmosphere? I seem to recall Samuel being somewhat put out after he and Acton had a discussion. It took place in the study, of course, and what it was about was not vouchsafed to me, but I was sure there were raised voices. Within days of this meeting Samuel had left the house, never to return, something which I had no good reason to expect.'

A small delicate handkerchief was produced to be put to her nose, as if tears were about to flow. Elisabeth wasn't fooled and she guessed Dirley wasn't either because, if the expression was one of sorrow, the eyes where as hard as agate.

'I so long to know what happened to him – some accident, I suspect.'

Mood is an odd thing, sensing it in another even more tantalising, as you search for reasons why the slight change in someone's demeanour indicates discomfort, as Elisabeth was doing now with Dirley.

'I think we would all want to know, Mrs Lovell. I do recall Acton told me, on your behalf, he sent out many parties in search for him.'

'All in vain,' came with the onset of genuine tears.

'Sadly true.'

Elisabeth knew she had been thinking on those exchanges to distract herself, but since they were inconclusive and she really didn't care what had happened to Samuel Lovell, she resolved to get out the clothes she would pack in a trunk, one which she would ask to be brought to her room in the morning. She must act as if all was going to be as it should; not to do so was to give way, as she had many times already, to feelings of despair.

Lifting John Hawker bodily was out of the question: he would have to get to his own feet as, once upright, even hands tied, only a fool would think him not capable of some trick. So Brazier took the end of the rope by which he'd tied his hands and threw it over one of the exposed beams. When the groans ceased and the head lifted a fraction, he took up the tension, which had Hawker's arms pulled off his back as far as they would go. Causing him pain was a plus; even more of a bonus was the way, over some time, it got the bastard first to his knees, then on to his feet.

'You,' was a snarl from Hawker as he faced Brazier.

This was immediately followed by an attempt to close, soon stopped by a hearty double-handed tug on the rope. This had him spin round and saw his arms so high up his back, it threatened to tear them from his shoulder sockets. It also produced a satisfying cry of real pain, which subsided when slightly lowered.

'Still want to kill me, Hawker? Pity there's no fire about, though if there was, it would be me setting this place ablaze and you trussed like a chicken and roasting.'

The string of expletives had Brazier smiling and he eased the rope again just enough to leave it uncomfortable.

'It is now my chance to do away with you, for which I daresay the good folk of Deal, if indeed there are any, would be deeply grateful.'

'Do your worst, Brazier,' Hawker gasped. 'I won't beg.'

'I never thought you would. Oblige me by taking a couple of paces backwards.' Refusal to budge saw the arms dragged up again, the only way to ease the pressure being to comply. As soon as he was right under the beam, Brazier looped the rope round his neck so he couldn't move his head. The rest in one hand, his knife was employed to cut it to the length he thought would serve.

'I could kill you but, odd as you will find, it being a sentiment of which you have no knowledge, committing murder – however justified I feel in doing so – does not sit well with my conscience. And there's another thing you lack.'

'Too lily-livered.'

'Killing people does not require courage, Hawker, what it needs is a black heart and in this you are truly blessed.' As he was talking Brazier first doubled the rope back on itself, the line laid over and under. He then fashioned two loops and drew the end through, pulling it tight, talking all the while. 'One of the things you learn in the navy is there's a knot for every purpose and I have just fashioned one for this.'

A pause and Brazier put his mouth close to Hawker's ear. 'I sense you're curious but determined to appear courageous. Odd, you're not a brave man but a bully and, I suspect, one who takes pleasure in inflicting pain.'

'Ten minutes with you,' he growled, 'one to one, an' you'd know about it.'

'Two minutes with me and swords and your guts would be hanging out.' The rope was put round his neck again and adjusted, so his arms were as far up his back as they could go, the loop pulled so the line over the beam was taut. 'What you have round your neck, Hawker, is a slip knot.'

Brazier pushed down the arms slightly, which tightened the knot till it was pressed into his flesh enough to make his eyes bulge, then eased it once more.

'This demonstrates to you what will happen if you try to free yourself, which cannot be done with your arms in the position they now occupy. The more you lower them, the tighter the knot will get around your throat, which to me, presents a neat solution to the problem you are.'

Another pause as Brazier moved round to look Hawker in the eye.

'Nothing to say? Well let me tell you the Excise has already been alerted by the High Sheriff of Kent to this night's attempt at landing contraband, now abandoned.' What followed was a hope. 'They are, most certainly, on their way.'

No reaction, just steady eyes holding a hateful gaze.

'It was never my intention poor local people seeking to earn a few pennies should be had up and face retribution for seeking to put food on their table. It's a pity the turds who do your bidding have to escape justice as well, but it's a price which has to be paid. But you, who tried to burn me alive, as well as four men I hold dear, must pay.

'You have two choices, both of them to my mind fitting. I have given you the means to hang yourself; all you have to do is drop to your knees and the slip knot will tighten, resulting in your strangulation. On the other hand, you can stay as you are to be arrested by the Excisemen, who will clap you in irons until you come up before a judge who will, when your crimes are exposed, and there will be witnesses, send you to the gallows.'

The eyes were still steady, the gaze remaining malevolent.

'So I leave it to you. Goodbye, Hawker, and when you get to the hell you deserve, I hope you are put in a fire, then you will know what you visited upon the poor soul one of your men clubbed in Quebec House.'

He made to leave, but paused. 'You must be wondering what will become of Henry Tulkington. Well, I would say his running of contraband is finished, for in finding you, the Excise will also discover the network of tunnels and storage chambers.'

A smile. 'I see in your eyes a question. How do I know all this? It will sadden you to find two of the creatures you got to do your dirty work could not wait to betray you. What it is to be a man no one loves.'

The expression told Brazier his exaggeration had hit home. 'But to return to Tulkington. For reasons I expect you will be able to discern, him I can neither kill nor serve up to justice. But it will soon be known he no longer has you to do his bidding, so perhaps there are those, beaten by you, who may wish to take revenge on him. I do hope so. Goodbye, Hawker. Enjoy choking, on whichever rope you choose.'

Brazier took up his lantern and left, now able to move swiftly, which he needed to do in order to be well gone by the time the forces of the law arrived. They would be armed and no doubt nervous, not the types to allow anyone to be in their line of fire. Passing Hawker's horse, he decided to unhitch it and take it with him; let Vincent Flaherty gain something from all the effort he'd put in rather than allow the Excise to sell it: the owner was profit enough.

He made his way back to where he'd left his sword, then on to the still tied-up packhorse, leading both mounts by lantern light, back the way he had come until, not far along the clifftop path, the shape of a figure rising out of a bush stopped him dead, soon followed by three more.

'Give you joy, Capt'n,' cried Dutchy Holland.

'You deserve the grating and the cat, the lot of you.'

'An' here's we thinkin',' Cocky called, 'you needed to be locked away for yer ain good.'

'Getting light, your honour,' Joe Lascelles pointed out, which was true, there was an edge of grey on the horizon.

This was a gift to Peddler. 'More'n can be said for you, Joe.'

'Back to Flaherty's,' Brazier said. 'And hope he has the means to give us breakfast.'

The experience of seeking to rouse out the people required to apprehend the smugglers was one John Cottin had not enjoyed. He found most of the Excisemen too far gone in drink to consider acting at anything approaching speed, this after a long period in which their superior questioned his right to call them out in the first place. It was with much huffing and puffing, along with threats to expose their laxity to the Riding Officer who paid their stipends, they agreed to venture out at all.

The garrison at Dover Castle refused to budge, and reminded him he required written orders, which could be no more than a request for assistance and, even if he produced one, they were not going to chase all over the countryside on the basis of some rumour.

'It is fact, not rumour,' he had barked at the captain being difficult.

'So you say, sir, but where is your proof?'

'I have it on good authority as we speak, a vessel is approaching St Margaret's Bay to land contraband.'

'And I know we do not answer to the likes of you anywhere, we answer to the Horse Guards, so if you want us to rouse out get an order from Whitehall.'

He and the disgruntled Excisemen finally got to the heights above the bay when the sun was coming up, to find it deserted. There was no ship, no smugglers and no sign of any contraband. But there was one positive: they found the way into the tunnel complex where they discovered, stored in large chambers, enough untaxed goods to make their activities a major coup.

Cottin returned to the Three Kings behind a seriously disgruntled coachman, who'd been up all night, ordered hither and thither, without any clue as to the why. He was even more dissatisfied to be paid off with his exact fee, his passenger too eager to get inside, have a bite to eat then to get his head down for a couple hours.

He had, after all, an important engagement, which he looked forward to now even more than he had hitherto.

CHAPTER THIRTY-ONE

The five-strong armed party, numbering six horses, which turned up at the gates of Cottington Court, were not going to brook any arguments about the right to enter. Faced with several muskets, added to a determined and pistol-waving Edward Brazier, Tanner did the only sensible thing. He unlocked the gates, scuttling back into his gatehouse, dragging his snarling dog, where he locked the door, thinking he was not employed to lay down his life.

Henry Tulkington, leaning back in the chair used for shaving, was unaware of what was coming until the sound of several sets of hooves had him jerk upright. He did this so quickly Grady had to withdraw the razor at speed. Elisabeth, distracted from her packing by the same noise and able to see out of her window once there, recognised the tell-tale navy scraper as well as the horse leading the party and her heart lifted. Already downstairs and in the dining room, only Sarah Lovell reacted with a look of concern; Dirley had no idea what he was hearing was unusual, so the thudding hooves got no more than a look of curiosity.

It was Peddler who opened the ornamental gates closing off the inner drive, glad to be back on the ground as the others rode through. It was an indication of the well-run nature of the estate that several stable boys came rushing out to take the horses, only to quickly

340

retreat back when they saw muskets being waved in their direction.

'Tulkington's coachmen,' Brazier called.

This sent Cocky and Joe Lascelles to see to the pair who resided above the coach house while Dutchy and Brazier dismounted in front of the portico, the one-time coxswain taking the reins of both mounts as well as Brazier's pistol, which was handed over with a wry grin.

'I don't reckon there's a weapon like this in the house. Pray I'm not wrong.'

With Grady occupied, albeit frozen with a razor in the air, the task of seeing to the front door fell to a footman who, without thinking, did what his superior might have avoided: he opened it wide as if the visitors were expected, which suited Brazier, who strode straight through to find Elisabeth halfway down the stairs and behind her Henry, still with soap on his face. At the word 'Betsey', she flew into his arms, while he, dragging a towel off his neck, screeched a command to get out of his house.

'I will go happily, Tulkington,' Brazier cried, whipping of his hat, 'but Betsey will be coming with me.'

'The devil she will. My man Hawker will be here soon and this time I will not hold him back.'

'Your man Hawker is, by now, either dead by his own hand or has been taken up by the Excise.' Brazier was vaguely aware of Sarah Lovell standing in a doorway to her side, as well as the outline of a larger person, but his gaze was on Tulkington. 'And know this: your operations are destroyed, your tunnels open to scrutiny, very likely by now swarming with Revenue men. If you've been lax in covering your tracks, they'll be at your door before the day is out.'

'Somebody throw this scoundrel out.'

Odd how this sounded more as though it came from a spoilt child than an adult, very different to the deep voice which demanded, as Brazier whipped out his sword, 'What the devil is going on here?'

Putting a little distance between himself and Betsey, he heard her say, 'My Uncle Dirley.'

If she wondered why he didn't respond, did not speak, Brazier could only have told her he was too dumbfounded. The man standing beside Sarah Lovell was the spitting image of his late father, perhaps a little older, maybe slightly more portly, but the likeness was striking.

'Uncle Dirley, this is Edward Brazier.'

He too seemed dumbstruck, his eyes wide open and filled with an image of himself as a younger man. It was with a less confident voice he muttered, 'Brazier?'

'The man I hope to marry.'

Direly seemed to recover somewhat. 'You're still married to Spafford.'

'Spafford?' Brazier barked; whatever else he was struggling with, this was fact. 'He's dead days past, along with his father.'

All eyes were suddenly on Henry, stood rock-still on the staircase, there being no notion of his coming closer when faced with a drawn sword in the hands of a man he was sure would run him through.

'Is this true, Henry?'

'I have no idea,' was just as weak.

Brazier scoffed. 'You were stood right by him when he was shot.'

Henry recovered a bit to sneer, 'How would you know, when you fled? A pity the man who shot at your back missed.'

'While I was denied any of this,' Elisabeth cried. 'You really are the most despicable pig.'

'And you, sister, are not far short of a whore.'

Sarah Lovell had her hands to her cheeks as Edward Brazier moved forward, sword up and angry, to send Henry speeding away. 'What in the name of all that's holy is going on here?'

'Lies, Aunt Sarah,' Elisabeth replied, her voice soft but no less accusatory. 'Which should not shock you for being yourself immersed in them.'

342

'How could I know about the fate of Harry Spafford?'

'No more than you could know about the fate of your own husband,' Brazier said.

'Enough!' Dirley barked, suddenly aware not only of a footman being present by the still open front door, but Grady appearing on the staircase, while the whole conversation must be reverberating around the house. 'Elisabeth, come into the dining room.' Seeing defiance, he added, 'And bring your Brazier fellow with you.'

There was no keeping Aunt Sarah out; she was first through the door as Elisabeth whispered, 'Is it true?'

There was no need to ask what, as he took and reassuringly squeezed her hand, calling out to his ex-coxswain, stood in the portico, as Elisabeth added, 'Have a care with my uncle, he's in league with Henry.'

'Door stays open, Dutchy, and keep the pistol where it can be seen.'

'Aye-aye, Capt'n.'

Inside the dining room, Brazier, given he was allowed time without distraction, was struck even more by the resemblance of this uncle to his father. The same thick grey hair, the sallow, olive-skinned nature of his countenance, the darker bags below the liquid-brown eyes, added to which he knew he was being studiously examined himself. The only thing missing was the parental smile.

'What do you know of my husband, sir?' Sarah Lovell demanded.

'Only what we've both been allowed to read of in a friend's journals.'

'You sent those letters?'

'Edward?' Elisabeth asked.

'Later, my dear.'

'What you said to Henry, sir, about tunnels?' Dirley asked.

There was a great deal left out of Brazier's explanation of the past few days, even more about the previous night while, in terms of reaction, what he did reveal had remarkably little effect on Dirley Tulkington. But the man talking had no idea of his profession, which demanded nothing show on his face regardless of how disturbing it appeared. Another unknown was the fact Dirley felt something of a sense of relief. Staying overnight at Cottington Court, running over how things had changed since Acton's day, he'd concluded his nephew was not someone he could rely upon, while he was certainly not a person to whom he was inclined to bend the knee. As already concluded, he could not represent his niece and stay connected to his nephew; he must choose one or the other with whatever consequences ensued, a question yet to be decided.

Yet as Brazier talked, with occasional interjections from Elisabeth to explain some of Henry's more egregious actions, he held back from interrupting until his curiosity could no longer be contained.

'I'm bound to ask where you come from, Captain Brazier?' The information was provided, though Brazier would have struggled to say why it was asked. 'And your father's given name?'

'Farley.'

The brown eyes closed and stayed that way while the timbre of the voice changed to one deep and soft. 'And where was he born?'

'I assumed in the same place, given I never enquired.'

'Your grandparents?'

'Dead before I was born, and I am damned curious as to why you're asking.'

The inquisitor was not a man to be put off. 'A farmer?'

'He was a naval surgeon.'

'Elisabeth, I wonder if you would mind leaving Captain Brazier and I to talk alone?' Instead of agreeing she looked at Brazier, who shrugged. 'And you too, Mrs Lovell.'

It was in an almost comatose state she departed, Elisabeth less willingly though assured by her uncle it was in her best interests. When she'd gone there were some pointed questions regarding John Hawker and what had occurred at St Margaret's Bay, many answered with reservations. But it was established by a man experienced in cross-examination that Brazier had been the architect of the whole catastrophe.

'I'm bound to ask, what are your intentions as regards my nephew?'

'Not your niece?'

'I reckon them fairly obvious.'

'I shall leave any retribution to those put in office to extract it. I've carried out that which I needed to do for my own ends and those of Betsey and I'll do nothing to endanger her well-being.'

'So Henry has nothing to fear from you?'

'Fear would only apply if he was man enough to face me with a sword or a pistol, which I think even you must know is never going to happen.'

'If you reckon he will be had up by the law you're mistaken, and the same applies to myself. We have been too careful to allow such a thing to occur.'

'We?'

'My half-brother Acton and I. The details of our association I will leave Elisabeth to explain, since she knows all there is to tell. But if you will take a seat, I'll relate to you something of our family background.'

'You're assuming this to be a matter which will interest me.'

'You wish to marry Elisabeth, do you not?' A firm nod. 'So the stock from which she hails must be of some importance.'

'Surely she can tell me herself?'

'Only what she knows, Captain.' In the face of a steady gaze Brazier took a chair and Dirley followed suit, the pair examining each other while harbouring their own thoughts. 'I'll first go back to my father, Corley Tulkington. No one prior to him is of much consequence.'

What followed was the description, to Brazier's mind, of an absolute rogue, who should have been hanged at Newgate several times over. There was enough about smuggling to establish how he'd gained supremacy, just as much of the violence which went with it.

'I sense from your expression you do not approve.'

'I can think of few who would.'

'Then you're naive, sir. Half the world we live in, or more, would see him as a hero. There are people who've expired from starvation on the very beach where Corley made his mark and who cared. Not anyone in authority. They expended their effort in stopping folk finding the means to exist instead of providing it.'

'If you think I favour dearth, sir, I must tell you I do not.'

'I'm pleased to hear it. But back to Corley, who was not only a success in running contraband but generous to those in need and a lusty fellow to boot. I suppose it would be fair to say he was free with his seed. One of his most remarkable paramours was known as the Spanish Lady. She wore a mantilla and held court in a tavern called the Saracen's Head. No one ever used her name and unkind souls would say she arrived with the Armada.'

'I assume not in the presence of your father.'

'Nor mine, Captain. The Spanish Lady was my mother and, when she was brought to her accouchement, she bore twins. Me, the first to emerge and named Dirley.' The pause was several seconds long. 'The other, whom it was soon noted as identical, was named Farley.'

Ignoring the palpable shock in Brazier's face, he continued.

'Corley, seeking respectability, eventually married Acton's mother, Elisabeth's grandmother and a lady of some position in society. Her family didn't approve, but as I say, Corley was lusty as well as, by that time, wealthy. I think both those traits appealed to her. There was no question of Farley and I being abandoned, even after our mother passed away. We were treated as equals, albeit Acton, our little half-brother, would be Corley's heir. I was put to learning the law, while my twin took up training in medicine.'

It was a dry throat which enquired, 'Medicine?'

'I noticed when you first clapped eyes on me,' Dirley continued, 'an expression remarkably close to recognition, while I saw in you a representation of myself and my twin brother as young men. Farley

346

was less than enamoured with the way the family made its income and told our father so, which saw a certain frostiness creep into their relationship. It was made worse when he stated his intention to marry a woman who would not have been a suitable companion as far as my father was concerned.'

'I think, as perhaps those letters I sent to Sarah Lovell show, such a thing could be highly precarious.'

'I won't confirm or deny what you imply in either case, but I will say we arose one morning to find Farley gone and with him what he took to be his inheritance, a substantial sum in money. Neither he nor it, despite extensive enquiries, were ever heard of again. What I conclude is this, Captain. Your real name is Tulkington and you are even more my nephew than Henry.'

'Not a suggestion or a relationship I would ever want to acknowledge.'

'But it does have one consequence. If my supposition is true, you and Elisabeth are first cousins only half removed, which in Canon Law could make the idea of your marrying her decidedly problematic.'

'Tell the slug who's too frightened to face me I shall send his carriage back once we have no further use for it.'

Betsey's trunk was lashed to the back and he and she had decided to ride into Deal, Peddler on the box and the rest of their party following, to find at the gate another carriage, that of Doctor Rudd, seeking entry, in order to treat Elisabeth. It took her to convince Tanner to open the gate.

'It puzzles me Doctor Rudd,' she said from within the carriage, 'I am perfectly well, never better, but I suggest you proceed. I suspect there's another in Cottington Court who may require your ministrations.'

Henry had not shown his face and was assumed to be hiding in his room. Dirley would have to fetch him out at some time, no doubt, to discuss what to do in light of what they knew, which could only be what they'd been told; going near St Margaret's Bay was too dangerous.

Asking about the connection, as Betsey finished her packing, Brazier had been given the whole background as related to her by her brother: the way everything was cut off from exposure, added to the protection afforded by Dirley's legal position. She naturally asked what he and Dirley had talked about, but Brazier demurred, there being more than one thing he'd have to tell her when the time was right: the demise of poor Lionel Upton and how it had occurred being one, obviously kept from her, as had that of Harry Spafford.

Time would be a healer in this. Edward Brazier's aim was to get her settled away from Cottington Court where they could, once everything was out in the open, discuss their impending difficulties and how to proceed. The first thing was to seek a clarification, given the degree of consanguinity, allowing them to marry, which could only be provided by the church. This took no account of how she would react on learning the details of their blood relationship.

He was worrying on this when they arrived at the Three Kings, sending Garlick into raptures of impending salacious gossip when Betsey's identity became known. Having settled her in her flower-filled room and with a promise to return in time for dinner, he was leaving to go to the Navy Yard, where his ex-barge crew were once more berthing, when he ran smack into John Cottin, in the company of William Pitt.

'Brazier,' Pitt remarked, in a demeanour hearty for him. Cottin for some reason looked embarrassed and sought to hurry Pitt past, which the King's First Minister was not having. 'Mr Cottin has been full of praise for the aid you gave him in proscribing the running of contraband. A most successful operation and a credit to our High Sheriff.'

'My aid?'

'Why yes, Brazier,' Cottin cried, seeking by his look to beg for no disclosure of the truth. 'Couldn't have enjoyed quite such a success without you. Most invaluable input, sir.'

'Odd,' Pitt added, 'when I asked you for the same assistance weeks past, you most unquestionably declined to have anything to do with ending smuggling.'

'Ending smuggling, sir. I wish you joy of it. The only way to clap a stopper on contraband is to reduce the duties you levy.'

'I think, perhaps,' Cottin blustered, 'we have struck a serious blow. The combination of the captain and I made the matter somewhat less daunting.'

There was such a temptation to drop Cottin in the steep tub, to tell the truth of how it had come about and who had done what, but he was debarred from doing so, on the very good grounds one disclosure would of necessity lead to another.

As was ever the way with the shamefaced, Cottin could not stop himself from gabbling on. 'Rest easy, Captain Brazier, your contribution has been laid out to your advantage.'

'It certainly has. Perhaps I can press upon His Majesty you're deserving of a command after all.'

He's been drinking, Brazier thought, while Cottin being beside him, with Garlick no doubt eavesdropping, debarred him from enquiring about Admiral Hassall and what his wife was up to.

'I'd be very grateful, sir,' was the required response, as Pitt referred to it himself. 'The other matter we discussed, perhaps we can dine together and talk over certain developments.'

'Of course,' was said. Not on your life or mine was what Brazier thought. 'Mr Cottin, perhaps you and I could have a talk sometime later today, perhaps just before I take dinner?'

The man physically jerked, and his voice was a gabble. 'Love to . . . must get back to my duties . . . coach journey booked . . . been away too long . . . work piling up of the most pressing nature, don't you know.'

Seeing Pitt leaving he wanted to dash after him, but a Brazier hand stopped him. 'Enjoy your inventions, Mr Cottin. I have found such things can come back to haunt you.'

'I must catch Mr Pitt to say goodbye.'

Brazier took his hand off the smaller man's chest. 'Just one thing. Where have you taken the man I left for you to apprehend, and was he alive or dead?'

'Man? What man? There was not a soul about in any condition by the time we arrived.'